Praise for Christine Feehan's Dark Carpathian novels

"A HIGH PRIESTESS IN THE WORLD OF VAMPIRE FICTION."
—*Romantic Times*

DARK POSSESSION

"Steamy and dreamy . . . Feehan's combo platter of danger, fantasy and wild, uninhibited romance continues to sizzle."
—*Publishers Weekly*

DARK CELEBRATION

"[A] sex-and-magic-filled treat."   —*Publishers Weekly*

DARK DEMON

"A terrific, action-packed romantic thriller."
—*The Best Reviews*

DARK SECRET

"The erotic heat . . . turns scorching."   —*Booklist*

DARK GUARDIAN

"A skillful blend of supernatural thrills and romance that is sure to entice readers."   —*Publishers Weekly*

DARK LEGEND

"Vampire romance at its best!"   —*Romantic Times*

continued . . .

Titles by Christine Feehan

MURDER GAME
PREDATORY GAME
DEADLY GAME
CONSPIRACY GAME
NIGHT GAME
MIND GAME
SHADOW GAME

HIDDEN CURRENTS
TURBULENT SEA
SAFE HARBOR
DANGEROUS TIDES
OCEANS OF FIRE

BURNING WILD
WILD RAIN

DARK SLAYER	DARK SYMPHONY
DARK CURSE	DARK GUARDIAN
DARK HUNGER	DARK LEGEND
DARK POSSESSION	DARK FIRE
DARK CELEBRATION	DARK CHALLENGE
DARK DEMON	DARK MAGIC
DARK SECRET	DARK GOLD
DARK DESTINY	DARK DESIRE
DARK MELODY	DARK PRINCE

Anthologies

LOVER BEWARE
(with Fiona Brand, Katherine Sutcliffe, and Eileen Wilks)

FANTASY
(with Emma Holly, Sabrina Jeffries, and Elda Minger)

FEVER
(includes THE AWAKENING and WILD RAIN)

DARK CURSE

A CARPATHIAN NOVEL

CHRISTINE FEEHAN

JOVE BOOKS, NEW YORK

THE BERKLEY PUBLISHING GROUP
Published by the Penguin Group
Penguin Group (USA) Inc.
375 Hudson Street, New York, New York 10014, USA

Penguin Group (Canada), 90 Eglinton Avenue East, Suite 700, Toronto, Ontario M4P 2Y3, Canada
(a division of Pearson Penguin Canada Inc.)
Penguin Books Ltd., 80 Strand, London WC2R 0RL, England
Penguin Group Ireland, 25 St. Stephen's Green, Dublin 2, Ireland (a division of Penguin Books Ltd.)
Penguin Group (Australia), 250 Camberwell Road, Camberwell, Victoria 3124, Australia
(a division of Pearson Australia Group Pty. Ltd.)
Penguin Books India Pvt. Ltd., 11 Community Centre, Panchsheel Park, New Delhi—110 017, India
Penguin Group (NZ), 67 Apollo Drive, Rosedale, North Shore 0632, New Zealand
(a division of Pearson New Zealand Ltd.)
Penguin Books (South Africa) (Pty.) Ltd., 24 Sturdee Avenue, Rosebank, Johannesburg 2196,
South Africa

Penguin Books Ltd., Registered Offices: 80 Strand, London WC2R 0RL, England

DARK CURSE

A Jove Book / published by arrangement with the author

PRINTING HISTORY
Berkley hardcover edition / September 2008
Jove mass-market edition / October 2009

ISBN: 978-0-515-14699-8

JOVE®
Jove Books are published by The Berkley Publishing Group,
a division of Penguin Group (USA) Inc.,
375 Hudson Street, New York, New York 10014.
JOVE® is a registered trademark of Penguin Group (USA) Inc.
The "J" design is a trademark of Penguin Group (USA) Inc.

PRINTED IN THE UNITED STATES OF AMERICA

10 9 8 7 6 5 4 3 2 1

*For my sister Anita Toste, who shares my love of strange
things, will stay up with me until all hours of the night
writing spells and making me laugh at childhood memories,
and who I have always loved and counted on my entire life:
This one is for you.*

ACKNOWLEDGMENTS

In a book as complicated as *Dark Curse*, there are so many people to thank.

First and foremost, special thanks to Dr. Christopher Tong, an incredible friend, who is a continual source of information. It was his brainchild to use the Carpathian language as the proto-language of the Hungarian and Finnish languages. Dr. Chris Tong (www.christong.com) is fluent in several languages, did undergraduate studies in linguistics at Columbia University and graduate studies in computational linguistics at Stanford University. He is currently writing a new book, *Beyond Everything*, and developing the World Meeting Place, a Web 3.0 (AI-based) site aimed at enabling the world's people to collaborate on solving the world's problems.

Thanks to Brian Feehan, who drops everything and brainstorms with me at the drop of a hat. You make my fantasy and action scenes come alive for me when I discuss them with you.

I have to thank Rachel Powell for introducing me to a wonderful woman, Diana SkyEyes, who was generous enough to share her knowledge with me at short notice and put me on the right path to aid my Carpathian women. Diana SkyEyes is an earth priestess with twenty years of practicing Moon Lodge and Wiccan traditions of alternative healing. She is a certified herbalist, musician and writer of healing songs. Any mistakes are my own as well as fictitious license used to enhance my story line. Thank you, Diana, for all your time and energy.

Thanks to my sister Ruth Powell, who has always stood for

children, and who is the only one I know who could create an ancient lullaby and make the words universal.

Thanks to my sister Jeanette and Slavcia, who were willing to discuss birth problems and how best to solve them using alternative medicines.

And, of course, thanks to Anita, who made all the work fun and reminded me of our early carefree days of laughter while we worked our own magic! Your talent for so many things always stuns and amazes me.

FOR MY READERS

Be sure to go to http://www.christinefeehan.com/members/ to sign up for my PRIVATE book announcement list and download the FREE e-book of *Dark Desserts*. Please feel free to e-mail me at Christine@christinefeehan.com. I would love to hear from you.

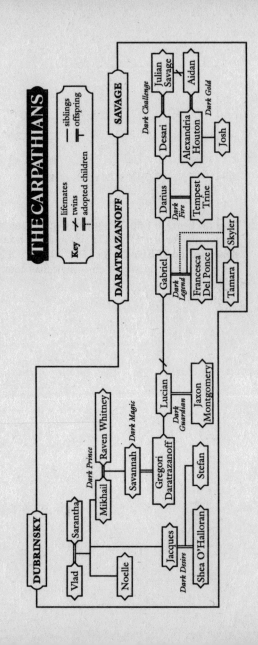

THE CARPATHIANS

Key ━━ lifemates
⋏ twins ━━ siblings
╤ adopted children ╤ offspring

DUBRINSKY

Vlad ⋏ Sarantha

Noelle

Jacques
Dark Desire

Shea O'Halloran

DARATRAZANOFF

Mikhail ━ Raven Whitney
Dark Prince

Savannah ⋏ *Dark Magic*

Gregori Daratrazanoff

Stefan

Lucian
Dark Guardian

Jaxon Montgomery

Gabriel
Dark Legend
Francesca Del Ponce

Tamara   Skyler

Darius
Dark Fire
Tempest Trine

SAVAGE

Desari

Alexandria Houton

Josh

Julian Savage
Dark Challenge

Aidan
Dark Gold

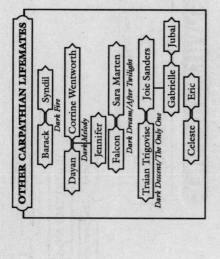

OTHER CARPATHIAN LIFEMATES

Barack ⋈ Syndil
Dark Fire

Dayan ⋈ Corrine Wentworth
Dark Melody

Jennifer

Falcon ⋈ Sara Marten
Dark Dream/After Twilight

Traian Trigovise ⋈ Joie Sanders
Dark Descent/The Only One

Gabrielle ⋈ Jubal

Celeste ⋈ Eric

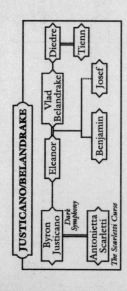

JUSTICANO/BELANDRAKE

Vlad Belandrake ⋈ Diedre

Tienn

Josef

Benjamin

Eleanor

Byron Justicano ═ Antonietta Scarletti
Dark Symphony — *The Scarletti Curse*

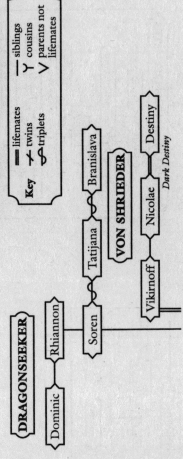

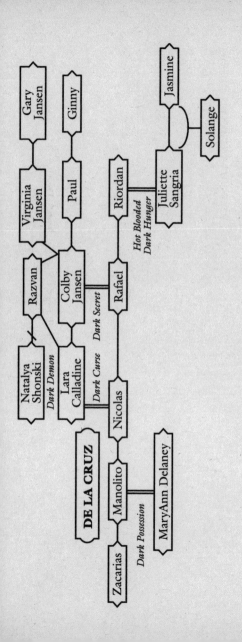

Prologue

The cold should have made her shiver, but it was fear, terrible bone-chilling fear, that seized Lara, causing such tremors they were impossible to control. She huddled on the floor of the ice cave, studying the walls of her prison. The ice was beautiful, walls thick and blue with amazing formations hanging from the ceiling and rising from the floor like a forest of multicolored crystal. She hunched down, watching the lights flicker across the ice—creating glittering, dazzling displays on the walls. All the while, her heart beat too fast and she choked on rising terror.

A soft whisper in her mind helped to steady her, to keep her centered and calm when she wanted to curl up in a ball and cry. She was eight years old now—today. She looked down at her arms and wrists, covered in bite marks, scars from teeth gnawing through her skin to get at her veins. Her stomach lurched. Today was the last day anyone would tear at her flesh and drink her blood. Today she would escape.

I am so scared. Even in her mind, using telepathic communication, her voice trembled.

At once she felt warmth in her mind. The sensation spread through her body, driving away the chill and giving her courage. *You will not be alone. We will aid you to escape. You must be brave, little one.*

Will you come with me, Aunt Bronnie? Will you both come? She knew she sounded plaintive and afraid, but she couldn't help it. She'd never been aboveground. The idea of going alone into an unfamiliar world was paralyzing. Without her aunts, she would have no way of protecting herself. They both had taught her, thrusting as many skills and spells into her brain and memories as possible, but she was still a child in a child's body. Thin. Weak. Pale. A mop of copper-colored hair she could never control and little else.

That may not be possible, Lara, and if we cannot, you must go by yourself. You must get far away from this place and hide your talents and abilities so no one will ever imprison you again. Do you understand? You cannot in any way appear different in the outside world.

They had told her of the world. Long, lonely nights they had whispered to her of places aboveground, of the sun and sea, of forests of trees, of living animals and birds that flew free. They had filled her mind—and her heart—with images so beautiful they had stolen her breath.

Why must I hide my gifts in the world outside? Lara shivered again, running her hands up and down her body in an effort to warm herself. It wasn't the temperature of the ice cave—she could control her body temperature when she remembered to think about it—but the idea of leaving was nearly as terrifying as the idea of staying. Here she at least had the aunts. Outside—she didn't even know what to expect.

It is always better to blend in, Lara. Xavier is a cruel man—there are others like him. You have great power within you and others will want it. Learn in secret and only use it when you must and for good or to save your life. You cannot let others know.

Come with me.

If we can, but no matter what, you must leave this place. You see what they do to us—what they will do to you. Your power will call to them and they will take everything from you.

Lara closed her eyes, the trembling turning into almost violent shuddering. Oh yes, she had seen. Torture. Horrible torture. Horrible black spells drawing forth demons with red glowing eyes and the sickening stench of evil clinging to them. She would hear screams until the day she died, the screams of others begging for mercy, begging to be killed.

She couldn't let her father or great-grandfather know of the power growing within her. She could never let on that the aunts spoke to her and taught her, filling her mind with everything they knew so that as the power in her grew, she would have the knowledge to accompany it. The two men would try to wrest everything she was from her, control her if they couldn't and, in the end, she would be like the others, torn apart while they still lived, experimented on, eaten alive piece by piece until madness and pain were all that was left.

Today was her birthday and she had to escape. She had to leave the only home she'd ever known and go out into a world she knew only through the memories of her two aunts, who had been imprisoned for so many years they had long ago lost count. Before that could happen, she would be forced to endure her father's and great-grandfather's sharp, wicked teeth one more time.

She covered her eyes and bit back a sob.

Lara. You are Dragonseeker. You can do this. We are strong. We endure. We do not ever succumb to evil. Do you understand? You must escape.

Auntie Bronnie always lectured her, but there was love in her voice. Worry. Determination. Auntie Tatijana sounded sad and weak, but the love was there as well, although these days, she rarely wasted energy on talking. Lara knew something was wrong, terribly wrong, and she was frightened of losing the two of them.

"I don't want to be alone," she whispered aloud into the freezing cold of the bluish chamber. She didn't say it in her mind to her aunts, because she didn't want them to know she was nearly paralyzed with fear of leaving. This terrible place of pain and death and cold was her home and here at least she had the aunts, and she knew what to expect. Outside—outside she would be alone in a foreign world.

Lara's body suddenly jerked upright. At the same time she felt the invader spreading through her brain like sludge. A cry escaped. Her instinct was to struggle against the command, but she forced her will to lie quiet, to pretend to be subdued. It was difficult when everything in her shuddered and withdrew from that spreading stain.

Do not fight. Do not fight, Aunt Bron's voice whispered. *Save your strength. Let him think he has control. We will all strike at the same moment. This will be the last time, child. The last time...*

Lara choked on the sob welling up. To have someone else inside of her, to feel evil invading her body, pushing at her mind and forcing his will on her caused bile to rise, flooding her throat and mouth with burning acid. She took a step. Another. Like a puppet controlled by strings. She couldn't prevent her instincts to fight. She resisted the invasive presence, trying to throw him out of her mind, a small rebellion that earned immediate retaliation.

Her body jerked again and pain pierced her skull, like ice picks drilling holes through skin and bone. The sensation of spiders crawling on her skin, hundreds of them, swarming, engulfing her, nesting in her hair, biting at her scalp, had her frantically slapping at her body. She opened

her mouth wide to scream, but nothing came out. She knew
Razvan—her father—had no patience with tears or pleading. It infuriated him to listen to screaming, or to a childish
voice. Her earliest memory was of him shaking her, snarling like one of the captured wolves he occasionally brought
into his lair to torment.

Whatever her memories, this was her way of life. The
aunts had told her a child should be loved and treasured,
never used for food, but it was only the memories they
shared of their mother's childhood that all of them could
really depend on. Not even the aunts had really experienced much more than what Lara's life was like. And
memories—especially ancient ones—could be faulty.

He is forcing me into the chamber. She tried to force
down the rising panic, to keep herself from fighting, from
exposing her abilities, but her sense of self-preservation
was strong.

You are coming to us, her aunt reminded her. *Think only
of that. You are leaving this terrible place to go to a new
life where they cannot touch you ever again.*

Lara nodded and lessened her fight response. She
couldn't lose it altogether or Razvan might suspect something was up. She was smart enough to know he sought to
control her through fear. If she wasn't afraid enough, he
would find a way to incite her terror so he could keep her
under his thumb and biddable.

She counted each step. She already knew the exact
number—she had made this journey many, many times
before. Thirty-seven steps through the corridor and then
her body would jerk to the right, and go through the
entrance into the large chamber where Razvan and Xavier
always held their ritual ceremonies. The long hall was
really a tunnel with a bluish ceiling and thick ice walls.
Under her feet the ice was slick and solid, almost crystal
clear, always gleaming brightly from the orbs of light in
the sconces. The light flickered along the walls, revealing

the rainbow of colors, gleaming like jewels embedded in the frozen world.

She loved the beauty, sculptures of orange-red and purplish-blue rising sharply from the floor, bursting into sparkling fountains frozen in place waiting for the light to hit them to come alive. She moved around the familiar shapes using short jerky steps until she was in the middle of the huge chamber. Huge columns rose to the cathedral ceilings, marking every few feet. Ancient weapons lined one wall and straight ahead, encased in ice, were two perfect dragons, one red and one blue.

Lara glanced up, her breath catching in her throat as it always did at the sight of her aunts, imprisoned not only by the ice, but caught in a powerful shape that was not their true form. She couldn't shift yet, but she felt she was getting close. The aunts had embedded the knowledge deep in her mind so that she wouldn't ever forget the process, but she hadn't worked up the courage to actually shift. And the aunts had forbidden her to try where Razvan or Xavier would feel the surge of power.

The red dragon had her great eye pressed against the ice. As Lara watched, the lid slowly closed and then opened again over the round orb. The small acknowledgment gave her the strength to look directly at the man who stood in the center of the room, a frown on his face. Razvan—her father—glared at her, beckoning with a long finger.

The lines in his face had deepened since the last time she'd seen him and that had only been a couple of days earlier. His hair had darkened from the coppery red to deeper brown, now streaked with gray. His eyes were sunken and beneath them were darker circles. The moment his gaze fell on her, he began to breathe harder, the air coming out in great puffs of excitement. In one hand he held a ritual ceremony knife and Lara's heart began to pound.

He has the knife.

Teeth tearing at her flesh was bad enough, but the sharp

blade slicing, metal against skin and tissue, invading her body and bringing with it the screams of past victims, screams she couldn't drown out for weeks afterward. The pleas for mercy haunted her dreams and clung like ice to her veins so that she felt she was going insane until time finally melted them away.

Lara couldn't help that spurt of adrenaline and the surge of power that came with it, the instinctive retreat, breaking out of the stumbling steps to withdraw. Razvan snarled, his lips drawing back to reveal his stained teeth.

"Get over here!" His face was a mask of hatred. "You are nothing, cheap fodder to feed the genius of my existence. Nothing! A worm crawling on the ground to service greatness."

He pointed to the ice and for a moment she thought to fight his power.

No! You must do as he says. He cannot know the power within you. He will imprison you as Xavier has done to us. This is your chance, Lara.

Aunt Bron's voice whispered, cajoled, pleaded and even ordered. All of that would never have been enough to overcome Lara's instincts for survival and her revulsion of the knife and Razvan, but there was stark fear underlying each word her aunt spoke to her. Lara allowed her body to bend, to go to all fours, to crawl across the ice floor, the cold piercing her knees. She allowed the sensation, not regulating her body temperature so the distraction of the cold helped to calm her.

Razvan stood for a moment, hunched over, whispering to himself, his eyes going from blue to green. Lara winced. Her eyes often changed color depending upon her mood, and it was the one thing that tied her to Razvan, the one trait she had to acknowledge they shared—and that meant the blood of a monster ran in her veins.

He stooped, a strange expression on his face as he glanced around the chamber. One hand dropped to the top of her head, his palm stroking what could have been a caress over her coppery curls. He spoke in a whisper, his voice rusty and hoarse. "Get out. Get out before you are consumed."

Lara blinked up at him, puzzled by the strange ritual he always invoked before he caught her by her thin shoulders and yanked her to her feet. His eyes glowed a ruby red, shining with madness as he turned her wrist up and slashed the blade across it.

She cried out, tried to suppress the shock of panic and pain as the knife cut through flesh to bone, freeing the screams of multiple victims, the shadows of life still clinging to the weapon that had tortured and killed them. Razvan pressed her wrist to his mouth and began to suck greedily, his teeth biting and scraping as if at a bone. He made hideous slurping noises, the sound mingling with the cries of the dead.

Tears burned behind her lids, blurred her vision and choked in her throat. The aunts were right, she had to escape. It mattered little what was waiting in the outside world, she couldn't survive this torment day after day.

Stay strong. He is nearly sated.

She clung to that, knowing that the aunts always were aware when Razvan was about to stop feeding. She felt weak and dizzy, her knees sagging. And then everything in her went still. The hair on the back of her neck rose. Goose bumps rose on her arms and a shiver of apprehension slid down her spine. *He* was coming. If Razvan was a monster, her great-grandfather was the living epitome of evil. She could feel his presence long before he ever entered the chamber.

Razvan shuddered visibly as he lifted his head and shoved Lara behind him. Lara swept her tongue across the wound, the healing agents in her saliva sealing her skin.

The scent of decayed flesh heralded Xavier's arrival. He entered, his emaciated body bent over, one hand wrapped around a walking stick as he shuffled into the chamber. The walking stick was a weapon of amazing power and could be—and often was—wielded to administer pain. The long robes covering the thin body rustled with every step, swishing across the ice floor, picking up crystals so that the hem collected shards and splinters of glistening white. The long white beard was nearly to the old man's waist. His image was blurry as he moved, but if she looked hard enough she could see the rotting flesh beneath the glamour.

Lara felt the surge of power and knew it emanated from the walking stick rather than from her great-grandfather. Razvan cowered from the old man as he approached. She knew Xavier was the oldest mage, the master of both white and black magic. His teachings had been the foundation of not only the race of mages, but of the Carpathian people as well. Her aunts had educated her in the terrible family history of kidnap, rape, murder and war. All because of this one man and his search for immortality.

Xavier stretched a thin arm toward her, his fingers like bones, the nails long and curled. He beckoned.

Razvan shoved Lara away. "You will not touch her. You have your own supply."

Come close, Lara, now, while they bicker over you. Come close to the wall and aid us in breaking free.

"I can no longer use them as you well know. They have become far too powerful to control. I need the book. We must find the book." Xavier stumbled closer to Lara, his clawlike fingers reaching for her. "Once I have the book, they will not be able to defy me."

Razvan swept Lara farther behind him. "This one is mine and you will not touch her."

"Do not presume to give me orders." The voice bellowed in the vast chambers. Xavier stood to his full height, Razvan shrinking before him. "I grow old, but I still have my abilities and you do not."

Lara inched closer to the wall, all the while gathering the energy in the room.

"You cannot even control your own children. As sick as they are they still defy you! You forced me to bring you my own offspring, but you cannot have this one. You kill them with your greed."

"You will give her to me." Xavier swung his stick up, the tip pointing at his grandson.

Lara seized the moment, pulling every scrap of energy from the stick she could and directing it toward the ice wall. At the same time, the aunts connected their power with hers. The massive wall bubbled outward toward the chamber. Great shards fell off as the ice spiderwebbed, and then fragmented.

"Stop them!" Xavier leapt away from the splintering ice as he yelled the warning.

A bright red dragon burst through the ice, claws stretched toward Razvan as the blue dragon bent its wing to Lara.

Now! Now! Climb on fast, Aunt Tatijana called to her.

Lara didn't hesitate. She jumped agilely onto the wing, scrambled up the sloping membrane and swung her leg over the dragon's back. Immediately the dragon reared back on its legs, great wings flapping violently, creating a windstorm, blowing both men backward. Xavier lost his grip on the walking stick. Lara concentrated on it, funneling the wind straight at the thick wooden staff. It rolled to the far side of the ice chamber. The blue dragon took to the air.

There is not much time. Go, Tatijana, flee while you can, Bronnie pleaded with her sister while she flung her body between Razvan, Xavier and Lara.

Lara could see both dragons were weak. Already their skin color was fading. The effort to keep the two mages at bay was already taking its toll on them. Sitting on Tatijana, she realized they were starved, had been starved for years. Xavier only allowed them the barest sustenance in order to keep them from being able to utilize their power. Of the two, Tatijana was the weakest. Bronnie tried to give her sister time to reach the surface and escape.

Lara looked down to see Razvan creeping toward the red dragon. Bronnie flapped her wings to keep Xavier on the floor and away from the all-powerful staff.

Look out. Lara tried to warn her aunt, but the warning was a heartbeat too late.

Razvan plunged the ceremonial knife into the chest of the red dragon. Tatijana screamed. The red dragon sank to the floor.

Get off. Run. I will hold them as long as I can. Tatijana extended her wing to allow Lara to crawl off onto a ledge far above the chamber.

Go with her, Tatijana, Bronnie entreated.

Come with me, Lara begged.

Tatijana shook her head. *I will not leave my sister. Go, little one. Run and forget this place. Do not look back. Be free and find happiness.*

Lara clutched the ice wall. She still had to find her way out of the maze of tunnels to the surface. She looked below one last time at the only home she'd ever known. Xavier regained his feet and held up his hand. The staff hesitated and then flew across the room to him.

"Be still or you will die," he commanded. "You fool," he hissed at Razvan.

The red dragon continued to fight, spilling blood across the ice floor in bright red streaks.

Xavier pointed the staff at the blue dragon. "Be still or I will kill your sister."

Bronnie ceased all movement and lay panting on the ice. The blue dragon settled next to her sister, nuzzling her with her long neck and tongue in an effort to save her.

Lara held back a sob by pressing her hand tightly against her mouth.

Go before her sacrifice is in vain, Tatijana ordered.

Lara ran.

a lot of mountains, but this one doesn't like us." He gave a nervous laugh. "It's getting dicey up here."

"No one says 'dicey,'" Lara murmured, running her hand along the face of the rock about an inch from it, looking for threads of power. The two men were not only her climbing partners, but her closest friends. At that moment she wished she'd left them behind, because she knew she was right. The cave was here, she just had to find the entrance.

"Whatever," Gerald snapped. "It's getting dark and there's nothing here but mist. The fog is creepy, Lara. We've got to get out of here."

Lara spared the two men an impatient glance and then surveyed the countryside around them. Ice and snow glittered, coating the surrounding mountains with what appeared to be sparkling gems. Far below, despite the gathering dusk, she could see castles, farms and churches in the valley. Sheep dotted the meadows and in the distance she could see the river running, filled to capacity. Overhead, birds cried, filling the sky and dive-bombing toward her only to break off abruptly and circle again. The wind shifted continuously, biting at her face and every bit of exposed skin, tugging at her long, thick braid all the while moaning and wailing. Occasionally, a rock fell down the slope and bounced off the ledge to the hillside below. A trickle of snow and dirt slid near her feet.

Her gaze swept the wild countryside below. Gorges and ravines cut through the snow-capped mountains, plants clung to the sides of the rocks and shivered naked along the plateaus. She could see the entrances to several caves and felt the strong pull toward them as if they were tempting her to leave her current position. Water filled the deeper depressions below, forming a dark peat bog, and beds of moss were a vivid green in stark contrast to the browns surrounding them. But she needed to be here—in this spot—this place. She had studied the geography carefully and knew, deep within the earth, a massive series of ice caves had formed.

The higher she climbed, the smaller everything below her looked and the thicker the white mist surrounding her became. With each step, the ground shifted subtly and the birds overhead shrieked a little louder. Ordinary things, yes, but the subtle sense of uneasiness, the continual voice whispering to leave before it was too late told her this was a place of power protecting itself. Although the wind continued to wail and blow, the mist remained a thick veil shrouding the upper slope.

"Come on, Lara," Terry tried again. "It took us forever to get the permits, we can't waste time on the wrong area. You can see nothing's here."

It had taken considerable effort this time, to get the permits for her study, but she had managed the usual way—using her gifts to persuade those who disagreed with her that due to global warming concerns, the ice caves needed immediate study. Unique microorganisms called extremophiles thrived in the harsh environment of the caves, far away from sunlight or traditional nutrients. Scientists hoped those microbes could aid in the fight against cancer or even produce an antibiotic capable of wiping out the newest emerging superbugs.

Her research project was fully funded and, although she was considered young at the age of twenty-seven, she was acknowledged as the leading expert in the field of ice-cave study and preservation. She'd logged more hours exploring, mapping and studying the ice caves around the world than most other researchers twice her age. She'd also discovered more superbugs than any other caver.

"Didn't it strike you as odd that no one wanted us in this particular region? They were fine giving us permits to look virtually anywhere else," she pointed out. Part of the reason she'd persisted when no caves had been mapped in the area was because the department head had been so strange—strange and rather vague when they went over the map. The natural geographical deduction after studying the area was that a vast network of ice caves lay beneath the mountain, yet the entire region seemed to have been overlooked.

Terry and Gerald had exhibited exactly the same behavior, as if they didn't notice the structure of the mountain, but both men were superb at finding ice caves from the geographical surface. Persuasion had been difficult, but all of that work was for this moment—this cave—this find.

"It's here," she said with absolute confidence.

Her heart continued to pound—not at the excitement of the find—but because walking had become such a chore, her body not wanting to continue forward. She breathed away the compulsion to leave and pressed through the safeguards, following the trail of power, judging how close she was to the entrance by how strong her need to run away was.

Voices rose in the wind, swirled in the mists, telling her to go back, to leave while she could. Strangely, she heard the voices in several languages, the warning much stronger and more insistent as she made her way along the slope searching for anything at all that might signal an entrance to the caves she knew were there. All the while she kept all senses alert to the possibility that monsters might lurk beneath the earth, but she had to enter—to find the place of her nightmares, the place of her childhood. She had to find the two dragons she dreamed of nightly.

"Lara!" This time, Terry's voice was sharp with protest. "We have to get out of here."

Barely sparing him a second glance, Lara stood for a long moment studying the outcropping that jutted out from smoother rock. Thick snow covered most of it, but there was an oddity about the formation that kept drawing her gaze back to the rock. She approached cautiously. Several small rocks lay at the foot of the larger boulders, and strangely, not a single snowflake stuck to them. She didn't touch them, but studied them from every angle, observing carefully the way they were arranged in a pattern at the foot of the outcropping.

"Something out of place," she murmured aloud.

Instantly the wind wailed, the sound rising to a shriek as it rushed toward her, blowing debris into the air so that it shot at her like small missiles.

"It's the rocks. See, they should be arranged differently." Lara leaned down and pushed the small pile of rocks into a different pattern.

At once the ground shifted beneath them. The mountain creaked in protest. Bats took to the air, pouring out of some unseen hole a short distance from them, filling the sky until it was nearly black. The dark crack along the outcropping split wider. The mountain shuddered and shook and groaned as if alive, as if it was coming awake.

"We shouldn't be here," Terry nearly sobbed.

Lara took a deep breath and held her palm toward the narrow slit in the mountainside, the only entrance to this particular cave. Power blasted out at her, and all around she could feel the safeguards, thick and ominous, protecting the entrance.

"You're right, Terry," she agreed. "We shouldn't." She backed away from the outcropping and gestured toward the trail. "Let's go. And hurry." For the first time she was really aware of the time, the way the gathering darkness spread like a stain across the sky.

She would be coming back early morning—without her two companions. She had no idea what was left in the elaborate ice caverns below, but she wasn't about to expose two of her closest friends to danger. The safeguards in place would confuse them, so they wouldn't remember the location of the cave, but she knew each weave, each spell, and how to reverse it so that the guards wouldn't affect her.

Ice caves as a whole were dangerous at all times. The

continual pressure from overlying ice caps often sent great frozen chunks of ice blasting out of the walls, fired like rockets, capable of killing anything they struck. But this particular cave harbored dangers far outweighing natural ones and she didn't want her companions anywhere near it.

The ground shifted again, throwing all of them off balance. Gerald grabbed her to keep her from falling and Terry caught at the outcropping, fingers digging into the widening crack. Beneath their feet, something under the ground moved, raising the surface several inches as the creature raced toward the base of the rocks Lara had realigned.

"What is that?" Gerald shouted, backpedaling. He thrust Lara behind him in an effort to protect her as the dirt and snow spouted into a geyser almost at his feet.

Terry screamed, his voice high-pitched and frightened as he tipped over backward and the unseen creature raced toward him beneath the earth.

"Get up! Move!" Lara called, trying to get around Gerald's sold bulk to throw a holding spell. As he swung around, Gerald's backpack knocked her off her feet and sent her rolling down the steeper slope. Her birthmark, the strangely shaped dragon positioned just over her left ovary suddenly flared into life, burning through her skin and glowing red-hot.

Two dark green tentacles burst from the snow-covered ground, slick with blood, the color so dark it nearly was black, emerging on either side of Terry's left ankle. The sound of bubbling mud rose along with a noxious, putrid stink of rotten eggs and sulfur, so overpowering the three of them gagged. The bulbous tops of the tentacles reared back, revealing coiling snake heads that struck with brutal speed. Two curved, venomous fangs clamped from either side through Terry's skin nearly to the bone. Terry screamed and flailed in terror as his blood dripped into the pristine snow. The small gap in the ground began to widen into a larger hole a few feet from Terry. At once, the tentacles retreated toward the hole, slithering across the surface, dragging Terry by his ankle. His screams of fear and pain grew louder, shrill and panicked.

Gerald flung himself forward, gripping Terry under his arms and throwing his weight in the opposite direction. "Hurry, Lara!"

Lara scrambled to the top of the slope. The mist whirled and thickened around her, making it difficult to see. She spread her arms as she ran, gathering energy from the darkening sky, uncaring that her companions might see, knowing she was Terry's only chance for survival. Never once since leaving the ice caves had she used the knowledge inside of her, the wealth of information her aunts had shared with her, embedding memory after memory in her mind—indeed, she hadn't been certain it was real. Until that moment. Power flooded her. Her mind opened. Expanded. Reached into the well of knowledge and found the exact words she needed.

"It's too strong." Gerald dug his heels into the earth and held on to Terry with every ounce of strength he possessed. "Stop wasting your energy and help me, damn it. Come on, Terry, fight."

Terry ceased screaming abruptly and began to fight in earnest, kicking with his free leg in an attempt to dislodge the two snake heads.

The vine threw more tentacles out, the greenish black stems writhing hideously, looking for a target. The teeth sank deeper into Terry's ankle, sawing at flesh and bone in an effort to keep their prey.

Lara flung herself forward, lifting her face to the sky as she muttered the words she found in her mind.

I call forth the power of the sky. Bring down lightning to my mind's eye. Shaping, shifting, bend to my will. Forging a scythe to sharpened steel. Hot and bright the fire be, guide my hand with accuracy.

Lightning zigzagged across the sky, lighting the edges of the clouds. The air around them charged so that the hair on their bodies and heads stood out. Lara felt electricity snapping and sizzling in her fingertips and focused on the thinner space between the long, thick bodies and the bulbous heads of the snake vines.

White light streaked across the short distance and pierced the necks of the creatures. The smell of rotting flesh burst from the vine. Both severed tentacles dropped limply to the ground, leaving the teeth, with the heads attached, still sunk deep into Terry's ankle. The rest of the tentacles reared back in shock and then burrowed beneath the dirt and snow.

Terry grasped one of the heads to pull it out.

"No!" Lara protested. "Leave it. We have to get out of here right now."

"It burns like acid," Terry complained. His face was pale, nearly as white as the covering of snow, but beads of sweat dotted his forehead.

Lara shook her head. "We have to get off this mountain now. And you can't take chances until I can look at it."

She took his arm and signaled to Gerald to grab his other one. They steadied Terry between them and began to hurry from the slope to the well-traveled path off to their right.

"What was that?" Gerald hissed, his eyes meeting hers over Terry's head. "Have you ever seen a snake like that before?"

"Was it two-headed?" Terry asked. Anxiety made him hyperventilate. "I didn't get all that good a look at it before it struck. Do you think it's poisonous?"

"It isn't attacking your central nervous system, Terry," Lara said, "at least not yet. We'll get you back down to the village and find a doctor. I know a few things about medicine. I can treat you when we get to the car."

The mountain rumbled ominously, shivering beneath

their feet. Lara glanced up at the swirling white mists. Above them, spiderweb cracks appeared in the snow and began to widen.

Gerald swore, renewed his grip on Terry and started sprinting along the thin, winding trail. "It's going to come down."

Terry gritted his teeth against the pain radiating up from his ankle. "I can't believe this is happening. I feel sick."

Lara kept her eyes on the mountain behind them as they raced, dragging Terry every step of the way. "Faster. Keep moving."

The ground shifted and rolled and small fans of snow slid in artful patterns toward the slope below them. The sight was dazzling, hypnotic even. Gerald shook his head several times and looked at Lara, puzzled, slowing down to look around at the undulating snow. "Lara? I can't remember what happened. Where are we?"

"We're about to be creamed by an avalanche, Gerald," Lara warned. "Terry's hurt and we've got to run like hell. Now move it!"

She put every ounce of compulsion and command into her voice that she could muster on the run. Fortunately both men obeyed, concentrating on getting down the steep slope as quickly as they could and asking no more questions. The safeguards protecting the cave were not only lethal, but they confused and disoriented any traveler stumbling across them. The warning system usually was enough to make people so uneasy they left the area, but once triggered, the safeguards fought to erase memories or even kill to protect the entrance to the cave.

It was definitely the place she had been looking for. Now she had to survive in order to come back and discover the long-buried secrets of her past. Gerald stumbled, and Terry screamed as the snake head slammed against a particularly dense pile of snow and ice, shoving the teeth farther into his flesh.

Lara felt the mountain tremble. At first there was silence and then a distant rumbling. The sound increased in strength and volume until it became a roar. The snow slid, slowly at first, but picked up speed, churning and roiling, rushing toward them. Lara forced down panic and reached into the well of knowledge she knew was deep inside of her. Her aunts had never appeared human to her, but their voices had been, and the immense wealth of information they had collected over centuries had been stored in Lara's memories.

She was Dragonseeker, a great Carpathian heritage. She was human, with courage and strength of the ages. She was mage, able to gather energy and use it for good. All of her ancestors were powerful beings. The blood of three species mingled in her veins, yet she belonged in none of those worlds and walked her chosen path—alone, but always guided by the wisdom of the aunts.

She felt strength pour into her, felt the crackle of electricity as the sky lit up with lightning. Once more looking over her shoulder, she sent a command to the wilds of nature to counteract the protective guard the dark mage had used on the mountain.

I summon thee, water ice, fit to my hand, provide me with shelter as I command.

Snow stopped movement abruptly, sprayed in the air, frozen in place, curled over their heads like a giant wave motionless in midair.

"Run!" Lara shouted. "Go, Gerald. We've got to get off the mountain."

Night was falling and the avalanche was not the worst they might face. The wind had stilled, but the voices remained, shrieking warnings she dared not ignore. They gripped Terry and half ran, half slid down the steep slope. Above their heads, the heavy mantle of snow had formed a wave, cresting over them, motionless like an ominous statue.

Terry left behind streaks of blood as they skidded over the icy surface. They were sweating profusely by the time they made it to the bottom. Locating their car was an easy task. In this particular area of Romania, most of the locals used carts with tires pulled by horses. Cars weren't a common sight at all and theirs, as small as it was, looked far too modern in a place centuries old.

Gerald dragged Terry through the meadow to where the car was parked beneath some naked branches. Lara turned back toward the mountain, let out her breath and clapped her hands together three times. There was an odd, expectant pause. The wave rolled, snow dropped. The mountain slid, raising a cloud of white spray into the air.

"Lara," Terry gasped. "You have to get these teeth out of my ankle. My leg burns like hell and I swear, something's crawling inside of me—inside my leg."

He sprawled on the small backseat, his skin nearly gray. Sweat soaked his clothes and his breathing came in ragged gasps.

Lara knelt in the dirt and examined the hideous heads. She knew what they were—hybrids of the dark mage, bred to do his bidding. She'd seen the beginnings of them in her nightmares. The snakes injected a poisonous brew, including tiny microscopic parasites, into their victim's body. The organisms would eventually take over his body and then his brain, until he was a mere puppet to be used by the dark mage.

"I'm sorry, Terry," she said softly. "The teeth are barbed and have to be removed carefully."

"Then you've seen this before?" Terry gripped her wrist and held her close to him as she crouched beside the open door of the car. He was sprawled across the backseat, rocking in pain. "I don't know why, but the fact that you know what they are makes me feel better."

It didn't make her feel any better. She'd been a child, dragged into a laboratory. The sights and smells had been so hideous she'd tried to forget them. The stench of blood. The screams. The grotesque tiny worms in a putrid ball, wiggling in a feeding frenzy, consuming blood and human flesh.

Lara took a deep breath and let it out. They didn't have much time. She needed to get Terry to a master healer who could handle such things, but she could slow the deterioration down.

Gerald looked around him, then back up at the mountain, now quiet and still. White mists swirled, but the voices were gone. Overhead the clouds grew heavier and darker, but the mountain looked pristine—untouched—certainly not as if anyone had climbed it and been attacked.

"Lara?" He sounded as puzzled as he looked. "I can't remember where we were. I can't remember how these snakes attacked Terry. Don't snakes need warm weather? What's wrong with me?"

"It doesn't matter right now. What matters is getting these teeth out of Terry's leg and getting him to the inn where someone who knows what they're doing can help him." Someone with natural healing skills, more than doctor's skills. If they were in the vicinity where she had been held as a child, then it stood to reason someone would know how to treat a mage wound.

She closed her eyes to block out the sight of Terry's gray face and Gerald's anxious one. Deep inside, where that wealth of knowledge lay, she found her calm center. She could almost hear the whisper of her aunts' voices, directing her as the information flooded her mind. The curved fangs had a barb at the tip.

Severed head that now does bite, fangs be removed with heat and light. Draw the poison that would remain, holding the harm, stop the pain.

"There might be someone much better at taking these out," Lara said. "We can get you to the inn fast and the couple

who own it might be able to find someone for us who has
dealt with this before."

Terry shook his head. "I can't stand it, Lara. If you don't
take them out now, I'm going to rip them out. I really can't
stand it."

She nodded her understanding and reached beneath her
jacket for the knife on her toolbelt. "Let's get it done then.
Gerald, get in the backseat on the other side and hold Terry's shoulders." More than anything, she didn't want Gerald where some of the tainted blood might spatter onto him.
The tiny microorganisms were dangerous to everyone.

Gerald obeyed her without question, and Lara studied
the first snake head. The hybrid was part plant, part living animal, and all frightening. It was meant to take over a
person, no matter what the species, and bring them under
the dark mage's control. It hadn't been just Carpathians
and humans he had tortured, but his own people as well.
No one, not even his own family, was safe, as Lara could
attest to.

She closed her eyes and swallowed hard, slamming the
door on memories that were too painful, too frightening to
remember when she had such a complex task before her.
She had rarely used her healing abilities on anyone else in
the last few years. In her childhood, she'd made the mistake several times, traveling with gypsies. She'd knit broken bones. Healed a wound from a blade that would have
killed a man. Removed harmful bacteria from children's
lungs. At first people would be grateful, but inevitably they
would come to fear her.

*Never show that you are different. You must blend in
wherever you are. Learn the language and the customs.
Dress the way they dress. Speak as they speak. Cloak who
and what you are and never trust anyone.*

She liked Gerald and Terry—very much. They'd worked
together for several years, but she'd been very careful never

to intrude on either of them, or to show them that she was different in any way.

"Lara."

Terry's pleading voice forced her thoughts to the task at hand. She steadied herself and gave him a reassuring nod. They were used to following her lead and it was natural to look to her now. She took another breath and let it out, pushing down the revulsion welling up.

The words to the healing chant rose out of that same bank of knowledge and she repeated them under her breath as she slid the razor-sharp knife beneath Terry's skin and found the barb.

Kuńasz, nélkül sivdobbanás, nélkül fesztelen löyly. Ot élidamet andam szabadon élidadért. O jelä sielam jŏrem ot ainamet és sone ot élidadet. O jelä sielam pukta kinn minden szelemeket belső. Pajńak o susu hanyet és o nyelv nyálamet sívadaba. Vii, o verim sone o verid andam.

The ancient Carpathian language she'd learned as a child came easily. She might be rusty, having never used it other than to murmur it to herself before she fell asleep, but the words, spoken in a chant, were always soothing to her.

As she whispered the healing words, she blocked Terry's pain. The fang was wicked—and nasty. It curved into the skin, growing wider, digging deep, and at the end, near the point, was a small barb, curving in the opposite direction. She had to slit the skin carefully to allow the points on either side to become loose enough to slide out without further damaging Terry's leg.

At first she used her human sight, blocking all other ability to see until she had the barb out. Only then did she allow herself to look with the eyes of a mage. Tiny white worms writhed and burrowed, swarming to the cells to reproduce as quickly as possible. Her stomach lurched. It took tremendous effort to shed her awareness of her own thoughts and physical self and become a blaze of healing white light pouring into Terry's wound to burn the organisms as quickly as she found them.

The wormlike creatures tried to hide from the light, and they reproduced quickly. She tried to be thorough, but Terry squirmed and moaned, distracting her, all at once reaching down to his other ankle, trying to yank the snake head free.

She found herself abruptly back in her own body, for a moment disoriented and panic-stricken. "Terry! Leave it. I'll take it out."

She was too late. He screamed as he yanked at the foul snake's head, tearing it loose from his ankle. The barb ripped through his skin and muscle. Blood sprayed the backseat of the car and shot across the seat, splattering Gerald's chest.

"Don't touch the blood with your hands!" Lara yelled. "Use a cloth. Get your jacket off, Gerald."

She clamped both of her hands over the wound, pressing hard, ignoring the burning pain as the blood coated her skin, burning to the bone. She fought past her own fear and panic to reach for the cool, centered place inside of her, calling healing light, burning white-hot and pure, to counteract the acid of the snake blood. The way her birthmark was burning there had to be vampire blood mixed in the foul brew.

Gerald ripped his jacket open and threw it away as the material smoldered with a grayish smoke.

Terry grew quiet as Lara sent healing light streaking through his body to the gaping wound in his leg. Bleeding slowed to a trickle and the tiny wormlike creatures retreated from the spreading heat Lara generated. She cauterized the wound, destroying as many of the parasites as she could before bathing her hands and arms in the same hot energy.

"Did you get any blood on you, Gerald?"

He shook his head. "I don't think so, Lara. It felt like it, but I wiped my hands and face and there aren't any smears."

"Once we get Terry to a healer, take a shower as soon as you can. And burn your clothes. Don't just wash them, burn them. Everything."

She backed out of the seat, helping Terry to swing his legs out of the way of the door so she could close it and rush around to the driver's side. Terry's coloring was terrible, but more important, she didn't like the way he was breathing. Part of his distress could be shock, the shallow, too-fast breathing of panic, but she feared she hadn't stopped the parasites from assaulting his body. He needed a master healer immediately.

She drove as fast as she could over the narrow, pitted mountain road, sliding through some of the sharper turns and bumping over the muddy holes. Dirty water sprayed into the air as the car fishtailed through mud and snow. All around them, the peaceful countryside seemed a sharp contrast to their terror and desperation.

Haystacks and cows surrounded them. Small thatched houses and horse-drawn carts with huge tires gave the impression of stepping back in time to a much slower-paced and happier era. The castles and abundance of churches lent the area a medieval look, as if knights on horses might come charging over the hills at any moment.

Lara had traveled all over the world searching for her past. She remembered little of her journey from the ice cave and once the gypsies had found her, she'd traveled all over Europe. Passed from family to family, she'd never been told where they'd found her. Coming to the Carpathian Mountains had been like coming home. And when she had entered Romania, she *felt* at home. This place was still wild, the forests untamed and the land alive beneath her feet.

The car slid around another corner and they were out of the heavier forest and into the peat bogs. The trail narrowed even more, winding on solid ground while the smell of the bog permeated the air around them. Trees swayed and drooped under the heavy weight of snow. Lights in the distance heralded farms and for a moment she thought to stop at one of the nearest ones for aid, but Terry had been bitten by a mage-bred snake carrying vampire blood. Healing a mage wound was difficult enough, but a hybrid with vampire blood—that required skills far beyond her knowledge or that of a human doctor.

Their one hope lay with the innkeepers. The couple had been born and raised in the area and had lived their entire lives there. Lara couldn't imagine that they wouldn't have some knowledge of the danger lying beneath the mountain. Over time, it became difficult to tamper with the same memories. And there had been something about the inn—something that had drawn Lara to it. A suggestion of power, as if perhaps there was subtle influence at work, encouraging tourists and visitors to stay at the homey, friendly inn.

Lara had allowed herself to be susceptible to the flow of power because it was the first time since the dragon had shoved her onto the upper cavern ledge that she had encountered the light, delicate touch of flowing energy. She had forgotten what it was like to bathe herself in the crackle of electric power, to feel it surrounding her, flowing through every cell until her body hummed with it. The inn and entire village gave off the amazing feeling, although it was so subtle she had nearly missed it.

"Lara," Gerald called from the backseat. "My skin is starting to burn."

"We're almost there. Go in and take a shower first thing." She didn't want to think what Terry was suffering. He was very quiet, other than making a soft moaning sound. "Gerald, when we get to the inn, we'll need to talk to the owners and ask who the village healer is."

"The owner's name was Slavica and she seemed very nice."

"Hopefully she's very discreet as well. She certainly seems to know everyone."

"Wouldn't it be better to ask for the nearest doctor?" Gerald asked.

Lara tried to sound casual. "Sometimes the local healers know so much more about plants and animals in the area. Although we've never encountered this particular species before, it's a good bet the villagers have, and the local healer probably knows exactly what to do to extract the poi—" She broke off and hastily changed her description. "Venom."

Lara pulled the car up the twisting road to the inn on the edge of town. The large, two-story inn faced the forest with its long porch and inviting balconies. She parked as close to the stairs as she could get and raced around to help Gerald get Terry out.

Shadows lengthened and grew as the clouds overhead thickened with the threat of snow. The wind howled and the trees swayed and rustled in protest. Lara glanced around her with sharp, wary eyes as she opened the door to the backseat and reached inside for Terry.

"I'll come back for the snake heads to show the innkeeper. Don't touch them," she cautioned.

Terry was nearly deadweight as he hung between them. Gerald had to practically carry him as they stumbled through the snow. The walkway was clear, but they took a shortcut, tramping across the front slope to get to the porch faster.

A tall, dark-haired man opened the door for them and reached to help. Even under the dire circumstances, Lara found him handsome, compelling even.

"Don't get the blood on you," she warned. "It's highly venomous."

The dark-haired man's gaze swept up to her face and froze, locking on to her. For one moment there was shocked recognition in his eyes and then it was gone as he got his shoulder under Terry to relieve her of the weight.

Lara whirled around, back toward the car. "Get him inside and ask the innkeeper to find a healer. I'll get the snake heads."

She rushed back down the steps, crossing the distance to the car in a run. As she yanked open the door, her birthmark, the one shaped like a dragon, began to burn hot against her skin. There was only one thing that brought forth the dragon's warning: Vampire. And he had to be close. She hastily donned her wraparound skirt and a cloak to cover her weapons. She closed the door and looked carefully around her, one hand sliding beneath her thick red cloak to find the knife on her belt.

2

The night was bitter cold. He shouldn't be feeling it—Carpathians could easily regulate body temperature, but he wanted to be cold. It was a feeling. Not emotion—but *something*. Cold was like bitterness maybe, and bitterness was an emotion. Maybe that was the closest thing to a feeling he would have before his death.

Nicolas De La Cruz walked the length of the village with long, slow strides, his face turned from the people who shared the walkways with him to prevent them from seeing his eyes. He knew the normally dark, midnight-black color glowed a deep ruby red. Icy cold swirled in the pit of his gut, and deep inside, where his soul should have been there was only a small black piece left—and that, too, was filled with holes. The centuries of hunting and killing the vampire had long since taken their toll.

He lifted his face to the swirling clouds laced and heavy with snow. This was his last night. He was done with his fight. He had served his people and his family with honor, held fast through the centuries and hunted more of his fallen comrades than most. Tomorrow he would walk into the sun and end his long, barren existence.

He was far from his home and his brothers. His oldest brother, Zacarias, would be unable to stop him from such a distance, in fact, wouldn't sense his end until it was far too late to stop him. He wondered how long it would take for the sun to burn him clean. A long time with the stains on his soul, but still, his brothers wouldn't have to share the intensity of the suffering of his last few minutes of life.

He shivered, grateful for the cold on his face and skin, grateful he could feel physical sensations. Emotions—he had lost those so long ago they were a distant memory, or maybe not really his memory at all. Three of his brothers had found lifemates and shared their newfound emotions with him. In some ways their happiness made it so much harder to bear being so alone.

He had come for one last walk through the village before meeting with Mikhail Dubrinsky—prince of the Carpathian people. He'd traveled far to deliver a warning, yet now, he wasn't certain it was safe for a face-to-face meeting—especially in the close confines of the local inn. Already heartbeats were loud, bombarding him with the need for rich, hot blood. Sharp teeth pushed against the inside of his mouth and saliva gathered in anticipation of the feast.

It wouldn't take much to let himself taste—just for a moment, one time—the hot rush of adrenaline-laced blood that would give him a glimpse of lost emotion. And a woman... He would love to feel a woman's soft skin, inhale her scent, pretend for just a moment he had someone who belonged to him, would look at him with love—genuine love—not that greedy heat that came the moment a woman knew his material wealth.

If he could feel regret, it would be not for the countless times he had to destroy an old friend, not for the many souls he'd freed and laid to rest, but that he'd never felt the true need for a woman. He'd never held a woman he loved in his arms and worshipped her with his body.

The whispers in his mind grew stronger, tempting him with the things he had never known in his long life.

Women had been attracted to his looks, his power and his money. He had used them for sustenance, but he'd never been able to know what it was like to feel the pleasures a woman could bring his body, the peace she could bring to his mind. One taste. Just one. He could sink his teeth into soft skin and feel the flow of life, hear the quickening rhythm of her heart beating in tune with his. She would fear him, his domination, his complete supremacy over her. Life or death. He had that power.

His heart slammed hard in his chest. His body stirred to life. He scented prey. A fragrance beckoning to him. Calling out from the beauty of the night. He had only to take that one last taste and he could experience everything before the sun rose and burned him clean. He turned his head and saw her standing in the shadows. The breath left his body in a rush.

Her skin was pale and flawless. Her hair was pulled back in a long, thick braid. Her eyes were wide, large and sparkling, glowing slightly. She seemed to be waiting for someone. A man? A low growl rumbled in his chest and he felt his body react to the thought. Detached as he was from his actions, he found it all interesting. He had never felt threatened by man or beast or monster, yet looking at this young woman, he knew he would fight to the death for a chance to taste her blood, to feel the softness of her skin, to hear her heart match the rhythm of his.

For the first time in his long life, he actually had erotic images of his own, not drawn from someone else's mind. They rose up to taunt him. This woman writhing and moaning, pleading with him to give her everything. He wouldn't feel a thing when he took her offering, but maybe, if he took her life at the same time, he would have that one moment...

Her head snapped around and her gaze locked on him. There wasn't the instant look in her eyes he had come to expect—woman spotting attractive male. She looked like a predator, gaze burning, mouth firm. Her body was all woman, dressed in layers of clothing, a high-necked dark sweater with long sleeves that covered her wrists. A pair of dark leggings that ran into serviceable boots covered shapely legs. A wraparound skirt was cinched at her small waist with a wide leather belt and hugged the fitted leggings but gave her ease of movement and a long, warm cloak hung from her shoulders to her knees.

There was something familiar about her, as if they may have met before. Try as he might, he could not look away from her. Always with women he had the upper hand, drawing them to him with his looks and dangerous air, yet he had the feeling this woman wasn't at all consumed with desire for him.

Again he had a visceral reaction deep in his gut. A need for her to want him. *Come to me now. Offer yourself to me.* There was shame in using the gift of his voice to entrap and enthrall her, it would have made the fantasy better to have her come to him of her own accord. Afterward he might even be able to convince himself she wanted him, but not like this, with compulsion.

Her body jerked. Her chin went up and the bright eyes smoldered. *As if she knew.* She began to walk toward him. He moved into deeper shadows, his heart pounding. He could already taste her in his mouth, feel her soft skin sliding against his. His blood surged hotly.

She was of average height and his size dwarfed hers, but she had womanly curves and looked strong. She moved with fluid grace, not at all stumbling and halting as if fighting a compulsion. For a moment the clouds parted and light spilled across her face. His gut knotted.

Stop! Go back. Get inside. He had to save her. His hands shook—actually shook—and damn him forever to hell, his body stirred, hot and hard and aching for her, when in all his years he had never had such a response. Her life—her very soul as well as his—was in danger. Even as he warned her, he took a step toward her. Wanting her. Needing her. If he touched her, if he got too close, they would both be lost.

A frown flitted across her face. She pressed her palm to her body, down low, and halted, looking confused.

Lara stared hard at the tall, wide-shouldered man coming toward her. He was the most classically beautiful man she'd ever seen in her life. His face was raw masculine beauty, his eyes so dark they were nearly black, yet when he turned a certain way, they glowed like rubies, causing a chill to race down her spine. He moved with unbelievable grace, his body flowing, ropes of muscles rippling subtly like a giant jungle cat on the prowl.

She didn't have reactions to men, no matter how hot they were. Her body remained as cold and as frigid as the ice chambers she'd spent the first few years of her life in, yet looking at this man, everything changed. Her breath quickened. Her pulse raced. Her stomach somersaulted and even her womb reacted, clenching hotly. But so did her birthmark. And her birthmark heralded the arrival of one thing—vampire.

The problem was, the mark seemed to have a short in it. One moment it burned with scorching heat and the next it went cool and lifeless. She had the blade of her knife up against her wrist, concealed by her long sleeve, the handle securely in her fist. She wasn't taking any chances, no matter how hot he was.

And then there was his voice. Velvet soft. Pure seduction. A night melody of dark promises, one moment beckoning, the next rejecting. The first time he spoke his command she had been certain he was a vampire drawing her to him to allow him to feed on her. The next moment he seemed to be trying to warn her off, yet he continued forward, his black eyes drifting over her face as if he owned her.

Nicolas couldn't stop walking toward her—as if he, not she, was the one under compulsion. He was going to have to call to Mikhail for help to save her. But he was so far gone, it was possible he would engage in a battle with the prince over her. And Mikhail couldn't be risked, not if their species was to survive.

Go! He warned her again, his voice low and firm, but he failed to bury a compulsion in his tone. As much as a part of him wanted to save her, the other part, standing off detached and greedy for one moment of true life, of *feeling* before he ended his existence, couldn't quite be noble enough to help her escape.

She turned her head, her gaze searching the shadows and rooftops for danger. He was almost on her when she turned back to him. Up close she was so beautiful. Breathtaking really. Her skin looked exquisite. Her scent was faint and alluring, drawing him. He felt almost in a trance, if that were possible for one such as him.

His fingers circled her wrist like a bracelet, light, yet made of steel. She moved then, whirling around, into him, her elbow connecting with his sternum. Nicolas barely felt the blow that would have rocked a human. Suddenly his arms were locked around her and his face was buried in the thick mass of her hair. It was soft. Heaven.

The blood in her veins ebbed and flowed like the tide, pounding through her, making him know he—and she— were alive. Not existing, but living. Standing there in the beauty of the night with the scent of the forest surrounding him as he took his last feast.

The whispers in his head turned to a possessive roar. This one was his alone. He didn't hesitate, he lowered his face to her shoulder, nuzzling the sweater aside to expose the bare flesh of her neck and the pounding pulse there. He made no effort to calm her, or put her under a compulsion. The adrenaline in her blood would heighten the experience, give him a rush of feeling so that he would always retain this moment. He sank his teeth deep and took the essence of her being deep inside him.

"Let go of me, you bastard," Lara snapped, shocked at the sudden pain, shocked that after all those years of swearing to herself no one would ever—*ever*—take her blood by force, she was locked in the arms of a vampire.

As a child, she had been used solely for food. Her father and great-grandfather had ripped into her veins and taken from her as if she were nothing, not human, not Carpathian and certainly not mage. She had been a food source and nothing more.

Rage swept through her. Shook her. Took her by surprise. She had never been so angry in her life. And yet, after the initial bite, the dark, erotic seduction made some part of her want to be a part of him, made her want to succumb to the fire and heat—to give her life for his.

Clenching her teeth, she fought the sensation of need and desire pulsing through her body. She wouldn't go that easily, or give in. She had no idea a vampire could be so cunning. One minute triggering an alarm, the next warning her off and then the bite. The absolute seduction of that bite.

She gripped the knife in her fist and tried to get a little room in order to move her hand toward his ribs, but she was facing away from him and it was difficult to feel where he was when lightning sizzled and crackled in her veins, robbing her of her ability to think.

Nicolas was so far gone in the ecstasy of her taste and shape and feel that it took a moment to register that she had spoken. *Let go of me, you bastard.* The words echoed in his mind, burst through his subconscious and took hold of his heart.

Emotion flooded in with dizzying speed. Fast and sharp and jumbled so that it was impossible to sort anything out. The love he felt for his brothers came tumbling into his heart and mind. Anger. Rage that he had been following an honorable path yet had been so close to turning. Shame. For the near brush with the monster he had been hunting for centuries. More shame for the sins he had yet to confess to the prince—sins committed against the leader of their people. Not in action, but in the hearts and minds of Nicolas and his brothers. Joy for the woman in his arms who would save him from a fate that would have dishonored not only him, but his family as well.

So much to try to sort out all at once. And all while his body was hard and hurting, his groin so full and thick the material of his clothes caused physical pain. He wanted her. Needed her. Had to have her. The taste of her was unlike anything he'd ever experienced. This woman. His lifemate. The woman he had searched for across several continents, the woman he had spent centuries looking for. The only woman who could restore his emotions.

He opened his eyes and her hair dazzled him. There in the darkness it burned bright red, but as he watched, his eyes played tricks on him, so that waves of colors glowed metallic and coppery. He couldn't find the strength of will to pull away from her, to stop the sweet fire sliding down his throat, tying them together in the way of his people. Somewhere, far off, he could hear his own mind screaming at him that he was losing his mind, that he had found her too late and that he was killing her, but he couldn't stop.

Pain ripped through his left side, startling him out of his trancelike state. He jerked his head up without swiping his tongue across the twin pinpricks at her pulse to close the wound. Blood trickled down her neck into the earthy tones of her sweater. He could see the garment, a dazzling color, hues of browns and gold, with red drops scattering and pooling in the yarn.

Color, after centuries of shades of gray. Beautiful, amazing color. He looked down at his side from where the pain emanated. The handle of a knife stuck out of his ribs. She stepped back away from him and spun to face him. Her eyes were twin jewels, burning bright, a deep emerald, not just green, but actually emerald. Even as he watched, the color swirled and changed, going from deep green to arctic blue. The blue was the color of the ice glaciers, clean and pure and ice-cold, but burning with intensity and fire.

He smiled at her. *"Te avio päläfertiilam. Éntölam kuulua, avio päläfertiilam."*

His voice was low, a dark seduction that slid over her senses, like velvet playing over her skin, arousing her. Lara had heard those words before, long ago when the aunts sang her to sleep. They sang of a great love story. A man—as dark as sin. A woman—bright as light. Only that woman could save him from the worst suffering of honorable death, or the worst fate of becoming the vampire. She had the power to restore his lost emotions, to restore bright, beautiful colors to the world. The love story had been the one beautiful thing in her life as a child and she had clung to it, needing something to hang on to.

Te avio päläfertiilam. Éntölam kuulua, avio päläfertiilam. You are my lifemate. I claim you as my lifemate. The words were so beautiful, so connecting, she could feel them echo in her heart and mind. They had been the words in her story and she dreamt of them, thought them romantic. But the man hadn't been so seductively beautiful and so utterly dangerous. And he certainly hadn't taken his lady's blood without permission. It was wrong. A violation she would *not* permit.

"Ted kuuluak, kacad, kojed." "I belong to you." *"Élidamet andam."* "I offer my life for you." As he spoke the words in that perfectly calm, soft voice, he gripped the handle of the knife and yanked it from his body. Blood gushed down his side. He held out the weapon to her, handle first.

Lara swallowed hard, raising her gaze from the wound to his face. There was no anger. No expression at all. Just a strange serenity that shook her. She moistened her suddenly dry lips and reached out to take the knife. Her fingertips brushed his. Electricity sizzled up her arm. He merely opened his arms wide, presenting his heart as a target.

"Pesämet andam. Uskolfertiilamet andam. Sívamet andam. Sielamet andam. Ainamet andam." His teeth flashed very white in the darkness. "I give you my protection. I give you my allegiance. I give you my heart. I give you my soul. I give you my body."

She realized he wasn't talking figuratively, but literally. He was offering to stand there while she drove a knife into his heart and took his life. This was no vampire. She had no real idea of what he was, but the words he was uttering were in the Carpathian language, a language as ancient as her aunts had been. And the words were a ritual that bound two halves of the same soul together. She had never believed in that love story, not truly, even though she knew the kinds of things that could be wrought with elements and energy and magic. But as he spoke each word in that soft, seductive tone, his black eyes glittering with possession and absolute determination, she could feel the ties forging like steel between them.

"Are you crazy? You have to be out of your mind. Don't stand there like an idiot. You need to stop the bleeding."

His eyes never left her face. *"Sívamet kuuluak kaik että a ted. Ainaak olenszal sívambin.* I take into my keeping the same that is yours. Your life will be cherished by me for all my time."

She flung her head up, her red braid whipping across her shoulder, glacier blue eyes crackling and glittering with anger. "Really? Is this what you call cherishing me?" She pressed a hand to her neck where the thin trickle of blood continued. "You *took* from me without permission. Without asking. Without one thought for how I might feel."

All the while she reprimanded him, her gaze kept dropping to the blood pooling at his side. He had to stop it. If he was Carpathian—and he had to be—he could close the wound on his own and keep his life's essence from flowing away.

"Te élidet ainaak pide minan." "Your life will be placed above my own for all time." His expression didn't change. He kept his arms outstretched, presenting her with a kill target. His black gaze never left her face. His expression was utter, absolute serenity, although his eyes blazed with a dark possession.

Fury shook her. "You won't have a life if you don't heal yourself."

"Te avio päläfertiilam. Ainaak sívamet jutta oleny. Ainaak terád vigyázak." "You are my lifemate. You are bound to me for all eternity. You are always in my care."

She hissed out her breath, teeth snapping together. "You don't just get to claim me and think it's all going to work out. Not when you've taken my blood without my consent." Her heart was pounding as she watched his life ebbing away with the flow of blood. "Do something."

"It is not my choice. Life or death is the choice of my lifemate. If you reject my claim, then you are condemning me and I willingly die by your hand."

Her blue eyes were twin chips of burning ice. "Don't you dare blame your death on me." But she was already springing toward him, unable to stop herself. Her throat nearly closed with fear as she clamped both hands over the wound in his side. She wanted to shake him. Literally just grab him and shake him until he saw how utterly ridiculous he was being.

So much for her romantic love story. "You might be the hottest man in the village, but your brain is about the size of a pea," she muttered under her breath. "Close the wound. I don't have that kind of ability."

"Then it is life you choose for me."

His voice was enough to make a woman want to strip and jump him, and the effect he had on her annoyed her more than anything else.

"You deserve to die just for being stupid," she snapped, but she didn't let go of his side, pressing tightly, making certain to clamp down and prevent further bleeding. "Now heal yourself."

He gave a slight, old-world bow. "As you wish."

That voice was seduction itself. Her body tingled, her breasts heavy and aching. She didn't want him touching her, or brushing her face or body with his black gaze. She could hear his heart matching the rhythm of hers. Air flowed in and out of his lungs in tune with hers, a soft sighing so that their breath mingled together. Everything feminine in her, everything she was, Carpathian, mage and human, rose up to meet the male in him.

"I wish for you to get yourself some psychological help. You can't seem to make up your mind whether you're a vampire or a hunter." She deliberately injected scorn into her voice.

His expression didn't change. He didn't even blink, but she'd scored a hit. They were connected now, all those unbreakable threads she felt between them allowed her to read his emotions and gave her an insight to the predator she was prodding. Her heart stuttered and her stomach did a funny little flip.

He didn't move, yet he was closer, much closer, his body pressing against the small palms of her hands where they were buried into his side. "Have no fears, *päläfertiil*, I have made up my mind."

She didn't like the sound of that—the soft purring in his voice that sounded more like a threat than a reassurance. She felt the heat suddenly bursting from his body, saw the flash of white light glowing around her hands. His flesh grew hot, although it didn't burn her, merely cleansed the blood from her skin. She dropped her hands abruptly and stepped away from him, looking up the long length of his body to his incredible face.

His body up close was too masculine, too strong, too everything. Wide shoulders, solid—he looked invincible—even though she'd managed to get a knife into him. She swallowed fear and took another step back.

"I have to go."

"We go together. You cannot pretend I have not claimed you and that you did not reject my claim. You chose life for me. Our souls are one."

Lara frowned. She had a vague idea of the ritual binding words from the story her aunts told her. The words were imprinted on the male before birth. Once uttered, they bound two souls together so one could not survive without the other once the ritual was actually complete. She didn't know what the rest of the ritual was, but if it involved sex with this man, she really wasn't up to the task.

She tilted her head and looked at him with a cool steady gaze. She didn't feel cool or steady, but she wanted him to understand her—to know that if she'd ever been serious about anything in her life, she was serious about this. "I know very little about your traditions or culture. Just stories my aunts told me when I was a child, but no matter what you've done to tie us together, know this: I don't know you. I don't love you. I don't care anything at all about you. I spent the first years of my life a prisoner and I will never—*never*—allow anyone to imprison me again. If you try to take anything from me by force, if you try to break my will or manipulate my mind, I will fight you with the last breath in my body. So you make up *your* mind—choose life or death for us."

His eyes darkened to obsidian, glittering with a sensual lust that burned through her body. He cupped her chin with gentle fingers and bent his head slowly. Mesmerized, she couldn't pull herself away. She could see the long length of his lashes, the tiny crinkled lines around his eyes, the straight nose of the aristocrat, the mouth sinfully carnal, but stamped with the mark of a man who could be cruel.

Her breath caught as his hair brushed her face. She felt his mouth on her neck. Hot. Burning. Velvet soft. His tongue rasped over the twin pinpricks at her frantically beating pulse, stopping the tempting trickle of her blood.

I choose life for us.

The words slid into her mind like a caress. She moistened her lips as he straightened to his full height. "Fine then. We understand each other." She turned to go back to the inn—to safety, because no matter what this man agreed to, she knew she wasn't safe with him and it wasn't entirely his fault.

Once more his fingers settled around her wrist like a bracelet. Warm. He stroked the pads of his fingers against the bare skin of her inner wrist, halting her. "I do not think you quite understand me and I would not want you later to say you were not in possession of all the facts."

Lara turned back reluctantly. "I'm listening."

"You are the one woman—the only woman—*my* woman. This is something I take very seriously. Your health. Your safety and your happiness. I will see to these things, but I will not share you. I will not allow others to interfere in our relationship. *No other.* Man or woman. If you have a problem with something, you tell me. If you are afraid of something, you tell me."

"I don't know you. And I don't trust that easily."

"I did not say it would be easy. I just want you to understand who I am."

She couldn't push down the rising panic. She saw him exactly for what he was. A predator. A hunter. A man who made decisions and expected those around him to follow his lead. Already the ritual words had bound them together. She could feel the pull of him on her mind—even on her body.

Lara let her breath out slowly. "I don't share my blood."

His lips curved into a small smile. She caught a brief glimpse of his white teeth and then that predatory smile was gone and he once again wore a face carved of stone. "I noticed."

Color rose in her cheeks. "I have to get back inside. I have a friend who is hurt. Maybe you can help him. You obviously know healing."

All warmth leeched from his eyes. "Your friend is male?"

She shivered, suddenly cold. "Yes. I came with two colleagues. We're doing research nearby and we're staying here."

"What kind of research?" There was a bite to his voice, a note of suggestion.

Now her entire body was blushing. She was annoyed with herself for the fluttery nerves in the pit of her stomach. She was trying to establish herself as someone to take seriously, yet each time she looked closely at him something inside her seemed to melt.

He scared the hell out of her. She had faced monsters, yet she hadn't been as afraid as she was at this moment. This man had changed her life for all time. He stood calm and resolute, implacable even, looking at her with possession in his eyes and a mouth that was so fascinating, she could barely tear her gaze away, yet she knew he was one of the most dangerous creatures living on the earth.

"Well, it's hard to explain. Mostly we do sexual research together. You know, sex in every culture down through time."

"Very funny."

"You deserved it. You had that tone."

"I had a tone?"

She swept her green gaze over him and began walking back toward the inn, very aware of him pacing beside her with the silent stride of a jungle cat. "Actually, I explore caves and I've been researching life forms in ice caves."

There was an edge of haughtiness in her voice. "So answer my question: Do you know much about healing? Or do you know someone who does? We were attacked by a hybrid—part plant, part snake—and very venomous."

He caught her elbow and brought her to a halt. "Did it bite you?" He was already running his hands up and down her arms, tilting her head this way and that. And then she felt the thrust of his mind against hers.

It was such a shock, the sheer intimacy of his mind merging with hers. There was nothing at all soft about him. He could erupt into violence with swift efficiency. When she had thought him one of the most dangerous creatures on earth, she hadn't even come close to understanding the killing machine that he was, yet he hid nothing from her. He didn't attempt to pretend to be different than he was, and she saw that he could. He could have appeared gentle and sweet, but he gave her the respect of showing her exactly who and what she was dealing with.

Lara inhaled sharply. Her aunts had told her Carpathians were powerful. They had presented them as heroic, hunters of the vampires, protectors of human and mage alike. She was unprepared for the ruthless, merciless mind of the hunter. And he was beyond any arrogance she'd ever known.

She couldn't prevent the tremor of awareness or the little shiver of fear. The heat of his body enveloped her, warmed her, driving out the cold of the night when she had forgotten to regulate her temperature. She attempted to retreat, slamming down the barriers in her mind. She had always been powerful, but it had been years since she'd had to utilize her abilities to conceal her mind from any other and she was slow and rusty.

"There is no need to hide yourself from me," Nicolas said. Not only was her body shivering, but so was her mind. He had triggered a well of fear, tapping into some long-ago memories of someone close to her who had misused and abused her trust. "I cannot lie to you, nor do I attempt to access what you will not give me freely. I look only for parasites and wounds. The snakes are more deadly than you can know."

She let her breath out, somewhat relieved. He hadn't examined her memories of that lost little girl. He didn't know who she was or what she was. There was always power in knowledge and she trusted no one—least of all the man who could make her body come alive when she had been frozen for so many years. She didn't trust anything that happened so fast, or that walked in an ancient land of enormous power.

"The snakes injected venom into my friend. There were tiny parasitic organisms in the venom and the blood of the snakes burned like acid." As she spoke, she moved away from him, a delicate feminine retreat.

Nicolas wanted to smile. He didn't smile easily. Hadn't smiled in five hundred years, but her girly reaction when she was trying to be a fierce warrior was so cute. *Cute.* He had never understood that word before. He'd heard it a thousand times but had no real concept of the meaning until that moment. Instincts told him she wouldn't appreciate being considered cute when she thought of herself as tough, so he kept his observation to himself.

She was shorter than most Carpathian women, barely coming up to the middle of his chest, but her body was all feminine curves. She considered herself overweight—he'd caught that small bit of information before he narrowed the flow of information to specifics. He didn't understand that either. She was perfect, but then he would have thought her perfect no matter what she had looked like. How could he not? She had restored his life, his very soul. He could feel real love for his brothers. He could feel real honor and a sense of duty to his people. She had turned a bleak, gray world into a dazzling wonderland. She was the epitome of beauty to him with her classic bone structure and the jeweled eyes of the Dragonseeker line.

Power crackled in her. This was no shy, retiring maiden, but a warrior prepared to fight him at every turn. She didn't know he had already won the battle. She was part Carpathian and her nature would draw her to him. The pull between them would grow over time and he would make absolutely certain that he was by her side while time worked its magic on his lifemate.

"Stop staring at me like that." She walked faster.

He kept pace easily. "I had no idea I was staring in any particular way."

There was joy in the night as well as breathtaking beauty. He marveled that he could feel it, see it, be one with it. The heavy clouds formed whimsical shapes, drifting overhead with the helpful push of the wind. The village breathed, hearts beating, children's laughter ringing out. Why hadn't he heard those sounds before? Sounds of life and love. Fathers murmuring, mothers calling, children laughing. He had lost the magic of life over the centuries and now it was there, flooding his senses.

Her eyes flashed at him. Green again. Green was her normal color, a dazzling emerald her red hair made deeper. Glacier blue was her power color then. There was satisfaction in discovering that small fact about her. He wanted to know everything about her all at once, but he had learned long ago the lesson of patience and it had stood him in good stead for hundreds of years. Time would reveal her secrets to him and each moment spent with her—finding out the little things, the intimacies of her true self—would bring joy to him.

He even enjoyed the unrelenting ache she brought to his body. It was another sign of being alive—of living and breathing and sharing his world with her. His soul had been so dark, so damaged, he had been unable to feel emotion, keeping pain at bay and guilt and shame, but it also kept away true life.

"You are a miracle to me. Maybe that is what you are seeing in my stare. Sheer wonder." He kept his expression calm, not allowing his joy to overwhelm her, but he did inject the dark seduction of black velvet into his voice so that it caressed her skin and slid deeper into her body, lighting little electrical sparks from breast to feminine channel.

She stopped so abruptly in the open doorway of the inn he nearly ran into her.

3

Lara scowled at Nicolas, her green eyes suddenly suspicious. "Are you a ladies' man? All sweet talk and syrup
with no substance? Because I'm telling you right now, I've
had experience with that kind of man and I can see right
through flattery."

She was lying. Looking him right in the eye and lying
her pretty little butt off. She had no experience with men.
And she couldn't stop blushing every time she looked at
him. The smile started in his mind and spread to his lips.
Genuine. Spontaneous. A miracle in itself that he could
smile—that he had a reason for smiling.

Nicolas wanted to carry her off to his lair and keep her
to himself for a year or two, learning every detail about
her. Desire rose sharp and painful. He kept his face without
expression. "I do not believe anyone has ever said I talk
sweet or that I am syrup in all the years of my existence."

She gave a little undignified snort. "Maybe not, but I'll
bet they called you a ladies' man."

"I am a Carpathian hunter of great skill but I am certain
I will have the necessary skills to become your mate."

She choked and turned away from him, stomping into the inn, her shoulders stiff. Nicolas moved in behind her, very close, aware as they entered that men turned to look at her. She was striking with her skin and hair, the glow many Carpathian women had, a sort of luminous quality combined with a fluid sexy walk that drew the eye. He flashed a message, letting them know without words that she belonged to him. Black eyes carried death as he looked directly at each man to emphasize the point. They looked away from her and two actually left, telling him the vibes he was sending out were just a little too strong. He was going to have to learn to manage his newfound emotions.

Nicolas followed her up the stairs to one of the rooms, taking the stairs two at a time. She reached for the doorknob. Nicolas's hand was there before hers. He inserted his larger body smoothly between her and the room.

"I will go in first." He had already scanned the room. Two unknown human males and Mikhail, prince of his people. Still, even with the prince, he wasn't about to take any chances on her safety. He scented vampire blood.

"It's my room," she objected, shocked at how smoothly, how easily he had taken over.

His black eyes moved over her face. "Yes, it is, and you seem to have a surplus of male visitors."

He didn't wait for an answer, but pushed open the door, ignoring her outraged little squeak. Mikhail had been fully aware of his arrival, his gaze shooting past him, but Nicolas's much larger body blocked the doorway, preventing Lara from entering. Nicolas took in the scene, the man writhing in pain on the bed. A second man holding his shoulders in hopes to calm him while the prince seemed to be attempting to heal the injuries of the male on the bed. Nicolas stepped aside to allow his lifemate entrance.

"Nicolas." Mikhail stepped forward to clasp both his arms in the traditional greeting of respect and honor between warriors. "It is good to see you." He didn't show the worry he had to be feeling that Nicolas De La Cruz had traveled personally from South America to bring him news. He understood that news couldn't be good or word would have been sent through the chain of Carpathians to their homeland.

"I bring greetings from Zacarias as well as my other brothers. I hope you and your woman are well."

Mikhail nodded. "I sensed a disturbance earlier."

Nicolas didn't change expression, nor did he look away. Of course Mikhail had sensed a disturbance. Nicolas had been close enough to turning that he had nearly taken his own lifemate's life. Fortunately, she had a knife and hadn't hesitated to use it. The blood was gone from Nicolas's shirt, but Mikhail wouldn't be easily fooled.

Nicolas turned to his lifemate. "Mikhail Dubrinsky is the prince of the Carpathian people," Nicolas explained to her before turning back to his prince. "Mikhail, this is *avio päläfertiil*." He put unmistakable possession in his voice even as he rested his hand on the small of her back.

Mikhail bowed slightly from the waist. "I am pleased to meet your lifemate, Nicolas, but what is her name?"

"Her name?" For the first time Nicolas looked bewildered.

"She does have a name, doesn't she?" Mikhail asked, clearly amused.

Nicolas looked down at the bright burst of red-gold hair and those brilliant jeweled green eyes. "What is your name?"

"You tied us together and you don't even know my name," she scoffed, trying to ignore the scent of tainted, rotted blood in the room. "You're absolutely crazy, you know that? It's Lara. Lara Calladine. And you?" Her heart was pounding too hard, knowing her life had changed forever. She couldn't think about it yet, keeping emotion light until she had time to assimilate what had happened and what she could do about it.

His slow smile nearly melted her on the spot, a distraction when the room felt "off" to her.

"Nicolas De La Cruz."

"You're Carpathian." She made it a statement, looking from one man to the other. "You both are." It was difficult to be conversing when she found herself shivering with cold, a little disoriented and slightly sick.

"As are you," Nicolas replied.

Lara shook her head. "Part, but not all."

His eyebrow shot up. "You are of the Dragonseeker lineage. No one could ever mistake your features or your eyes for anything else."

Her heart leapt. "Then you know my aunts? Have you news of them?"

Nicolas wanted to give her good news. The joy and hope on her face was astonishing. "I am sorry, *päläfertiil*, I know only Dominic as full Dragonseeker. There are two females, Natalya, Vikirnoff's lifemate, as well as my brother's lifemate, Colby, who carry Dragonseeker blood. It is a great lineage and one of the most revered in our history."

Lara looked to Mikhail. "Have you heard of my aunts?"

Mikhail shook his head. "I am sorry. I do not know which aunts you speak of. There are no full-blooded women in the Dragonseeker line. Rhiannon was the last and she is lost to us. How are you related?"

She opened her mouth and closed it abruptly. She was part mage. She knew the story of Rhiannon, the last daughter of the Dragonseeker lineage. She had been the lifemate of a great warrior who had been murdered by Xavier, the high mage. Xavier had kept Rhiannon prisoner and alive, forcing her to give birth to his children. The triplets Soren, Tatijana and Branislava were born of the unholy union. Soren had escaped into the world and joined with a human woman. He had two children, Razvan and Natalya. Lara's father was Razvan. She was a direct descendent of the

Carpathian's worst enemy, the man who had betrayed their trust and started a war that ultimately had led to the near extinction of mage and Carpathian alike. Her mother had been mage, so mage blood ran strong in her, along with the Dragonseeker blood.

Lara shifted her gaze to Terry, who lay on the bed moaning and rocking back and forth. She forced herself to look at him when she wanted to run. She had seen young mages who had been deliberately injected with the parasites rotting from the inside out. The scent of death was already oozing from his pores.

She cleared her throat. "Were you able to clear his blood of the parasites?"

Terry's body jerked and he focused on her face. "Lara. You're back. It hurts like hell. What do you mean parasites?"

"The right leg is easy enough," Mikhail said out loud, "but the left is giving me a few problems." He glanced toward Nicolas, using the common telepathic path used by the Carpathian people. *She did not answer my question.*

Lara stiffened. They were communicating on the path her aunts used with her. She had always thought that there had been a chance she made the aunts up. That the trauma of her childhood had produced a break and she had created an imaginary world for herself, but there was no way the prince and Nicolas could communicate on that *exact* band.

She is not here to be interrogated. Nicolas's tone was mild, but he shifted subtly, placing his body between Lara and the prince.

A flicker of amusement showed in Mikhail's eyes and then was gone as he turned back to the writhing man on the bed.

"He pulled the snake head out before I could stop him. The snake's fangs are curved with barbs at the ends. I think the barbs carry the venom, and when he ripped them loose, he allowed the poison to pour into his system." She glanced toward Nicolas and used their private mental path. *It seems a little rude to be discussing me when I'm standing right here, but thanks for sticking up for me.*

Mikhail's head snapped around, his black eyes glittering. Lara drew in her breath. She hadn't spoken telepathically to anyone but the aunts in years and she'd been sloppy, allowing the channel of energy to spill over enough to warn Mikhail she was speaking with Nicolas. Annoyed with herself, she bit her lip hard, reminding herself to stay quiet and blend in. One could hide in plain sight if one were adept enough at it.

"Terry, don't worry, we'll be able to make you feel better," Lara assured, still avoiding looking directly at him. She had to go to him at least and hold his hand. What sort of friend was she? She steeled herself, stiffening her spine.

The sight of him writhing in pain triggered memories of her childhood. Healthy, living blood smelled like life, sweet and flowing. Death brought a metallic tang. But tainted blood was rotting, putrid, the stench offensive and sickening. She couldn't get away from the smell, even with all the little tricks her aunts had taught her.

She made a move to get around Nicolas to go to the man on the bed, but Nicolas seemed to move with her, shifting almost imperceptibly. Lara didn't catch how he did it, but when she tried a second time, his solid mass continued to block her way.

"Mikhail and I will do what we can to heal your friend, but you need to stay back until we know what we are dealing with."

Lara opened her mouth to protest, but closed it without speaking. His voice was low, so low she doubted if either Terry or Gerald caught what he said, but there was a tone there, one of complete command. He was enormously strong and she didn't know what powers he had, but she sensed danger. Now, in front of so many others, wasn't the time to test him or his resolve. It would mean pitting herself against him openly, and the aunts had drilled into her not to draw attention to herself. The few times she had done so in the past, she'd met with disastrous results. She let her breath out in a small hiss between her teeth. In the end, she might feel guilty for using the ready excuse, but the blood on the bed sickened her. She allowed Nicolas to dictate to her.

Nicolas kept his smile to himself. She thought she was hiding her displeasure, but her hair swirled with bands of color, red and blond streaks. The red came out when she was upset or angry and right now her hair was streaked with flame. The color of her eyes had gone from green to glacier blue, glittering like ice at him, but she said nothing, simply stepped back as if she was obedient and sweet.

He bent over the mutilated ankle. There was nothing sweet about his woman. She might hide her true nature from the others, but she was a little tigress with claws and fangs, ready to do battle when situations warranted. His life had gone from barren and gray to exciting in the blink of an eye. Her reaction to his high-handedness made him want to find something else to do to make her hair crackle and her eyes glow at him.

There were masses of parasites in Terry's system, and Nicolas frowned as he focused on the clogged blood. He glanced at Mikhail. *Have you ever seen anything like this before?*

Not to this extent. I have sent for Gregori. He is our greatest healer and is this man's only chance at survival intact. Mikhail glanced back at Lara, deliberately including her in the conversation. *I am sorry. I know he is a friend of yours.*

Lara's stomach knotted. She pressed a hand to it. This was her fault. She had taken Terry and Gerald with her to find the cave, because she hadn't thought it was real. She had begun to doubt herself. Somewhere deep inside, she had suspected the cave might really be there when she had first gone for a permit after studying the mountain's geology. There had been an excitement she couldn't suppress and she should have known she was on the right track. If she had believed in herself more, she wouldn't have exposed her friends to such danger. *Can you save him?*

It wasn't that Mikhail and Nicolas exchanged a look, both were bent over Terry's ankle, examining the wound, but she felt something pass between them. It wasn't words, not even on a private telepathic path, because Nicolas was keeping his mind open to hers.

Vapor poured through the open window, a steady stream of white mist filling the room. At once the air was electrified. Lara felt the hair on the back of her neck rise. She stepped back, away from the window toward the door. She shouldn't have worried. Nicolas was there immediately, inserting his body between her and the mist, and for once, she wasn't offended. She wanted nothing to do with whatever was coming in through the open window.

Energy was something a mage learned to manipulate from birth. She had seen many young mages working on using whatever was available to them for simple or complex tasks. In the years of observing studies and experiments, she rarely had felt the amount of energy pouring into this room, and never had power been seeking another like a magnet and surrounding that one person as it was now. The vapor continued to stack into the shape of a large, transparent man, but the energy raced toward the prince, seeking him out, bathing him in large waves—giving him untold power.

Nicolas, Terry and Gerald didn't seem to notice anything at all. Maybe it was just that she'd always been sensitive to the presence of energy because, as a child, it had been her warning that she was about to be dragged from her chamber and her flesh torn, her blood consumed. She shivered, feeling queasy.

Pressing a hand to her rolling stomach, she backed away

from the prince and the man shimmering with transparency. Her skin crawled. Her wrists burned. She felt the sensation of spiders crawling over her skin. Lara brushed them away, coming up against the wall. The temperature in the room dropped significantly and she couldn't stop shivering with cold.

The stranger swung around to look at her, his eyes slashing steel. "Dragonseeker," he said aloud. "The blood runs strong in her."

Bile rose. She choked, barely able to drag in enough air. The walls of the room undulated, curved, formed tunnels, thick and blue around her.

"Gregori, we do not have much time," Mikhail said.

Fear became a monster, blossoming, growing, building inside her until she could barely see straight. The floor shifted under her feet. So much power. The scent of decayed blood so strong. The man on the bed was beyond screaming now, moaning continuously.

Gregori nodded, but those silver eyes continued to bore into Lara, shredding her guards, her very carefully placed shields, seeing right through her to reveal every one of her secrets. *You have much power running through your veins.*

Her body jerked, her mind flinching away from the invasion. Those light, piercing eyes. She had seen eyes that color on only one other person. Fear shook her. For one moment his face wavered, and she found herself staring at a different face, one all too familiar from her nightmares. Gasping, she whirled around, seeking a way out, but the cold ice walls were too thick to penetrate. She was trapped. Her wrist throbbed and burned.

Lara? What is it? Nicolas stepped toward her.

Stay out of my head! Not only did she reject the contact, she threw him out of her mind, slamming a barrier hard and fast, gathering the energy in the room around her like a protective cloak. Her hands rose, an automatic gesture of protection, weaving fast with astonishing expertise.

Wall of light. Shield of gold. Rise up now. Come forth, come hold. Protect using knowledge deep within, meant to protect and abate the sin. Let not the demons from the past continue harvesting, let them fast.

Thunder roared, shaking the room. A solid wave of light and red-orange flames burst from the barrier of pure energy.

Look out! Nicolas called out the warning, throwing his body in front of Mikhail.

Gregori was already in motion, diving across the room to cover the prince.

Light banded and flashed in waves, bursting into bright rockets, hot flames a towering wall of red-orange, nearly blinding them. The men threw up their arms to shield their eyes. The wall of energy hit all three Carpathian males with the force of a freight train, tossing them as if they were no more than bits of flotsam on the waves of the raging sea.

Gregori and Nicolas took the brunt of the energy, both absorbing it rather than fighting, trying to shield the prince from most of the impact. Even as Nicolas was thrown backward, he was already shifting in midair, leaping to cover his lifemate should Gregori meet the attack on the prince with a death threat. He slammed into Lara hard, power clinging to him in ropes, lighting up the room as he flashed through the air. He drove her backward, taking her to the floor, his larger body blanketing hers.

She tried to roll, but he caught her wrists, preventing her from using her hands to weave spells, slamming her arms above her head and pinning her to the floor. "Lara, look at me."

She went absolutely still beneath him, her eyes unfocused. Her body was ice cold, alarmingly so. Nicolas didn't hesitate. He thrust his mind into hers, following her along the path of her memories.

The smell of decayed blood was strong. The scent

mingled with decomposition of rotting flesh. Then he heard the screams. Moans. The continual cry of someone in agony, not just physical, but tormented mental agony. Nicolas ventured down the ice-cold hallway. It opened to a large chamber. Overhead the ceiling was high and long columns reached from floor to ceiling. Splashes of red cut through blue and sprayed across the left wall where a man was chained to the floor. He was naked, convulsing, his eyes glowing with madness while tiny white parasites fed on his flesh. Nicolas recognized him as one of their bitterest enemies—Razvan, grandson of Xavier, the oldest and most powerful of all mages.

Chained beside Razvan was what was left of a woman lying motionless, her face set in rigid horror, her mouth open wide as if she'd died screaming. The parasites fed on her while Razvan desperately tried to beat them off of the body. His hands were bloody from pounding the ice. He looked up abruptly and Nicolas followed his tortured gaze to the tow-headed child with streaks of red in her hair huddled in the corner, her fist shoved in her mouth to keep from screaming. He was no judge of the ages of children, but to him the little girl appeared to be no more than three or four. The child's eyes were on the woman's face and she sobbed softly.

Momma.

Everything in Nicolas stilled. Deep down rage began and fought its way to the surface. He wanted to grab that child and rush her to safety, but all he could do was save the woman he was holding in real time. He caught Lara's face firmly in his. No child should ever have been subjected to such a thing.

"Avio siel, my soul, come back to me." He whispered the command to her, burying a strong compulsion along with the order itself. "You are safe, Lara. I am your lifemate and I will always protect you to my last breath."

Her cloudy, almost opaque gaze shifted to his face.

"Yes. Look at me. Focus on me. Let me lead you back."

In the ice cave of her memories, he didn't wait for the child to respond to him. With exquisite tenderness he lifted her, covering her eyes, burying her little face against his chest, soothing her with his voice as he turned his back on that horrific scene and walked out.

Lara's long lashes fluttered. The wild, pale blue of her eyes darkened as she looked at him. She drew a breath. Nicolas eased back, pulling her into a sitting position. She looked around her, alarm creeping into her expression.

"Did I hurt anyone?" She ducked her head, refusing to meet his eyes.

"No one was hurt." He kept his voice low and soft, reassuring even as he caught her chin with firm fingers and forced her to maintain eye contact. "No one here would ever harm you."

Her heart beat too fast. He laid his palm over her breast, sending warmth into the glacier cold of her body and slowing her heart to match the even, steady beat of his. She struggled to draw breath into her lungs and he bent his dark head so their breath mingled until hers slowed to a more relaxed, effortless flow of air. Her gaze remained locked with his and he had the impression of tears, but none formed in her eyes.

"I will block the smell for you." *Gregori, do not look directly at her, there is something about your eyes triggering a childhood memory.* "You should have told me it was bothering you. As your lifemate, it is my duty to protect you from such things."

"I'm a big girl, all grown up."

She had felt him then, in her memories, carrying the child that was her from the ice cave. She had felt his comfort and now, even with her lower lip trembling slightly from fear, she didn't move away from his touch. He leaned forward and very gently brushed her mouth with his. He held her gaze for another long moment, his mind moving in hers, making certain the nightmare world of her childhood had receded enough to allow her some peace.

"Are you all right, Lara?" Mikhail asked.

His voice was as gentle as Nicolas's, she decided. He must think she was on the verge of a breakdown. And maybe she was. But Nicolas had blocked the smell of decayed blood and flesh, replacing it with the fresh scent of the forest. She even could feel a slight breeze on her face. Aside from total humiliation, she was fine. She steadfastly tried to avoid looking at the healer, but she knew, like the proverbial moth, she would be unable to help herself.

Lara took Nicolas's outstretched hand and allowed him to pull her to her feet. "I'm fine, thank you. I hope no one was hurt."

"If I were hurt, I'd get a new second." Mikhail grinned at her. "Don't let him intimidate you. He practices that look every evening down by the lake."

Before she could stop herself, her gaze traveled to Gregori. His silver eyes made her queasy, but she forced herself to look at him. "I'm not intimidated, but I am sorry. I didn't mean to hurt anyone."

"No one was hurt, little sister," Gregori said, keeping his gaze on Terry. "If we are going to help your friend, we have to hurry."

Lara's heart leapt. She had all but forgotten Terry and Gerald, who were witnessing her bizarre behavior as well as her abilities to use energy. She shouldn't have worried. Neither seemed to be paying attention. One of the three Carpathian males had blocked their senses and given them false memories of what had happened.

She was very ashamed of her behavior in front of these men. She hadn't even taken care of her friends. Squaring her shoulders, she took a step toward the bed. The presence of the parasites had opened the floodgates of her childhood memories, none of which were pleasant.

"Guard the door," Nicolas ordered, once more putting

his solid mass between her and the bed. "We do not want the innkeeper or her husband to come into the room. It is too dangerous."

She tried not to look relieved, nodding her head and stepping back to allow them room. She leaned one hip against the door and watched the healer at work. She had never witnessed a master healer performing his arts before and was fascinated by the complete concentration and efficiency he used. He shed his body without hesitation, leaving only pure healing energy in his wake.

Mikhail lit candles and the aromatic scents filled the air, aiding in the healing process. Gregori left his own body and entered Terry's, working to drive out the quickly multiplying hordes of parasites working to consume the young man's body.

It was amazing to watch the seemingly endless energy being sucked out of Gregori, draining him of all strength, even with the other two Carpathian males working with him. His face turned gray. He swayed with weariness, and time passed with infinite slowness.

Outside the window, snow began to fall, first a few flakes, and then at a much steadier pace. The inn grew quiet as patrons went to bed. Gerald shifted position often, but stayed, holding Terry's shoulders and talking soothingly to him. Terry ceased moaning after an hour and by the second hour he was resting far more comfortably.

Gregori came back into his own body, staggering, sitting on the floor abruptly, pale and drawn. He shook his head. *The parasites are multiplying as fast as I am destroying them. I am uncertain whether I can reduce the numbers fast enough to eventually get rid of them.*

Mikhail casually tore at his wrist with his teeth and extended his arm. Lara's gaze was immediately riveted on Gregori's mouth as he placed it over the wound. Her stomach knotted. Thunder crashed in her ears.

I will work with you, Nicolas volunteered.

As will I, the prince added.

No! Both Carpathian males reacted violently.

You cannot, Mikhail, Gregori said. *We cannot chance the tainted blood anywhere near you. The parasites sense your presence as it is. They swarm to whatever side is closest to you in the hopes of contaminating you.*

We will need your blood to aid us, Nicolas added with a flick of his dark gaze toward Gregori.

Gregori sighed as he allowed Nicolas to pull him to his feet. *He is not a baby, Nicolas. He's a grown man who knows the Carpathian people cannot exist without him. If he is destroyed, our species will die out. As much as we want to believe someone else could take your place, Mikhail, you, as well as our enemies, know it is not true.*

Not necessarily, Mikhail objected. *Savannah carries my bloodline and she is carrying twins. Raven carries my son, although she is having problems again.*

We cannot take chances. Lucian, Gabriel or Darius can easily take my place as your second, but there is no other male to fulfill your position. There was an edge to Gregori's voice.

It was evident to Lara that they had had this discussion many times. She found the conversation very interesting and it helped to take her mind off the ragged tear in Mikhail's wrist. He had swept his tongue across the wound, but she could still see teeth marks and faint smears of blood. Her stomach lurched and bile rose. Her body temperature dropped abruptly.

There is my brother, Jacques. Mikhail's voice had grown quiet, matching that edge to Gregori's voice.

Who still does not trust his mind without that of his lifemate. There can be no risk to you, Mikhail. Gregori flicked him a glare. *Do not give me grief over this again, Pops.*

Mikhail choked and took a step toward his second, who just happened to be his daughter's lifemate. Terry's face twisted into sudden malevolence and he flung himself at the prince, growling, spittle running down his chin. Gerald seized his shoulders in an effort to restrain him, but Terry was amazingly strong for someone so injured, fighting free and leaping with outstretched hands, already curved into claws at Mikhail's eyes.

Nicolas waved his hand at exactly the same moment Gregori did. Lara whispered a shielding spell, her hands weaving a complicated pattern. Terry slammed into an invisible barrier. Teeth rattling, eyes spinning in his head, he rammed his skull over and over into the shield protecting the prince.

Gerald staggered across the bed, trying to control him, but Terry punched at his face, still growling like a rabid animal. Gerald fell back across the bed and Terry resumed head-butting the invisible wall to get at the prince.

Lara reached for Terry's mind in an attempt to calm him. She touched his mind gently, in reassurance. At once a boiling ball of parasites reacted to her presence, twisting and thrashing in a frenzy of venomous need. One moment she was in Terry's head, the next she found herself thrown out, a hard male shove sending her careening out of Terry's brain.

She spun around to glare at Nicolas. She was beginning to recognize his touch. He didn't spare her a glance, his entire attention on controlling Terry. She glanced over at Gregori. The healer actually had Mikhail pressed against the wall, but the concentration on his face indicated he was with Nicolas, restraining Terry.

Terry lay back on the bed, eyes unfocused, but his body calm, no longer fighting. Lara let her breath out slowly. Gregori motioned to Mikhail to leave and Mikhail flicked one look at him. He wasn't going anywhere and it was evident on his face—in his eyes.

"Get to work," Mikhail ordered.

Gregori shrugged his broad shoulders and once more, using pure healing energy, entered Terry's body.

"What's going on?" Gerald asked, scrambling off the bed and moving around the Carpathian healer toward Lara.

Nicolas glided, cutting off Gerald's route. "You have blood all over your shirt. You should go take a shower."

"He's right, Gerald," Lara agreed. "It isn't safe. Burn your clothes. Anything you were wearing today."

Gerald halted, glanced at Terry, yanked the door open and hurried out to his room across the hall.

Lara leaned one hip against the wall and watched as Nicolas joined Gregori, the two of them working furiously, in tandem, to save Terry's life. And it was a struggle for his life—for his soul. The parasites were desperate to take him over, to possess his body and mind and turn him to their master's bidding.

The men worked nonstop, and time slipped away. Both grew paler until they were nearly gray in color and eventually sank onto the bed beside Terry. Mikhail once again calmly tore at his wrist and pressed his offering to Nicolas.

She tried not to look at the bright red blood. She tried not to see Nicolas holding the prince's arm, his fingers gripping as the life force flowed from Mikhail into him, yet she was mesmerized and couldn't look away.

Her wrist burned. Her lungs burned. She shivered, her body cold no matter how much she tried to restore and equalize her body's temperature. The walls around her curved and took on a bluish tinge. She sucked in her breath, trying to focus on the wall above the prince, but her gaze—and mind—were continually pulled back to the sight of the blood where it trickled down on his arm, smeared a little on Nicolas's fingers and dripped to the floor.

Her stomach lurched. Desperate, she locked on to Terry's face. That, too, was a mistake. She imagined the parasites swarming through his bloodstream to his every organ, launching a massive attack, fighting the healer and Nicolas for possession of him.

Sweat beaded on her forehead. Terry's face wavered, his boyish features changing, morphing until he was undeniably handsome, with blazing turquoise eyes and midnight black hair spilling across his forehead. The hair streaked with waves of silver. The eyes opened and locked with hers.

Her breath caught in her lungs. Agony there. Awareness. Impotent fury. Fear. So much fear the room filled with it. The walls bulged outward, unable to contain such terror.

Run. Run, Lara. Hide. She heard the sob in his voice, the overwhelming horror.

Nicolas found himself shivering with cold in an ice chamber. Chained to a wall, arms and chest burning from links coated with acidic vampire blood, Razvan fought to maintain possession of his own soul. Agony lived in his eyes and his black hair banded with platinum.

Lara. The voice whispered with love. With fear. With despair. *Baby. Run. He is coming and I cannot protect you.*

Nicolas felt terror rising, choking him. He swung his head to peer into the corner. The female child was older this time. Maybe four or five. She huddled against the wall, trembling, tears running down her face, her heart beating so loudly he could hear it above his own steady rhythm.

Dragging footsteps came from behind. Nicolas turned and saw a hideous creature, part skeleton, part man, coming toward them. Skin hung in places yet was drawn tight in others. All flesh was decayed and rotting. A few long strands of gray hair tufted from his bald head. A straggly beard hung to his chest, but vermin crawled in and out of the dank hair, moving continually. His nails were yellow and long, curving back on his gnarled hands. Rotted, black teeth flashed in a macabre, evil smirk. His eyes were alive in what was left of his face, a slashing light of glowing, silvery madness.

Fear escalated until Nicolas's own heartbeat began to

change, hammering hard in anticipation. His lungs burned for air.

Nicolas! Mikhail's voice became a sharp command, demanding he return to the present. *Peace, little sister. You are safe,* the prince added, attempting to calm Lara.

Nicolas knew only one way of keeping Lara from her nightmarish memories, the flashbacks recurring with even sharper images in the confines of the room. He caught her up in strong arms, thrust his mind fully into hers, taking complete command. Dragonseeker ran strong in her veins and she certainly was capable of shifting with his help. He dissolved them both and took her out of the room, out of the inn and into the fresh clean air of the night.

4

Lara stood in the center of a very warm chamber, deep beneath the earth. Water rushed from the walls of the cave into a deep, steaming pool. Sconces on the walls spilled light from scented, flickering candles, throwing shadows on the crystal walls. The breath left her lungs in a little rush and she spun around in a circle, fingers curling around the hilt of her knife in her belt at her side.

She moistened her lips and turned to confront Nicolas. "Exactly where am I and how did I get here?"

"Before you get all crazy on me and throw that knife you have in your hand," Nicolas drawled, "you are not a prisoner. I left a path in your mind so you can find your way out anytime you need or want to go. This is the safest and most peaceful place I know of. Safeguards are in place for your protection. There is a bed in the next chamber where you can rest."

She searched her memories and found the way out, carefully placed as if she'd actually entered the cave a thousand times and knew every chamber and hallway. "I have a room at the inn." She didn't relax her grip on the knife.

"It is occupied with several men at the moment. I thought perhaps you would enjoy this retreat a little more."

His black hair spilled across his forehead, drawing attention to his very black eyes. The urge to sweep the silky strands aside was so strong she took a step away from him to keep from reaching out.

"That doesn't explain how I got here or why you didn't consult me."

He shrugged powerful shoulders, causing an intriguing and very sexy rippling effect under his shirt. She tried not to stare.

"I carried you here. We shifted into mist so we could travel undetected and much faster."

Lara nearly choked. "I don't shift."

His eyes gleamed at her, amusement softening the edge of his mouth. "You shifted without even a hint of a problem. I thought you had been doing it every day."

She flashed him her fiercest scowl. "Then why don't I remember?"

"Do you have memory lapses often? Is this something I should be aware of and watch out for?"

"Ha ha ha. You think you're really funny, don't you? I have never shifted in my life and certainly not into mist." And she'd tried, a thousand times, over and over, until she finally believed she had made up her childhood.

"You know how. It is there in your mind."

"It is?" For a moment she forgot she was annoyed with him. She didn't want to revisit memories locked away, to find out, but if she could shift, it would certainly be a useful talent. Her aunts were shifters. They had been trapped in dragon form, but that wasn't their natural form. She should have known they would have provided her with that skill as well as languages, healing and magic. "I didn't know."

"Well, you certainly have the knowledge. You need help, of course, because you are not fully Carpathian, but that is easy enough. You have barriers in place. Protections.

I found your own," he said in a matter-of-fact way, but he was watching her closely. "But there are guards made by others. A male's touch. Two women. They did not want you to remember your childhood."

The two women had to have been her aunts—but the man? Her father? She knew no other men. Why would her father put up a barrier to her earlier memories, but allow her to see him feeding off of her? Her stomach lurched and she turned away from Nicolas, unwilling for him to witness more weakness. She often had nightmares, but no one had ever been around to see the results. And the flashbacks—if that's what they were—she'd never seen Razvan chained and a prisoner before.

"I don't understand any of this."

Why was she seeing Razvan as the victim instead of herself? Nothing seemed to make sense anymore, not even her own behavior. Now she couldn't explain why her aunts and someone else—someone she hadn't known had been in her head—didn't want her remembering her childhood.

"I can't imagine why they would erase my memories," she murmured. She couldn't get the sight of the ravaged face of her father from her mind.

"Not erase, protect," he clarified. "The memories are still there for you to discover."

"Was it real? What we saw, was it real?"

He lifted a hand and the candles flickered. The aroma of soothing lavender, honey and lilac filled the chamber. He wanted to make her feel better, but one did not lie to a lifemate. "Your memories have been suppressed, but not tampered with. They are very real."

"You saw it then, the same memory I did?" Triggered by blood and parasites and those horrible silvery eyes. She ducked her head, letting her breath out in a little rush before inhaling the fragrance of the candles.

"Yes. I recognized the marks on him from the chains. My brother Riordan was captured and held by such chains.

It is difficult to hold a Carpathian prisoner. I believe who-ever is behind this has been perfecting his technique." *And using your father to experiment on first.*

Lara caught his thought before he censored it. She looked around for a place to sit. Immediately there was a low-slung chaise with soft cushions in front of her. She didn't question how it got there, but sank down onto it, fearing her legs wouldn't hold her up much longer.

"I don't understand this, Nicolas. If your brother had those same chain marks, was he Xavier's prisoner? Tell me about your brother."

"We live in the rainforest in South America. It has been our home for many centuries now and our family is well established there. Riordan was on patrol, as we seem to be getting more and more activity..."

"By activity, do you mean Xavier?"

He shook his head, noting that she kept rubbing her temples. He touched her mind to find a headache pounding there. "No, I mean vampires. The jaguar people share the Amazon with us, and the vampires have banded together to try to destroy the Carpathian people. They wanted to rid themselves of one of our allies, so they began corrupting the jaguar species. Riordan stumbled across evidence of their presence and, in tracking them, fell victim to a false call for aid."

Nicolas moved behind her and reached out to press his fingertips against her temples. Lara stiffened and jerked her head away, eyeing him warily over her shoulder.

"Let me," he said softly. "There is no need for you to be in pain."

She held her breath, uncertain what to do, and that was rare for her. Nicolas kept her off balance with his close proximity. They seemed to share the same air. She felt him under her skin and every single cell in her body was acutely aware of him.

"It is a small thing, removing your headache."

And it made her feel small and petty to deny him. She shrugged. "Tell me more about your brother."

"He was held captive in a laboratory."

"It is the same, then. They were experimenting on him. Surely it isn't coincidence."

"Mostly they experimented on animals, but once they had Riordan, they chained him to the wall, using chains coated in vampire blood, much as you remembered seeing Razvan chained. The blood burns like acid, burning without mercy. It is very painful. They kept Riordan drained of blood and weak with a poison injected into him."

Lara frowned, almost grasping another memory, one of needles, but she let it slip away.

Nicolas pressed the pads of his fingers over the pulse throbbing in Lara's temples and held them there, infusing warmth and healing energy. He could feel her instant sympathetic and identifying reaction to his brother's captivity. "He is safe and very happy now," he added. "His lifemate rescued him and brought hope to our family, a belief that if it happened to Riordan, if he could find his lifemate under the unlikeliest of circumstances, then perhaps the rest of us could as well. We managed to hold out longer than we ever thought possible."

Because his family carried tremendous gifts, they also were burdened with a far more dangerous element. While all Carpathian males grew dark over time, especially those born warriors, the De La Cruz brothers were born with the darkness already strong in them. They had been consumed by it rapidly, glorying in the training, the battle and hunt and most of all the rush of the kill.

"How does that work?" Lara asked curiously. "The aunts said the seed of the vampire was in the Carpathian male."

"That is one way to look at it. Certainly all Carpathian males are capable of choosing to give up their souls. We wander in barren worlds with only our memories and touching the minds of others who still feel and see the beauty of our surroundings. It is difficult to fight the need for emotion, any emotion."

"Is my father a vampire?"

Nicolas was silent for a moment, his hands dropping to her shoulders to ease the tension from her with a massage. "We do not know what your father is. One moment we think he is dead, and then he pops back up somewhere. He has many faces and has committed numerous crimes against our people, but no one knows for certain what is happening in the enemy camp. You may be our greatest clue. You and your lost memories."

"What do my memories mean? All this time I thought my father was a demon. He took my blood, ripped open my wrist, my neck, my veins. He treated me as if I was nothing but a meal for him. That's what I remember."

"We do not know or understand the time line. Perhaps there was a time when both of you were prisoners together."

"It doesn't make sense that my aunts would suppress my memories of him as a prisoner. What would be the purpose? And you said there was a male's weave in the barrier. I only know of my father and Xavier, but you would feel the taint of evil if either of them had woven a shield. What would be his purpose in leaving me only memories of him feeding on me? Why would they all want me to think my own father was the worst kind of monster?" Lara dropped her face into her hands.

Nicolas stayed behind her, as still as a cat, his hands continuing to massage the tension from her shoulders. "Perhaps the true memories are worse than believing your father was wholly a fiend."

"You recognized him. Is he still alive?"

"We believe he is."

"When was the last time you saw him?"

"He possessed the body of an elderly woman at the inn

where you have a room. There was a celebration of sorts and the lifemate of the prince's brother..."

Her breath hissed out in a rush between her teeth and she whirled around to face him. "Say her name. She has a name."

He shrugged his shoulders, unperturbed by her annoyance. "Shea, Jacques Dubrinsky's lifemate, was with child. The elderly woman attacked with a poisoned, barbed needle and would have killed her had not my brother, Manolito, stepped in front of Shea to protect her. Fortunately he survived the attack."

She made a small sound and turned away from him again, the soothing aroma of the lavender and honey unable to combat the news of her father's treachery. "Shea was pregnant and Razvan tried to murder her and her unborn child."

"It appears so."

She shook her head. "I'm so sorry. I didn't think beyond what he had done to me, but I should have."

Nicolas moved, glided really, a blur she barely saw or felt until he was standing in front of her, lifting her chin with gentle fingers. "You are not responsible for anything Razvan has done. He carries his choices on his own shoulders."

She managed a small smile. "Thank you for that. And what of my aunts? Do you know anything at all of them?"

"I am sorry, Lara, but I have heard no news of them being seen alive. If they are truly your aunts."

"Great-aunts," she corrected. "But I always called them my aunts."

He smiled. "I did assume that. If they are your great-aunts, that would make them Rhiannon's daughters. We know Rhiannon had triplets with Xavier. Two girls—your aunts—and Soren, your grandfather. Soren was murdered by Xavier some years ago. No one has ever seen the girls. What do they look like?"

"I only saw them in dragon form. They were weak and

sick. Xavier used them for blood, and kept them in a weakened state. He was very afraid of them. Often, if one was unfrozen, he would hold a knife to the other's throat. They saved my sanity, whispering to me when things got very bad, distracting me when I was used for feeding."

"You are certain they were Rhiannon's children?"

"The love story they told me was of their mother, Rhiannon, and her true lifemate. Xavier murdered him and held Rhiannon prisoner, forcing her to have his children, triplets. He believed he could be immortal, living on the blood of the Carpathians. I'm certain the things they told me were true, at least they said they were." She looked at him. "You were able to bind me with the ritual words. How would they know the Carpathian marriage ritual if they weren't Rhiannon's daughters?"

"Dominic, Rhiannon's brother, has sought news of her for many years now. We were informed of her death at the hands of Xavier, and he has been hoping to hear of his nieces. This news will sadden him."

"They could still be alive," she said. "It's possible. They helped me escape the ice cave, and maybe they managed as well. They were very powerful. Xavier kept them weak, but they were smart. They might have found a way. That's what I've come back to find out. I'm going to hunt for evidence of what happened to them."

Nicolas drew in his breath sharply. "The ice caves are too dangerous. The last visitors barely escaped with their lives. It is not a place you should enter."

She kept her eyes on the water in the pool gently lapping at the ring of rocks. "Have you been down there?" She didn't much care one way or the other what he thought. She intended to go to the cave and find out for herself what had happened to her aunts.

"Not personally, but all Carpathians share knowledge. Vikirnoff and his woman fought shadow warriors, vampire and mages alike when they were there."

She frowned and glanced up at him with a quick flick of her lashes. "His woman? Not that again. Does she have a name? Do women hold so low a place in your estimation that you can't be bothered to learn their names?"

He bent down, placing his lips against her ear. "I think you are trying to pick a fight with me because you are upset over the flashbacks you are experiencing. You have been in my mind enough to know I respect women, and would give my life to protect them." He tugged on her long braid. "I have to see the prince and will get news of your friend. I also need to feed and you must as well. Stay here and relax. I will bring you food and something to drink and we can figure this out together."

The feel of his warm breath against her ear, the mesmerizing brushing caress of his lips sent a shiver down her spine. Her breasts tingled, nipples tightening. She pressed her teeth together in a little snap.

"I do not want anything at all to do with blood."

"I figured that out." He straightened and moved away from her, gliding across the cave floor in that peculiar silence that reminded her of a stalking jungle cat. "Do you feel comfortable enough to stay here on your own, or will being underground trigger more flashbacks?"

She sent him her most fierce scowl. "I'm a caver. I explore caves all the time. I had *one* small problem for just a moment seeing those disgusting little parasites. I'm fine now. *Perfectly* fine." She deliberately took a slow look around. "It's quite beautiful here."

It was, too. The walls were veined with minerals and crystals. Candles of all sizes were everywhere. The pool looked inviting. The air smelled fresh and soothing. Beyond the chamber she was in, she could see a bedroom of sorts set up quite like a room in an aboveground home. Clearly Nicolas had tried to provide a tranquil, safe place to rest.

"The safeguards are in place. They are the newest

patterns to keep out enemies trained in our ways. You will be safe. If you have need of me, you have only to reach out," Nicolas said. "I will hear you."

"How is it possible we can communicate the way we do?" Lara asked curiously. "We aren't using the telepath common to all Carpathians. I thought that was established with a blood bond. You took my blood, but I didn't take yours."

He was more than aware of that fact. Need roared in his ears, thundered through his heart, surged through his veins and pounded painfully in his groin in hot demand. He took a breath to keep his body relaxed, his mind calm when the primitive side of him wanted dominance. "You are my lifemate and I have bound us together. The rest will come in the right time."

"And if it doesn't?"

He shrugged. "Then we do not survive this life and will go to the next to try again."

She watched his large frame waver into transparency, and then fade away until he was nothing but mist streaming from the chamber. Only then did she realize she was holding her breath. She stood and stretched, trying to get her tight muscles to relax. She shouldn't be relieved to be here, she should be angry. Nicolas had taken her away from her friends without her consent, but if she was being honest, she couldn't breathe in that room. She couldn't think clearly there. She wasn't a strong enough healer to rid Terry of the parasites. Without her present, the Carpathians would call in more of their kind, and Terry would have a better chance.

She sighed, knowing they would erase her friends' memories to keep them safe, but it was the only way. And maybe that was why her aunts had erased her memories, or at least sealed them up. She took off her clothes and folded them neatly, setting them on top of a flat rock before wading out into the hot mineral pool to ease the tension from her body. Water enveloped her thighs, chasing away the chill of bad memories.

Lara swam across the warm bubbling pool, aware of the instant relief of her headache and the terrible knots of tension in her neck. She sighed, lay back and closed her eyes.

~

Nicolas circled the forest with a lazy flap of his wings. He had shifted into the form of an owl, better to travel the distance faster. He still had much to do. It was imperative to speak with the prince and deliver the message he had traveled so far to bring. He took his time in the air. For the first time in hundreds of years, he enjoyed the incredible sensation of flying, rather than taking it for granted.

The feel of gently falling snow, the sway to the trees as the breeze whispered through them, even the scent of the crisp air, all brought joy to him as he spiraled down to the forest floor to the appointed meeting place. He had contacted the prince to insure Lara's human male friend was still alive and arranged a meeting with Mikhail while he was there. He had chosen the forest because the Carpathian Mountains had a special magic.

As he shifted, his boots sinking into the icy crystals and layers of vegetation beneath, he felt the instant connection to the earth. His species were of the earth, needing the richness of the soil for rest and rejuvenation. They felt a kinship with the plants and tall majestic trees. The animals and birds were brothers in nature and Nicolas drank in his surroundings, allowing himself to be overwhelmed emotionally by the ability to simply feel.

He waited in the comfort of the thick forest for Mikhail. He almost wished he'd had the meeting with the prince before his emotions had been restored. Overhead an owl settled onto a tree branch, wings fluttering before spreading out and swooping toward the ground. At the last moment, the owl shimmered and took the form of a man.

"You are pacing, Nicolas," Mikhail said as he took the ground in a smooth stride. "That cannot be good."

"I bring news, Mikhail, and no, it is not good. My brothers all send greetings and Zacarias has asked that I renew our family's pledge of loyalty and defense of you and our people."

"That has never been questioned."

Nicolas met the knowing black gaze of his prince straight on. "When your father ruled, and we were young and filled with arrogance and importance, we often sat around the campfires discussing options other than blindly following traditional Carpathian ways. My family and the Malinov family were close. We protected one another in battle and we shared memories as our time came and emotions faded. We spent a great deal of time together."

Mikhail nodded, but remained silent—waiting—knowing that Nicolas rarely carried on conversations unless he had something important to say.

"The Malinov brothers had a sister, a bright, beautiful girl totally revered by all of us."

"Ivory," Mikhail said and instantly pulled up her image in his mind. Tall, slender, hair like black silk flowing to her waist. She had been beautiful inside and out. Wherever she went, she brought a fresh, soothing breeze with her that could bring peace to the hearts of even the eldest warriors, the darkest hunters. Of course he remembered her. Poems had been sung about the legendary Ivory.

"Her parents died soon after her birth and our two families raised her together," Nicolas continued. "Ten elder brothers, battle-hardened and stern. It must have been difficult for her, but she was always smiling and singing and making the world seem a cheerful place even as colors and emotions faded from our world. Ivory could restore a semblance of what was lost to us when we were in her company. But she wanted to study, to go to the school the mages provided. She was so bright and her mind demanded stimulation. Power hummed in her veins and she needed the knowledge to better use such a great gift."

Mikhail knew the story, but didn't stop Nicolas, knowing instinctively he needed to retell it, to remember the small details that needed to be said, but more important, to give his news the only way he could.

"We believed Xavier was betraying the friendship of the Carpathian people. The debate raged among our people and we wanted our women to be protected. Vlad tried hard to keep peace when many of the ancients were becoming bothered by his increasingly erratic behavior. We could not stop the others from allowing their daughters and lifemates to study, but we refused Ivory unless we attended with her. And we were called to battle, so she was left alone."

Without protection. Nicolas didn't say it aloud, but the thought was there in his mind. Even now, hundreds of years later, he remembered that moment as if it was yesterday. Ivory, his sister-kin, the only relief from the stark barren existence, smiling at them bravely, tears in her eyes, yet warmth and love seeping into minds and hearts as she watched them go. She kept her fears to herself, leaving them all with what comfort and happy memories she could provide.

"I am telling you so you know our frame of mind, Mikhail, at the time this dark deed was done," Nicolas said. "Not to offend you or place blame on your name. I know you gave the order to destroy your own brother when it was necessary. But in truth, Vlad should have given that order years before."

A muscle ticked in Mikhail's jaw, but he said nothing, simply waited.

Nicolas rubbed the bridge of his nose and met Mikhail's gaze. "Your brother was twisted and Vlad knew it. Your brother wanted Ivory, even knowing he wasn't her true lifemate. Your sister, Noelle, carried the same strain of madness."

Mikhail nodded. He hadn't ordered his sister's death any more than his father had ordered his brother's—and Jacques had paid the price. "So much power running through our veins can corrupt and twist, Nicolas, just as in any other family."

Nicolas nodded. "It is true. When we learned a vampire had killed Ivory, we searched for her body to attempt retrieving her from the shadow world, but we could not find her. We had lost the one bright light in our lives, and there was no relief from the madness of our existence. So late at night, around the campfire, we plotted how to bring down the Dubrinsky family and end the reign of a man who was no longer fit to lead. Our two families had discovered the ability to link and share power in the way the Daratrazanoff bloodline can do. At the time, we believed that because we could do as the Daratrazanoff line could, there must be another family that could be the living vessel for our people."

"A living vessel must be able to hold all knowledge and power—past and present—for our people. He links all Carpathians together telepathically as well as physically through his mind," Mikhail said. "I know of no other family who can do this."

Nicolas sighed. "It stood to reason if we could do as the Daratrazanoffs could that there would be another family that could hold power. We know your family carried madness, tainted with a need for control over the opposite sex, and we believed we could find another more worthy leader."

"And you came up with a way to destroy us?" There was quiet acceptance in the prince's voice.

"Yes." Nicolas said honestly, still unflinching. "With the Malinov brothers. And they are implementing that plan.

We believe they have been doing so for hundreds of years. First as Carpathians and now, perhaps, as vampires."

Mikhail paced a short distance from Nicolas and returned. "I will call in our hunters."

Nicolas reached for Lara, found her floating peacefully in the pool chamber. He nodded. "I think we have no choice."

Warriors, heed the call to council. Mikhail sent the call immediately.

The two Carpathians exchanged a long look, took two running steps and leapt airborne, shifting into the bodies of owls, racing across the snow-laden clouds to the ancient cave of council. The two predatory birds dipped wings as they flew through the entrance and raced down the long corridor to the council chamber.

Nicolas hadn't been in the cave for centuries but it still gave him the same sense of pride, honor and camaraderie as it had in days of old. The sacred council chamber was large, rounded, with a narrow, natural chimney in the center. Script on the wall was in the ancient language, the code of the warrior, the one he had lived by throughout the centuries. Honor. Mercy. Integrity. Loyalty. Deadly purpose. Their code—their way of life.

The walls of the cave were a deep midnight blue, almost like the darkest sky, great stalagmites rising from the floor in a semicircle, tall, nearly shooting up to the high ceiling where stalactites grew in downward spirals, each glistening with sparkling deposits of colored minerals. Crystals in various geometrical shapes erupted from walls and covered the floors in giant prisms. The interior blasted them with heat from the magma chambers beneath them, forcing the Carpathians to regulate their temperature.

At one time, the cavern had been flooded with hydrothermal water, rich in minerals, leaving the deposits behind, until great, glowing crystals had formed. The crystals aided the warriors in focusing clearly on the coming battles, strategies and solving problems as well as the daily rigorous mental and physical training all Carpathian warriors were sworn to continue.

The first chamber opened into a second one, much smaller, completely enclosed and ringed inside with lava rocks. Purifying steam curled from the inside of the second chamber, beckoning to them.

Many single males crowded the cavern, dark, tall, eyes cold and distant. With his new emotions, Nicolas felt despair for them. Warriors without hope, who lived on honor only, battling not only the vampire but—worse—the call of the vampire. He took a breath and let the cave work magic on him.

Nicolas stood in the center of the crystalline cavern, in the place so many legendary warriors had stood before him. "It will be difficult to face my brother-kin when shame hangs over our family name for the first time."

Mikhail shot him a look of exasperation. "It is a little arrogant to feel shame for things that happened hundreds of years ago, Nicolas, as if you are the only ones to ever make a mistake. You and your brothers have proven your loyalty over and over. Manolito saved my life and then the life of Shea and her unborn child. Should I hang my head in shame for all the errors in judgment I have made over the centuries? If I did, I would never see the sky."

Nicolas shrugged, a small humorless smile flitting across his face. "We came up with a plan to overthrow your father, a way to bring down the reign of the Dubrinsky family. Mikhail, the things we planned were idle, angry talk to begin with, but when we sat around that campfire and fleshed out the details of a long-term battle plan, we committed treason against you and our people. There is shame in that."

Mikhail frowned. "If you had destroyed the Dubrinsky line, who did you believe would carry the power and knowledge of our people?"

"As we are able to perform the duties of the Daratra-zanoff family, we were certain there had to be another family and we intended to search them out. Of course, later we abandoned the plan, so no one ever approached any of the other lines to see if they could be a living vessel."

"And did you suspect any other lineage of being capable?"

"You sound as if you would step down immediately."

"In a heartbeat," Mikhail said and then sighed, shaking his head. "There is no one right way, Nicolas, and just because my family's line must bear the leadership does not mean we have all the answers. I am as fallible as any Carpathian. Every time we lose a child. Each time one of our women miscarries or a child dies. I consider it my failure and my shame that I have not found the answer to our dying race. I sit protected in my home while my warriors go out to battle evil, losing pieces of themselves along the way. Good men, better than I, stand between me and danger at every turn. Would I step aside and allow another to lead? In a heartbeat—especially if he were smarter than I."

Nicolas shook his head. "We were wrong, Mikhail, as you are now to think that way."

Mikhail sent him a small, twisted smile. "I thought to end my life. Before Raven, before I found my lifemate, I thought to end my life so I would not have to see the complete extinction of our species. You and the other warriors who served my father are far older, have hunted longer, endured longer, yet I could not continue under the weight of my failures. Was that not far worse? Was that not an act of cowardice?"

Nicolas shook his head. "I believe it was an act of desperation. I walked the streets this very night intending to meet the dawn, yet I did not trust myself to make it one last night. It is the way of our people, Mikhail. Every hunter faces that moment, yet we do not have the added burden of an entire species resting on our shoulders."

Mikhail clapped him on the shoulder. "We are flawed men, my old friend. Every last one of us. We sin and our women redeem us."

Nicolas answered with a wry grin. "That is the truth."

"Tell me of your lifemate. Where did she come from? The Dragonseeker blood runs strong in her."

Nicolas's white teeth flashed in a real smile, one that lit his eyes. "She is the daughter of Razvan, and she is amazing. I cannot even begin to describe the way I feel inside. I barely know her, but I want to spend every moment with her. She just came out of nowhere at the perfect moment and saved my life, my sanity and my soul. I look around and I don't know how I survived all these centuries without her. The world is alive again for me. I had forgotten the beauty of nature. In truth, I had forgotten what it feels like to truly love my brothers."

Mikhail let out his breath. "Another child with Dragonseeker blood is most welcome. As for the joy of lifemates, I have had Raven in my life for many years now, and yet each time I awaken from the earth, I am overwhelmed anew by the gifts she has given me."

Nicolas cleared his throat. "I am uncertain that my lifemate sees a reason to be with me."

"There is no reason for our women to be with us other than the way we are able to bind them. They are light to our darkness, and the darker our souls, the stronger the woman must be. Guard your lifemate well, Nicolas. She is a treasure beyond price."

Nicolas turned Mikhail's words over in his mind. There was no reason for their women to accept them other than the binding words that locked their souls together. His hold on Lara was fragile at best. He needed time to establish his bond, to form some sort of trust between them, although truthfully, he felt she should follow his lead without question.

He glanced around him, feeling the subtly flowing

influence, the focus of the crystals, the energy of the cavern with the magma flowing far beneath it and the snow gathering a thousand feet above. Nicolas spread his arms wide. "And this place of power. I had forgotten the beauty of this cave. And the clarity one has when in it."

Mikhail nodded. "There is no other place on earth quite like this. Ice and fire meet as one. Passion and control. The earth always holds the answers for our species." He looked around him at the wondrous display of nature. "Hopefully we will come closer to finding answers this night."

5

As Mikhail spoke, the Daratrazanoff brothers arrived. Four of them. All tall with striking looks, flowing black hair held back with leather ties. Faces cut from the same classic mold. Wide shoulders, broad chests, narrow hips, a warrior's straight posture and easy, fluid movements.

Darius, the youngest brother, was every bit as battle-experienced as the eldest. Intelligent, cunning, able to do the impossible. He had the black eyes of the Carpathian race, and the grim mouth that came with too much knowledge of death. Beside him were Lucian and Gabriel, legendary twins who had hunted and battled for the Carpathian people. Gabriel flashed a smile of greeting as he clasped arms with Nicolas. Lucian and Darius remained expressionless, although their eyes held genuine warmth when they greeted their prince.

The very petite woman beneath Lucian's shoulder was his lifemate, Jaxon. Pixie face, short platinum hair, dark shrewd eyes, she had been a cop, maybe even still was, but now hunted the vampire alongside her lifemate. Nicolas

disagreed violently with the modern idea that women—
even trained women with the ability to fight—should ever
be allowed to place themselves in danger, but Jaxon wasn't
his woman. She belonged to Lucian, their most legendary
warrior, and yet he allowed her to fight beside him. Perhaps
it was sheer arrogance on the warrior's part, a confidence
that he could protect his lifemate no matter what, but Nicolas felt she should be kept far away from the vile creature
that was the undead.

Women were to be protected and cherished, not put at
risk on a battlefield. A hunter couldn't be worried about protecting a lifemate when he battled the vampire. In ancient
times, most lifemated pairs ceased hunting altogether
rather than risking death for both. It was one of the main
bones of contention between the De La Cruz and Manilov
brothers and Vladimir Dubrinsky. Even then, their birth-
rates had been declining. None of them had believed the
women should be allowed to fight when they didn't have
the edge the males had. Not strength—but darkness itself.

Nicolas hid his true feelings behind a calm mask as he
greeted the fourth Daratrazanoff, Gregori. Second in command to Mikhail, the man was without mercy when it came
to enemies of the prince. He was a ferocious guardian, yet
was known far and wide as the Carpathians' most gifted
healer. Instead of the glittering obsidian eyes of his brothers, his were slashing silver, eyes that weighed and judged
a man. He looked fit and healthy, not at all pale from fighting to save a human from parasites.

"Thank you for what you did this night for Lara's
friend," Nicolas said. "How is he doing?"

A frown flitted across Gregori's face and was gone, a
huge show of emotion for him. "I did my best to rid his
body of the parasites, but how much damage they did, I
cannot say. I am hoping for a full recovery, but not expecting it. His friend is staying with him, and Slavica, the
owner of the inn, will check on him periodically. Should he

have need, she will call." Gregori looked around the cave, warmth creeping into his pale eyes. "It is long since I have come to this place—too long."

His brothers nodded their agreement.

New arrivals forestalled further conversation as Jacques Dubrinsky, the prince's brother, entered. He had midnight black hair, black eyes, a thin white scar circling his throat, another on his jaw and cheek and it was said a jagged rounded scar on his chest. Carpathians rarely scarred, which meant the wounds dealt him must have been fearsome indeed. He had been a victim of torture that had nearly driven him insane. Even now, he stayed mostly to himself.

Nicolas stepped forward to greet him, clasping arms.

"Bur tule ekämet kuntamak," Jacques said. "Well met, brother. It has been a long time since I have seen you. How is Manolito?"

"Manolito is very well and has found his lifemate. Her name is MaryAnn Delaney. I believe you know her. And your woman? And the child?"

"Shea is doing fine and we are having the naming ceremony in a few days. Our son grows strong."

"That is good news," Nicolas said. "The best of news for all of us."

The flutter of wings heralded two more Carpathians. Vikirnoff Von Shrieder and his lifemate, Natalya, shifted together. Nicolas clasped Vikirnoff's arms, a little taken aback that Natalya had answered the summons to the warriors' council. It had not occurred to him that Vikirnoff, an ancient warrior of tremendous prowess, would allow his woman to place herself in harm's way.

He glanced at her. The woman had bright red hair and eyes that changed from brilliant green to blue. She had the mark of the Dragonseeker stamped all over her, the classic looks, the brightness illuminating her skin, the bands of color in her hair. She was known to be a fighter—and also the sister of Razvan, Lara's father. He stepped away from Vikirnoff, afraid he would be unable to maintain silence on the subject of women fighting when Natalya would be such a prize to Xavier should she be captured.

Nicolas shook his head and then caught Gregori watching him with his piercing silver gaze. He knew exactly what Nicolas was thinking.

"And I agree," Gregori said, as he walked past Nicolas to position himself beside Mikhail.

"Agree with what?" Mikhail asked, turning away from where he'd been talking with Darius. "And with whom? It is not all that often you agree with anything."

"I think one of the topics we need to place under discussion is the welfare of our women and children—*all* of them—including the women who believe they have the need to fight vampires."

Mikhail bared white teeth. "*O jelä peje terád.* Sun scorch you, Gregori, you are not getting me in trouble with my lifemate and daughter. I am not doing your dirty work for you…" He included Nicolas in his glare. "Either of you."

Gregori shrugged. "Swear all you want, it is an issue you have to face."

"Me? Oh no, you don't. I refuse to take all the heat on this. If we are getting into it, all of you are voicing your opinions loud and clear. The women would rise up like my worst nightmare."

"I am serious," Gregori insisted. "If we are going to bring in the full council, then we should address all issues."

Mikhail nodded his head. "I know it must be discussed, Gregori, but you and I both know the old ways are long gone. Even then we had a few women warriors."

"Not lifemates," Nicolas interjected. "Never women who could bear us children, or that when lost would take their mate with them."

Mikhail shrugged. "In the old days very few lifemates were warriors. Times are different. Our species is on the brink of extinction."

"All the more reason to protect the few women we have," Nicolas said. "Sometimes old ways are good, Mikhail. Our women did not take up arms just to show they could."

"These women did not start out as Carpathians. Our species *looks* human and when we bind a human woman to us, although she is converted by blood, she thinks like a human. Through the centuries human women have had to fight for their rights..."

"That is a weak argument," Gregori broke in. "What do we do here in this chamber? We swear our loyalty to our people. We swear to serve them, whatever the sacrifice calls for. Our lifemates have never done that. They do not understand that in order to save our species from extinction, they must sacrifice, too. We have a handful of couples, less than thirty, Mikhail. Our children do not mature for a good fifty years. Do you really believe that we can afford to lose one woman? One pair?"

"No, but I also know that we are in a war with enemies surrounding us from all sides. We cannot afford to be divided either."

"We are not divided," Gregori said. "No man wants his woman fighting."

Mikhail shook his head, a slow smile touching his mouth. "So you think we should tell our women to be quiet and let us make decisions for them? It is not the men who will be divided, it is our women. From us. Free will. Have you forgotten that small little detail? We take that away when we bind them to us. Do we continue to do so after they are our lifemates? I suppose we can reduce them to little more than puppets who do our bidding at our will. But I know both Raven and Savannah would walk into the sun before submitting to such enslavement."

"*O jelä peje terád.* Sun scorch you, Mikhail," Gregori

growled. "You have become modern and liberal in your old age."

Nicolas turned away from the prince as another couple entered. Nicolae, Vikirnoff's brother, with his lifemate, Destiny, hurried in. Nicolas wanted to get a good look at the woman who had been captured by a vampire when she was just a young child. She had endured the torture of a vampire's blood, riddled with cell-eating parasites, for years. Medium height, very curvy, with sculpted muscle, thick dark hair and enormous blue-green eyes, she flowed with grace and the fluid step of a trained fighter. He noted her eyes were restless, moving around the cavern, taking in every detail, noting exits and entrances, the chimney and labyrinth of tunnels.

Destiny was best friends with Manolito's lifemate, Mary-Ann. She saw each person in the room, sizing them up, her gaze resting on him just a little longer. Nicolae, her life-mate, was very tuned to her, Nicolas noted with approval, placing himself between her and the men without lifemates in the room. Like most Carpathian males, Nicolae was tall and muscular with long black hair and cool dark eyes.

"You are Nicolas, brother to Manolito." Destiny greeted, moving toward him, forcing her lifemate to keep pace in order to protect her.

It was a classic mistake women made, forgetting that anyone could be a danger, even here, in this sacred place of power. Nicolas sighed and shook his head. His woman would learn her place and every security measure he could think of for her.

"How is MaryAnn?" Destiny asked.

"She is happy," Nicolas answered. "I have news to share, but want to wait until we have all gathered. I brought you a letter from MaryAnn." He slipped his hand inside his shirt.

Destiny's eyes narrowed, became cool and watchful. She shifted slightly onto the balls of her feet, turning just slightly, a subtle movement that put her in a good position to defend herself and attack if necessary. As if choreographed, her partner shifted at the same time, a few steps between them, giving plenty of room. This was a fighting team. Even Nicolas, for all his absolute opinions on the subject of women hunting vampires, could see they were in perfect sync. It still didn't make it right.

He took the letter from inside his shirt and handed it to Nicolae as a courtesy. One warrior to another. Nicolae turned the envelope over in his hand, obviously scanning it before handing it to his lifemate.

"Thank you," Destiny said to Nicolas. "I appreciate you bringing this to me personally."

At first he thought she meant to be sarcastic because he had handed the letter to her lifemate, but then he realized the couple really was in perfect harmony. She didn't seem annoyed by his protection, but rather accepted it as her due.

Another Carpathian male arrived. It was Dominic, of the Dragonseeker clan, great-uncle of Razvan and great-great-uncle to Lara, although Carpathians rarely made a distinction. As Lara referred to the aunts, she would refer to Dominic as "uncle."

Nicolas studied his stern face. The Dragonseekers were one of the most powerful lineages in all of the Carpathian community. He was tall with broad shoulders and metallic green eyes, a legacy of his clan, eyes of seers, changing color with mood or in battle. In the last battle to save Mikhail and the Carpathian race, he had suffered severe burns across his shoulder, down one arm, up his neck to one side of his face. The scars were there if one looked closely, faint evidence of the horrific charring of his flesh. Strangely, the scars added to his aura of danger. His green gaze took in everything, then settled on Natalya for a brief moment.

Dominic strode over to Mikhail. Gregori moved to

intercept, reminding Nicolas that Dominic was one of the ancients who had not sworn his allegiance to Mikhail. He had served Vlad in the old days, but had only returned recently. He had fought beside the prince, even offering his life to save him, but there had been no sworn blood oath. Jacques moved into position on the other side of his brother to ensure protection. Nicolas found himself moving into fighting range just in case. No one could afford to take chances with the prince's life anymore than they could with their women.

Dominic bowed slightly. "*Én jutta félet és ekämet.* I greet a friend and brother," he said as he clasped Mikhail's forearms.

"*Veri olen piros.* Blood be red, Dominic," Mikhail returned formally, the greeting literal, meaning he hoped Dominic would soon see in color.

Dominic's shoulder shrug was eloquent. He had not found his lifemate in all the centuries of his existence and he wasn't holding his breath.

Julian Savage, a tall, heavily muscled, unusually blond Carpathian with golden eyes strode in with Barack, another male at his side. "I bring regrets from my brother, Aidan," Julian greeted. "He and Alexandria have returned to the United States. He would have come had he been within hailing distance. Dayan is on the way. He is checking the skies for the taint of the undead."

Falcon came next, with two tall, unknown Carpathians at his side. One looked familiar, an ancient Nicolas was certain he had come into contact with over the years, and the other was completely unknown to him. He had spent a great deal of his time in South America, away from his homeland and out of touch with the Carpathian people. Excitement surged in him at the thought of being among the great men of his time, once again standing solidly shoulder to shoulder as they had in the old days.

Dayan, guitar player for the Dark Troubadours and

father of one of the few female children, arrived with Traian and his lifemate, Joie. Nicolas crossed his arms over his chest, biting back his disapproval. He saw some of the others glance at the women and shake their heads. He wasn't alone in his belief that the lifemates of the women should take charge and insist on safety before anything else.

Others arrived, some in pairs, some alone. Nicolas recognized a few of the men, but most were strangers to him. The Carpathian Mountains were no longer his home, although his homeland spoke to him, the soil rich and inviting. And he had missed this sacred place and the call of brothers to council.

The last to arrive was a tall man with a face that could have been carved in stone. He entered quietly and stood a little apart from the others. Nicolas recognized the signs of aloofness, a man who had seen countless battles and knew many were to come. A man without a lifemate, driven by the madness of the dark spreading across his soul. He was Dimitri, guardian of the wolves, and he stood straight and looked other warriors in the eye, but he stood alone.

The Carpathians gathered into a loose circle. Gregori waved his hand to light the candles placed along the curved walls of the chamber. Instantly the giant crystals burst into life, radiating muted colors. This was the one sacred place a hardened warrior could go, one who skated the edge of madness, and still feel a semblance of peace. Perhaps it was the hallucinations close proximity to the crystals combined with the intense heat produced, but once the candles were lit and the hallowed rituals had begun, the hunters close to succumbing to darkness were revitalized for a short time.

Some warriors claimed the barren gray world was more difficult to endure after the brief reprieve, but Nicolas had always found the warriors' cavern a world of comfort that made sense in the craziness they lived. In long centuries that often ran together, the rituals were comforting, the old, traditional ways reassuring.

"We have much to discuss," Mikhail said. "Thank you all for coming. Nicolas has brought us news that will help us understand the mindset of our enemies."

The heat of the cave seeped under Nicolas's skin, in spite of his ability to regulate his temperature. Already he felt the crystals working on him, healing the small wounds in his body, providing clarity to his mind. Everything became sharper, much more focused, and the feeling of camaraderie deepened, so that he wanted to hear each warrior's opinion and could listen with an open mind to all views.

Mikhail moved to the center of the crystal circle, standing beside a large bloodred column of crystal minerals. Rising from the floor nearly to Mikhail's shoulder, it was one of the smallest in the room, but came to a point as sharp as a razor. He held his hand over the point of the crystal and the room grew instantly quiet, the Carpathians almost breathless in anticipation. When he spoke, he used the ancient language of his ancestors, the language still spoken by all their people.

"Blood of our fathers—blood of our brothers—we seek your wisdom, your experience and your counsel. Join with your brother-warriors and lend us your guidance through the blood bond. We pledge to our people our unwavering loyalty, resolve in the face of adversity, swift and deadly retribution, compassion for those in need, strength and endurance through the centuries and above all, we will live with honor. Our blood connects us."

Mikhail dropped his palm over the point of the crystal and it cut through his flesh easily. Rich, red blood immediately coated the top of the column. "Our blood mingles and calls to you. Heed our summons and join with us now."

As the blood of the prince mingled with that of the warriors who had gone before, the crystals were illuminated, throwing off lights and color like the aurora—swirling reds lit the room, emerald green banded in waves across the wall. The ever-changing spectacle pulsed with life, recognizing the prince of the Carpathian people.

A low murmur rose into a strong chant as the gathered Carpathians began their age-old ritual. "*Veri isäakank—veri ekäakank. Veri olen elid. Andak veri-elidet Karpatiiakank, és wäke-sarna ku meke arwa-arvo, irgalom, hän ku agba, és wäke kutni, ku manaak verival. Veri isäakank—veri ekäakank. Verink sokta; verink kaɲa terád. Akasz énak ku kaɲa és juttasz kuntatak it.* Blood of our fathers—blood of our brothers. Blood is life. We offer that life to our people with a blood-sworn vow of honor, mercy, integrity and endurance. Blood of our fathers—blood of our brothers. Our blood mingles and calls to you. Heed our summons and join with us now."

Gregori stepped in front of Mikhail and dropped to one knee. "I offer my life for our people. I pledge my loyalty to them through our blood bond." He dropped his hand on the crystal point, allowed the precious gift to mingle with Mikhail's blood, with the blood of every ancestor who had gone before. Then he offered his hand to Mikhail.

"As vessel of our people, I accept your sacrifice." Mikhail solemnly answered the pledge, taking the blood offered so that he could always find Gregori wherever he might be, any time, any place. It made the hunter vulnerable. Should he choose to give up his soul and turn vampire, he could be more easily tracked. Many chose not to participate, knowing the consequences. Gregori had often urged Mikhail to make the ritual mandatory, but Mikhail believed in free will.

Gregori rose and Lucian came forward to take his place, placing his hand over the crystal, mingling blood with that of his ancestors and kneeling before the prince to swear his allegiance and give his blood to the prince as a symbol of his vulnerability.

Nicolas held his breath as Jaxon, Lucian's lifemate,

followed him to the pillar. This was a warrior's most sacred ritual. Of the three female hunters, she was the least experienced. If the crystal rejected her, his argument to keep the women protected would be much stronger.

The cathedral-like chamber filled with the sound of male voices. The music of the crystals harmonized with the chant, producing a strong and haunting melody. Steam swirled as Jaxon approached the dark red column. She looked small and fragile beside the centuries'-old crystal's wide circumference. Without hesitation, she dropped her palm over the sharpened point. The hum of the crystals changed subtly, but continued as strong as ever, simply adding in a softer, more feminine note. As Jaxon knelt in front of Mikhail to swear her allegiance, her skin took on a luminous glow.

Nicolas stepped up next. He had performed this ritual many times in the past, but his memories had dimmed over the centuries, leaving him unprepared for the magnitude of feelings pouring into him. The moment his blood mingled with that of his ancestors, his soul called to the soul of the warriors who had gone before—and they answered, filling him with strength, clearing his mind so that every detail was clear and vivid.

His heart beat with a different rhythm, he heard the ebb and flow of blood running through veins like the endless steady ebb and flow of the tide. He felt the energy the crystals generated for healing, for clarity. Beneath the forest of crystals, hundreds of feet below the chamber, he felt the pool of rich magma feeding the heat into the cavern. The heat and fire fed the needs of his body, heightening his hunger for his lifemate. The ancient warriors murmured to him in the language of his people. *Eläsz jeläbam ainaak. Kulkesz arwa-arvoval, ekäm. Arwa-arvo olen gæidnod, ekäm.* Long may you live in the light. Walk with honor, my brother. Honor guide you, my brother. The voices continued, encouraging him to walk on the path of the warrior as they had done before him.

Mikhail took his blood and he felt the instant connection to the Carpathian people, men and women alike, the unity of strength and purpose. Nicolas went back to his place in the loose circle, feeling strengthened, and much more bonded with the other Carpathians than he ever had.

One by one, the warriors and the remaining women followed suit until only one warrior remained.

Gregori looked past his prince, to the man left standing, arms folded, back to the wall, near the entrance. His silver eyes met Dominic Dragonseeker's metallic green in challenge. A hush fell in the cavern. The hum of the crystals became louder, more insistent, as if calling to the last warrior.

"No man should be forced to swear allegiance, Gregori," Mikhail reprimanded softly. "Dominic, you have always served our people with your loyalty. No one, least of all me, questions your honor. It is enough that you swore a blood oath to my father."

Before Gregori could reply, Dominic shook his head, his steps measured and steady as he walked forward. "These are difficult times and one cannot tell friend from enemy. Gregori would not be worthy of his position if he did not guard you well. These years I have sought my lost sister, but I know that she is dead, long gone from this world and I cannot save her, nor would she want me to call her back from the shadow world. At last she is with her lifemate and by the moon, I hope she is at peace. It is time to once again embrace my duties to our people."

He dropped his hand over the crystal and blood swirled a deep red in the midst of so many other shades. The aurora filling the chamber changed color as well. Steam swirled and some of the giant crystals glowed a soft white light, as if the moon itself had entered the cavern and shone brightly above Dominic in appreciation. "I offer my life for our people. I pledge my loyalty to them through our blood bond." He offered his hand to Mikhail.

Mikhail took the offering, ingesting the blood. "As vessel of our people, I accept your sacrifice."

Dominic stood. "Someone must go into the camp of our enemies and find out what they plan next. Our women and children are at risk and we cannot ignore the fact that we have fewer than thirty women to rebuild our race. Our women must accept their responsibility to our people." His gaze rested on Natalya and then flicked to each of the women in the chamber. "They cannot place their precious lives in more danger just for the sake of doing so. I am volunteering to go to the camp of the enemy and gather information."

Mikhail shook his head. "They know who is with them through a blood bond. The parasites they inject into their systems call to one another. We found that out from Destiny."

"Gregori has the blood and I can ingest it."

Destiny gasped, one slim hand circling her throat. "You cannot. It eats at you every waking moment."

"You have no protection," Gregori added. "You have walked a darkened path for too many centuries and the parasites would eventually push you beyond your endurance. With no lifemate to guide you back, it would be suicide—more than that, you would mostly likely succumb to the call of the undead."

"That is why I want you, your brothers, Nicolas and Dimitri to take my blood. I believe, with the Dragonseeker heritage, I have more of a chance to last longer, perhaps even a year, before I succumb. If I cannot walk into the sun, then there will be six of our most experienced hunters able to track me."

Mikhail shook his head. "We cannot afford the loss of your bloodline, Dominic."

"You have Natalya and Colby. Possibly young Skyler. And now this new young woman, Lara, who is lifemate to Nicolas. The Dragonseeker line will continue. I have not found my lifemate in all these centuries and I have grown weary. Allow me to give this last service to our people. I will do my best to walk with honor and go into the sun before it is necessary to hunt me, but if not, the preparations will already have been made. I will allow these hunters access to my memories so they are fully aware of how I function as a fighter. Hopefully that will give them an edge."

The protest swept through the chamber. The crystals hummed louder and gave off a multitude of colors. Mikhail rested his hand on the bloodred column. He drew in a deep breath and let it out.

"Perhaps we should shelve this discussion until we have heard what Nicolas has to say."

"Forgive me, Mikhail, but you cannot allow me to hear anything Nicolas or anyone else has to say. If I go, I cannot know your plans. I cannot hear one word of strategy. We are in a war and the very existence of our species is at stake. The choices here will be difficult." His gaze sought out and rested on the three women—Natalya, Jaxon and Destiny. "Difficult for all of us. We have to make sacrifices and know what is the best use of every resource we have available to us. The choices are not easy, nor will they be popular, but they have to be made. I am expendable. I have the blood that will fight against the call of darkness the longest. My lineage was not given the burden of other bloodlines." His gaze flicked briefly to Nicolas and gave him a warrior's slight bow of respect.

Nicolas shook his head, his throat suddenly clogged. Dominic was a living legend, much like Lucian and Gabriel. He knew—and understood—the curse of darkness on the De La Cruz brothers. They struggled to maintain honor and always had in the face of that creeping stain.

Now, when he must stand before the council admitting he and his brothers had a hand in plotting the conspiracy to bring the downfall of the Carpathian people, Dominic was acknowledging the terrible burden the De La Cruz brothers had endured over the centuries.

"No one is expendable," Gregori said. "Not a single warrior, certainly not one of your expertise and wisdom."

Nicolas remained silent as each warrior gave his or her opinion. In the sacred chamber, with their blood mingling with their ancestors, the steam purifying them and the crystals focusing and clarifying their minds, all were heard with great respect. But he knew Dominic was going to ingest the blood and sadly, he agreed it was the right thing to do, the only thing when their entire species was poised on the brink of extinction.

Dominic was right. The Carpathians needed to know what Xavier and his coalition of vampires and jaguar-men were up to. They needed a spy in the camp. The Malinov brothers would never be able to resist letting a Carpathian as powerful as Dominic join their ranks, and certainly Xavier would consider it a huge coup. The turning of Rhiannon's brother would be a victory for him.

His eyes met Mikhail's. The naked sorrow there was reflected in his own gaze. Mikhail knew as well. Dominic would listen to the gathered warriors, but in the end, nothing would change his mind. Someone had to go and Dominic was the logical choice.

For one moment, the lines in the prince's face were etched deep. His mouth was set and he looked older, tired, weary of the burden resting on his shoulders.

The chamber grew quiet. Mikhail straightened to his full height, his black eyes glowing a deep red. His face changed completely, so that he looked majestic, every inch the leader of the warriors gathered to make momentous decisions. Steam swirled and several crystals softened color until it appeared the moon shone deep beneath the earth, spotlighting their leader. The aurora colors swirled with life, streaks of bloodred moving through an ocean of color.

"You honor our people with your bravery, Dominic," he said. His low voice carried throughout the cavern. "It shall be. The Carpathian people will never forget your sacrifice."

Dominic stared down at his closed fist, then one by one opened his fingers. One nail lengthened and he drew a thin line across his wrist, holding his arm out to Gregori. Gregori remained still, his face an expressionless mask. Mikhail lifted his hand—an order, a decree. First Gregori, and then Lucian, Gabriel and Darius came forward and took the blood sealing Dominic to them. Dimitri stepped forward and then it was Nicolas's turn. He took his place beside the warrior he considered one of the greatest of all time.

The prince, in the name of good for the Carpathian people, was sending Dominic to an existence far worse than any Carpathian could conceive. The De La Cruz lineage had been cursed with darkness, but they had also been gifted with enduring strength and honor. In the centuries past, no Dragonseeker had ever succumbed to the whispers that grew louder as one lived longer without hope, without emotion. This then, was the last of a great line of warriors, sent to spy in the enemy camp with the poisonous blood of the vampire eating him from the inside out.

Nicolas met Dominic's gaze, steady and true, refusing to look away from greatness. He couldn't save him, but he could send him away with honor, and give him the respect due him. Dominic gave him his blood and then clasped his arms in the way of the warriors.

"*Arwa-arvod mäne me ködak.* May your honor hold back the dark," Nicolas said softly. "Fight fiercely."

"*Kulkesz arwaval.* Go with glory," Gregori said. "*Joŋesz arwa arvoval.* Return with honor."

Mikhail stepped close. "*Jonesz arwa arvoval.* Return with honor." He clasped Dominic's arms hard and they stood toe to toe.

"It is the right thing," Dominic assured in a low voice as he gripped his prince's forearms. "The only thing. Give me a couple of weeks and have someone start the rumor of my turning. Make sure it is subtle. It would be news, the first Dragonseeker to succumb to the darkness. People would talk, but the news cannot come from anywhere near you. Talk will get to them and the Malinov brothers will seek me out in an effort to recruit me."

Gregori pulled the precious vial of blood from a small box and handed it to Dominic, who pulled the stopper out and drank without hesitation. The silence in the room was complete. Even the crystals ceased humming. No one moved or spoke until Dominic gave them a slight bow and took his leave—alone.

Destiny choked and turned her head away, burying her face against her lifemate. "It is like a razor is ripping through your insides," she murmured, the memories vivid and sharp.

Nicolae put his arms around her and held her to him, speaking softly, his tone low, but comforting.

Something soft inside of Nicolas rose to the surface as he watched the two. Nicolae's body posture was not simply protective, but loving. And when she turned her face up toward his, he could see the love shining back. He didn't have that. He didn't even have Lara's respect, let alone love. Nicolae had a treasure, a gift, something so precious—a lifemate was beyond comprehension—but with being so gifted, he should never be foolish enough to risk her.

Mikhail faced his warriors. "We have much to discuss before this night's end. Nicolas has brought us news of our enemies and their plans. He will speak this night. A young woman has arrived in our village and she is Nicolas's lifemate. He has made his claim and bound them together, although the ritual is not complete." His gaze rested on Natalya. "We believe his lifemate, Lara, is the daughter of Razvan."

Natalya let out a single, small sound. Her twin brother had been lost to her for many years. She had believed she killed him in a recent battle, but he had returned, possessing an elderly woman's body, to attack Shea and her unborn child.

"There is reason to believe that Razvan has been used for experiments, that possibly he was a prisoner for some time before he succumbed," Nicolas added.

"I want to talk to her," Natalya said.

Nicolas shook his head. "We have not completed the ritual. She does not trust us and has bad memories of her father. I do not want her distressed. She needs time."

Natalya's eyes went from deep green to ice blue. "She would want to talk to me."

Nicolas shrugged his shoulders, a casual ripple of muscle that put Vikirnoff just a little in front of his lifemate. "It matters little to me at this point. She does not know about you and I am not going to tell her until we have sorted out our lives. I have a very tenuous hold on her at the moment, only through our soul bond, and I will not risk it."

Natalya opened her mouth to protest, but Mikhail suddenly whirled around, his entire demeanor changing, his expression stricken as he stared for one heartbeat at Gregori, and then his brother. Without a word, his body shimmered and he leapt into the air, shifting as he did so.

Gregori's face went pale. "We will discuss the things we have gathered to talk about as soon as possible. Hopefully we can reconvene this meeting on the next rising. I must go with Mikhail to Raven now." He was gone nearly as fast as the prince.

Lucian and Gabriel stepped forward, facing the other

warriors. "Go with honor. We will meet when the prince summons us."

Nicolas didn't wait for Natalya or Vikirnoff to corner him, he simply shifted into the body of an owl immediately and took flight for home—and Lara.

6

Lara opened her eyes, savoring the heat and soothing bubbles in the mineral pool against her body. She had drifted off to sleep in the warmth. The water lapped at her skin, the sensation like tongues rasping at her breasts and throat. She blushed. She didn't have sexual thoughts or fantasies. She wasn't made that way, yet all she could think about was the width of Nicolas's shoulders, the black silk of his hair and how it felt against her skin. His breath was warm, drawing her like a magnet. She felt... unsettled... uneasy... restless. Her body felt tight and unfamiliar.

If this was what he did to her, he could stay away. On the heels of that thought came instant protest. Despite the soothing sound of water falling into the pool, or the heat enveloping her body, her mind emphatically rejected the thought of never seeing him again, reaching for him—rushing to him. He had been gone so long and an unfamiliar part of her, that was growing stronger by the moment, longed for his presence.

She took a deep breath needing... *Nicolas*. She sought the connection before she could stop herself.

I am here.

The relief of his touch was immediate. She didn't want to need the reassurance of the touch of his mind. *If this is what you do to me, I don't want any part of it.* She had learned to be alone. Never be different. Blend. Try not to stand out. And *never* need anyone.

It is the pull between lifemates, Lara. It is natural. When your aunts told the story, did they not tell you about the needs burning between a bonded pair?

She couldn't help but laugh softly, mostly with relief at hearing the steady sound of his voice. *They probably thought I was a little young for that sort of revelation.*

You have a point. But consider that Carpathians are nearly immortal. If we did not have such a need for one another, life might get boring.

She found herself with a genuine smile. She doubted life would be boring with someone like Nicolas, although she had no idea, now that he'd tied them together, how they were going to manage. But it wasn't her problem, she reminded herself, it was his. He had uttered the words of the binding ritual.

The love story between Carpathian lifemates that her aunts had told her had been her only information on how relationships worked. Back then, it had been a fairy tale, now she thought maybe she was in the middle of a nightmare.

What do you know of your mother?

When Nicolas asked the question, Lara reached for the answer, but there was only a blank empty space in her mind. *I don't remember her.*

He moved inside of her. Lara felt his presence, sharing her mind, not just her immediate thoughts. Wincing, she threw up a shield. *I'm uncomfortable with you doing that.*

Why?

There was curiosity in his tone, but no remorse. No acquiescence. Certainly no reassurance that he wouldn't do it again. A small frisson of fear skated down her spine. What did she really know of this man? And why was she accepting him so easily?

I have alarmed you.

A little. I don't trust so easily.

He sent her a small rush of warmth. *That is a good thing. I would not want you to.*

Lara swept back her long wet hair and ducked under the water again, coming up to wade across to the flat rocks where she could sit. The cave was beautiful with gems and crystals sparkling in the flickering lights. Water lapped at the rocks in a gentle rocking motion, the sound almost a lullaby. She realized she felt a measure of peace for the first time in her life. *Tell me about yourself.* She crossed her arms under her breasts and tilted her head back to watch the light show the candles gave off.

I have four brothers. I have spent much of my life in the Amazon rainforest. You would like it there. It is beautiful and wild. I cannot wait to return and see it in vivid color. Nor can I wait to look upon my brothers and feel, for the first time, in my heart, not just in my head, the love I have for them.

She could feel the love he had for his family. She caught glimpses of four very intimidating men, handsome, with that same dangerous edge that Nicolas had. *Four brothers? Did you grow up with them?* There was no way to disguise the wistful note in her voice.

She had been out in the world long enough to know what a family was supposed to be, and she longed for one of her own. Maybe that was why she was so susceptible to Nicolas. She ached with loneliness. She had always needed the cool interior of the caves to hide the fact that she couldn't really take too much sunlight so she had little contact with others. If she had to work in the morning hours or late afternoon, she could manage with long sleeves and sunblocks, but she rarely set to work until evening. She told her colleagues she had an allergy to the sun. During the afternoon, she could barely manage to function, so she found that caving was a perfect solution to all of her problems—and deep in a cave, she didn't have to watch others interact with their families.

Growing up with my brothers was always interesting. We all believed we were smarter, faster and had to prove it to one another. We did some crazy things.

She caught images of several boys falling from the sky at alarming rates of speed from alarming heights, each struggling to shift right before hitting the ground. Each boy tried to beat the time of the one who had gone before. It was a dizzying, frightening scene. *Your poor mother. Five crazy sons. I didn't think about what raising a Carpathian child would be like—especially a boy.*

The thing she found the most interesting was that the oldest boy in the memory was already a man in human years. She could tell by Nicolas's recollection that they were still fun-loving children, yet they looked grown.

Flying is the best feeling in the world, soaring high, riding a thermal, diving through the clouds. I had forgotten the pure joy I had as a child until you came into my life. I will take you this next rising if you like.

She could hear the joy in his voice—felt the emotion pouring into her mind, allowing her to experience some of what he was feeling. She hadn't ever felt like he had. Her earliest memory was of her aunts whispering to her, trying to console, disembodied voices she thought for a long time were in her own head.

That would be fun. Who wouldn't want to go flying?

Lara pressed further into his mind, huddling there for a moment, basking with him in those long-ago, forgotten moments. She caught glimpses of other things. Something dark and grotesque moving fast out of the trees toward him. His eldest brother, Zacarias, calling out a warning, calling out instructions even as he raced to place himself between Nicolas and the monstrous being rushing from the trees.

Lara gasped and drew back. *What was that?*

Vampire. Nicolas injected a soothing note into his voice. He was still a good distance from her and needed to find sustenance before dawn broke. *My first kill. We were teaching Riordan, my youngest brother, shifting on the run, and the undead attacked me. I was a distance from my brothers. I think he thought I had detected his presence, but he was a huge surprise. I barely escaped with my life. Zacarias gave me instructions while I was fighting him off and I managed to destroy him before he got to us, but you would have thought I was the only hunter in the world that day. I was stuck on my own importance.* He injected a little laughter into his voice.

To Nicolas, Lara felt… *frightened*, or maybe it was edgy, he couldn't put his finger on her sudden withdrawal, but that brief glimpse of a vampire had triggered something in her mind. He didn't like that she was alone in the cave with what could possibly be another flashback of her childhood. Something—and he was fairly certain it was the parasites—had brought long-buried memories to the forefront. Now that the barrier had gone, he suspected she would be able to remember pieces of her past.

I will be there soon. He didn't want her to feel alone, not ever again.

Below him, a farmer crossed a small pasture to a makeshift barn. In the body of an owl, Nicolas changed his flight, circling to make certain the man was alone and there was no danger, scanning the region for the dead spots that might indicate there was a vampire present, before beginning his descent.

Lara sank back into the water, puzzling out why she felt so edgy when only moments earlier she had felt safe and cocooned in a world of heat and aromatic fragrances. This cave was far different from the ice cave. She often caught glimpses of her past—secret little vignettes of a shivering, terrified child, listening to the ominous crack of ice weighted with tremendous pressure. Everything in her memories was cold and barren and frightening. Here, she felt protected and safe, the world sparkling with gems and soft lights, yet...

Nicolas drew her to him with the sound of his voice, low and sexy and oh so very commanding. His physical beauty, intensely male, the burning possession in his black eyes, the force of his personality totally focused on her was all a little overwhelming and thrilling. Even his childhood memories—they were beautiful, the laughter, the camaraderie, everything she'd ever wanted. There was a brightness in all the boys.

A chill ran down her spine. *Until the vampire had come out of that forest and attacked Nicolas.* She stood up once again in the shimmering pool, her arms crossed over her breasts, her heart beating too fast. Darkness in Nicolas had risen to meet the vampire. There had been nothing at all bright in Nicolas at that moment. That dark blotch grew and spread, consuming him until she couldn't tell hunter or the undead apart. As if alive, as if a separate entity, the darkness in him had leapt forward, eagerly reaching for the hunt—for the kill. There had been no hesitation, not on his part. Even as that shiny young boy he had embraced that rising darkness, losing himself in it as he rushed to meet the attacking vampire.

She pressed her fingertips to the strange birthmark low on her body, the dragon that warned her when a vampire was near. Earlier, when she had first encountered Nicolas, the dragon had gone hot and cold. Nicolas had triggered the warning with the darkness in him. She swallowed the lump in her throat, her heart slamming now so hard she could see the rise and fall of her breasts, feel a choking in her throat. Remembering that same flash of hot and cold, mixed signals that frightened her as much or more than a steady burn. Her father had often produced that same odd, faulty response whenever she was close to him.

Her pulse thundered in her ears, heart hammering so loud she could barely hear the water pouring from the wall. What was wrong with her? Her stomach lurched and she staggered, her wrist, throat and neck burning painfully. Nicolas appeared charming, but what did she really know of him? He hadn't argued with her. He had even been polite when she'd shoved a knife in his ribs, but she really knew nothing at all about him.

Terror welled up. She had lived life with humans, good-natured, uncomplicated, genuinely nice people for the most part. No, they hadn't understood that lost child and they'd given her from family to family, continually on the move, but they had cared for her basic needs and no one had tried to use her for their own gain. She had almost forgotten a world of deceit, of betrayal, of kill or be killed.

She reached out again tentatively, the lightest of touches, her mind seeking his. At once she was consumed by hunger, by the need for blood. She heard the ebb and flow of life surging and pounding as a farmer hauled a calf from a cow's laboring body. She heard the heartbeat, steady and strong, scented the good health, a large masculine physique toweling off the calf while murmuring to the cow. She crept closer, scenting the blood from the birth. It only added to the need building in her, the hunger raging now, taking hold and directing her. She ran her tongue along her teeth, and felt a lengthening and sharpness just past her incisors. Her heartbeat increased, began to take on the rhythm of the unsuspecting farmer bent over the cow.

Merged with Nicolas, she felt the smooth, silent glide, stalking prey. A dog tried to bark, but Nicolas/she stopped it with one quick, commanding flick of a hand. Adrenaline rushed through her. She felt the movement in her veins, a high like no other. Blood thundered in her pulse, roared in her ears. Then she was on him, that one moment of recognition, the heart rate jumping, the mind rebelling, only to be taken over completely by Nicolas—by her.

Ultimate power. Life or death. Teeth sank deep and the rich taste burst through her, into her, filling organs and tissue with strength and energy. Lara gasped and pulled her mind away, stumbling through the water toward the rocks where she could steady herself.

Need and hunger poured through her body, overwhelming with its intensity. She fought it back, but knew, once that need was there, only blood would satisfy it. He had awakened the one thing in her she had always tried desperately to suppress.

Nicolas was taking blood from a human being. Using that person as cattle. Worse, he was controlling his victim's mind and he'd done it without using spells and potions. He was that powerful.

Her wrist ached and burned. She looked down and saw her flesh torn open—chewed—as if teeth had gnawed and ripped. Blood splashed onto the boulders and droplets hit the pool. Her neck ached where Nicolas had sunk his teeth into her and she covered the spot with her palm. It came away smeared with blood. The illusion was so strong she stared in horror before she realized it was illusion.

Slowly, Lara looked around the cave. How had she let this happen? No matter how warm and beautiful, a prison was still a prison. A predator was still a predator. She'd been mesmerized by him. She'd recognized the danger in him from the start, but somehow he'd made those concerns vanish from her mind. Was he controlling her? Manipulating her mind?

Shivering, Lara staggered out of the pool, looking around for something to dry herself off with. Where had she planned to sleep? In the ground with him? On the bed with him? With him? Why hadn't she even considered that? She wasn't stupid, yet she'd followed him here without question or protest. What woman would go off alone with a stranger for the night where no one knew where she was? Nicolas De La Cruz exuded sex from every pore. His walk, the roll of his shoulders, the dark eyes burning so intensely—he was a sexual man and she was sure he didn't expect to sleep in a bed with a woman without possessing her body.

Lara dragged on her clothes, heedless of the way the material stuck to her still-damp skin. Panic rose, and she spun around, determined to find the way out. He'd given her directions—were they real?

Do not be foolish, Lara. The sun is rising. I will be there soon and we can discuss this calmly. You are merely having a panic attack and there is no reason for it.

The calm voice grated on her nerves. He was condescending and arrogant. She had every reason to panic. Any sane woman would have done so a long time ago. Using the directions in her mind, she sprinted out of the glistening chamber into a long corridor.

I forbid you to risk yourself. Wait for me.

This time that thin veneer of civilization cracked and she could feel the edge to his voice. Her stomach lurched. She gasped and pushed herself harder, increasing her speed, using her night vision in the dark confines of the cave. She couldn't think about how deep she was or the maze of tunnels that ran miles beneath the mountain. The only objective had to be to get out as fast as she could. She rounded a corner and the corridor divided into two paths.

The air is heavy in the cave, difficult to breathe, to run fast. Each step is harder. You are sinking into sand, your legs heavy. You are so tired, Lara. Why not sit and rest. Your mind is confused and the directions are fading from your memory.

The voice was low and insidious, filling her head, the compulsion spreading through her body. She stumbled, confused, and halted, twisting this way and that.

It is becoming difficult to see in the dark. You should stay still.

Stop it! "Stop it!" Lara repeated, shouted aloud.

Her voice echoed through the caverns, disturbing returning bats. The creatures took to the air, wheeling and fluttering, thousands of them, filling the spaces around her. It was difficult to breathe, and impossible to move. She stood there, trembling, waiting, held prisoner by the mesmerizing voice. She felt the surge of power in the chamber heralding his arrival, and the bats immediately renewed their aerial acrobatic performance.

Lara forced herself to take a breath. She had to resist him. She could see in the dark. She was unafraid of bats. The earth pressing down on her didn't bother her, yet here she was cowering in the cavern, afraid to move, her body feeling clunky, leaden.

I am mage. I am Dragonseeker. You will have to do more than trick me with your voice, Carpathian. Fury burned through her, scorching the shackles of compulsion into ashes.

I can do much more. Do not arouse the demon in me, Lara. Dawn is breaking. The sun is rising.

He was close. She sensed him coming closer. Tilting her chin, she called energy to her, lifting her arms and clearing her mind, accepting the power so that her hair crackled and a faint glow threw the cave into soft light, agitating the bats more.

Those that fly and are of the night, protect me now with winged flight. Gather together, become as one, remove yourselves with the rising sun.

The bats circled, fast and tight, the ball growing larger as they obeyed her command, rising upward and streaming toward a recess in the dark cavern. Lara struck hard at Nicolas, sensing his weakness with the rising sun, retaliating with another spell.

Whispering voice inside my head, I fear you not, nor your leaden web. Voice that seduces, whispers and binds, I return the intent to thine own mind. Let the words stop and take away, that which would hinder or hamper my way.

The moment the last words left her mind, she was on the move, running fast, throwing up barriers and shields in her mind, to prevent Nicolas access. He tore each wall down easily, shredding her defenses as fast as she built them. Each time he penetrated into her mind, he sent compulsions to slow her step, to misdirect her the wrong way, confuse her so that she thought she was disoriented and she retaliated with more spells to counter each thing he did.

She fought him every step of the way, aware as she did, of his enormous power, of how he held back when he could have crushed her resistance. Instead of giving her confidence, his restraint only added to her fears. What did he want from her? Her Dragonseeker blood? She knew it ran strong in her veins, rich and filled with energy and power and immortality. Her father had told her many times how valuable and unique the strength in her blood was. Her great-grandfather had stalked her repeatedly, his grotesque body crawling with worms, rotting flesh sloughing off as he pursued her in an effort to claim her blood for himself.

Now, here in the cave, she felt the same terror blossoming as she ran, her heart pounding too hard, and she could smell the strong odor of decomposing flesh. She gagged, a sob welling up, as she threw one look over her shoulder to see if the old man again pursued her.

Shadows moved. A hand stretched out, closer and closer. She felt hot breath on her skin, her neck. The twin marks over her pulse throbbed. Was Nicolas creating an illusion, twisting buried memories? Was he despicable enough to do such a thing? Or was Xavier really there, chasing her through the underground passages?

He is not there. Your mind is playing tricks on you because you are allowing yourself to panic. I would never use your memories against you. He is not there. Nicolas would not allow her to be so terrified, remembering the monsters chasing her in ice caves.

She didn't know what was true or what wasn't, nor did

it matter anymore. She had to be free. Lara redoubled her efforts. She was betting on the fact that she could be out in the early morning sun with little repercussions. A sunburn. A few blisters. Her eyes would burn and bother her for a few days, but surely a Carpathian as old, with a soul as dark as Nicolas's, would have to seek cover before she would. She had to make it to the entrance and find her way to the village.

She could see, just ahead, a bloom of dim light. Her heart leapt. She was going to make it. Lara drew in a deep breath and pushed herself to go faster. Her lungs burned. Her throat hurt, her legs cramped. There was a stitch in her side. She pressed her palm there and forced her body forward. The entrance was wide and rounded, mostly rock shaping the way in. Light spilled a few feet into the corridor, illuminating the narrowing tunnel.

Lara stepped into the pool of light just feet from the opening. A shadow fell over her. A tall dark man with wide shoulders filled the entrance, blocking her exit. Nicolas stood there, his body still, arms folded across his chest, his jaw tight, mouth cruel, eyes as black as night, burning with some inner fire that threatened to consume her.

Lara halted abruptly a few feet from him, a roaring in her ears and a vice around her heart. Guilt edged her mind, but she refused to accept it. "I want to leave. Get out of my way."

"Where would you go when the sun has already risen?" The question was issued in a mild voice, yet it carried the sting of a lash.

He was furious. She could feel anger radiating off of him, although his expression remained blank and his voice quiet.

She lifted her chin. "I have a room at the inn."

"Which is occupied at the moment. It would be dangerous for you to go there and you are very aware of that. Also, the inn is a great distance away and you would burn in the sunlight. You cannot shift without me and risking your life getting off this mountain is ludicrous when there is no reason for it."

"I want to leave this place."

"We will leave together in the evening when it is safe to do so. For now, I brought food and drink for you."

"I've said I want to leave." Lara's hand fluttered to her neck, her palm shielding the twin marks over her pulse. She could feel his mouth there, his breath warm—no—hot, the brush of his lips, soft and sensuous against her skin.

"You are obviously not thinking clearly, Lara," Nicolas answered. "It is dangerous for you to leave. I cannot allow you to place yourself in harm's way." •

"That isn't your choice," Lara snapped. She detested that he sounded rational while she was beginning to sound hysterical. This was madness, yet he stood there, real and solid, preventing her from leaving the cave—just as she'd been prevented as a child. She fought down panic, determined to try to be reasonable in an unreasonable situation.

"It is not only my choice, and my right, but my duty as your lifemate."

She touched his mind, more because she couldn't help herself than because she wanted to. As before, he was entirely open to her, allowing her to see both predator and man. He was angry at her defiance, certain of being right and unused to anyone questioning his authority. He was a dominant male, centuries on earth, a highly skilled hunter and it was an affront to his pride that his lifemate question not only his ability to protect and care for her, but worry that he might harm her in some way.

He didn't like anyone defying his orders, let alone his woman, and he had no intention of allowing her to leave the cave when he deemed it dangerous. As far as he was concerned, she was slightly hysterical and completely irrational.

Lara forced down panic and took a deep breath. Nowhere

in his mind could she see that he was attempting to control her mind. There was some relief in that, although she was fairly certain, unless she could convince him otherwise, that he had no intention of letting her leave.

"I think we don't understand each other. I appreciate you trying to take care of me, but I've been doing that all by myself for some years now. I don't need nor want you telling me what is good for me."

"Obviously that is not the case or we would not be standing here at the entrance to a cave in broad daylight." He glided forward, one step, two, turned slightly and raised his hands.

Lara felt the surge of power, saw his arms lift and knew he was sealing and safeguarding the cave, which meant no one would get in—or out. Panic hit hard and she leapt forward toward the light spilling into the cavern. She caught a glimpse of his face, all sharp edges, beautifully carved, very masculine, the light throwing the details into sharp relief and highlighting the smoldering anger in his burning black eyes.

Alarm shot through her, but it didn't matter, nothing mattered, except getting out of the cave before he sealed the entrance. She ran fast, using a burst of blurring speed, speed she hadn't even known she was capable of. Desperation drove her past Nicolas. He reached out so fast she couldn't actually see him move, snagging her wrist, whipping her around and bringing her body up hard against his.

She struggled instinctively, trying to free herself from his grip, but he was enormously strong, his body hard like an oak tree. The light faded as the entrance sealed, plunging them into darkness. With the light, the air surrounding them seemed to diminish, so that she renewed her efforts, swinging at his chest, pounding until she felt battered and bruised.

Nicolas tightened his grip on Lara, taking care not to hurt her, but she was wild, fighting him with her fists and attempting to use magic. He could feel the energy pounding in her, trying to escape, just as she was trying. He surrounded her with soothing calm, holding her close to him, swamping her with reassurance.

"Lara, stop," he hissed softly. "You are only hurting yourself."

She wanted to hurt him. To move him. To make him understand what he was doing. Energy crackled in the air. Her hair glowed with bands of brilliant red, snapping and popping with electricity. The ground shook and undulated beneath their feet. The mountain groaned, rumbled. Dirt trickled from the walls and several smaller rocks fell and rolled.

Nicolas wrapped his arm around her head to protect her, sheltering her body with his. "Breathe with me."

His voice was calm. She hated that he was calm when she was filled with chaos and panic. She felt his breath warm against her cheek as he bent his head toward hers.

"We have to get out of here before the mountain comes down on top of us," she said, not understanding why he wasn't feeling the same panic when all around them the mountain creaked and groaned and debris fell. "This is an earthquake."

"It is not natural. You are causing it," Nicolas said. "Look at me, Lara."

She couldn't prevent herself from obeying, lifting her face, her gaze colliding—then locking—with his.

"Your eyes have changed color. You are generating a tremendous electrical current. Even your hair is banding with color, all signs of power. You have to calm yourself."

"Open the entrance." *Because I'm capable of bringing the entire mountain down on both of us and would rather do that than be a prisoner.*

He shook his head. "Do not force me to protect you from yourself." *I am quite capable of doing whatever it takes to keep you from harm.*

He looked as ruthless as he sounded. There was no give in him—no mercy. Not in his eyes, not on his face and certainly not in his mind. He would force compliance without a second thought. Lara had sworn she would never again feel helpless and vulnerable, as she had when she was a small child, but there was no point in matching her physical strength against Nicolas, and little point in challenging him with power.

"Do you really believe you have the right to dictate to me?"

He shook his head. "No. But I have the right to protect you. I am not threatening you. You are the one putting both of us in danger. It is my duty to protect you. Your fears are groundless. You have looked into my mind and find nothing there to alarm you…"

She made a derisive sound and once again tried to jerk away. He retained possession of her arms, holding her body close to his to prevent the occasional disturbed rock from striking her.

"I found plenty to alarm me. You're every bit as dark as a vampire."

She expected him to deny the charge—she wanted him to deny it—but he simply nodded his head, his gaze still holding her captive.

"That is so. All Carpathian males who hunt eventually become as dark as a vampire. How could we not when we take the lives of friends and family? When we are judge, jury and executioner? Did you think there wouldn't be a price to pay for what we do? There is always a price, Lara, and we accept that when we take on the job."

She let her breath out slowly, forcing her mind back under her own control. "Please let go of me." Breathing deeply, she managed to pull back the power spilling from her, reining in the waves causing the disturbance in the cave.

"I can take you back to the chamber much faster."

"I would prefer to walk." She tugged backward, trying to put a little space between her and the heat of his body. He was too big, too solid, too masculine, mostly he was just too powerful, swamping her with his complete confidence.

He let her go the moment the earth beneath them and the walls surrounding them ceased rippling and the last rock tumbled to the ground.

Lara took another breath and looked down the dark corridor. "I wish you could understand that I don't think I can actually stay here all day." It was hard to get the words out, to try to reason with the unreasonable.

"I realize you are having flashbacks, but I will help you get through this."

His arrogance set her teeth on edge. As if he could solve her inconsequential problems when she couldn't do it herself. Lara stepped past him and began walking along the narrow corridor. At once candles sprang to life in sconces above her head, throwing shadows along the walls of the tunnel. The light didn't dispel the fear in her mind. She was a prisoner, any way she looked at it, and she had promised herself it would never happen again—and it wouldn't.

The narrow corridor expanded outward several feet past a veil of stalactites—thin, dark daggers of brown and gold sharpened to lethal points. The hanging spears glittered with earthy tones, so long and thick she had thought the corridor closed, impenetrable on that side, but she could see more corridors, a maze of trails leading in different directions beneath the mountain. He could have gotten her lost, but he had been true to his word, giving her the directions to get out, even though he had no intention of allowing her to leave.

"In the story of lifemates that my aunts told me, the couple seemed to be very much in love. I don't really see that happening between us," Lara said, her back and shoulders stiff. "Do you?"

"Of course." There was complete confidence in his tone.

Nicolas paced easily one step behind her, his body so close she could feel his warmth. She sent him a small frown. His breath was on her ear, one hand brushed the small of her back. She tried not to feel the pull between them, that physical chemistry that persisted no matter what. Maybe she was drawn to the very danger in him she so strenuously objected to, but whatever it was, when he was so close to her, it was difficult to think straight. "It was only a story my aunts told me. Maybe it isn't even true."

"It is true. I could not have bound us together had the words not been imprinted before my birth. We 'marry' our woman immediately to protect the species from extinction."

"How lovely for the woman." Sarcasm dripped from her voice. Watching over her shoulder, she caught the faintest of smiles. It didn't quite reach his eyes, but it infuriated her. "Don't you think it's wrong that you can utter a few words and change a woman's life whether she wants it or not?"

"No. Why would a woman want to be with a man like me? It is the only way to protect our species from certain extinction. If you were not tied to me, you would not so easily have come with me."

"I said I wouldn't be a prisoner." She walked faster.

Nicolas kept pace with her easily. "And you are not a prisoner."

She shook her head. "We don't even talk the same language."

It was impossible not to breathe him into her lungs. He was too close. He walked so silently she kept turning her head to see if he was there and she'd catch him. Real. Solid. Frightening. Fascinating. So male. Utterly handsome. He was almost too good-looking to be real. But his eyes gave him away. Hungry. Cunning. Intelligent. A hunter of prey. He made her pulse race and every alarm bell shriek. He made her aware of him as male and of herself as female. And he made her lose focus. She didn't have a clue how to handle him—but she knew absolutely she wouldn't allow him to turn her into the puppet her father had wanted.

His hand brushed the small of her back, his fingers trailing along her spine. "I think we will manage just fine, Lara. Give it time."

7

The chamber was even more beautiful than Lara remembered, a dazzling display of gems and crystals of various colors. The water sparkled as it poured from the wall into the pool, the droplets like thousands of diamonds falling from the sky, but the warmth and beauty of the cave no longer made her feel safe and comforted. A cage was still a cage no matter what it looked like. She preferred the glacier-blue ice caves, cold and desolate, because she knew exactly what to expect there.

She moistened her lips and steadied herself. Yes, she had strong Carpathian blood running in her veins, and she burned like hell in the sun—she figured that was just the luck of the DNA draw—but she wasn't fully Carpathian like Nicolas. She wasn't a hunter who had killed over the centuries. She wasn't close to turning vampire, as he was. And that meant she simply had to bide her time and wait. She wasn't concerned with the safeguards at the entrance. She was a talented mage and had watched carefully as he had woven the strands for the safeguards.

She searched for a safe topic of conversation. Anything

that would keep him from touching her mind and discovering her plan. "Did you see the prince? Did he tell you how Terry was doing?"

"I spoke with Gregori, our healer, and he said your friend has a good chance of surviving. He would not say that if it was untrue."

"Gregori looks less like a healer than anyone else I could imagine."

"I suppose he does. You obviously had seen the parasites before."

She had shared that memory with him, she had no choice but to admit it. Lara nodded. "Xavier experimented often, trying to find ways to strengthen his ability to command others to his bidding." She couldn't stop the shudder that ran through her body. "His creatures were ravenous and often escaped his commands. They ate human flesh."

"Your mother?" He asked it softly, his voice gentle.

She swallowed the sudden lump in her throat. She hadn't thought of her mother in years. She'd never been able to conjure up a picture of her in her mind, not even a scrap of memory. Not the color of her hair or even her scent. She hadn't known she had a mother until the parasites combined with the silver of Gregori's eyes had triggered a long-forgotten memory. "Yes, but I didn't remember her until now."

"She was mage." He made it a statement.

Lara frowned. Now that he said it aloud, she recalled her aunts referring to her mother as mage. Why hadn't she remembered that before? Why hadn't she remembered that her mother had curly hair? She touched her own hair. She had been born with white hair, although a red tint had developed very early on. Little corkscrew curls had been all over her head, thick and springy, impossible to control. Her mother's hair had been like that as well. "Yes, she was. I vaguely recall pulling on her curls."

The memory of her mother lying on the floor of ice,

parasites attacking her dead body, made her sick. She pressed a hand to her mouth, found she was trembling and paced closer to the warm pool. The sound of the waterfall soothed her, allowing her to draw a few deep breaths so that she could change the subject. She didn't want to remember anymore.

"You were gone a long time. What did you do tonight?" *When you weren't controlling other people's minds and stealing their blood without their consent.* The thought came unbidden and she kept her back turned so he couldn't read her expression. She didn't trust herself at all. He was used to reading opponents, and right now, whether he knew it or not, they were locked in a battle for life.

"We held a warriors' council this night. The vampires have banded together and are trying to destroy our species. Humans would stand little chance against them. Just making them believe vampires exist would be nearly impossible."

Her heart jumped with shock and she turned to face him in spite of her resolve. "Vampires are too vain and selfish to band together. They only hunt in pairs when one has become the puppet of another. I know that to be true. My aunts told me exactly what had to be done to kill them if I ran across them, and they told me the vampires despise everyone, including each other. That is why the Carpathian hunters will always have the edge when fighting."

"That has always been true, down through the centuries," Nicolas agreed. "But it is no longer so. Someone has found a way to band them together and we are in for a long, bitter war for survival."

She didn't question why his dark gaze stayed on the gentle lapping of the water in the pool against the smooth boulders. "Xavier? Do you think he's still alive? He was so old even twenty years ago, but he was good at getting the necessary Carpathian blood to continue his life."

"We believe he may still be alive and has formed an

alliance with five brothers, powerful Carpathians who we think have turned vampire."

"If Xavier is still alive, then my aunts could be, too. I have to get into that cave."

His head jerked up, black eyes burning over her face. "That cave is dangerous. Going there is foolish. If your aunts were alive, we would know it. They would have the ability to call to our people for aid."

"If that were true," Lara snapped, sarcasm dripping from her voice, "then they would have done so when I was a child. They were kept weak and sick."

"Those who entered the cave saw the bodies of two dragons encased in ice—dead."

Lara's stomach churned and she pressed a hand to her abdomen. "Xavier kept them encased in ice. He froze his blood supply, very clever, wouldn't you say? Do you know what kind of pain a person goes through when their body is recovering from being frozen?"

Nicolas gentled his voice. "Lara, I will go to the ice cave myself and check for you, but it is best if you stay far from that place. Xavier left protections—dangerous ones, including shadow warriors. It would be suicide for you to go there."

Lara pressed her lips together tightly. What was the use of arguing with him when she planned to escape anyway? Of course she would go. How could she not? Her aunts would never have given up searching for her, nor would they let danger prevent them from going to the one place that would yield the bodies as well as clues.

She cast around for something—anything at all to say. She could see the corner of the bed in the next chamber, a massive old-fashioned bed with a carved head- and footboard. She didn't want to go into the other chamber or even acknowledge it was there. Already, she could feel the tension rising in the cavern.

Glancing at him from beneath a screen of long lashes,

she moved a little farther out of reach. He seemed to fill the space of the chamber, although it was quite large with high ceilings. It was impossible not to feel the sexual pull. He was too handsome, too sensual, the combination of the way he moved—going from utter stillness to a streak of action—was sexy. Power was in the flow of his body and etched into every line on his face. His brooding eyes could melt Lara and when he turned the intensity of his black gaze on her, focused on her completely, her body ceased belonging to her and reached for him.

She had tried to put off thinking of the consequences of Nicolas's claiming her as his lifemate. Maybe in a secret part of her she hadn't really believed that by uttering a few words he could change her life forever, but she felt the connection—and sexually it was just plain frightening. To go from not being even mildly interested in men who she was friends with and knew, to having her body flare out of control for a man she didn't even like was horrifying.

She had been helpless as a child and vowed never to be so again. She'd spent years of her life controlling everything around her so she would never have the vulnerable, helpless feeling again. She looked around her at the cavern walls. Here she was nearly twenty years later and she was right back where she'd started, only this time, her own body betrayed her.

"Stop being so afraid of me, *päläfertiil*. I will not take anything you do not want to give me."

In the flickering candlelight he looked a little wolfish. She crossed her arms over her breasts wishing her gaze wouldn't drift down his hard, masculine body and that he didn't have that knowing look on his face. He was Carpathian, with heightened senses, and he would know her body was aroused—worse, he could probably smell her fear.

Her chin lifted. If he could smell her fear, then what was the use of denying it? "You bound our lives together without consent. That tells me you take what you want and really could care less about what I want or how I feel."

"Is that what it tells you?"

She couldn't help the small glance she shot at the passage leading to freedom. It was only a few precious feet away, but it might as well have been miles. "You don't have to sound so patronizing. Do you really think things are the same as way back when you were born? What is it now, five hundred years?"

He bared his white teeth in what could have passed for a smile, but was more of a warning. "You are a few centuries off, but I get the point. We have the right to claim our lifemates. If you do not fight the inevitable, the transition will be a lot easier and smoother."

Her eyebrows shot up. "Really? For who? I must have some rights in this situation. Surely I can talk to someone who can advise me. The prince, maybe."

The tension in the cavern went up a notch. He didn't change expression, but tiny red lights flickered in the depths of his eyes. "If you want to know something, you have only to ask me. Lifemates do not deceive one another."

"You said you wouldn't make me a prisoner, yet you have. You gave me the way out, but then you refused to allow me to take it."

He stirred, going from stillness to muscles rippling beneath his thin shirt, as if a great cat stretched and unsheathed his claws. The air left her lungs in a little rush and she actually stepped back, although he had remained stationary.

"The sun will burn your skin. You cannot expect me to allow you to hurt yourself simply because of an unfounded fear. That goes against my entire nature."

"I don't think you understand something as fundamental as freedom, Nicolas," Lara said. "You're big and strong and have enormous power. When have you ever had anyone telling you what to do? I can't imagine many people in your lifetime have dictated to you."

"It is not the same thing." He gave a small sigh. "I have never had to do this before, and it is something I do not enjoy."

"The 'it' being someone disagreeing with you?"

"Arguing for no good reason. I cannot permit you to burn for the sake of defiance. What kind of a lifemate would that make me? Would you truly prefer someone who cared nothing for your health and safety?"

"You say lifemates don't lie to one another. Can you truly say you refused to let me leave because you were worried about my skin burning, or was the reason really because I dared to defy your orders?"

He moved then, a fluid glide that sent a shiver of fear skittering down her spine. He looked like a caged jungle beast, fierce and impatient and all too dangerous. "I refuse to answer such a question. I left my mind open to you, allowing you to see everything, including my motivation. There is nothing more to say on the subject."

She drew in a deep breath, feeling his anger smoldering beneath the surface, but she couldn't quite bring herself to apologize, not even to soothe him and keep him thinking she was accepting her fate with grace.

Nicolas broke the silence first. "You have not eaten."

"I'm not really very hungry. It's been a long night." She winced as soon as the words were out of her mouth. She didn't want him to suggest they go to bed.

"I know you need blood, Lara, there is too much Dragonseeker running in your veins for you to survive without it. If you have problems with the idea of taking blood from a human, what do you do? Animal blood has never sufficed."

Lara shrugged. "Blood banks. I don't have to control people as if they were puppets." She sent him a telling look and then paced around the chamber to put a little distance between them.

He seemed to be everywhere, his presence dwarfing everything else. When he stopped moving, he went absolutely still. She could see the hunter in him. Patient. Motionless. Waiting. And he could wait forever. Panic rose and she crushed it down. No, he only seemed invincible, just as Razvan and Xavier had seemed all-powerful when she was a child. She had escaped them when she thought it impossible, and she could escape this man as well. She just had to keep thinking.

Nicolas folded his arms across his chest. "Without blood we die. Is it not better to take what we need without scaring the person and then leave him without knowledge that we have done so, than terrorizing someone when it is completely unnecessary?"

Nicolas watched Lara swing around, her hair crackling with energy, her eyes going aquamarine. "I *felt* that farmer's fear, that one moment before you took over his mind. And earlier, in the street, when I first met you, you made no effort to keep me from knowing what was happening when you took my blood." Her hand slid to her belt, to the knife there, her only weapon should he attack her again. The smooth handle felt reassuring.

"You cannot have it both ways, Lara. Either you want me to control his mind and keep him from being frightened, or you want me to just feed, uncaring of how the donor feels."

"Why not use a blood bank?"

He sank down onto the edge of the boulder beside the mineral pool. "You already know the answer to that. The blood does not work for us. We can survive, but not thrive. I fight vampires. I need to be at full strength at all times. What would you have me do?"

Lara pushed both hands through her hair in agitation. "I don't know. Something else. Something more respectful. People shouldn't be used for food like that. They have feelings. We aren't just mindless puppets."

"You are not human."

Her chin rose. "I may have a hodgepodge of blood running in my veins, like most humans do, by the way, but without a doubt, I think like a human. I know what it's like to be kept prisoner and dragged out so someone could tear my flesh open and drink my blood. They didn't care if I was scared, or repulsed. They didn't care what I thought or felt. *I* didn't matter to them any more than that farmer mattered to you."

His dark eyes drifted over her face, taking in every detail. "Should our species give up our lives because we should not take the blood of others without consent? We are careful and respectful."

"It didn't feel very respectful to me." Mentally she kicked herself. She was supposed to be stringing him along. She needed to use her trick of distracting, banal conversation, a sugary voice, even inject humor, all tools she had found invaluable when she was growing up. Conversation sidetracked people.

Confrontation put them on edge and warned them they were dealing with someone of power. Her body reacted to her moods. The families she lived with eventually became uncomfortable with a child whose hair and eyes changed color when she was upset. She didn't blame them for thinking she was a child of the devil; many of them were superstitious and, quite frankly—well—she was a child of the devil or the closest thing to it—at least the great-great granddaughter of the devil.

Nicolas reached for her hand. His palm slid along hers—skin to skin. Her stomach flipped. His fingers tangled around her fingers and her heart began to pound out of control. She took a deep breath and looked up at him. Instantly she felt trapped—captivated—by the intensity of his gaze. He turned her hand over and brought it to his chest.

"I have lived centuries, Lara. I was born with darkness already crouching inside of me and I fought it back every moment of my existence with nothing but honor. I am not making an excuse, I just want you to understand. This night I was too close, and you saved me. We're bound together, but the ritual is not complete. I may have been rougher than I intended with the farmer, but if I didn't calm him before he was aware, it was not intentional."

She moistened her dry lips. Deep inside where self-preservation lived, she heard herself screaming, "No, no, be quiet, don't engage," but it was too late, the words were already tumbling out of her. "There was a rush, when you seized him, I felt the rush pour into you. You're addicted to it. It's amazing to be all-powerful over someone else, for that one moment to hold life in your hand and choose for them." She tilted her chin at him, tugging away her hand. "Maybe that's what kept you going on these years, not honor."

Nicolas stepped back, fury sweeping through him. His mind touched hers and he drew away, horror sweeping through him as he stepped back a few paces, just out of arm's length when he wanted to grab her and shake her. How dare she dismiss so easily his centuries of service, his fight against the darkness rising like a monster every day of his life. Worse, what kind of a lifemate would deliberately leave her mate vulnerable, completely helpless out of selfish convictions that weren't even logical or reasonable? He could see her plan as plain as day—she was waiting for the sleep of his people to overtake him and she would leave him alone and without safeguards.

He hadn't felt anger in centuries, now it welled up, a black wall of rage. No one questioned his authority, and they never questioned his integrity. She had done both in the space of a few moments.

His black eyes glowed hotly and his breath left him in a long, slow hiss. "You think to leave me when I succumb to the sleep of my people? You would do that? Leave me here, unprotected and without safeguards, knowing I could do nothing at all if I was found? You know what anyone would do should they find my body, yet you would betray me in such a way."

The waves of anger coming off of him swamped her, sent her stumbling back away from him. He looked every inch a wolf, white teeth bared, mouth set in cruel lines. There was no mercy in him for his enemies, and the moment he saw she intended to expose him to danger, she became his enemy.

A scream welled up, but she bit it back, turning on her heel and running—to where, she didn't know. She only knew if she stayed, the full brunt of his temper would be on her and he looked as if he could kill her.

He was on her fast, a lion bringing down prey easily, jerking her to a halt and spinning her around to face him. She threw up her free arm to protect herself from blows that never came. He caught her upper arms and gave her a hard shake. "I do not beat women, although if one needed it, it would be you."

Keeping a firm grip on her, he dragged her through the cavern to the chamber where the bed stood out so prominently. The sound of her heart thundered in both of their ears. He tossed her easily onto the mattress, one hand running through his thick hair.

"Don't you touch me." She crawled to the farthest corner near the headboard, away from him.

He moved fast, a blur of speed, towering over her, showing her she couldn't escape. "You think I could not make you want me? You are my lifemate. Your body responds to mine no matter what your ridiculous mouth is saying." The burning in his gaze turned to speculation. "Do you want to pit your power against mine? I could make your body mine easily, and you would crave me night and day. Perhaps it would simplify both our lives."

Lara could feel the instant tingling in her body, every

nerve ending reaching for him, and she was horrified. Her entire body was on fire just from the intensity of his gaze and the low seductive tone he used, as if he was already brushing her bare skin with the warmth of his palm and pads of his fingers. She had no doubt in her mind that he could enslave her sexually and that she would be no more than a puppet living with this man. He was every bit as cruel, every bit the monster, only packaged differently.

The feel of her blade was reassuring against her hip. If not him, then herself. She searched for a way to disarm him, to dispel the tension between them. Her plan was still good, if she could just keep him calm an hour or so longer. The sun had to be up fairly high. She was feeling a bit lethargic herself. No matter how powerful, he couldn't stay awake forever. He would have to go to ground and sleep.

"I wasn't going to leave you without safeguards."

"Your safeguards must be known to every vampire and mage from here to the sun and back. And do not try to lie to me. I did not see your intention to guard my body while my spirit rested. You did not even think about it."

She wanted to refute his accusation, but in truth, she'd thought only to get away. Before she could suppress it, her temper flared. "Who guards their captor? Now who is being illogical and unreasonable? You can't have it both ways." Her hair banded with stripes as her stomach churned with impotent anger.

His black eyes glittered ominously as his hand snaked out, caught her wrist and yanked her over, so that her cape fell open, exposing the scabbard on her belt. He ripped the leather free, tearing the knife from her belt and hurling it through the archway to the pool. It landed with a splash and disappeared beneath the steaming water.

Lara had the strangest reaction. There was a part of her that wanted to curl up in the fetal position, there was a part that wanted to fight tooth and nail, but there was also the most horrifying reaction, a shiver of anticipation that made her womb clench and set wings fluttering inside her stomach.

"Is that so I won't stab you through the heart when you go to sleep?" She fed his anger because she feared the dark seductive velvet in his voice—the burn of desire smoldering in his eyes. She feared the reaction of her own body to him and more than ever was afraid that he could enslave her will.

His smile held no humor, nor did it light his eyes, but was a mere flash of strong white teeth. Her heart tripped as she saw the slight length and point to his canine teeth. The effect was subtle but it was there. She tried to make herself smaller as he settled on the bed beside her. One large hand cupped her face, forcing her to look at him, to stare into his mesmerizing eyes.

"You tried stabbing me once. You chose life for us and I expect you to keep your word." As he spoke, his thumb slid back and forth across her bottom lip.

She jerked her head up. "You're trying to intimidate me."

Swift impatience crossed his face. "I do not think I have to try very hard. I left my mind open to you, gave you complete access, trusted you with everything I am, and you, in turn, closed your mind to me, accused me of heinous crimes and mistrusted me from the beginning. I grow weary of this argument."

She hoped he was. She hoped he was so weary he'd go to ground and leave her to make her escape. She kept quiet. His body crowded close, so close he seemed to be everywhere, surrounding her. He took her hand again and held out his other palm. Veins of minerals appeared in the walls of the chamber, glowing briefly as if hot. She blinked at the sudden bright light. There was a tug on her arm and something heavy and warm snapped in place around her wrist. She opened her eyes to see him enclosing his wrist in an iron shackle, tying them together.

Lara's face went pale. She jerked her arm away. "What are you doing?" With her free hand she tried to push the iron bracelet from her wrist, but it was snug.

He paid her no attention, murmuring under his breath. She felt the surge of power and knew he was layering on safeguards, binding the shackles with magic so she would have no hope of getting them off if she didn't act fast.

Forcing back a sob, Lara countered his magic. *Iron that binds and fastens tight, I seek to unlock that which holds me tight. I summon thee mineral, blend with light, forge me a key to undo this plight.* Power surged as raw minerals from the earth blended with fiery light to form a key.

Nicolas twisted quickly, pushing her to the bed, holding her arms down to keep her hands from rising to direct energy into patterns and to prevent her from grasping the key as he threw out a spell of his own.

Cease this action, intended to unbind, I take in your energy making it mine.

The key disappeared in a burst of light. At once she knew he had bested her. He was centuries old and she was rusty in her practice. She had forgotten that in the early days, when Nicolas was young, mage and Carpathian shared secrets. She was helpless, completely under his domination, a prisoner unable to escape. She blinked up at him, wanting to punch his face, but terrified of the repercussions. He leaned close, so close she could see the long dark lashes that veiled his smoldering eyes. His lips brushed the side of her mouth.

"You look like a trapped kitten, about to hiss and spit fire at me. Go to sleep. We will sort this out the next rising."

With that, he lay back, dragging her with him, rolling onto his side, his eyes closing—dismissing her. Lara held her breath, waiting, not knowing what to look for. It didn't take long. His breath left his body in one rattling exhale and he lay completely motionless. She was chained to a dead man.

The trembling started somewhere in her legs and ran up

her body so strong she was afraid she would go into convulsions. She lay staring at the ceiling, her heart beating too fast, too loud, her chest hurting, lungs burning from lack of air, her mind screaming. She was a prisoner with no control, no power, no say over her own life. It was only a matter of time before he would demand sex and she would succumb to his wishes because she would be unable to stop her body from needing his.

She shuddered. From there, he would take her blood. It was the nature of all Carpathians to take blood and she had sensed, more than once, his desire to take hers. She'd rather be dead than to live enslaved. She couldn't survive without control in her life, without a say in what she did. She couldn't allow herself to be used for food, or, as she feared would happen, sex and food.

Lara thought of her past, the few memories she did have of her childhood and knew she could never relive those times as an adult. She lay awake as the sun rose to its height and her body became so leaden she could barely move. When the sun began to sink, she began trying various spells to rid herself of the iron shackle binding her to Nicolas, but no matter what she tried, she couldn't counter his guards.

She stared up at the gem-studded ceiling without seeing it, tears swimming in her eyes. There was so much left undone that she'd promised to do, but it was too late. Her first promise had been to herself and she refused to even consider anything else. She just needed to work up enough courage to escape in the only way left to her.

Nicolas awakened, drifting, taking one shallow breath every few minutes, allowing his mind and spirit to find peace in the quiet of Carpathian twilight—not fully gone, but not far from the surface. Lara had hurt him and he couldn't remember the last time anyone had ever done such a thing:

He hadn't known anyone could. He knew he should wake fully and face her, but he needed to sort out his unfamiliar emotions. She had certainly pricked his pride when she'd accused him of being addicted to the rush of his power. Honor had sustained him these long centuries, not addiction, and it was the only thing he had to offer her. She had stripped him of even that with her careless accusation.

He had wanted to throttle her, yet at the same time, the need to kiss her, to dominate her body with his, had risen up like a terrible demon possessing his mind. She should have been grateful for his honor. Without it, she would have found herself naked and writhing under him. She owed him deference and respect. She was so young and inexperienced in all things. She should rely on his wisdom and trust him. He had done nothing but try to protect her, but she persisted in acting like so many of the women, demanding foolish and dangerous things without thinking them through.

His chest felt heavy, a strange sensation when he should have been weightless. His wrist burned and ached. Fear skittered up his spine and found its way into his consciousness. His spirit reacted, reaching for his body, abruptly taking possession. Nicolas came aware instantly.

He heard the sound of ragged, thready breathing and smelled—*death*. He shifted his body, and felt Lara, ice cold, lying beside him. Turning his head, he saw her face, eyes wide and unseeing, staring at the ceiling. A wave of his hand dissolved the shackles, allowing him to roll over and come up on his knees beside her, reaching for her limp arm, his heart nearly stopping, then beginning to slam hard and fast in his chest. Her wrist was torn open, obviously a deliberate attempt to end her life. Her own teeth had ripped the ragged tears, opening her vein so that blood ran down the side of the bed.

Veriak ot en Karpatiiak. Köd alte hän. By the blood of the prince. Darkness curse it. What has she done?

Swearing, he brought her wrist to his mouth, using his tongue and healing saliva to seal the vein and sweep closed the wound. *Lara! Come to me.* It was a demand. And he was furious that she would do such a thing.

What was she thinking? Didn't she know what would happen? *Lara!* Desperation was setting in. She'd been like a wolf caught in a trap, willing to chew off her foot, or end her life rather than be captured and held prisoner. He had lain beside her, angry, righteous, and all the time, she had been quietly ending her life.

He gathered her into his arms, rocking her gently as he shed his physical body to enter hers. She needed blood. Fast. Her body labored, her mind had already shut itself down to keep from brain damage. Had she been human and mage without Carpathian, she would already be dead.

He found her spirit, flinching from his light—from him. *Come to me, o jelä sielamak. Light of my soul, stay with me.*

His arrogance had driven her to this. He hadn't seen her as a person, so much as *his.* His savior, his possession, his to do his bidding. He'd been so sure of himself, so certain of his rightness. Nicolas De La Cruz, informing his brothers how they should handle their lifemates, so certain he knew best for everyone around him, after all, he was faster and smarter and had lived so much longer. And yet his own lifemate, the woman he had sworn to protect, to make happy, he had driven to this—taking her own life rather than submit to him.

He crooned to her, wooed her, soothed her as he gathered her spirit to him to prevent her from going so far he might not be able to bring her back. Keeping her secure, he returned to his own body.

He had needed her to know who was in charge. He needed to establish his dominancy like some conquering warrior, to prove to her that when he said something she should listen because he knew best. This was his failing.

He hadn't taken the time to know her, to understand her, or even to give her credit for keeping her word. She had chosen life for them and she placed herself in his hands for all time, trusting him. And he'd destroyed that trust—and them.

He hadn't seen her as someone separate from him, with her own thoughts and feelings. His family had been cursed "too" everything. Too smart. Too fast. Too assured. Too dark. There in the darkness of the cave, deep beneath the ground, holding the ice-cold body of his lifemate, he admitted the truth to himself.

He lengthened his nail and drew it across his chest, opening his vein. He couldn't even promise her he wouldn't repeat his mistakes, the darkness in him may have gathered strength over the years, but it had been there from the beginning. Even with his lifemate close, it was a living, breathing entity inside of him and it demanded those around him go his way. *I will fight my nature as much as possible, Lara.* He murmured to her softly as he pressed her mouth to the wound over his heart. *I will be all things to you. Come back to me and let me show you I can be what you need.* He had only considered how much she must change to be what he needed. How had he been such a fool?

She didn't respond. Not to the scent of his blood, and not to his coaxing words. In the end he had to resort to a command, wincing as he did so. How could she ever resolve living with one such as him? How could he protect her from his own nature? Even now, when she so clearly chose death over living with him, he imposed his will on her.

Juosz és olen ainaak sielamet jutta. Drink and become one with me. Live with me. I will never be perfect, but I will do all within my power to make you happy. Drink and live. It was a command—a compulsion—and he put every bit of power he could summon into the directive because he was not able to let her go. He would choose life for her and spend the rest of the time they had trying to convince her he had done the right thing.

Her mouth moved against his bare chest. He was unprepared for the strange reaction of his body. The heat exploding into fire. The fullness in his groin. The burn of need in his veins. He threw back his head and absorbed the feeling, took it deep and held on to it. The call of one lifemate to another. His soul had called to hers and hers had answered. Their minds sought one another, needing the constant closeness between them. Now his body was calling, determined to awaken hers. Where was his heart? Did he even have one? Was that part of the curse of the De La Cruz family? Maybe they really didn't have hearts—or maybe it was just him. Although right now, right at this moment, he felt like his was breaking. He ached for both of them.

His life force flooded her starving body, organs and tissue and brain greedily reaching instinctively for nourishment—for life. He made certain he not only gave her enough to replace what she had lost, but enough for a formal blood exchange. Their first true exchange and it was much needed. He had to find a degree of control to combat the darkness that had grown so strong over the last few centuries. His one fear had been that of turning vampire, becoming the most loathsome of evil creatures, yet now, with his lifemate to provide the light to his darkness, he should have been free of worry. Without the formal blood exchange, even with the claiming ritual, until they met as one in body as well as soul and mind, he was a danger to everyone—but mostly he was dangerous to her.

Nicolas cradled Lara in his arms, close to his chest, still rocking. The sun had gone down some time ago and the night was on them. He had no idea when she had managed to harm herself or how long she had lain awake contemplating harming herself, but her spirit was a long way from her body.

"*O jelä sielamak.* Light of my soul, come back to me."

She struggled and at first he thought it was to stay away from him, but then he realized her spirit was trapped elsewhere. She had drifted away on a sea of blood and wherever her spirit had roamed, past or present, or the shadow world, she was trapped in a web she couldn't get out of. Without hesitation, he merged his mind fully with hers, following the path to find her and guide her back to the land of the living.

8

Nicolas shivered. It was cold. For the first time in his life, when he tried to regulate his body temperature, it was impossible. The cold was mind-numbing. And there was so much fear, wave after wave swamping him. Fear was not an emotion he was intimate with and the waves were overwhelming, keeping him off balance, his stomach churning and his heart beating too loudly. He didn't question that he shouldn't have a heart—or hear one, not while he was without his body, he simply accepted whatever happened and continued after her.

He found himself in a child's body. She was so tiny, her heart wild. Terror—her terror—settled into his mind, filling every corner, every compartment until he breathed it in and out, until it was living inside his very soul. He stared through horrified eyes at a man chained to the wall of ice. A young woman sat beside him weeping as she tried to wipe the beads of sweat from his face.

Razvan/*father.*

Nicolas breathed through the terror and tried to focus

on what was happening. Razvan was nearly drained of blood, weak, barely able to talk coherently, his voice low and trembling so that the woman leaned close and pressed her ear to his lips in order to hear him.

"Shauna, get her out before it's too late. You have to let her go."

Lara's mother shook her head, tears running down her face. "She's too little, Razvan, she'll never make it on her own."

"Better she die than let him get his hands on her."

"I can't bear it. I can't bear to lose you and her. There has to be another way."

"I will need blood and you've already given me too much."

"She hates giving blood. She's too young to understand," Shauna said, but she was already lifting the little girl with copper curls onto her lap.

Instead of feeling comforted, Nicolas was swamped with Shauna's fears as well. Living in the body of the child-Lara, he struggled against the arms holding him tightly, fought, kicking and biting as Shauna extended the child's arm toward the man lying pale and ravaged. His heart felt as if it might explode. He tried to shift, to get away from the teeth coming at his small, exposed wrist. He had always been fast and strong, his powers honed at a very early age when few boys could even think of shifting, yet now he was powerless to free himself. He could only wait, watching those teeth come closer and closer to his flesh.

His body shrank away from the hot breath. He heard whimpering and felt Lara's spirit desperately fighting to free itself. The small arm was already covered in scars. This wasn't the first time and it wouldn't be the last. There was no escaping those sharp teeth tearing through her skin to get at her tiny veins.

Nicolas pushed Lara behind him, shielding her as those teeth tore into his wrist. Pain blossomed, stole his breath, punched him in the gut. His vision darkened and blurred. He couldn't minimize the pain as he always had done, he had to let it wash over and through him, accept it to keep from passing out. Even as a child he'd been able to control pain over the many mishaps of shifting too close to the ground or slamming into a tree while flying. Although a man, he was merged deep with Lara, reliving those early years and he was as helpless as she had been. Merged so deep with her, he was not Carpathian, able to push pain aside: He had to suffer through it as she did.

He felt each individual tooth, felt skin rip, tissue and muscle, felt the puncture into his vein and the flow of his life force from his body. His spirit shrank until he felt small and vulnerable beyond even his scope of imagination. At the worst moment in his life, he had never felt this helpless. The lips sucking blood from his body felt greedy and ravenous. His body became leaden, his heart struggling to find a beat while his lungs labored for air.

"Stop! Stop, Razvan," Shauna cried and pushed at the mouth clamped around the little wrist. "You're going to kill the baby."

Razvan jerked back. Tears spilled down his face. "I'm sorry. I'm so sorry, Lara. Shauna, this isn't safe. I can't stop myself anymore. I'm becoming like him."

"No you're not," Shauna said fiercely. "You're not like him. You'll never be like him." She rocked the baby back and forth trying to sooth her.

Razvan leaned over and closed the wound with a swipe of his tongue. Nicolas knew the healing saliva wasn't quite right, wasn't quite able to numb the flesh or heal properly, which was why the little wrist had scar tissue everywhere and why Lara felt the pain of each bite as if knives were ripping at her.

"Hurry now. She must go. He will be coming any moment."

Razvan inched his body aside to reveal a hole in the ice. Where the ice had been white or bluish in color, it was now red with pink edges. He had tunneled into the wall of ice using his own warm blood to carve a tiny passageway.

Shauna hugged the child to her, squeezing tight, sobbing quietly as she did so. Abruptly she thrust the girl into the tight channel and shoved her. "Go. Hurry. Follow the water out."

The ice pressed down on the little body, scraping at skin. He felt the lacerations and tears as he scooted forward. There was no turning around. When he tried to scoot back rather than go into that smaller, darkened warren with the scent of blood heavy in his nostrils, his body simply wedged in tighter. Panic began to take hold. Nicolas fought to shift, to become smaller, anything to get out of the tunnel. The heavy ice weighed down on him. Above and all around him, the ice creaked ominously as the heavy pressure constantly shifted the walls.

Nicolas couldn't draw air into his lungs, his head was buzzing from lack of oxygen. He felt as if he was suffocating. He knew Lara was experiencing the same reaction and he was totally helpless to come to her aid. He felt overwhelming tenderness for Lara the adult who had suffered as a child, and rage and aggression, at his own impotence in protecting her from reliving it. He tried to pound at the ice, using sheer will to break her free, but there was no escaping the tight space. He only bloodied his fists.

For the first time in his life he experienced claustrophobia. He felt trapped with no way out. His enormous strength didn't work. No magic spell saved him. He couldn't weave energy and use it. No matter how hard he tried to use sheer force to crack the ice and break out, he was in a three-year-old female body that didn't have his powers. It was impossible.

Lara's spirit stirred. Merged so deeply together, it was nearly impossible to tell where one started and the other left off. Their souls were bound together. *Go.* Her whisper was weak. *There is no need for you to live this with me. I survived it before, I will again.*

He wasn't certain that was true. She barely was alive, and in any case, there was no way he would abandon his lifemate to relive whatever experiences she must in order to come back to him. He had thrown her into the past and he would shield her with everything he had in him in order to protect her from the worst of her memories. No matter what it took, he would stand in front of her. *Rest, o jelä sielamak. Light of my soul, I will not abandon you here.* The tenderness in his voice surprised him, as did the ache in his heart.

Something sharp pierced his ankle, stabbed deep, all the way to the bone. His body suddenly jerked backward. Ice tore the skin from his shoulders and hips, from his arms. He tried to kick back to remove whatever had penetrated his ankle, but all that did was cause excruciating pain. His body was ripped backward through the tunnel fast, peeling the skin from his body as he was pulled back through to the ice chamber.

He fell onto the chamber's hard floor, horror filling him as he saw the most monstrous of creatures—Xavier. Shauna lay on the floor, blood seeping from her mouth and nose. Already dark bruises stood out on her skin. She reached for the little girl, but Xavier kicked the woman away and yanked Lara/Nicolas up by the coppery curls. He carelessly tossed the child against the cavern wall, smashing her small body without thought.

Xavier was a mass of decomposing flesh, serrated blackened teeth and pitiless silver eyes. Nicolas watched with horror as the monstrous demon stomped the woman repeatedly, her ribs, crushing them, her face, breaking bones, her legs, pulverizing them.

Razvan struggled against the chains, so that they cut into his body and blood ran in rivers to drip onto the ice. He screamed, a hoarse, hopeless yell, bloodred tears streaking his face. "It was me. Don't touch her. I'll do anything. Please. Please." He fell back weeping, his fists pounding into the ice until they, too, were bloody.

Xavier ignored him, continuing to kick and stomp Shauna's body. "Look at what you've made me do," he yelled to Lara. "Look at her. Your mother, taking your punishment. You deserve this treatment. You did this. You've made her suffer." He reached down and yanked the child by her hair, dragging her across the floor to fling her facedown beside her mother. "Steal her last breath, you ungrateful brat. What are you good for except for food? You've killed your own mother."

He spat on the body and reached into the pocket of his long tunic, pulling out a jar of wiggling white parasites. "My friends will gladly clean up *your* mess, although it will take a few days. Feast," he said and threw the parasites onto Shauna's limp body. The grotesque bugs immediately swarmed over her mother.

Xavier reached down and caught up Lara, his silver eyes glittering with maniacal glee. Laughing, he snapped a chain around her waist, locking it to her father's chain before he hobbled away. She had little room and was forced to sit beside her mother's body while her father rocked and moaned as they watched the parasites slowly consume her.

It could have been hours, or days that Nicolas sat, traumatized by the brutality of the Carpathian's worst enemy. He had thought he knew evil intimately in the centuries of hunting the vampire, but this was far, far worse. Xavier had murdered his grandson's wife in front of the man and their child. Even more, he forced them to watch the slow consumption of her body by the ravenous parasites. It was no wonder that Lara had flashbacks when she saw them combined with Gregori's unusual eye color. And it was no wonder that her aunts and father had buried her memories deep.

We are with you, Lara, a voice whispered softly. *Do not fear, we are near. Do not look at the body on the floor. That is no longer your mother. She has gone to a safe place where the monster cannot reach her.*

Nicolas concentrated on the voices as they whispered encouragement, told stories and tried to aid a young child in dealing with the incomprehensible. Without her great-aunts, Lara would have either given up or gone insane. He found himself holding on to their voices, letting the soothing compulsion wash over him as the next vignette of Lara's childhood began.

The fear cycle was always first, he realized. Her spirit traveled up the path of her childhood, inching her way from her past toward the surface—and him. She managed to advance a couple of years before the web of horror entangled her again, effectively holding her prisoner in her memories.

At six she was thin and small, barely fed and alone constantly. She had a tiny cubicle, slept on the ice floor with only a thin blanket and her growing ability to regulate her body temperature. It was difficult for her to sustain heat, and the constant shivering prevented her from gaining much weight. The aunts were the one stabilizing influence, talking to her day and night, whispering of far-off places, teaching her as much as a child could comprehend and implanting lessons and truths for times when she was older and could possibly grasp the knowledge and wield more power.

He learned they were kept drained of blood as Razvan was, often frozen, encased in ice, that they suffered horribly when thawed and that Lara felt every moment of their agony along with her tortured father's. It was only their voices that kept her sane.

He moved toward the surface with her, cradling her spirit, breathing warmth into her mind in an effort to reconnect with her. He needed her trust and he'd blown it in the worst possible way. He understood that now, understood what it was like to feel small and helpless—and without hope. He understood fully why she had chosen the only way out to her and that he was responsible for driving her to feel helpless all over again.

The moment fear swamped her, coming at her like a tidal wave, he knew she was trapped again in a significant moment of her life. She was aware the moment he stepped in front of her spirit again, surrounding her with his protection, allowing the waves of terror to engulf him.

Don't. Just go, get out while you can. We may never be able to leave this place.

I will not leave without you, Lara. It is my sin, my failing that sent you back here. I will not leave you here. If we stay, we stay together.

And he meant it. He embraced that child's body as she sat crosslegged on the floor, drawing a picture of a dragon on the ice wall. There was amazing detail for a child. Her little fingers grasped the small tine of a fork and carved scales with painstaking care over the dragon's body and long tail. She took her time, humming to herself, lost in her art.

A small whisper of sound alerted her. Lara tensed and slowly lowered her hand from the drawing, looking over her shoulder. Razvan's broad shoulders filled the doorway. His eyes were dark with sorrow, his face ravaged. One moment he looked a handsome man who had seen too much pain, the next his body hunched as if under a terrible burden. His face contorted and his eyes rolled back in his head as he fought some unseen foe.

"Lara, get out. Run, baby. Get out. He's in me, he's taken over my body and I can't throw him out. Go."

Even as he warned her, his voice changed back and forth, going from concern to cackling. Although it appeared to be Razvan standing in the doorway, Lara smelled Xavier, the rotting corpse of a man who refused to die. Nicolas felt her stillness, the instant pounding of her heart, the terror seizing her mind. She stumbled back on all fours to crouch against the wall.

"What is this?" Xavier/Razvan asked, standing in front of her drawing.

Lara/Nicholas stayed silent, keeping her hands behind her back, fear stamped on her face. Nicolas pushed her behind him as Xavier whirled around and struck him, knocking him off his feet, sending him flying.

"Answer me," Xavier/Razvan hissed with displeasure.

Lara/Nicolas picked himself up. "My best friend."

Razvan's face contorted as though he was fighting again. His body shook and a bloodred tear trickled down his face. For a moment he held out his hand, but abruptly, the fingers curled into two tight fists and he sneered. "Friend? You think those dragons are your friends? Why would such a powerful creature ever befriend the likes of you? You're worthless, totally worthless."

He cackled, the wicked sound sending chills down Nicolas's spine, and the voice was all Xavier now in Razvan's body. Once again, Nicolas felt that hopeless vulnerability, knowing he couldn't stop this man. He was a six-year-old child, anemic, fragile, alone, with no hope of escaping. As he watched, the dragon on the wall began to pop out, first one clawed foot, stretching and reaching, the talons curling sharply. The head emerged, the eyes blinking for a moment before glowing red. The tail slashed and the dragon broke free, landing on the floor a few feet from Lara.

Nicolas pushed her farther behind him, corralling her

spirit and shielding her as he felt her cringe in anticipation. This was going to be bad. He knew it wasn't just physical warfare, this was psychological, a deliberate attempt to defeat all hope, using a childhood make-believe friend that took the form of her comforting aunts against her. Possessing her father's body so that he did the ultimate damage to her, betraying all trust, ensuring she had nothing at all to hold on to. And he couldn't imagine what Razvan suffered, obviously some part of his mind aware of how his body was being used to torment his child.

The dragon swung its head back and forth, eyes spinning and then focusing on the child. It leapt on Lara/Nicolas, hissing and spitting. At the last moment Lara/Nicolas spun around and the claws ripped at his back, tearing deep gouges. He went to the floor, curling up in the fetal position as the dragon bit at his legs and slashed at him with its spiked tail.

Possessed as he was by Xavier, her father laughed and kicked at him, encouraging the dragon to spout flames until she screamed and Nicolas screamed with her.

Do not resist. Let him take what he wants from you. The feminine voices were in unison and Nicolas was instantly aware of Lara trying to kick out with her feet, not toward the dragon, but toward her father.

The dragon renewed its assault in a maddened frenzy of teeth and talons. Nicolas felt every shred in his skin, felt the rakes on his back as muscle tore beneath those sharp claws. The bites were painful, but shallow. The worst was the fire, spraying over his head, frying his sensitive skin, raising blisters instantly.

Suddenly impatient, Xavier/Razvan waved his hand and the dragon melted at his feet. He leaned down and jerked Lara/Nicolas to his feet, his teeth ripping open his wrist and sinking down to gulp greedily at the rich blood. Nicolas bit back a grunt of pain as his arm throbbed and burned. His stomach turned over and once again his vision blackened around the edges.

Lara suddenly resisted, swinging her arm in a tight arc and sinking the sharpened tine into Razvan's throat. Xavier screamed and threw her away from him, clamping his hand to his bleeding neck. Lara swept her tongue across her wrist and backed up slowly.

Nicolas wanted to hug her to him. In spite of the pain and the sheer hopelessness of her situation, Lara fought back, refusing to let a monster crush her spirit.

Xavier flew into a rage, spittle running down his face as he ripped her clothing away, his hands weaving a complicated pattern. Water poured down on her from the ceiling, she was lifted from her feet and flung back into the ice. The wall opened to receive her, molding around her back, buttocks and legs, freezing her skin to the ice itself.

Only then did Xavier grow quiet. He placed food and water a distance from her. "If you want to eat or drink, you'll have to tear yourself from the wall. If you don't, I'll leave you there to rot and send my little friends in to eat your body."

Nicolas watched him shuffle out, leaving the child in excruciating pain with blood running down her legs, with her back already painful. He wanted to weep, to smash something, to gather her close and hold her against his heart and protect her always. And more than anything, he wanted to kill Xavier.

Again time meant nothing to him. He drifted on a sea of pain until the voices came again. Soft. Insistent. Encouraging. Singing of hope. Whispering endearments. Voices he could latch on to, voices that saved him from complete despair.

He found himself ascending once again toward the surface with Lara's spirit. Her light was a little brighter, but she felt battered and bruised—as did he. He tried to hurry, anxious that she not relive another event. He'd had enough—seen enough—experienced enough. He never wanted to feel that helpless and vulnerable ever again. He shepherded her, surrounding her with warmth and reassurance, feeling her reluctance as they moved closer to breaking free.

Lara was more afraid of him than of her past. She'd already lived through her childhood and survived. He was the devil she didn't know and in their relationship, he had all the power.

I am all you think I am, but I can learn. I will learn. I have many sins, päläfertiil, not the least is arrogance, but I am not above admitting my mistakes. Come with me. Come back to me and give me a second chance.

He had accepted—from the first moment he heard her voice and knew that she had saved him—that she was in his care. He had resolved to do the best that he could for her—see to her every physical comfort. He hadn't expected resistance or mistrust on her part, but in truth, it hadn't mattered to him—his heart was not involved and he knew without a shadow of a doubt that he could have all things his way. He even believed it to be his right. Somehow in this new night, he knew things were changing. The hard stone in his chest slowly began to beat the same rhythm as hers. He knew he was growing more and more protective, and feeling more and more tenderness toward her.

Something caught at her, jerking her spirit away from him, stalling the process of recovery. He worried now that he had found her too late and she had retreated too far, or had actually embraced insanity to escape the madness surrounding her. He sped after her, following her to the web where her spirit lay entangled by strands of memories rushing together to surround and capture her.

She was a year or so older, her hair bright under the flickering lights. He could see the beginnings of the

Dragonseeker legacy woven into the color of her hair, the red glow and blonder highlights. Her eyes were by turns deep sea-green and a brilliant blue. She stood to one side in the great chamber with its cathedral ceilings, hiding behind a column, making herself small, obviously trying to avoid being seen by Xavier and Razvan as they faced each other.

Lara. The voices whispered in her ear. *Xavier cannot ever know that you are aware of what he is doing to your father. He would kill you. You cannot tell your father, even to ease his mind, because when Xavier possesses his body, or Razvan is under his command, he will reveal all of your secrets.*

If I tell my father I know he doesn't want to hurt me, maybe he will fight even harder. There was hope—and a little defiance in that childish voice.

He will betray you. He will not mean to, but he will be unable to stop himself.

You have been prisoners far longer. Lara was angry now, unbelieving. *Xavier can't control you.*

Razvan has been tortured, Lara, experimented on, over and over. His health and strength are gone. Xavier uses you against him. Xavier still doesn't understand the power of your blood. Once he does, there will be no chance of escape.

Nicolas felt the stubborn streak in Lara. She didn't answer her aunts, refusing to deceive them with an outright lie, but determined that she would go to her father and confess she knew Razvan was being manipulated against her.

As if sensing Lara's stubborn will, the aunts tried again, speaking in perfect unison, their voices soft and melodious. Nicolas recognized the threads of a compulsion woven into the pitch. Both women were weak and the suggestion wouldn't work on a stronger mind, but Lara wasn't healthy and her spirit had been beaten down.

Lara, you cannot give any information to your father that Xavier would use against him. Razvan wouldn't want you to. He has sustained Xavier all these long years and fought against him because his Dragonseeker blood is strong. Xavier knows he will soon give out and must find a replacement. If now, when he is at his weakest, you give him information that Xavier could harm you with, he will feel he has lost all honor.

The child that was Lara squeezed her eyes closed, not really understanding the whole of what the aunts were telling her, but she knew she couldn't reassure her father that she understood Xavier either possessed his body or forced him to comply using a combination of drugs and magic with his orders.

Nicolas felt Lara slip further away from him, the overwhelming despair she was feeling stronger than ever. She stared at her father with a wistful expression. He had a strong urge to pull her into his arms and hold her close, but he had no real body and she still didn't trust him. He understood why now. He understood her need for control and freedom. And he understood her absolute repugnance of anyone taking her blood.

Razvan looked weak, his once handsome face ravaged by pain and suffering. The lines were etched deep and the chains wrapped around his legs and arms had left permanent burn scars from the vampire blood they were coated in. He sagged against a column, not even fighting to get away from Xavier, who took a small vial from his tunic pocket. Nicolas felt Lara tense, her small spirit shrinking back.

Interested, he stepped in front of her to block her, ready to take the brunt of whatever had happened at the age of seven. Xavier clearly experimented on Razvan and he was learning all sorts of pertinent information not only about his lifemate, but things that would be useful to the Carpathian people. Nicolas now wished he could stop Dominic from proceeding with his plan. If Xavier had felt compelled to try his experiments on Razvan because he had Dragonseeker blood running in his veins, Dominic would surely be a huge prize. Most of the experiments seemed to be centered around controlling the Carpathians or finding a way to imprison them yet still keep them alive.

For the blood. Lara's voice whispered to him, in her adult voice, not the child's. *He wants your blood in the same way you want it from your sources. He will hold you prisoner and drain you dry. You would be nothing but a food source to him.*

He softened his tone to tenderness, his heart reaching out for hers. *Lara. I do not want you for your blood. Come back to me. Am I really worse than this place in your past?*

For a moment he thought he had won this first battle, but then Xavier moved and the child was back, shuddering as her father was. She shrank back behind the column as Xavier hobbled across the floor of the ice cave, holding the vial in his gnarled fingers.

"You should have given me what I asked for. Giving me your sister was so little to ask in return for your life and the lives of your children." The old man clacked his tongue in reprimand. "And so many children. You betrayed your poor dead wife with your body. All those young, nubile women so willing to lie with you and give you children so you could suck the life out of them."

Razvan stirred. "You sucked the life out of them and you forced betrayal of my wife. She knew the truth, knew you used my body. Let me die, old man. I've served you for far too long and am of no more use to you."

Lara's body jerked in instant denial. The child shook her head hard, the red-gold spiral curls flying in all directions. *Don't leave me, Father. I cannot bear it.*

He will stay alive for you, Lara, the aunts crooned in unison. *You are his only reason to continue his existence.*

Nicolas found the blend of feminine voices soothing. Without them, Lara, and most likely her father, would have gone insane years earlier. The two imprisoned women were keeping hope alive. How could they do it when they had been prisoners and fed on from the time they were young children? The Dragonseeker blood in them had to be very strong.

Razvan lifted his head, his gaze darting around the chamber, seeking the child he knew had to be witnessing the confrontation between him and his grandfather. Lara froze, pressing as close to the column as she could get to avoid being seen.

Xavier let his breath out in a long, slow hiss. "I believe we can still get a few more children out of you before I'm done with you. My armies can now identify one another and even hide their existence from the foolish Carpathians thanks to you. And I can hold even the strongest prisoner and feed on the blood of the most powerful immortal, again thanks to you. I will not be hasty in getting rid of such a useful tool. You may not have the pure blood I need yourself, but you pass it on to your children."

Nicolas remembered from so many long centuries ago that Xavier had always loved to be the center of attention. He thought himself brilliant and powerful and wanted everyone around him to know that he was. He loved to brag. Nicolas had always considered him to be narcissistic. Xavier thought the world owed him its allegiance and respect. He believed he was entitled to any woman he wanted to have. Long before Rhiannon disappeared, many young mage women had lived to serve his every need or want. Xavier often had regaled the Carpathian men with tales of his sexual prowess and exploits, never realizing how little respect they had for him because he didn't hold his women in high esteem.

Now, having to hide for centuries, Xavier had no one to brag to other than the very ones he imprisoned. It was obvious he enjoyed Razvan's pain. Nicolas was certain he despised Razvan because the Dragonseeker ran strong in him. Xavier was mage. He wanted to be immortal and he wanted others to fear and admire him, but he thought himself far superior to the Carpathians. Razvan was too close to a Carpathian in his enduring strength and his code. He had protected his sister and tried desperately to protect his children, all the while being tortured and used for experiments. Yes, Xavier would despise him, because he hadn't broken Razvan, and that continued defiance would cost his grandson dearly.

"You could have escaped when you got free so many years ago," Xavier pointed out, "but like a dog crawling to your master you returned to me."

Razvan shook his head. "You manage to change history to suit yourself. As I recall, I followed you to the United States because you were going to kidnap a child and bring her back here. You were unsuccessful, weren't you?"

Xavier erupted into a maddened rage, beating at Razvan with a thin whip, over and over until Razvan hung limply from his chains.

Impotent rage swept through Nicolas. He couldn't bear to see Razvan so helpless, beaten by a monster for trying to save a child. He shook with the need to strike back, desperate for his own power, hating his inability to save Razvan. The emotions were so strong that it took him a few moments before he realized he was feeling the child's passionate need to help her father every bit as well as his own sentiments.

She leapt out from behind the column and raced across the ice. Nicolas barely had time to push to the front when she kicked Xavier hard behind the knee. The old man tilted ominously, and then crumpled to the floor of the cave, howling. Lara tried to pull the chains from her father's arms, the vampire blood burning through the pads of her fingers. Nicolas felt the pain stabbing like a knife all the way to the bone, robbing him of breath. She whirled around to the man, trying to pick himself up off the floor, crouching down, patting at his tunic pockets to try to find the key to unlock the chains.

Xavier slapped her hard, sending her flying. Nicolas actually felt the Dragonseeker blood in her surge to the fore to aid her body in its catlike movements. Lara was obviously unaware of the way she landed on her feet, a seven-year-old child, untrained, yet already moving with physical prowess. She rushed the old man again.

This time, Xavier was ready for her. He threw her down and lashed her repeatedly with the whip, drawing thin red streaks across her body. She rolled and covered her head as he lashed her viciously.

"You want him free? You want that, girl? He'll smell the blood and come sniffing at you like a hungry hound. He hasn't had blood in days and he'll tear into you." The old man kicked her and shuffled across to her father.

Razvan fought at the chains, threatening Xavier and calling out to Lara to run. Nicolas couldn't get up. The pain of the whip, the burns and he was certain a cracked rib were too much for the small body they occupied. He could only lie there helplessly, covering Lara's spirit, doing his best to shield her while Xavier stabbed a needle into Razvan's neck and dispensed a yellowish liquid.

Xavier stepped back from his grandson and watched with gleeful eyes. "She wants you free, Razvan, and I grant her wish."

Tatijana! Branislava! You must come to her aid. Please, please get her away from me. Block her mind, block my mind. I cannot bear to harm her again. This is too much, even for me.

Nicolas heard the plea in his head and Lara's small body tried to push itself up. He could see Razvan's face contorting. Saw Xavier step away from him, his expression cunning. Razvan's eyes glowed red and his teeth lengthened.

Fear consumed Nicolas, ate him from the inside out. He scrambled with Lara, trying to dig into the ice for purchase to get away, but only slipped. Razvan lifted his head and sniffed the air—scenting the blood, just as Xavier said he would. He turned his head slowly until his mad eyes focused on Lara.

She whimpered and tried to crawl away. Growling, he was on her, licking at the drops of blood beading on her skin from the whip marks. She fought, trying to push him away, but he pulled her arm to him and sank his teeth deep into her wrist. She screamed.

Nicolas felt the slice through his skin, the tearing of muscle and tissue, the puncture into his vein. It burned. More than physical was the agony of knowing he was so helpless. No matter how he fought, no matter how many blows he landed, there was no escaping those teeth gnawing at his flesh, or gulping at his blood.

Every moment made him weak until he felt he couldn't lift his arms to ward off his inevitable death. He almost welcomed death. It was preferable to being so powerless. His heart jumped in alarm. This, then, was how he had made Lara feel. Hopeless. Filled with despair. So weak and vulnerable instead of making her feel powerful and cherished. This was the sin he would carry for all time.

Xavier pushed Razvan away and jerked Lara's arm to his mouth. The pain of his teeth was worse than Razvan's. His grandson pushed back, clawing at Lara and growling as the two men scuffled and fought over the prize. Lara wept softly until her body was too weak even for that. She lay panting, wheezing, her lungs struggling for air as Xavier controlled Razvan using magic, caging him in a field of energy and walking him back to his chains.

The old man turned to look at the child sprawled on the floor, his face a mask of fury. "You dare touch me? Kick me? I give you food. Life even. Ungrateful little brat." He reached down and hauled Lara up by her hair, the long red-gold curls framing her face.

Energy crackled and light sparked around his open palm. Shears appeared, sharp and wicked. Without preamble he hacked at the curls so that great chunks of silky hair fell to the floor of the ice cave. Lara screamed and writhed, trying desperately to wiggle free. Xavier took a firmer grip and kept cutting, all the while humming.

Horrified, Nicolas shoved Lara aside, knowing Xavier was purposely humiliating her, cutting the hair as close to her scalp as possible. Long strands of black hair began to rain down to pile on top of Lara's head, until the long thick strands of midnight black covered every inch of silky red.

Carpathian hair grew fast, long and thick and luxurious, almost like the pelt of an animal, and few ever cut their hair. It was a sacred tradition in their culture and the ancients especially had an aversion to a shorn head. Nicolas was no exception. As the chunks of hair fell, he felt sick inside.

Lara's spirit stirred. Whether she liked it or not she was his lifemate and as her distress weighed on him, so did his on her. She pushed deeper into his mind, allowing him to pull her away from the childhood memories. Nicolas didn't hesitate, treating her sudden capitulation as a gift. He surrounded her spirit and took them fast from the past to the present, understanding completely why the aunts and her father had blocked her memories. He had lived them with her and he was shaky and sick inside.

Nicolas held Lara in his arms, looking down into her face, breathing for both of them, calling her name softly.

9

Nicolas looked down into Lara's eyes, now opaque. Glass eyes. Unseeing eyes. He had forced her spirit close to the surface—he still surrounded her there, refusing to let her go—but she had not committed herself to life. She refused to commit herself to him.

I cannot blame you, Lara, but I am asking for a second chance. Come back to me.

She flinched. First her spirit, and then her physical body. She saw him as the enemy, a man who would imprison her and take her blood. Crave her blood. Need it. Hunger after it. The knowledge flooded his mind and as merged as they were, as honest with her as he insisted on being, he couldn't deny those things. He would crave her taste. She was his lifemate and part of their bonding—a huge part of their lovemaking—was the exchange of blood. It was a reaffirming of the love and commitment to one another, not only of the heart and mind and soul, but the physical life as well.

He pressed his forehead to hers. *We will find a way to satisfy both our needs. We have only to make that commitment.*

He was a man who always was certain of his every move, who knew what to do under any circumstance, yet suddenly he was off balance, uncertain of the right thing to say or do. He had never in his life, even as a boy, felt helpless or vulnerable; he'd had no way of understanding her at all, or the trauma she'd dealt with.

He could hold her as he was doing, rock her gently back and forth, feeling lost. *I have no words to make this right.*

She was still, too still. He felt almost desperate. *My life was so different from yours. I had parents who were loving, four strong brothers who always had my back. I have always had enormous strength of body and will. My skills were superior to many others and, I think, from an early age, I developed a very unflattering arrogance. I was always able to get my way no matter what I wanted.*

He brushed his lips against her eyelids, feeling them flutter, a whisper of movement much like the gentle grazing of a butterfly's wings. Was she listening? Did he have a chance of bringing her back to him? Or would she be forever caught in a half-world where he couldn't quite reach her?

I was there with you this time, Lara. I learned what it is like to feel helpless, to feel small and filled with despair.

There was a small silence. He found himself holding his breath. She was aware of him, she was close—so close his every instinct was to grab her and jerk her the rest of the way into the land of the living, but he fought that dominant side of his nature and waited as patiently as any hunter.

There was a stirring in his mind. *I did not want that for you.* Her lashes fluttered and she opened her eyes. Sorrow and guilt mixed with fear. Her gaze drifted over his face and then up to his hair. Her body jerked as if struck.

Nicolas looked down at himself. He was covered in blood from the whip marks and gouges, and his ribs were bruised from the kicking. There were wounds on his wrists, deep punctures and gaping lacerations. Still holding her, he reached one shaky hand to touch his shorn head. His hair was gone, leaving only patches.

His heart leapt and then he took a breath and let it out. "Lara, *fél ku kuuluaak sívam belső*. Beloved, you must come back fully to this world."

Her gaze continued to drift over his face, blue-green eyes swimming with tears, melting that stone-cold spot deep inside him he had never quite managed to make function.

I am not beloved.

He captured her hand with gentle fingers and brought her knuckles to his mouth. "You gave me back my soul, *päläfertiilm*, and now you have restored my heart." He placed her palm over his heart. "It beats again, and it is beating for you."

He was covered in fresh whip marks that were already fading, but he had to see for himself what Lara's body retained of those childhood years. She wasn't fully Carpathian and he doubted if her injuries had healed the way his already were doing. She had had years of abuse. Why hadn't he already discovered that?

Nicolas turned her hand over to examine her wrist. The multitude of scars piled one on top of the other. Slices and punctures and gouges formed a bracelet. The fresh tears had come from her own teeth trying to open her vein to escape the darkness in him. His gut knotted at the sight. It had been the scar tissue from the continual childhood abuse that had saved her life, but like a wolf willing to chew off its leg when caught in a trap, she had been more than prepared to do the same.

The sight of those marks shamed him as nothing else could have. He had relived only a small portion of her life and it had left him shaken and sick inside. She had endured years of it. He pressed her wrist to his mouth. Her entire body jerked and she whimpered softly, closing her eyes, several tears tracking down her face.

Trust me, o jelä sielamak. Light of my soul. "Trust me, Lara." He kept his voice low, mesmerizing without being hypnotic. He breathed warm air over the rough band of scars and then lowered his mouth to her wrist. His tongue stroked a healing caress over the rigid skin. His lips brushed back and forth in a small, soothing motion. He whispered a healing chant, rhythmic and beautiful to the ear, the words ancient and flowing in his melodic voice.

She stopped resisting, but he felt her holding herself very still as if waiting for betrayal. His heart wept for her, for that small child who had been made to feel so helpless, and for the grown woman whose lifemate had carelessly made her feel exactly the same way.

He turned her other wrist over and performed the same ritual, a slow bathing of her skin with the healing agent in his saliva, all the while watching her face, her eyes, for a sign of withdrawal. There was no movement one way or the other. She became completely still, too frightened to even blink up at him, a wild animal trapped.

"I am not going to hurt you," he assured, keeping his voice soft, intent on drawing her wholly back to the surface. She hovered there, ready to flee back into a place of childhood horror rather than be imprisoned as an adult. "Stay with me, Lara. Let me show you how a Carpathian man cherishes his woman."

He pushed aside the long rope of bright hair to examine the marks at her neck. His were there, two small puncture wounds and a small strawberry. He pressed his mouth there, sweeping his tongue across the mark of possession to heal it completely. Where before it had been important to him for the world to know she was his, now it was important to him that she be free of any reminder of her childhood. She shuddered, her body stiff, but again, her spirit seemed to hover there, just waiting.

Do not be alarmed, Lara, I need to examine your back.

He chose to use the more intimate form of communication, mind to mind, so that his motives would be absolutely clear to her. *I have to take a look at your back and legs.*

The urge to see for himself was a need, had grown into a monstrous compulsion he couldn't fight. His body was covered in thin white stripes already healing, which meant, he was certain, that she carried scars all over her body, constant reminders of being helpless and humiliated. His hands were gentle as he laid her facedown on the soft blankets he'd fashioned for her. It took moments of thought to have her skin gleaming beneath the flickering candlelight. She was so tense she was shaking, but again she lay quiet under the caressing pads of his fingers.

Her back was crisscrossed with white ridges and lines. The pattern continued all the way down her buttocks to the backs of her legs. Most were shallow and faint, but scar tissue had formed over a few of them. He knew, from the fire in his back and legs, that he bore the same marks, although within another hour, they would disappear from his body as if they'd never been.

His eyes burned and he closed them for a moment, despising himself for not knowing this, not taking the time to know every inch of his lifemate's body, know every bit of her past in order to secure the happiness of her future. He had vowed to cherish her, to place her happiness above all things and, even without the lifemate bond, honor should have dictated that he do so. He had been consumed with his own importance, his own desires and his belief that he was always right and others owed him their allegiance.

Nicolas bent forward and pressed his lips to the middle of a particularly deep scar. *Forgive me, päläfertiilm. There is no excuse I can offer to you, nor will I. Words will not repair the damage I have done to you, only actions.*

His tongue swirled over the white slashes, and then traced each deep ridge. In his mind, merged so deeply with hers, he chanted the healing words of his people, words filled with power. As he did so, he waved one hand so that aromatic candles filled the chamber with soothing, curative scents. Across the mineral pool, herbs floated, releasing their fragrance to add to the therapeutic environment.

Nicolas swept one hand through his hair, feeling the chopped edges, his stomach knotting in protest of his shorn head. Dismissing the disturbing sensation of helpless anger, he bent closer to Lara's back and began the slow task of tracing each individual scar with his tongue. He doubted if, after all this time, the marks would disappear completely, but certainly they would fade until it would be difficult to see them. He wanted that for her.

He wasn't foolish enough to think that if he could make them disappear from her body, the trauma would be gone from her mind—they both would live with the damage done to her, but... *I will not make mistakes.* Amusement slipped into the velvet of his voice. *Not the same mistakes anyway...*

A muffled sob escaped. She trembled from head to toe.

Lara. He whispered her name like a soft entreaty. *Do not fear me. I know I was wrong.*

Not you. Me. I was wrong. The aunts have always said where there is life, there is hope. It was cowardly to retreat. I didn't think what you would do or what would happen to you. I honestly didn't know you would follow me and try to bring me back. Another sob shook her.

He pressed kisses along two thin streaks, his tongue following the path of the whip marks to ease those lines from her body. *If you had not, I would never have learned what it was like to be helpless. I would have said I understood, but how could I have had true understanding? I might have been compassionate and felt sympathy, but I would never truly understand. No, päläfertiilm, it had to be this way so I could become a true lifemate to my other half.*

Lara wanted to believe his low, mesmerizing voice, but

she hadn't recovered her courage. She was terrified of a future with this man. Right now he was moving his mouth and hands over her body, stirring her into a torturous physical ache when she was so frightened she didn't know what to do or who to turn to. He held power over her, whether it was what she wanted or not. He seemed to understand, his voice was a seduction of promise, his hands and mouth a hypnotic blend of seduction and soothing warmth.

She lay facedown with her eyes closed, absorbing the feel of his hands smoothing over her skin. It was incredibly sensuous to have him lapping at her body with his tongue with long, slow caresses that made her body shiver. He wasn't trying to be sensual, it was just natural in his touch, an intimate stroke of his tongue, or maybe it was the pull between lifemates. She knew he wasn't trying to arouse her body; she was firmly in his mind and could feel his intentions to heal her, to take away reminders of abuse.

His hands shaped her hips, the pads of his fingers traveling over the curve of her buttocks, his tongue following the thin white stripes. Now she could feel his hair, the illusion of his shorn head gone, so that the long length of it fell like silky rain over her bare skin. Her womb tightened and her hips moved restlessly.

His entire focus seemed to be on her—on her body, her skin. His hands ran along the sides of her breasts, her ribs, shaped her hips and slid smoothly over and beneath her bottom to stroke beneath each cheek and down her thighs. The leisurely exploration was slow and gentle and all the while his tongue lapped at her scars. She could feel the brush of his lips as he planted little kisses along the path of her spine and into the small of her back. Her body vibrated beneath his touch, every nerve ending aware of him.

A sound escaped, somewhere between a moan and a slow hiss of need. She pressed closer to the pillow, tears burning in her eyes. How could she want him this way when he had taken her dignity, her independence, so hard-won after a childhood of abuse? But her body was on fire for him. Every touch of his hands, every lap of his tongue, even the brush of his hair sent flames dancing over her skin and built the hunger blossoming inside of her.

I am almost finished, o jelä sielamak. Light of my soul, stay still for me. Because if she didn't, his body was going to go up in flames. He had started out with only a thought to heal her, but his groin was full and aching, pressed tightly against her thigh as he worked.

Nicolas tried to keep the feel of her satin skin and the rounded curves of her body from affecting him, but it was impossible. Her body trembled, her legs moved restlessly and he scented the call of mates, but a small sob escaped, muffled and restrained. He remained deeply merged with her, reading her distress.

It is good to want your lifemate, Lara. Enjoy the feeling, do not fear it. Just because we both desire one another's body does not mean we have to act on that desire. You are safe with me. I wish only to heal you, not to add to your fears.

There was a small silence. He held his breath waiting for her response.

I'm not ready. There was apology and guilt in her voice.

How could you be? You have to trust before you can give your body into my keeping. There is no need to be upset because I want you. You are my lifemate. His tongue touched the back of her thigh in a slow, intimate dip into a whitened dimple. *I am supposed to want you as you are supposed to want me.*

Lara rubbed her face against the pillow, arousal teasing her thighs. *I guess that is the one thing we don't have to worry about.* Every stroke of his tongue intensified the need building. She was very confused, torn with fear, afraid to commit to him, yet her body betrayed her—wet, weeping with hunger, calling to his, breasts sensitive, feminine channel inflamed and needy.

He took his time on the backs of her calves, not rushing when his own hungers grew with every brush of his skin against hers.

This is not about sex, Lara, this is about healing. When I make love to you, there will be no doubt what I am doing. But you will not be confused and afraid. You will come to me willingly or not at all.

That was the trouble: she was willing—at least her body was, and that felt like a betrayal of herself. She had allowed him to draw her back, in essence to agree to commit her life to his again, yet he still seemed to have all the power.

"The true power lies with you," Nicolas objected, reading her fears easily. He sat up, waving his hand so that a soft material covered her bare skin, keeping her from feeling so exposed and vulnerable. He gathered her back into his arms, cradling her body to his. "A woman is the greatest treasure a man can have." He could feel her body trembling and she looked up at him through troubled eyes veiled with thick lashes. "You really are too weak to be taken to the inn, but if it would make you feel better, I can do so. My fear is that if we are attacked, we would be very vulnerable there."

He needed blood—and so did she. As weak as she was, he doubted if she could go more than a couple of hours before he would be forced to give her another exchange and he was uncertain how best to broach the subject with her.

"I'm not afraid of being here."

That hadn't been the trouble, Nicolas knew. And he caught her desire, hastily suppressed, to be in the open where she could feel free. He didn't want to move her, at least not until she was significantly stronger.

Nicolas settled against the headboard of the bed with Lara in his arms. He rested his chin on top of her silky hair and held her in his arms, close to his chest. His heart was beneath her ear, a steady rhythmic beat meant to reassure her. She wanted to be outside in the open. A small smile touched his mouth and he directed his attention to the high ceiling of the cavern.

The flickering candles suddenly snuffed out, leaving behind complete darkness. Immediately the sensation of the room growing and expanding struck them and then the dark was lit by a thousand stars. Lara gasped, lifting her gaze to sparkling constellations scattered across the ceiling. The sky turned a midnight black, a perfect backdrop for the glittering stars. A faint breeze swept into the cavern, bringing the scent of wild flowers and freshly cut grass. She blinked and found that the stalagmites, large columns of minerals deposited from water dripping over the centuries, had twisted into thick tree trunks, branches spreading across the chamber floor to twine with one another and form a forest. Leaves fluttered in the breeze, creating a whisper of sound.

She leaned back and gazed upward, spellbound. "It's beautiful."

Nicolas couldn't take his eyes from the rapt expression on her face. For the first time since he'd met her, he'd done something right.

"See that constellation up there?" He pointed to a grouping of stars. "Watch it."

At first the stars remained stationary in the sky and it was difficult to distinguish what he meant by constellation, but then an outline emerged, twin dragons slowly taking shape as the stars began to glow brighter, forming the bodies, sweeping tails and heads. One dragon stretched, leaning forward, lifting a clawed foot in a graceful movement. The second dragon threw back its head and let out a stream of roiling white vapor. As she watched, the gasses began to spin, drawing together as if pulled by gravity to form a long, flowing opaque tube.

The dragon pumped its wings, the stars shaping its body glowing white-hot. Its twin rose up on its hind legs and fanned the sky, spreading stars in all directions.

Her soft mouth curved into a tentative smile, even as she leaned back against him. She was already exhausted, unable to sit up she was so weak. He laid her against the pillows and slid to one side of her, propped up on his elbow, continuing to build the illusion of being outside the cavern in open air.

The crystals in the room began to vibrate, sending the leaves dancing and the tree trunks humming. Flowers covered the floor, springing up all over, lining a path that led from the bed through the archway to the chamber with the pool. The archway disappeared under vines as they wound around one another and climbed up the walls.

Lara kept her gaze fixed on the stars. The dragons leapt about playing with carefree abandon, their antics making her laugh.

"You try it," he said.

She shook her head. "I can't do that."

"Of course you can." Nicolas caught her hand and laced her fingers through his, pointing as he did so to a group of stars just above the heads of the dragons. "Choose a cluster that reminds you of an animal."

She swallowed visibly and Nicolas could feel her body vibrate with tension. In her mind she traced the dragon that she'd drawn on her wall. It had leapt out at her and attacked viciously. The solution to their problem might be simple enough in theory, but it would take time and patience. He needed to make her feel the power running through her body and in her mind. She was Dragonseeker, from one of the legendary and most revered bloodlines. Knowledge, not only of ancient Carpathian ways and abilities, but mage as well, had been dumped into her mind. She had tremendous potential. He had to show her that power.

But she might try to leave me. The thought came

unbidden and he felt the darkness in him rise to take the bait. Even his teeth lengthened. Now that his emotions were involved as well, he was more dangerous than ever. He fought back the need to dominate and leaned closer to her, pressing his lips against her ear so that they brushed the velvet soft lobe.

"You have every ability, that of your aunts, your father, and mine, in your head. You have only to find the right information and put it to use. You mind is merged with mine. Follow what I did and you will have complete control of the illusion. That is all it really is."

Lara shivered, her blue eyes swirling with green. Her hair banded with color, going to a deep red. "But it seems so real. If I touched it, I believe I would feel scales."

"Of course, or I have not done my job properly."

Lara reached toward the sky with one hand. The stars seemed very real, as did the surrounding forest and meadow of flowers. She cast another nervous glance toward Nicolas, reminding him again of a wild creature cornered and fearing for its life. She was ready to defend herself if necessary; he could feel her mind preparing for trouble.

"Try the cluster of stars up there on the left. My pair would like to have a little one to play with."

"I lost control of my drawing once," she admitted in a low voice.

He felt the bites on his arms and legs as if those sharp teeth were tearing into his flesh all over again. He took her arm and kissed the small, faded scars. "You will not lose control this time, and if you did, I am here to help you."

She held his gaze for a long moment and then turned her attention to the collection of bright stars forming the outline of what appeared to her to be a dog. She concentrated, drawing with her imagination, choosing the stars for the outline of the body of a young dragon. More slender, smaller and more compact, but with outstretched wings and a long spiked tail. She paid much more attention to detail than Nicolas had and that fascinated him. She had lived her childhood with her aunts imprisoned in the form of a dragon and she had obviously studied them.

Her dragon had rows of sharp teeth, yet kind eyes. The mouth was slightly open and a steady stream of vapor poured into the night sky, creating more stars. The head bobbed and the tail twitched. Lara smiled, but her body remained tense.

"Your dragon is amazing, much more detailed than mine," Nicolas said.

The smaller of his two dragons flapped its wings and bent its wedge-shaped head toward Lara's baby. The two dragons touched noses and the baby tumbled over backward. Lara's soft laughter filled the chamber—and filled his heart. His stomach muscles tightened and his groin pooled with hot blood, going hard and full in a rush of emotion.

"We need something else," Nicolas said. "Let me see what I can do."

He chose a longer, thinner constellation, using the stars to form the figure of a woman wearing leggings and a skirt.

"You're making me." Lara pointed to the head. "Don't forget my hair."

He rubbed his chin along her shoulder, injecting a teasing note into both his voice and his mind. "Have a little patience."

Her returned smile was tentative, but it was there. Nicolas deliberately fashioned the hair awkwardly, giving the two sides different lengths.

Lara nudged him, laughing aloud. "You aren't an artist."

"I am more of a musician. You do the hair."

She chose several bright stars, connecting them so they appeared to be long strands of hair blowing back from a heart-shaped face.

He caught her chin between his fingers and tilted her

face this way and that, studying her facial structure. "Your chin is not pointy."

"Maybe not, but the star is right there in perfect alignment."

He waved his hand and another star appeared parallel with the first one.

"That's cheating."

He dropped a kiss on top of her head. "But much more like you. You have that tiny little indentation right there..." He brushed the spot with the pad of his thumb. "...that I absolutely love." He leaned in to graze the corner of her mouth and then that tempting spot with his lips.

Her heart hammered hard in her chest, but he only stretched lazily and slid off the bed to face the forest of trees. He lifted his arms and the music started. First the low beat of a drum, then the soft sound of a guitar. A piano joined in, followed by several wind instruments.

Lara closed her eyes and let herself drift on the music. It was quite beautiful, obviously an original piece. There was more to Nicolas than the aggressive hunter she first thought him. The water flowing out of the wall and into the pool added to the soothing feel of the forest and music. She felt him sink down onto the bed beside her.

"I have to go out for a short while, Lara," Nicolas said. "I must feed." He stroked his hand over her hair. "I would not do this, knowing it may upset you, but you are very weak and I need to bring you to full strength."

She moistened her lips, concentrating on the strains of music, her pulse jumping at what he meant. She knew it was true. She could barely lift her arms. If she was going to find the bodies of her aunts, or at least find the answer to what happened to them, she had to regain her strength. And now there was the puzzle of her father. The child hadn't seen the truth of his terrible existence, but the woman had. She had to find the same answers for him. If it was possible that he was alive, she needed to find him and free him.

"Lara?" Nicolas leaned close to her, smoothing back her hair with a gentle hand. "Do you understand what I'm saying to you?"

She forced her eyes open to meet his gaze. It was now or never to see if he had really changed. She pushed herself into a sitting position. Instantly he was there with his strong arms, propping her up, pushing air and pillows around her until he felt her comfort.

She made herself say it out loud, her gaze steady on his. "You want to give me blood."

He didn't look away and he kept his mind firmly merged with hers. "I need to give you blood," he corrected, allowing her to see the truth, to feel his hunger for her, for the taste of her, for the excitement of holding her close to him and feeling the incredible bonding between lifemates. More than his personal hunger to exchange blood with her, she felt his even stronger need to make her healthy again.

She moistened her lips. "I need to go back to the ice cave," she blurted out. "That's the reason I came here in the first place. I have to go back. Not you. Not the other Carpathians, but me. My aunts kept me alive, no, they did more than that. They kept me sane, and I suspect they kept my father sane as long as they could. I owe them and I need to go find them. Dead or alive, finding out the worst, it doesn't matter, I have to do this."

She clung to the mind merge, reading his reactions, refusing to flinch away from the dominating, very powerful demon who rose on a tidal wave of darkness to protest. His curse, he had said. She saw him so clearly now. Nicolas would never be anything but what he was, and that was a forceful presence who had confidence in his decisions. He would always believe in protecting her first, keeping her safe, but he was also struggling to give her a sense of confidence. He saw her as an equal, but one who needed to be guarded and governed. He was determined to grow beyond that. She saw and felt his struggle to fight back his first reaction. The protest welled up in him strong—violent even.

"You are not going to make this easy for me, are you?" he asked with a small sigh.

"I have to go into the cave. I'm asking you to understand."

"That I can say without reservation. I do understand. Truthfully, *I* have to go back to that cave. I was there with you, sharing the horrors for a small time, and their voices helped not only you cope, but me as well. You are my life-mate, a gift from the gods, and they kept you alive and sane for me. I understand the need to know their fate. If they are dead, I will recover their bodies and bring them home. If they, by some miracle, are still alive, and I find proof, I will never stop until they are found."

For the first time she reached out to him, taking both of his hands in hers, her gaze never wavering. "I have to go myself, Nicolas." She repeated each word with distinction, watching it sink in, watching his instinctive reaction.

He looked so incredibly handsome and dangerous with his black glittering eyes and smoldering, sensual features. His hair was long already and tied back again with a leather thong, making her wonder for a moment if he had deliber-ately brushed the strands across her bare skin. She felt her color rise at the thought.

"Read my mind, if you need to. See why it's so impor-tant to me. Just because I'm a woman doesn't mean I don't have the same needs that drive you to protect those you love. The aunts were the only real support I had in my childhood. I didn't remember my father at all until I redis-covered the ice cave."

"*Köd alte hän.* Darkness curse it." Nicolas hissed the oath between his teeth. The problem was—he did under-stand. How could he not? He didn't want to, not when the mere thought of Lara in that cave made him crazy. It was too dangerous. What kind of a lifemate would he be if he didn't protect her? All of his life he had ranted about the males being too lenient with their women, being wrapped around their fingers... *O jelä peje teräd.* Sun scorch it. He was going to address the warriors' council and demand that Mikhail forbid the women to hunt the vampire. If he allowed those blue-green eyes to sway him from what he knew to be the right path...

He groaned. "Do not do this to me, Lara."

"I know it will be difficult for you. If I learned anything about you, merged together as we were, I know this is asking something huge of you—to put aside your need to keep me safe, but I have to ask you. In return," she moistened suddenly dry lips. Her body trembled and then she raised her chin. "I don't expect you to be the only one sacrificing. In return, I'll try to accept your need of my blood."

There it was. The offer. The lifemate howled with absolute joy. The demon rose, hungry, insatiable, punching him hard with a fierce, possessive desire. Blood surged hotly in his veins and pulsed in his groin. If she said it and he accepted, she wouldn't—couldn't—go back on her word.

The demon, the arrogant, dominant hunter rejoiced. The lifemate stepped back and assessed the situation. She was pale, trembling, wringing her hands together. The price was far too high for both of them and finally, there was something he could do for her.

He took a deep breath—let it out slowly. His hands framed her face and he shook his head. "Not like this. Not a bargain between us when you are repulsed and frightened by the very thought. When I take your blood, Lara, it will be with love, an expression of love, a ritual between man and wife as old as time. If I cannot make you comfortable enough to trust me to accept the bond willingly, then I do not deserve you as a lifemate." He held up his hand to stop her from answering. "That is not to say I will not insist on you accepting my blood and if an exchange is necessary, I will tell you. You will have the option of my controlling you for those few moments so you do not fear."

Lara's fingers wrapped around his wrist. "What if I can't do it?"

"Then I must help you."

"And the cave?"

This was his gift to her, the only one he had to give. Everything he was rebelled, hard knots twisted in his gut. "I will take you."

There was a small silence while she stared into his eyes, seeking the truth. He felt her moving in his mind. The music continued, the breeze moved through the trees and the dragon stars danced overhead.

"Do you mean it?"

"I am your lifemate. Seek your answer in my mind."

She tilted her head to one side, her gaze locked with his. Just as he had lived her earlier life and finally understood what it was like to feel helpless, vulnerable and humiliated, she had been merged with him and was beginning to understand that Nicolas had spent centuries guarding everyone around him. It was inherent in his nature. And to allow her to put herself in danger was an enormous concession—more, it went against everything he had ever believed in or stood for.

"You're an amazing man, Nicolas."

"Do not call me amazing until I get you out of that cave in one piece. We will plan carefully for every emergency. And you will do as I tell you. I have long hunted our enemies and, although you know the caves, and have seen how brutal they are, you have never fought our enemies."

She nodded. "I have no intention of doing anything else," she assured. She lay back against the pillows, too tired to sit upright. "Do it now, while the music is playing and I can look at the stars. If you don't, I'm going to pass out."

He had almost been waiting for her to lose consciousness,

or at least to go back to a state of drifting. He didn't want her to fear him, not now when he had made a little progress. She was beginning to trust him a little, reaching toward him, maybe even taking a few small steps to meet him somewhere close to the middle.

The problem, Nicolas knew, was there was no middle for him. He didn't know how to compromise. He could only hope that his desire to understand her and make her happy would help him overcome his need for complete dominance. He understood then why the ritual words were imposed on the male. She didn't promise to cherish and put his happiness first—he was already taking over her life, changing the course of it for all time. The male had to make the sacrifices to make the union work. After all, he was the one who benefited most.

He reached for her without further preamble, pulling her tense body onto his lap and cradling her against his chest. "Listen to the wind blowing through the trees, *päläfertiilm*. Hear the music of my soul calling to yours." He stroked back the silky fall of her hair and gently turned her face to his chest. His shirt melted away, leaving the heavy muscles exposed.

"When you take blood from your lifemate, it is an offering, a gift. You are not hurting me, just the opposite. I feel great physical and emotional pleasure from the exchange. The giving of blood is an offer of life, my life for yours, the sharing of the same skin, as we do physically when we make love or physically when we merge mind to mind. A true offering is erotic with a lifemate. Between warriors it is literally a gift of life. The truth of a blood exchange is far different than the corrupted concept Xavier made it."

Lara closed her eyes to better hear the velvet seduction in his voice. Although he had used the word "exchange," she knew he had no intention of taking her blood, although the desire beat at him. She wanted to succumb completely to that voice, to her lifemate, to give him back something when he was struggling to find a bridge between them. If he could give her a gift of such magnitude, she could find it in herself to be as equally courageous.

In truth, it wasn't that difficult. His body was hot and hard. His arms—enormously strong. His heart beat a steady rhythm and her heart followed his lead. She felt light and feminine, her body aching, inner muscles tightening and arousal teasing her thighs and feminine sheath. Her breasts ached for attention.

Lara let herself drift on a tide of rising desire. She nuzzled his chest, his bare skin beneath her cheek, before lifting her lashes to look into his eyes. She felt stunned by the raw hunger there, the sheer intensity of his need. Her mind sought and found his as her pulse pounded and blood surged hotly in her veins. The rush of heat took her by surprise. Her teeth felt sharp, her body edgy. The sound of his heart thundered in her ears, the ebb and flow of life through his body filled her with excitement.

For a moment she was repulsed by her own nature, the need rising to take the essence of his life from him, but his gaze was so hot, so hungry, his hunger fueled her own. She closed her eyes, nuzzling his chest, her lips sliding over his bare skin, tasting. Her tongue darted out, a leisurely foray over the muscle. His body jerked. Against her bottom she felt his shaft, steel-hard, thick and rigid, pressing tightly into her.

A soft moan escaped her throat. She moved against him restlessly. He felt male. Strong. He felt like her other half. Her body smoldered with heat. Longing rose, a helpless desire to taste him—every inch of him. A tidal wave of need swept over her, taking her with it. She lapped at his hot skin. Once. Twice. Her teeth lengthened more in anticipation. Her mouth filled with a tangy spice.

She bit down gently, a small experimental bite. He shuddered in response, his arms tightening possessively, his shaft jerking. She opened her eyes once more, locking her gaze with his, drowning in his hunger. She sank her teeth deep. Nicolas threw back his head and moaned sensually, a husky sound that sent tremors through her body.

And then the addictive taste of him flooded her senses. Power. Energy. A rush of lust so strong her body shook. He simply gathered her closer, one hand supporting her head, holding her to him. Power soaked into her organs and tissue, sizzled through veins and arteries to center in her most feminine core to pulse there with rising hunger.

Everything about him was more vivid, every one of her senses was sharper, so that when she inhaled she drew him into her lungs. She heard the rhythm of his heart calling and her heart answered.

He whispered to her in her mind, his voice slightly husky, so sensual she began to play erotic images in her head—in his head.

Nicolas groaned again, fighting for control. He had wanted to show her a sensual experience, but she was pushing the limits of a centuries-old restraint. *Lara. O jelä sielamak. Light of my soul, you have to stop before it's too late and there is no going back.*

He didn't want her to stop. His hand slid up her rib cage to cup the weight of her breast in his palm. One thought and her clothes would be gone. He could have her, be inside the haven of her body, take them both all the way to paradise.

Her hips moved, she pressed back against him, her bottom sliding intimately over his shaft, the friction sending shudders of pleasure through his body. In another minute the decision would be out of his hands. Right now, in the ecstasy of taking her lifemate's blood, her body was on fire, welcoming his, but she wasn't ready to take that next step and he refused to take advantage—if he could restrain himself.

Reluctantly he left the warmth of her breast and slid his palm between her mouth and his chest. *Enough, fél ku kuuluaak sívam belső. Beloved, you have to help me.*

She swept her tongue across the twin pinpricks, her gaze a sexy, drowsy combination that only increased his desire. She reached one hand up to curl around his neck, bringing his mouth to hers.

His heart stopped as her lips feathered across his. Back and forth, a slow, light touch that stole the air from his lungs.

"You really are the most amazing man, Nicolas."

Even her voice was a seduction. He wasn't going to live through this. His lungs burned, his groin ached and every muscle was tight with sexual tension.

With even more reluctance, he put her aside, laying her body on the bed. It took some doing to get his normally graceful body to move so that he could stand up and pace a little away from her to give himself a reprieve. He had to get out into the cool night air and regain his control.

"I have to go, Lara. You rest until I return." It was cowardly to retreat, and he could see by her face she didn't like it, but it was the only safe avenue open to him.

10

"You're going to leave me here? You don't want to talk about what just happened between us?" Lara's hand trembled as she pushed back the silky fall of hair from her face.

Nicolas was in a heightened state of sexual awareness. He was hungry, starving even, and the scent of her drove him crazy. He could already taste her in his mouth. The demon in him roared to life.

He stepped back away from the bed, turning his head so she wouldn't see the red flames he knew would be flickering in his eyes. He curled his fingers into his palms, the sharpened nails digging deep. Teeth sharpened and when he spoke, his usual low voice held the hint of a growl. "Now is not the time to talk with me about sex, Lara. I am not a saint by any means."

She studied his averted face. Her gaze drifted down his body to the thick, impressive bulge pushing at the front of his jeans. There was a heady power in knowing she had driven him to the edge of control, yet she wasn't ready to face the consequences. Nicolas was desperately trying to give her time and truthfully she needed it. She took a deep breath and pulled back from the edge of the precipice she was so tempted to jump off.

"I don't want to be left alone," Lara said. "Not again. Not even when you've made the cave so beautiful. I need to be out in the fresh air with you."

Nicolas shoved his hands through his hair and paced back and forth, reminding her of a trapped jungle cat. Muscles rippled beneath his thin shirt and there was a fluid grace to his every stride. Abruptly he came back to the bed, towered over her for a moment and then he crouched down. "*Fél ku kuuluaak sívam belső*. Beloved, I am in desperate need of blood. I had planned to close down the sharing of our minds so you would not have to experience it. I cannot very well take you with me and have you watch something that distresses you, no matter how necessary."

She pushed herself up, surprised that even with the infusion of his blood, she felt a little weak and dizzy. Ignoring it, she forced herself to stand. "Take me to the inn then. I can visit with Terry and Gerald. I want to see if Terry is doing better. I feel responsible. I never should have taken them along."

He didn't want her near either man, and certainly not until he made certain the parasites were completely gone from Terry's system. He didn't want to share her, not now, not with anyone until their bond was complete, but she needed to be grounded. She needed to feel as if she didn't come from some tainted line. He was wrong to keep her family from her just because he wanted to be the only one she relied on.

He took a breath and let it out, determined to do the right thing no matter the cost to himself because all this goodness wouldn't last. He knew himself better than that. The darkness was as much a part of him as breathing. "I can check on your two friends for you, but I actually have something better for you to do if you really think you are up to it."

"What?"

He reached for her hand, tugged until she extended her arm and he could bring her fist to his chest—right over the twin marks over his heart. "Razvan has a twin sister and she is alive."

Lara blinked up at him. At once he felt the push of energy. The music filling the cavern went silent. Her hair crackled and streaked, and her eyes, looking up at him, went from that deep emerald green to glacier blue. "How long have you known this?"

He looked down at his hands then back up to meet her probing gaze. "I did not tell you right away because I wanted to give us a chance to come together as lifemates. You need to trust someone and I wanted it to be me."

She was silent a moment, her blue eyes on his face. A small sigh escaped. "You really do like control, don't you?"

He shrugged his broad shoulders. "Yes."

"Don't do that again. Don't hold back information from me because of something that stupid. Do you really think I would trust my father's twin sister so easily after seeing what my great-grandfather and my father were capable of doing?"

"I do not know her, but I have heard she is a great warrior. She fights the vampire beside her lifemate."

Lara pushed a hand through her hair. "Are you certain she's Razvan's sister?"

"There is no doubt. I can take you to her. She's a good person, Lara. And your father, whatever he is now, appears to have been misjudged. He appears to have been a good man at one time. Natalya, that's her name, can tell you much more about him."

She looked up at him and Nicolas felt a strange melting

in the vicinity of his heart. She looked pale and vulnerable, her eyes enormous. There were shadows there, and dark circles beneath her eyes. He wrapped his arm around her and drew her against his body, holding her close to comfort her. It amazed him how right she felt in his arms.

Nuzzling the top of her head with his chin, he rocked her gently. "If it is too soon for you, Lara, we can wait before you talk to her."

She didn't exactly melt into him, but she did put her arms around his waist and hold on. "I don't know what I want to do."

"She's been in the cave."

Lara stepped back, looking up at him. "When? Recently?"

Nicolas nodded. "I do not know too much other than what my brothers told me. Manolito, my brother, fought beside her during a recent battle." He took a breath. "It was thought she killed Razvan with her sword, but he turned up again, or at least he appeared to, possessing a woman's body and striking the blow that sent Manolito to the shadow world."

Lara turned away from him to hide her expression from his watchful eyes. Of course she had to go see her father's twin sister. But she didn't know if she was strong enough to learn about her father. It was much easier to think of him as a monster than a man tortured beyond all endurance. She couldn't imagine the psychological torment of knowing one's body was used to harm others. That would be worse than physical torture.

"And if it's true," she murmured aloud, "I just left him there." She raised a stricken gaze to Nicolas. "That's why he helped bury my memories of him, isn't it? And the aunts agreed to it because they didn't want me to know I was abandoning a father who had tried to protect me. I would never have gone had I known he was a prisoner, being tortured and abused."

She rubbed her wrist. Nicolas had managed to reduce the scarring, but some of the ridges were still there. She brushed her thumb back and forth in a soothing gesture, without realizing she was doing it until she noticed Nicolas's gaze drop to her wrist. Embarrassed, she put her arm behind her back.

"Does it hurt?"

The gentleness in his voice constricted her throat. She shook her head. "I think it's a habit." But it had hurt for years, burning at times, painful for no reason.

"You didn't abandon him, Lara. You were a child, eight years old. Consider it from his point of view. If he was innocent and trying to protect you, the relief he would feel, the freedom from allowing Xavier to use him against you, would have been tremendous for him. Had you stayed, his suffering would have been far more."

"You don't know that."

A small smile softened the edge of his mouth. "He is Dragonseeker. His every instinct is to protect his family, especially his women and children. If Xavier really possessed his body, using him to impregnate women, if he really murdered your mother in front of him as it appeared he did, and if he controlled Razvan, forcing him to take your blood, then Razvan has suffered the torment of the damned for centuries. That would be the worst a Carpathian male could suffer. Your father would have rejoiced to have you out of there and out of Xavier's control."

She pressed her lips together. His hunger was beating at her, yet he stood there patiently trying to reassure her that leaving her father to be tortured and maybe murdered had been a good thing. "Let's go, Nicolas. I'd like to meet my aunt."

"Do you want to try shifting? An owl, perhaps?"

Her jeweled eyes gleamed at him. He had said she was capable of shifting with his help and she wanted it to be true. She was certainly willing to try. "A dragon."

He nodded. "Of course, what else would you choose?" He grinned at her, a teasing invitation to fun. She'd never seen him smile like that, and it made him look younger. "You are already familiar with the dragon's body. The most important thing with shifting..." He held out his hand to her and began to walk with her through the cavern into the labyrinth of tunnels. Candles sprang to life on the walls ahead of them as they hurried along. "... is to remember to keep the image in your head at all times. It has to become automatic so that you do it without really thinking about it and that takes practice. I want you to keep your mind merged fully with mine. Once you shift, excitement and joy—I cannot even begin to describe the feeling for you—sets in and it is easy to lose what you are doing. So keep your mind firmly in mine so I can help you if you need it."

She smiled up at him. "Don't worry, I don't exactly want to fall out of the sky."

He laughed softly, shocking himself. He wasn't a man who laughed often—if ever. He was slowly discovering that with her companionship, Lara also brought a joy in the sharing of everyday things. He tightened his fingers around hers, keeping her close to his side as they moved swiftly through the tunnel. "I did not notice that you scanned the area periodically for vampires. It is very necessary for survival to make that a habit."

"Isn't that a rather faulty system now?"

His eyebrow shot up. "You have been absorbing the information in my mind." He was pleased with her. With everything going on, it hadn't occurred to him that while merged with him she would be seeking as much information as possible to help with her own survival.

"Of course. You seem to have a lot of experience hunting vampires."

His boyhood story intrigued her and Lara had tried to delve a little deeper, at first to see if Nicolas always embraced the fight with the undead. Did he get a rush when he fought? When he killed? She had found the answer and it worried her, but it also fascinated her that he felt no fear—none—when he fought. She had spent her life afraid, always looking over her shoulder, terrified that others would discover her differences and condemn her, terrified that Xavier would find her again. She wanted to be like Nicolas, facing the worst without fear.

"Not all Carpathian males were raised to be hunters. In the old days we had a community and many men were craftsmen. They did woodworking and gem-calling. They worked with herbs and candles to develop our healing powers. Some were sword-makers. They did incredible, beautiful work with weapons. My family was bred as warriors. Many of the skills of our ancestors are imprinted on us. So if you are born into a lineage of warriors, you have skills and reflexes already built in. In other words, you already have an advantage before you even begin training. Where a gem-caller or sword-maker has other skills imprinted, those skills are not at all useful for fighting."

There was a small trail of water running across the path. Without missing a stride, Nicolas caught Lara around the waist, lifted her over it and continued walking as though nothing had interrupted them.

When the small, secret thrill at the strength in his arms subsided, Lara slipped her hand back into his. "And the darkness in you? How exactly does that come to be?"

His fingers tightened around hers. "Does it frighten you?"

Her gaze flicked to his face and then sought out boulders blocking the entrance to the tunnel. Excitement was building at the prospect of shapeshifting. "A little," she admitted.

He lifted an eyebrow.

Lara shrugged. "Well, maybe a lot. You're very sure of yourself."

"I have lived a long time." He brought her fingers to his lips. "But all this is new to me and I have found that I am learning as we go. Feel free to clue me in when I am making mistakes."

"Have no worries there," Lara said. She tugged at his hand, halting him before he could avoid her question by bringing down the safeguards. "I really want to understand you better and I can't if I'm worried all the time that you might become a vampire."

"That is no longer a possibility, Lara," he assured. "You are the other half of my soul, the light to my darkness. Once found, your light guides and protects me. I have no doubt I will always be a difficult man, but I will not turn vampire." He jerked his chin toward the boulders, his eyebrow raised in challenge. "Do you think you can remove the safeguards?"

A smile slowly formed. "A test. You're challenging me."

"I am also timing you."

It was her turn to raise an eyebrow. She spun around toward the entrance and lifted her hands into the air. Every stroke of the pattern he had woven was recorded in her mind. The aunts had drilled it into her to observe even the tiniest movement, a flick of a finger, a small nuance that made the difference of getting it right the first time and surviving.

She could feel his eyes on her and the intensity of his gaze sent a shiver of awareness tingling down her spine. She had to really concentrate to block him out, to make the long graceful movements and the short, subtle ones accompany her soft murmured words. It was a silly chant really, one she had made up and used repeatedly as a child to help her learn how to weave and undo warding spells. Her hands moved swiftly, gracefully, following each thread of unseen light, seeking out each knot and double-checking the threads in the weave of the pattern.

Spider, spider, spin your web, absorbing now these unseen threads. Spider, spider, throw your line, remove all that would harm or bind. Spider, spider, clear the way, protecting now this entryway.

The boulders rocked back and forth for a moment, shimmered and disappeared. Lara spun around, grinning at him. He was there—too close—right on her in fact. She hadn't heard or felt him move, but as she turned, she turned right into his arms, her face raised toward his. Their gazes locked. A frisson of awareness—of arousal—raced from breasts to thighs.

His fingers curled around the nape of her neck, his thumb sliding over her cheek as he bent his head toward hers. His other hand slid down to the small of her back, urging her body close against him. Lara didn't pull away but neither did she lean into him, nervous and unsure of herself and him.

Do not be afraid of this, Lara. It is just a kiss. I am asking only that in this you do not fear me. His thumb feathered across her cheek, his black gaze holding hers. *I do not want you to ever fear I will take anything from you that you are not willing to give.*

His words played over her skin, floated on his warm breath. She could see the length of his lashes, the cut of his sensual mouth. He gave her time to pull back, lowering his head slowly, inch by inch, until his lips feathered over hers, back and forth, soft as velvet. Air backed up in her lungs and her heart beat too loud.

I'm not a coward. She whispered the words in his mind and moved into him, adjusting her body fully into his.

No, you are not.

He pressed a kiss to the corner of her mouth, teeth tugged on her full lower lip until she wanted to groan with pleasure. He flicked his tongue against her lips, and then licked, as if savoring her taste. His hand put even more pressure on her back, and her body went soft and pliant, molding to his until she felt they shared the same skin. His mind opened to hers, his emotions pouring in.

She was instantly drenched in a flood of desire. Hot. Passionate. Yet at the same time, there was a tenderness so intimate tears flooded her eyes. She could feel his elation that she met him halfway, his intense need to protect her, his determination to be a good lifemate to her, to make her happy and confident.

She also felt that darkness swirling close to the surface, the demon rising to claim her. He ruthlessly pushed it down, holding the animal side of him in check. He was beginning to need her—not the Carpathian needing a lifemate and not the demon roaring to claim her. Nicolas, the man, longed for her smile, for one shared moment of happiness—for a kiss. And that was a seduction in itself.

She nipped him back, grateful he held the wild, dominant side under close rein, desperate for his mouth on hers. He licked her lips again and she opened her mouth to catch the exotic taste that was just Nicolas. Strangely, the tangy flavor of his blood still lingered on her lips, inside her mouth, and she secretly longed for his blood again. She was ashamed of that secret craving, hiding it behind a barrier she was thankful he didn't probe.

The moment Lara opened her mouth to his, his tongue swept inside, claiming her. Coaxing her. He was gentler than she would have liked, more tender than she had the strength to stand against, and hotter than she thought possible. His mouth was like a haven of erotic secrets, hot and wet and filled with velvet promise.

Flames danced over her skin, a million wings fluttered inside her stomach, her womb clenched and muscles tightened. He swept her away on a tidal wave of pleasure so that to anchor herself she wrapped both arms around his neck and tunneled her fingers into his thick hair. He tasted like an aphrodisiac, one she could easily become addicted to, all male, heat and desire, a world of sensual pleasure she wanted to drown in.

Nicolas pulled back first, pressing his forehead against hers, breathing her into his lungs. "I cannot think anymore and I need to be able to have a clear head when we fly together."

"Are you saying I mess up your head?"

He kissed his way down to her mouth again, biting at the lower lip he found so intriguing. "That is exactly what I am saying."

She laughed. "I like that idea. Your head could use a little messing up."

He bit down again, this time causing a small sting of pain. He instantly traced over the bite with his tongue, removing the sting as fast as he'd caused it.

"Ow!" Lara pulled away, not wanting to admit to herself that that little bite excited her even more. She needed a little distance from him. "I want to fly." She started to leave the cave, hurrying in a vain attempt to outrun the arousal twisting through her body.

His fingers settled over her wrist, bringing her to an abrupt halt. "The first lesson is to always scan before you go out into the open. You are looking for blank spaces."

"I thought we decided that vampires were becoming more adept at hiding themselves." Annoyed at herself for not remembering, she rubbed the small dragon birthmark over her left ovary, relying on it to warn her.

"No matter how adept they become, we use every tool we can to give ourselves the advantage. I know you really want to do this, but it is always necessary to protect yourself."

Lara nodded. She'd been too distracted by him, not the promise of flying. "I'm sorry, that was careless of me." She wished, just once, that he'd be distracted enough by her to forget everything else but her.

"Reach out with your senses and feel the night. Merge

with me if you need to and see how spaces should feel. After a while you will be uncomfortable, your mind and skin prickly if you sense the undead near. They are a toxin to our environment and we are sensitive to all things of the earth."

She reached out as directed, letting her senses expand. It took a little experimentation, but she felt triumphant when she achieved it. She sensed animals, and people. The wind whispered in her ear secrets of the night. "I think we're all right to go."

He nodded, his fingers sliding from her wrist to her hand and walked her from the cavern to the edge of the cliff.

Lara shivered with excitement. The night was overcast, with large gray clouds, heavy with snow, but everything sparkled, both in the sky and on the ground below, as if she was surrounded by a world of diamonds. "I've never seen the night like this before. I always thought I should want to be able to walk in the sun, but seeing the night like this, I can't imagine what I was thinking."

"Why would you want to be out where the light hurts your eyes and the sun burns your skin?" There was real curiosity in his voice. "The night belongs to us. It is our world and the best part of it. Who would ever want the sun when they can have this?" He spread out his arms to encompass the night. "I might wish that I was not quite so vulnerable when the sun is high, but I would never give this up for the ability to see daylight."

Lara frowned. "I guess being raised where my skin burned and all the children could play and swim, but I had to hide away, made me long for something I couldn't have."

He wrapped his arm around her waist, pulling her to him to drop a hard kiss on her pouting lips. "Let me show you why the night is so much better. Aside from the obvious advantage, that it suits our physical hungers..." His voice held a suggestive tone and he smiled unrepentantly when she flicked him a quick glance. "...the night is just plain fun. Have you ever had just plain fun?"

Lara looked out over the valley far below them. She could see the bogs shimmering with ice crystals, the meadows capped with white powder. The world had a shimmery quality she'd never noticed before.

"Take a deep breath."

Lara did so. She drew the fresh, crisp night air into her lungs.

"Do you feel the energy? It surrounds every living thing. Tune yourself to it, the energy feeds your power, so you can use it to build whatever you need fast."

"Carpathians use energy differently than mages," Lara explained. "I've been mage-trained, I don't know how to just control it through me."

Nicolas shook his head. "You have been doing it all along, when you get upset. At the inn, you blasted us out of fear. You gathered energy and used it against us. For now, you need to feel the power, the way it feeds you subtly."

He lifted his arms to the night. In the distance, a wolf howled. Another answered. One by one several more took up the lonely chorus. "There. Hear that?"

"The wolves?"

"One wolf. That note that sounded different. There is a Carpathian running with our brethren tonight. You need to really listen, not just hear. You have the abilities, now you need the training and practice."

Lara looked below her toward the darkened interior of the forest. "Carpathians run with the wolves?"

"Of course. We take the form of a wolf, choose a pack and are accepted into it if we desire. We will do that if you like, but first, you need your flying lesson."

Lara shifted restlessly from one foot to the other while he explained—in detail, in *tedious* detail—how she had to keep the image at all times in her head or she would fall from the sky.

"Okay already," Lara said when he began to go over the instructions again. "I got it all the first time."

His black gaze smoldered at her. "Do not be overconfident."

She sent him a saucy grin. "You aren't going to let me fall."

She closed her eyes and pictured the dragon in her mind. It had been years since she had seen her aunts, trapped in the form of a dragon, but she remembered every detail of their large, scaled bodies. She held the shape in her mind, the wedged head and large, jeweled eyes. Out of nowhere came a rush of energy, flooding her body, turning her warm. Muscles contracted and expanded. She felt her body bend and begin to reshape. Shocked, she pulled back from the edge of losing herself, so startled she nearly lost the image.

Nicolas was there immediately, just as she knew he would be, merged solidly, holding the image for her. She felt the brush of scales against her arm as his body changed. She waited a heartbeat and then she embraced the change, throwing herself into it, not wanting him to change his mind. She wanted to fly. And then she was crouched on the edge of the cliff, staring out over the valley with new vision. She spread her wings wide, standing on two legs, flapping her wings and creating a wind that blew out into the clouds.

Careful, Nicolas cautioned. *You are scaring me, Lara. Pay attention.*

You sound like an old hen. I'm just trying the whole thing out. This is so cool.

She was going to give him a heart attack. He felt like a mother hen, trying to watch over a baby chick. He was supposed to be the rooster, crowing and everyone falling into line instantly. If he was in his normal form he'd be sweating by now and sweating wasn't something Carpathians did much of.

Do I just step off the edge and flap my wings?

His heart bottomed out when the female dragon stepped to the edge as if to launch herself over. He leapt in front of her, pushing the smaller dragon back as he hovered in the air. *Let the dragon take over. You are still thinking as you. If you want to fly like a dragon, you need to become the dragon.*

How? I'm still me.

You are and you are not. You are there inside, but it is only your spirit left. Merge with your dragon and let it have free reign. Once you get a feel for flight and the way your dragon sees and thinks, you can allow your spirit to emerge a little more. Always, always remember to hold that image in your mind no matter what is happening around you.

Lara's dragon nodded its wedge-shaped head. *Move back and let me try.*

Nicolas, inside the large dragon, found himself smiling at the demand in her voice in spite of himself. He found he liked the little bite in her voice. He backed away from the ledge, all the while keeping his mind firmly in hers. Tension vibrated through his body as she stepped off the edge, great wings flapping frantically.

Let your dragon take over. He would give her a couple of seconds. If she couldn't let go enough to allow the dragon to take over completely, he would have to seize her mind and take complete control.

Don't you dare. I'll get the hang of it. Stop distracting me.

He felt the seeds of panic as the little female spiraled out of control. Every instinct screamed at him to take over her mind and right her, but he fought it back, holding on by a thread to give her a little more time as his dragon dove headfirst after its mate.

Deep inside the body of his dragon, Nicolas groaned as he realized Lara had a problem with giving up control. He should have anticipated and prepared for it. She had seconds before the illusion of giving control to her dragon became a reality as Nicolas would have no choice but to take over. The ground rose up to meet her as his male dragon went streaking after her. Nicolas fought hard to give her those few extra precious seconds.

And just that suddenly, Lara took a deep breath and let go of herself, turning control over to the dragon. Instantly the wings of the female dragon stopped the wild flailing and folded close to the body, stopping the spin. Then the wings came out, and with one powerful, coordinated stroke, the creature rose gracefully into the air.

Childlike laughter rang in Nicolas's ears. A vise seemed to squeeze his heart at the sound of that young, carefree voice. She had never had a childhood, never been able to play or laugh, to feel the freedom of the wind in her face, to look down at the tops of the trees and the glistening meadows, to somersault in the night sky and just have fun. Now, sheer exhilaration sent her singing through the sky. The wind flew in her face, cool and brisk, and he felt the joy in her.

Nicolas! This is… amazing.

Yes, it is. She was amazing. She did something to him inside he hadn't expected, turning him inside out with her simple happiness of the moment. In a way, he relived his own first experience of flying, but somehow, he enjoyed hers even more. She had never tasted true freedom. This was her first real exposure to the beauty of their world and he wanted her to enjoy every moment of it, to see the night in the way he did.

Nicolas was astonished to find he was beginning to need her for more than to calm his demons, or spread light through the darkness—he needed to hear her laughter, to see the childlike delight in her sparkling dragon's eyes. He found himself admiring her courage. She had risen from the ashes of cruelty and horror yet maintained a sweetness and hope that he had never imagined could be possible under the circumstances.

Flying through the night sky with her, it suddenly occurred to him that she might be a better person than he, that where duty and honor were ingrained in him, he thought himself superior to those he protected, but Lara truly did care. She cared about her two friends, and her aunts, and was beginning to worry about the father she had believed for years was a monster. He had protection to offer her, but what else?

He had thought finding his lifemate made him entitled to her, that she would worship the ground he walked on—that she *should* worship him, yet he hadn't considered that he might lose his heart to her. The possibility hadn't entered his mind, not even for a moment. She was supposed to lose her heart, but he would remain the same. Now, everything was changing inside of him and he felt off balance—and vulnerable. He didn't want to lose her and not because she was the other half of his soul and could save him. He simply didn't want to lose her, and the stirrings of that emotion terrified him.

Nicolas! Come on. Let's race to that huge gray cloud.

He let her get a head start, holding his dragon back to a more leisurely pace until she got several yards away. Then she built up a great deal of speed. The female dragon shimmered with metallic reds and gold, her scales gleaming whenever the moon managed to sneak out from behind a cloud and illuminate her as she sped across the sky. She gave off a halo of light, glowing, an age-old call, female dragon to her male.

Nicolas was so startled he nearly lost his image of the dragon. Lara's female was calling to her mate, and in her innocence, with her spirit still dwelling on their kiss, Lara was inadvertently heightening the female's drive for her mate. Lara was unleashing a storm of hunger so intense

Nicolas could feel his own instinctive reaction—his own demon rising.

No! He tried to hold back the male, but his dragon roared, tearing himself free of Nicolas's control, diving after his mate, powerful wings creating a windstorm as he flew after her. Lara's laughter washed over and into him, her mind rubbing intimately up against his in her excitement. She was innocent in her enticement, entirely unaware she was arousing the heat in the male—and in him.

The ground below seemed far away as the dragons rose sharply into the sky, dancing as the star dragons had done, performing an aerial ballet. Swift and lithe in the air, Lara soared free, growing more confident as she felt the dragon's strength. The creatures held power and magic and she identified strongly. She tried a series of rolls and then glided through the air before somersaulting in a graceful acrobatic display.

Nicolas felt his dragon gathering himself—waiting—watching as he chose the moment he needed to capture her in midair. There was no stopping the male, unless he took both of them out of the sky. He was almost as enraptured as his dragon, counting the beats of the wings, as the male increased his speed, circling to come in at an angle just below her. Hot blood surged through his veins, filled his groin, lust punching hard and mean. The female spread her wings wide and the male made his move, sending his large body into a roll, coming upside down below her, belly to belly, wings wrapping her in a tight embrace, his talons locking with hers as he took possession of her body, burying himself deep.

Nicolas felt Lara's shocked excitement as the two dragons spiraled toward earth, heads entwined, wings tight around each other, talons locked, the male plunging over and over into the female. Lara and Nicolas were separate from the dragons, only their spirits held in the physical bodies, yet both felt every heated stroke, the love of two mates expressed in dizzying passion in the air. Nicolas wanted Lara with that same intensity his dragon felt for his mate. The dragon passion only increased his need. He stroked Lara's mind, a soft intimate brush, showing her without words how he felt.

Without warning, a bolt of fire speared through the air, impaling the coupling dragons, entering straight through the male dragon's back, passing through his belly to the female and out her back. The male trumpeted, the female screamed, blood sprayed into the air, droplets scattering across the cloud, mingling with the snow falling to the ground.

The male tried to hold the female, talons digging deep even as he lost strength with the great flow of blood. The ground was coming at them fast.

Nicolas seized Lara's spirit, ripping her from the female dragon, shifting to mist and abandoning the mortally wounded dragons.

We can't leave them. Lara was horrified. And then she coughed. More droplets showered the clouds, falling like rain to dot the white landscape in red.

We have no choice. He held her to him with his ruthless determination, blocking out everything but the danger they were in. *They are part real, part illusion. We are all real. We have to get to safety.* He was wounded as well. Already in need of blood, he had given to Lara twice, he couldn't afford to lose much more—not and fight the undead.

Thunder cracked, the roar shaking the ground as a lightning bolt simultaneously slammed from ground to sky, narrowly missing them. As it was, the shock wave threw them apart, and sent Lara tumbling toward the rocks below.

Nicolas reversed direction, masking her blood, shifting the air to cushion her and bring her down gently, even as he left himself exposed to draw the vampire's fire. It wasn't long in coming. Sensing an advantage, the undead revealed himself, swooping across the sky, streaking as fast as he could to get to the wounded hunter.

Lara landed softly in a snowdrift, holding up her hands to assure herself she was back in her own skin. The moment she moved, she felt pain knifing through her body and looked down to see her stomach coated in blood. She was sprawled naked in the snow, crimson streaks smearing the pristine whiteness around her.

Looking up, she saw Nicolas shifting back to his own body, meeting the vampire in a crashing blow that sent both tumbling out of the sky. Her heart nearly stopped, then began to pound so hard, blood splattered onto the ground. She had to do something. She pushed herself shakily to her feet and raised her arms overhead. She couldn't stop the vampire, but she could give Nicolas a few precious moments.

Ropes of silk, strong as iron, come forth now to hold and bind, legs of eight, fast to spin—spin your web, hold fast within, weaver of the web hold tight, that we may stay, stand and fight.

Spiders dropped from the sky, raining down on the vampire as he fell. The vampire became entangled in the spider threads, shiny and thick, like the poisonous webs she'd practiced weaving in her cave when she first thought she might stop Xavier with such a thing.

The more the vampire fought the sticky ropes of silk, the faster the spiders spun and wrapped him up, giving Nicolas time to land in a crouch, scoop up precious soil from beneath the snow and press a hand front and back to stay the bleeding.

Use the soil, Lara. You are Carpathian enough for it to work. Mix it with your saliva and press it into your wounds.

She did need to stop the bleeding and weave clothes for her shivering body. She couldn't go into shock in case Nicolas needed her. She fell to her knees and dug through the snow until she uncovered the soil beneath. It took a moment to force herself to mix saliva with the dirt and pack her wounds, but she did it, all the while watching as the vampire hit the ground hard a few hundred yards from her.

Snarling with rage, red eyes glowing, the face was a mask of fury. He turned those soulless pits her way and bared his savagely sharp teeth.

Get out of here, Lara. Go now. Run to the village.

Leave him? How could she do that? She stretched her arms to the sky, needing clothes to cover her so she'd at least feel as if she had armor against the vile evil that tore through the silken spiderweb. Once more she turned to the snow spiders, calling on them to begin spinning their gossamer threads for her warmth this time.

Spin little spinners, weave little weavers, fit me tight. Spin and weave with your crystal light. Fit to me a second skin so that I might feel warmth again.

Hastily she ran across the ground away from the vampire, in the direction of the village. She made it into the tree line and stopped to drag on her clothes.

11

Lara spun around, turning in circles, trying to find Nicolas and the vampire. One moment they had both been there and now she couldn't see either one of them. Cursing, she ran back out from the trees. The soil may have stopped the worst of the bleeding, but it didn't take away the pain of torn flesh. She could barely breathe with the pain, yet she managed to shove it aside in her anxiety for him.

Nicolas! The moment she called to him she was afraid she had distracted him at the worst possible moment.

Several yards away, just over a rise, she saw snow blast up into the air. She sprinted, or at least tried to, sinking ankle-deep into the powder. She needed snowshoes on her feet, or at the very least, the ability to run across the surface. Weaving a pattern with her graceful hands, Lara leapt as if she were a snow hare.

Strings of sinew, finest bone, bend and shape, form and hone. Weave and place upon these feet, lightest paws of a snow hare be.

Lara felt a tingling, stretching sensation in her feet as she landed back in the snow and hurried across the meadow toward the rising slope. The pain in her back and stomach grew with every step, but she forced her body forward, afraid for Nicolas. He had taken the brunt of the attack. Now she could hear the vampire snarling and growling. The sounds were hideous. Nicolas was totally silent, making her pulse pound and fear clutch at her.

Instinctively, her mind reached out to connect with Nicolas and found—a killer. There was no hint of her charming lifemate, so intent on courting her. There was no mercy, no gentleness, nothing but a killing machine made of sinew and bone, honed by centuries of battles and a mind made for combat.

She skidded to a halt, pressing her palm to her mouth. Did she want to see him like that? Know him like that? The killer was as much a part of him as that smooth, charming man, the one who had kissed her senseless and taken her on the wildest ride of her life, and he was in a fight for his life—both of their lives.

She knew evil when she saw it, and the vampire had the same peculiar odor as Xavier's pet mutations—the parasites. She pushed down the gathering bile caused by just the stench alone, and forced her body forward. She couldn't leave him wounded to fight a battle with such evil when she might find a way to help him.

Lara dropped down on her belly and scooted the rest of the way up the rise to peer over the snowbank. Below she could see sprays of crimson streaked across the sparkling snow, as if someone had thrown red paint in slashing lines in every direction. A lone tree, bent under the weight of the snow, stood as a sentinel watching the age-old battle between vampire and hunter.

Nicolas stood a distance from her, tall and straight, his hair flowing behind him, his eyes glowing with power. In spite of the injuries—now open where the vampire obviously had raked down his chest and belly with talons, tearing away the soil patch—Nicolas moved with fluid grace, a blurring speed she could barely comprehend, as he streaked across the snow to slam his fist deep into the chest of the vampire.

The vampire screamed and clawed at Nicolas's face, but the hunter had already leapt out of reach, using his tremendous speed. It hadn't been his first attack. Lara could see three deep wounds on the undead. The two combatants circled each other.

"Your woman will be fodder for animals. They'll eat her flesh and drink what I leave of her blood."

Nicolas didn't reply, didn't engage in conversation. His gaze never left the vampire. His breath came slow and easy, although Lara couldn't imagine the agony he must have been in with his severe wounds. There was something about him. She couldn't help but admire the lone warrior, facing an enemy with such confidence, nothing in his mind but absolute victory.

She wanted to be like Nicolas. She wanted that confidence in herself, to know she could handle any situation alone if necessary. She didn't want to be afraid anymore. She could see how Nicolas had gotten the way he was—he *had* to be confident to the point of arrogance, he had to believe in his own abilities or he would have never survived.

The vampire spat a mouthful of blood, hate twisting his features. Twice his gaze shifted toward the sky and both times Nicolas feinted a movement, bringing attention back to him. The third time, Nicolas moved again with that same blurring speed. The vampire turned his head at the last moment, meeting the attack with a shriek, shapeshifting to avoid the enormous strength that smashed through bone and sinew to reach for the vulnerable, blackened heart.

Nicolas hit the undead as he tried to shift, half-vampire form, half-wolf. The muzzle elongated, razor-sharp teeth driving straight at Nicolas's face. Lara bit back a scream of fear and buried her face in her hands. Her body began to shake so hard her teeth rattled. How could he face that? He hadn't even flinched. She peeked out between her fingers and saw his face, a mask of blood, his arm buried deep into the cartoonish werewolf's chest.

The creature was nearly seven feet tall, and he caught at Nicolas with clawed hands, jerking him back, shrieking as Nicolas refused to let go of the heart. The vampire shook him, slamming a fist into his chest repeatedly in an effort to dislodge those burrowing fingers. The eyes went cunning and she saw the gaze lock on Nicolas's throat. Her heart nearly stopped, but she flung her hands up, weaving a hasty pattern of protection.

Ore of earth, forged by fire, circle cast by need-desire, form this metal into a ring of hard titanium.

The pattern glowed white-hot and then cooled as it formed a protective circle around Nicolas neck just as the werewolf thrust its head straight toward Nicolas's exposed throat. Saliva and blood dripping, the muzzle gaped wide, and then clamped down hard with a frightening crunch just as Nicolas yanked his arm back. A terrible sucking sound made Lara's stomach churn, but she fought back the need to get sick. The werewolf's teeth sank hard and deep, hitting the titanium collar. The vampire roared as its teeth shattered into pieces and the heart was drawn completely from its rotted cavern. He lumbered after Nicolas, who was backpedaling, throwing the blackened organ onto the snow and calling down the lightning at the same time.

Thunder cracked and a white-hot bolt of energy slammed into the heart, incinerating it, and then jumped to the vampire. He glowed, burst into orange-red flames, sending noxious fumes into the air. The vampire burst into ashes, and Nicolas directed the energy bolt to burn everything until it disappeared. Only then did he sag a little, reaching into the energy to bathe away the acid blood from his arms and chest.

He turned toward her, his expression a dark mask, his

eyes brooding, hooded, concealing his thoughts as he took a step. Nicolas staggered and recovered. Lara stood up slowly, her entire body shaking. There was blood everywhere, and he had wounds on his face, chest, abdomen and back. How he could be standing, she didn't know.

He glanced skyward, and leapt the distance between them, crowding her body behind his as he faced the trails of mist forming out of the lightly falling snow. The mist began to shimmer and a tall man with nearly waist-length black hair came striding out of the snow.

"Nicolas?"

The black eyes took in the wounds as well as Lara pushed behind him. The gaze jumped from her red-gold banded hair to her eyes swirling between green and blue.

"I did not recognize the vampire, Vikirnoff," Nicolas said. "He was fairly young. No more than three or four hundred years old. Why are they turning so young?"

Natalya was quickly making her way to stand by Vikirnoff. She always was near her lifemate, especially if a vampire was in the area. Nicolas didn't want the couple there. It was petty of him and made him feel ashamed and even stupid that he wanted more time alone with Lara. He had always been so self-assured, but now he feared losing her, feared she would leave him—or stay with him because of the lifemate bond, but never find it in her heart to love him.

It was pitiful to think that he wanted love from her. He had been self-sufficient all of his life and it made him angry to think he needed her. Yet here he was afraid—*afraid*—she would ask sanctuary from her kin.

Nicolas turned to Lara and held out his hand. "Let me take a look at your injuries." He pulled her to him and lifted the hem of her sweater.

Lara caught at his wrist and glanced toward the strangers, obviously uncomfortable. "The fire spear cauterized the wounds for the most part. I lost a little blood, but not enough to worry about, especially once I packed it with soil. But you're a mess." She touched his face with gentle fingers.

Fél ku kuuluaak sívam belső. Beloved, allow me to see. I must heal you before I can see to my own injuries.

Give me a minute. Her fingers sought his, tangled and held on.

Nicolas tried not to be so happy about her clinging to him. He brushed his lips against her forehead before performing the introductions aloud. "Lara, this is Vikirnoff and his lifemate, Natalya. She is your blood-kin."

It set his teeth on edge that he was so petty that he rejoiced she was distressed in the company of her father's sister, but he couldn't help the rush of satisfaction. Nor could he help the need to heal her wounds without a moment's delay. It hurt to see her injured. He swung around to face her, his palm sliding beneath her sweater to press his hand over the wound. At once heat leapt from him to her. Startled, she looked up at him with her enormous green eyes and he felt dizzy—drowning.

It was a strange feeling to be so off balance and he didn't like it much. Nicolas slid his hand away as fast as he'd touched her, stepping to her side so that he could draw her beneath his shoulder, one hand sliding around to her back where his fingers snaked beneath the sweater to lie over the wound.

Natalya stared at her twin's daughter, her eyes filling with tears. "You look like him—like me—us." She leaned back against Vikirnoff for comfort. "I'm Natalya, Razvan's twin sister."

Lara swallowed the ball of fear blocking her throat, locking her body so she didn't stumble back and away as she wanted to do. She reached behind her until she found Nicolas's wrist to steady herself. "I don't look anything at all like him," she denied. Aware she sounded like a child—even her voice was higher pitched—she took a steadying breath and tried again. "He had dark hair streaked with gray. Mostly he's gray. And his face is etched deep with lines, not at all smooth. He's thin, and white."

Carpathian men do not go gray unless they are tortured beyond endurance. It takes… much… to produce gray hair, thinness and deep lines.

You have deep lines.

I have been in countless battles and made many kills. More and more I believe your father has been fighting Xavier to save not only his family, but perhaps all Carpathians.

We are not Carpathian.

Dragonseeker blood is strong. You are Carpathian.

A single sound of distress escaped before Natalya could stop it. She touched her tongue to her lips and made a visible effort to recover from the news of her brother. "We need to help your lifemate. He needs his wounds healed and blood fast. Perhaps you would care to accompany us back to our home?"

Lara's fingernails dug into his palm. Nicolas brought her knuckles to his mouth and nibbled on her skin to distract her. "We were on our way to visit with you when we were attacked. Thank you for the invitation." *Yes or no?*

Her eyes met his, her nod nearly imperceptible.

"Thank you, we will come."

Vikirnoff casually brought his hand to his mouth and tore open his wrist, extending his arm toward Nicolas. Several bright drops of blood splattered onto the ground. Lara gasped as the sight hit her like a blow. She closed her eyes, unable to watch as Nicolas took the proffered wrist.

Nicolas hesitated. "Natalya can take you up to the house," he offered.

Lara kept her eyes closed, trying not to draw the scent of blood into her lungs. Her stomach lurched, but she shook her head. "I'll wait for you." *Just get it over with.*

Nicolas politely closed the ragged tear on Vikirnoff's

wrist. "Thank you, but I can wait until we are out of the open."

Vikirnoff opened his mouth to protest. His gaze brushed Lara's ashen face and he shrugged. "We had better hurry then."

Natalya glanced at Lara sharply, then at Nicolas's ravaged body. Her lips tightened but she didn't voice a protest. Nevertheless, Lara knew she wanted to and that one, small glance shamed her. Nicolas had fought to save their lives, and had done so without flinching from the task. His body bore many deep wounds, but he only had considered taking care of her injuries, slight in comparison to his, yet she couldn't stand the sight of him taking the blood necessary to restore his strength and take the pain from his wounds.

It is no one's business but ours why we both choose our path. Nicolas flicked a warning glance at Natalya that had Vikirnoff bristling.

Natalya put a restraining hand on his wrist and shimmered, shifting into mist, before taking to the air. Vikirnoff followed her.

"I'm sorry." Lara blinked back tears burning in her eyes. "I feel so ashamed."

"There is no need for that. You may have saved my life with your quick thinking." Nicolas touched his neck where the collar had stopped the vampire's teeth from ripping him open. The bite wouldn't really have killed him, and he had been prepared for the shock and pain of it, bracing himself to give himself the time to rip the heart from the chest, but she certainly had cut short the battle, giving him those precious few seconds longer. "That was quick thinking and ingenious on your part."

The praise in his voice made her color rise. "Can I help you heal? I'm not the best healer, but I have some skills." She had no idea how to help him with the injuries, but he looked so alone and she hated being the one to make him feel that way. She wanted to show solidarity, even though her inability to watch him take blood delayed his getting help. She felt awkward asking, but she couldn't let it go. "I know the Carpathian healing chant. My aunts learned it from their mother and they taught it to me, but I don't really know how to actually heal wounds very well. Maybe you could teach me what to do, just in case this happens again."

He smiled down at her, his expression tender. "It will happen again. Here, we can gather the richest soil we can find, mix it with our saliva."

"The healing agent in yours is probably much stronger than mine."

She chose a spot directly under the trees. She wanted a place where flowers grew in abundance. The plants were dormant, but the soil lay beneath the snow, black with minerals. She mixed the soil and saliva and made a compress for the wounds.

Earth with healing properties, flower beneath the earth do see, twine your essences, fill these wounds gently, apply your healing boon.

She breathed into the mixture, chanting softly in Carpathian, unaware she did so. She added her own special blend to aid in healing him.

This man is a shadow but of the light, help him to heal to resume his fight.

She was a little hesitant, afraid of hurting him, but she pressed the mixture carefully into the gouges on his chest and into his abdomen with gentle fingers. There was a small silence as she worked carefully, making certain to cover every scratch. She could barely breathe with the feel of his skin beneath her fingers, with the heat of his body so close. He remained very still, almost holding his breath, but her heartbeat followed the rhythm of his in exact synchronization.

"How long do you leave this on? I can't get past putting dirt into a wound." Her voice trembled a little.

"I should be able to clean it off in a few minutes." His hand cupped her chin and raised her face up to his. The pad of his thumb slid over her lower lip in a little caress.

Lara's gaze locked with his. Her breath stilled in her lungs. A shiver of excitement whispered down her spine. There was raw hunger in his burning black eyes, a desire that seemed to match the sudden smoldering in the pit of her stomach. Heat spread. Arousal skimmed over her thighs and breasts.

Nicolas bent his dark head toward hers. His lips brushed over hers, featherlight, a question, a demand, a soft entreaty and a firm insistence. She answered, drawing him into the soft haven of her mouth.

I'm so glad you're safe. Her voice was shy.

Nicolas let his lashes fall, blocking out all sensation but the wet, velvet heat of her mouth. He could get lost there, eating her up, drinking her in. Molten lava poured into his veins, thick and hot, fueling every desire.

He deepened the kiss, took more of a command, pressing her a little to see if she would respond. It was getting more difficult to keep his hands off of her when the demons roared and his body hardened into one unrelenting ache. Everything inside of him knew Lara was the other half of his soul, the keeper of his heart. He feared she would never feel the same.

Her hands came up to curl in his hair, but she was tentative in her response, a little shy, not quite swept away as he wanted. He let it go. This wasn't the time or place, and she wasn't quite ready for that next step with him. He would have to be satisfied that she was reaching for him, even meeting him part way.

His hands were gentle as he allowed them to slip from her face. He loved the sexy, slightly dazed look in her eyes.

"Can you shift again?"

She blinked several times, her small teeth biting into her lower lip. She nodded.

A slow smile softened the hard cut to his mouth. "Follow the image in my mind and hold it. Each time you practice you will become more adept at it. When we get to Vikirnoff's home, it will not take more than a few minutes to make things right."

She knew he meant taking blood from Vikirnoff. He was swaying a little, she noticed, and the lines in his face seemed etched a bit deeper. There was no reprimand she could find in his mind, no looking down on her because she couldn't abide the thought of his taking someone else's blood. She found the genuine acceptance he gave her humbling and maybe a little healing. She breathed a little easier. "Let's go then. I don't want you to have to wait any longer than you already have."

He took a step to his right, holding mist uppermost in his mind and in hers. She felt the change almost immediately. The rush of adrenaline nearly stopped her from shifting, but she pulled back and let go of her physical body. It was much easier to accept the change this time and she was both exhilarated and proud that she managed to shift into mist and streak across the sky with Nicolas. She knew he was holding the image for her, but she didn't care. She'd done the impossible and it felt like a huge milestone to her.

I've learned a lot tonight, Nicolas, thank you.

He brushed her mind with an intimate warmth that poured over her like warm honey. Her heart contracted. He was finding his way inside her, past every barrier she'd erected from childhood. His gentleness was so unexpected when he was such a dangerous, arrogant man. He made her feel as if she were the only important person in his life. He didn't care if Natalya didn't approve of her—she was enough for him just the way she was and his acceptance went a long way toward making her feel much more confident in herself.

The house was built into the mountainside, so artfully arranged it was nearly impossible to see it until one was right upon it. Lara and Nicolas shifted on the rock steps leading to the cool shade of a porch, all built out of the same stone. Lara enjoyed the feel of going into a cave. The front looked like a home, with windows and a door, but made out of the mountain itself. The house itself was well lit with bright hanging lights, marble floors and gleaming polished wood everywhere.

"You have decided to settle here," Nicolas said, looking around the warm room.

"Unlike you and your family," Vikirnoff said, "my brother and I only spent the last few years hunting together and never in one location. Prior to that, we moved from region to region filling in where no ancient was posted. It will be nice to have a home after so long. Nicolae and Destiny are settling here as well. We will be able to help guard the prince and the women and children in the hopes of rebuilding our people."

Lara was grateful for Nicolas's hand on the small of her back, connecting them. He was also in her mind and it steadied her to face Natalya, who did look so much like herself. If Razvan had looked like her at one time, he no longer did, but Natalya could have been her mother—or sister.

Natalya waved her toward a deep, comfortable-looking chair. "Please sit down. It's amazing to finally meet you."

Nicolas took her hand as she sank into the thick cushions, his thumb sweeping over her palm in a gentle caress. *Will you be all right for a few moments without me?*

Her stomach lurched. When had she become such a coward? Was she so thrown by the scent and sight of parasites and silver eyes that she could no longer cope on her own? Maybe it had been death in those eyes and the scent of decay? Whatever childhood trauma she had dredged up refused to go away. The door had cracked open and she had to deal with it.

She glanced up at Nicolas. He looked so calm, so in

control, so at peace while she was churning with doubt. He had to deal with her past as well.

We will do so together. Again he flooded her with warmth, making her feel a part of him and not so alone.

Yes, we will. And I'll be fine. Don't worry about me.

Nicolas bent to brush a kiss across the top of her head. *Reach for me if you need me, otherwise, I will keep us separate.*

She moistened her lips. Of course he would think to pull his mind from hers to prevent her from "seeing" or feeling what was happening as he took blood. She nodded to indicate she understood, managing a small, reassuring smile.

Natalya watched Nicolas leave the room with Vikirnoff. "Is he good to you?" she asked abruptly. "The De La Cruz family has a certain reputation and they live by their own rules."

The question startled Lara and she was uncertain how to answer. "We've only just met."

Natalya nodded. "And he bound you to him, but the ritual isn't complete. Do you know what happens to the man if the ritual is completed?"

Lara shook her head. "I know only what my aunts told me in stories. I was a child and my memories of most of those years are vague, so I'm guessing some of it could be inaccurate as well. I often don't know what is real, planted by them, or my imagination."

"It must be very confusing for you."

"Yes, but I'm learning a lot."

"I'm sorry I make you uncomfortable. I'm extremely happy to meet you, after all, you are my niece. Colby, who is a lifemate to Rafael, is your half-sister. Razvan was also her father."

Tension locked her muscles and stretched her nerves. Natalya had deliberately inserted the information into the conversation to see her reaction. Lara kept her face carefully blank. "I've been having a few flashbacks that may indicate that Xavier possessed Razvan's body in order to seduce women and get them pregnant, so he could feed on the blood of Dragonseekers."

Natalya winced. "He wanted to use me that way. Razvan convinced him that I didn't have strong enough Dragonseeker blood to be useful. He protected me my entire childhood and throughout the years after. I didn't realize what was happening to him until recently and then I thought he had somehow turned vampire or was in league with them." She leaned forward, her blue-green eyes locking with Lara's. "Do you know if that's true? Do you know if he's still alive?"

Lara bit down on her lower lip. What did she really know about Razvan? Her childhood memories had been faulty. She remembered little until the trauma of seeing the parasites. Was he evil? Had he turned evil? Was he even still alive? There were so many conflicting pieces of memories rising now that she didn't know the truth. "I can't help you, as much as I'd like to. I don't have any answers. I see things that indicate to me that Xavier not only possessed Razvan's body, but he injected him with something that took his will—not his mind completely because he tried to resist, but ultimately, it appeared as if Xavier was making him do terrible things and Razvan was unable to overcome the combination of drugs and spells that Xavier wove."

Vikirnoff and Nicolas came back into the room, catching the last part of the conversation. Nicolas didn't look quite as drawn. He sat on the arm of Lara's chair, his body positioned protectively toward her. "Possession and taking over minds, making people into puppets, was Xavier's forte. No one had his skill and he continued to perfect it over the years. It was one of the things the prince and he disagreed on. Some things shouldn't be done." Nicolas tangled his fingers in Lara's hair. "Xavier felt the Carpathian people used mind control to get their way and he had every right to do so as well. It was difficult to argue with his logic."

"Because there was truth in it," Lara said.

Nicolas nodded. "At the time, I felt we were using our mind control for good, and he wanted to use it to further his own ends, but lately I have learned that I certainly used it for my own selfish purposes. It is much easier and faster when I want cooperation so I just do so without thinking."

Vikirnoff made a sound of disgust. "To ease someone's fears is not the same thing as making them do things they would never ordinarily do," he objected.

"Such as give blood?" Lara asked.

Vikirnoff shifted forward aggressively. Natalya put a gentle hand on his arm. "You have scars on your wrists, Lara. I found a ceremonial knife that had been Xavier's and when I accessed the memories, there was one of a young girl Razvan was using to feed from. Xavier came in and tried to take her blood as well and she was able to escape the cave with the help of two dragons."

Nicolas's hand curled around the nape of Lara's neck. "That was Lara. Her aunts were caught in the form of dragons and were too weak to escape as well. We are going back to the cave to determine their fate as well as to try to figure out what happened to Razvan."

Vikirnoff sat up very straight. "That cave is one big trap, Nicolas. We barely escaped with our lives. Xavier left guardians and there were signs that the chambers are still in use at times. We have been watching it closely, but no one goes in there, it is far too risky."

Nicolas's long, strong fingers began a slow massage on her neck. "We are well aware of the risk, Vikirnoff, but we cannot live with ourselves if we do not find out the answers to our questions. The aunts risked everything to save Lara. And the evidence that Razvan has for centuries—not a few years, but centuries—endured torture. He is Dragonseeker, which means there is the possibility that he could survive."

"We saw him attack Natalya," Vikirnoff pointed out. "He was in her head, tracking her, trying to lure her to him, to use her against us."

"But was Razvan in his own mind? Or was it Xavier possessing or controlling Razvan? Lara and I need to find the answer to that question. And her aunts have been imprisoned long enough. Dead or alive, and we do not expect to find them alive, we want to bring them home."

Vikirnoff took Natalya's hand. "You knew Razvan better than any person alive. Could this be possible? Could it have been Xavier controlling Razvan?"

She closed her eyes briefly and shook her head. "I don't know, Vikirnoff. I truly don't know. He only came to me in my dreams. How could Xavier intrude on dreams?"

"How can Xavier find a way to imprison and keep from suicide one of the most powerful Carpathian women? Rhiannon's lifemate was murdered, yet Xavier managed to force her to have triplets with him," Nicolas pointed out. "I knew Rhiannon and her lifemate. She would have followed him if she could have."

Lara cleared her throat. "The aunts talked about her often. She was held prisoner by Xavier and once she had the children, she stayed alive willingly to help protect them and teach them as much as she could about the Carpathian and mage cultures. She imparted knowledge to them at a fast rate because she knew eventually Xavier would murder her, and he did."

You didn't tell me this. Nicolas's voice slid into her mind with ease.

I'm getting bits and pieces now. Now they just come to me. She didn't know if she was happy about it or not.

Nicolas didn't like her feeling so confused. In close proximity to Natalya, Lara was already edgy. She hid it well, but she was uncomfortable, her memories still too raw. Twice she rubbed her wrist, although he knew it was habit more than pain, but the gesture served as a reminder of her traumatic childhood.

"I want to go with you," Natalya said. "To the cave. I *have* to go."

"Natalya," Vikirnoff cautioned.

"No, it's Razvan. I have to see if there's a chance we're wrong about him. Maybe we'll find something, a clue to what's been happening."

Vikirnoff muttered something under his breath. "The cave is a death trap. You were there, Natalya, you know it is."

"He kept me away from Xavier. I could be the one with the nightmare childhood. I could be the one he experimented on and fed off. Razvan saved me, Vikirnoff. I love my brother and if I can at least clear his name so his children think better of him, then I owe him that much."

Vikirnoff shook his head. "It is insanity to go back there. You know that."

Nicolas understood exactly how Vikirnoff felt. The last thing he wanted to do was to take Lara back to the underground labyrinth that Xavier had created. *I have to go, Nicolas. If it was your family, you would go.*

The problem, he decided, was that once your heart was involved, all logic went out the window. It mattered little that he knew it was dangerous, but now he understood her needs and that made the decision not quite as easy as it had been when he had no emotions. His eyes met Vikirnoff's, for the first time understanding the difficulties with keeping women safe.

"The caveman method had value," Vikirnoff stated.

"I agree," Nicolas said, sighing inwardly. *I said I would take you. I do not go back on my word.*

"Then we go tomorrow night?" Natalya asked.

"The night after," Vikirnoff corrected. "I want to do a little reconnaissance before we go and we have to attend the warriors' council. Jacques's baby will be named in the warriors' circle. It is important we all attend to support Jacques and Shea. Should something ever happen to Shea, Jacques could not survive it. Their son would have need of our entire community."

The warriors' council... where he had intended to support Gregori in their bid to keep women away from fighting. Nicolas nearly groaned aloud. "Have you heard news of the prince's lifemate? I assumed she was having problems again."

Natalya looked down at her hands, her expression sad. "Not only is Raven having problems, but evidently Savannah is as well. It doesn't look good. Gregori is working with both of them and Syndil has been working with the surrounding soil, but both women are bleeding, their bodies trying to reject the babies."

A burst of pain in Lara's head had her wrenching her hand free of Nicolas in order to press at her temples. Her mind seemed to splinter for a moment, and a door cracked open. She had a brief glimpse of a sobbing woman, blood on the floor and piles of dirt around her. Xavier stood over her smiling with satisfaction.

"Sometimes we must make small sacrifices for the greater good, my dear. One lost child to ensure that the death of many continues is not too small of a price to pay."

Bile welled up and she stood fast, pushing Nicolas away from her and rushing from the house to stand outside in the fresh, cold air where she could breathe. Nicolas came up behind her, placing gentle hands on her shoulders.

Lara shook him off, taking a step forward, breathing fast. "Don't. Don't say anything yet." He had seen that small vignette of her past. She had felt him there at that first burst of pain, before either realized what was happening.

"You cannot possibly think you are in any way responsible for anything Xavier has done. He wanted immortality and he was angry and bitter that he did not have it and the

Carpathians did. He wanted every power our species had as well as his own. When Rhiannon's lifemate was murdered and she disappeared, we knew he had been plotting against us for years. Of course we had no way of knowing the extent of the damage or what he had done. He is a master mage, and undeniably powerful. The seeds of hatred and his descent into madness began centuries before you were ever born."

"His blood is in my veins." She gestured toward the house. "In her veins. He set out to destroy an entire species in the foulest way he could think of." She looked at him then, her eyes sad, shamed. "You know that's what we saw. More experiments. He's done something, has been doing it all along, to make the women miscarry, to make the children die." She tilted her head in challenge. "You don't know him the way I do. You can't kill him. You can't stop him. He is the most despicable creature on the face of the earth, the most evil."

Nicolas understood what she meant. Xavier had murdered his own son. Had kidnapped, raped and forced Rhiannon to bear him children and then, after using her blood for years, had murdered her. He had imprisoned his grandson and experimented on him, tortured him and used his children for a blood supply. He had murdered his grandson's mage wife. There was nothing he could find redeeming about Xavier. He'd never liked him in the old days when the mages and Carpathians had a strong alliance.

"It isn't all mages, you know," she said softly. "My mother was mage."

"Fél ku kuuluaak sívam belső," he whispered.

Beloved. Was she beloved? Could someone as strong as Nicolas possibly really understand, accept and love someone as damaged as she?

His mouth curved even as he kissed her again. *We both know I am not without my faults, as much as I would like* to pretend otherwise. *You need to eat this night. We will go to the inn.*

She nodded. "I want to check on my friends anyway. Let's go."

Nicolas glanced back at the house. *Lara needs a little time. I will take her to the inn to get some food. We can meet after the warriors' council and check out the cave before we bring the women.*

A feminine voice gave a small huff of disdain. *The women?*

Lara's voice echoed her aunt's. *There you go with your women theme. I suspect you have hidden issues, Nicolas.*

You have no idea. She was feeling benevolent toward him now, but after the warriors' council, she wouldn't be too happy.

12

The inn was bustling with activity when Nicolas and Lara arrived. It was always necessary within the village to keep up the pretense of being entirely human. Many Carpathians often went to the dining room and appeared to be eating dinner. It wasn't difficult for Nicolas to shift into immaculate clothes, giving Lara a long, swingy dress that swished around her ankles.

Lara patted her hair, surprised that it was down in a long freefall of red-gold silk. She glanced up at the tall handsome man who made her feel beautiful. His male beauty struck her, a mixture of danger, animal and pure sensual male. She swallowed the sudden need rising and managed a quick smile. "Did you remember makeup, too?"

He tangled his fingers with hers and brought her hand in a possessive gesture to his chest as they entered the lobby area where even the villagers often gathered for drinks. "Of course."

As close to him as she was, she instantly felt the difference in him. The moment they stepped inside where there were others, he went from her gentleman to fiercely, primitive male. It happened in a heartbeat. He even smelled different, a combination of musk, spice and wild outdoors. The cut of his mouth was sensual, yet held a cruel, warning edge. His heavy-lidded eyes brooded, drifting over the competition as if marking each man. The hand at the small of her back was distinctly possessive. He even moved that scant fraction of space closer to her, so that he seemed to be everywhere, dominating her space.

Or maybe the difference was in her. She was intensely aware of the darkly handsome man prowling at her side, all raw sexuality and power. Women turned their heads and stared at him with greedy eyes. Their gazes followed her with some disdain and a lot of envy. She was certain she didn't look woman enough to handle a man as blatantly sexual as Nicolas.

The moment she thought it, he brushed across her body with warm air, as if he'd breathed on her bare skin. Her nipples tightened and heat rushed through her bloodstream. She glanced up at his face, at the raw hunger in his dark eyes each time his gaze slid over her. She touched her tongue to her lower lip and instantly his gaze was riveted there.

"You have to stop," she whispered, a blush creeping up her neckline to bring color into her face. "You're making me..." She broke off, hardly able to breathe properly. She'd never felt quite like this before—excited—sexy—wanted. It was amazing and practically incomprehensible that she could draw the undivided and completely focused attention of a man like Nicolas De La Cruz. She wasn't adventurous. She wasn't beautiful. She certainly wasn't sexy, although he made her feel that way and it was a little intoxicating.

She was all too conscious of his fingers splayed wide just above the curve of her spine. Heat spread from every pinpoint as they crossed the bar to the dining room. Music pulsed in the bar and a few couples swayed to the beat, holding each other more than they danced. A few feet from the arched entrance, Nicolas stopped abruptly, his fingers settling around her wrist to swing her in front of him.

Her breath caught in her lungs as he pulled her into his arms. She fit perfectly, her body going soft so that she melted into him, so close she was nearly sharing his skin. Hard muscles rippled and prowled, a heated, seductive slide that sent a shiver of awareness down her spine and had her breasts aching. She felt the hard bulge pressing tight into her stomach, the thick, unashamed evidence of his desire for her. Her mouth went dry and her stomach muscles knotted.

Nicolas bent his head, his lips skimming her exposed neck and the pulse beating frantically in rhythm with the music. "Relax for me." His voice was rough with a mixture of seduction and lust, almost as if he was making love to her instead of dancing with her.

His tone sent a million butterflies winging in the pit of her stomach. Moisture dampened her thighs and sent an electrical current spiraling through her body. It was her first real experience with such an overwhelming sexual reaction and her emotions were all over the place. Every single nerve ending seemed to have flared into life. Every cell was very aware of Nicolas moving so close to her.

"I don't know how to... I've never..." She didn't know whether she was telling him she'd never danced and had no idea what she was doing, or whether she was trying to tell him she'd never had sex and didn't know the first thing about tempting a man.

Nicolas tightened his hold on her, his arm locking her against him as they executed several intricate dance steps across the floor. She felt as if she was floating in the clouds, light and airy and in perfect tune with him.

"You are temptation itself." His lips brushed against her earlobe as he whispered the words.

Teeth nipped, the smallest of bites, leaving her breathless. Arousal fingered her breasts, her thighs and teased at the junction between her legs. He was seducing her, there on the dance floor, and she didn't even want to resist. She touched her tongue to her lower lip, fighting nerves, determined to see this night through.

She wanted him, wanted to belong to him, in spite of his arrogance and domineering ways. When her mind was merged with his, she could see his determination to learn, to make her happy, to be the man she needed. How could she not want him? Aside from that, she found him to be the sexiest man alive.

He turned her, brought her back into the shelter of his body and just the way he did it, so commanding, strong and protective, sent another rush of heat surging through her bloodstream. His scent enveloped her, the spicy male tang that was exclusively his mixed with the scent of musky male arousal making for a potent combination. The slide of his hands caressed the sides of her breasts, her rib cage and tucked-in waist before settling over her hips to pull her tighter against him.

Another surge of moist heat dampened her thighs. Her breasts ached, felt swollen and needy. Every muscle tightened to the point of strain. She couldn't think anymore, swaying to the throbbing music on a rising tide of desire, in a hazy fog of sexual enthrallment.

He bent his head again, this time to nuzzle her neck, his tongue touching the pulse pounding so frantically. Ordinarily she would have instantly retreated, but the small series of licks accompanied by the gentle scrape of teeth sent her temperature soaring. Flames danced over her skin, centered between her legs and filled emptiness so that her body craved more. His lips were unbelievably warm and firm, his teeth a torment, wracking her body with longing. She could barely breathe, her heart pounding loud enough for both of them to hear.

Nicolas recognized the danger the moment he stepped in close proximity to other men with Lara. The binding ritual wasn't complete. She could still slip away from him. The call of the demon rose to a wild, demanding roar. He saw every shift of the eyes, the way the men watched her as they moved together in perfect rhythm across the dance floor. He scented the heightened sexual awareness.

Lara didn't realize how alluring she was, a mixture of innocence and fantasy. Her skin glowed, her eyes classic bedroom eyes, large and soft and enthralling. A man could drown in her eyes—he was drowning. And having other males in such a close environment was triggering the beast. He could feel it clawing at his gut, making demands to claim his lifemate, make her irrevocably his. More than that, his own fears of losing her heightened his animal instincts, the primitive side of him that demanded he take what was his. He was walking a thin line, trying to court her as she deserved and at the same time, remain stable when his lifemate was just out of reach. It was never easy for a male to balance civility with his own predatory nature and coming to the inn made for a volatile situation he hadn't counted on.

He drew a deep breath into his lungs and scented— Lara. Her feminine call sent blood pounding in his groin. The feel of her soft breasts nestled against his chest nearly drove him mad. He was desperate to hold her, to touch her, to touch all that satin skin. Each moment in her company had escalated his need of her. Need had built so slowly at first, and his desire to court her had kept him from realizing how the fire in him had grown and spread until it was a storm threatening his control.

His shaft pounded with blood and his hammering heartbeat. His need was brutal now, a continual, unrelenting demand that was merciless. His erection wasn't going away anytime soon, not even if he had the opportunity to bury himself deep in the haven of her body. And through it all, each time he looked at her, each time her shy gaze met his, it tripped a strange sensation in the region of his heart.

He wanted to be equally as tender as he did violent. He wanted her to want him with every cell in her body, in the same frightening way he needed her. He had had an utter misconception of lifemates, or maybe it was just different with Lara. He had thought she would save him from the darkness and the chemistry would be good, that they would have several lifetimes to find a way to love one another. He hadn't expected her to touch him in places that he thought were stone cold. He hadn't expected to feel such tender, protective emotions so fast or so strong, but she was really light to his darkness, in all the ways he hadn't expected.

His lips drifted over her pulse, as he inhaled her scent. Her long silky hair slid over his face, a few strands tangling in the shadow along his jaw. He pressed her hips into his body, massaging the terrible ache that refused to go away. Touching her wasn't enough. Even now he could feel his teeth lengthening and sharpening as his entire being demanded he assuage the hunger rising in direct proportion to his sexual needs. He was on the very edge of his control.

Eyes glowed with red flames. His teeth touched her pulse, scraped back and forth in a mesmerizing rhythm. He was close—so close to taking what belonged to him, making her his, yet she had been willing to escape into death rather than be forced.

He had never experienced such raw, primitive lust, welling up, a fever of hunger so sharp and brutal he could barely think straight. His soul had been long ago punctured with holes until there was only darkness there, black and ugly and filled with death. But she had spilled shining light across it and somehow, by some miracle, he felt hope. And his heart, centuries gone from the world—longer even than his soul—she had restored so that he could feel soft inside when he'd forgotten if he ever had.

A small groan escaped his throat and he fought harder, urging the demon to settle down, to be patient

and wait—that Lara was worth waiting for. And in the
end, what he really wanted was for Lara to give herself to
him. To want him. To make the commitment on her own
because she had genuine feeling for him. His teeth receded
and that hazy red disappeared from his sight as the music
faded away.

Lara stood swaying, her body tight against his. He could
hear her heart beating the exact same rhythm as his. He
lifted his head slowly, reluctant to allow her out of his arms.
"You need to eat something." It was mundane—true—but
so far from what he wanted to do he could barely get the
words past the need clogging his throat.

She nodded, but stood there, so close to him her soft
body was imprinted on his hard one. She tilted her face
to look up at him. Her eyes were shy, but glowed with an
inner light that made him intensely aware of his sexuality. Her skin was luminous, her eyes bright, her body like
warm silk beneath his roving fingers.

"Lara?"

She lifted her hand to his face, her touch gentle, tender even. "I want to remember this moment always. I don't
have many wonderful memories, but dancing with you is
an incredibly beautiful experience and I want to savor this
night."

Merged with her, he could see the truth. She wanted
to hug their time to her, hold on to it to take out later and
replay, moment by moment, no matter what happened in
the future. Her response brought a surge of hot blood that
nearly destroyed his hard-won control, but along with it,
his heart responded, a painful ache of longing to be loved
by this woman.

His hand slid down to the small of her back to guide her
to the dining room. He cleared his throat. "I hope we make
many such memories together. I will enjoy every one."

"Before anything else, I need to check on Terry and say
hello to Gerald," Lara said.

Nicolas felt the instinctive animalistic reaction swirling in his gut at the idea of Lara in a small room with her two male friends. He nodded his head, forcing a smile. "Why not use the house phone to call them first? Make certain they are up to visitors?"

The hard knots in his belly relaxed when Gerald told her he'd just gotten Terry to sleep and was going to bed. After reassurances all was well, Lara promised she'd come by earlier the next evening to see them.

Nicolas unashamedly used his influence to secure a table in the darkest, most secluded corner of the room. A single candle lit the table with a soft glow and he dimmed that as well as blurring their images to prevent anyone from interrupting their time together. He held the chair for Lara to slip into and then took the one closest to her, blocking her body from any prying eyes that might manage to slip through his thin shield.

Lara felt cocooned in Nicolas's heat, caught in a sexual web that seemed to only increase, even as he casually summoned the waitress.

"What looks good to you?" He ran the pads of his fingers up and down her bare arm in a slow caress, almost as if he didn't realize he was doing it.

Just the deep timbre of his voice sent a heat wave through her body and, in combination with his touch, she swore flames licked at her skin.

Lara cleared her throat. "Something light." She wanted to leave, to be alone with him. She wanted desperately to explore the sensation of fingers trailing up and down her arm, all over her body, in her body. Desire rose so fast and sharp she felt the walls of her feminine sheath clench with slick, hot heat. "I'm not really very hungry."

He murmured something to the waitress she didn't catch, didn't care. She could only look at him, the pure lust etched deep into his too-handsome face, the dark hunger in the depths of his eyes. Knowing it was there for her, that his entire focus was on her, added to the building excitement. Her nipples pushed against the fabric of her dress, rubbing with each subtle movement.

Nicolas leaned toward her, and sent a stream of warm air bathing her breasts right through her dress. She felt the lick of his tongue curling around her nipple. Gasping, she drew back, color stealing into her face as she realized there was a small wet spot right over her engorged nipple.

"No one can see us," he murmured. "I have to see you like this—wanting me."

"I think you've managed to accomplish that already." Even her voice was different. Husky. Sexually charged. An invitation. She couldn't take her eyes from him, mesmerized by the sheer, naked longing on his face. She had never, under any circumstances, imagined a man looking at her like that, let alone a man such as Nicolas De La Cruz. "You have this way of making me feel as if you are so focused on me you don't see another woman in the room."

"Why would I want to see another woman? You are the only one who matters to me." He continued to absently brush his fingers up and down her arm, absorbing the warm, silky texture of her skin. "You are *my* woman."

His softly spoken tone, like black velvet rubbing over her exposed skin, caused her womb to clench and moisture to gather at the junction of her legs. She twisted her fingers together in her lap beneath the table as trembling began to work from her toes to her head. The music seemed to be playing in her head, or maybe it was the rush of her own blood keeping time with his.

She felt starstruck, unable to speak when her body was shaking with need of him.

Nicolas tugged on her arm until she gave up her hand. His long fingers stroked over the ridges on her wrist, now much fainter than they had been. "Promise me if I drive you to feel so hopeless again, if anything or anyone does, you will tell me." He brought her hand to his chest, over his heart, his fingers still stroking those long caresses up and down her bare skin. "I know I am not an easy man to take, nor will I ever be, but I want only to secure your protection and happiness."

She managed a nod. "I promise."

He leaned closer to her, his lips inches from hers. "And I want to feel your body under mine and hear you scream with pleasure. I plan on taking my time, having you over and over all night long until neither one of us can stand up, until you cannot think, only feel. I want to give you every sensual experience that I can." He brought her hand to his mouth. "I have waited several lifetimes for you, Lara."

His voice was gentle, low and very sensual, his black gaze hooded, but there was nothing gentle in his eyes. Turbulent. A violent storm raging. A hunger that was so sharp and savage he looked ready to throw her onto the dining room table and rip her dress from her body. The thought added to the temperature rising fast inside of her. Between her legs she was so hot she felt on fire. He hadn't really touched her, yet she wanted him almost beyond imagining. The lines etched in his face spoke of control—only by a thread and a part of her wanted to shatter that control, to know what it was like to be thrown on the table and taken by a man whose hunger for her was insatiable.

She blushed and hastily looked down at the table as the waitress approached.

She cannot see you clearly. His voice brushed intimately against the walls of her mind, making her entire body tingle with awareness. She wanted to be out of the inn and into his bed. She could barely breathe anymore with desire swamping her.

The waitress placed the bowl of vegetable soup in front of her and left without speaking. Nicolas kept possession of her hand. Lara dipped the spoon in the bowl, took it out and then began making little waves with it.

"Are you afraid of me?"

Her gaze jumped to his. "Not of you. I've never had sex before. You seem very experienced."

A slow smile softened the edge of his mouth. "I had many centuries to learn technique and speculate what I would want to do with my partner, should I ever be so lucky to have one. Our males can be quite obsessed with the idea of sex, but as a general rule, it is not fulfilling without our lifemate. Perhaps that is a safeguard for our women as well as the other women around us. My sexual appetite is raging and if just anyone could assuage it, I am not certain how long I could stay in complete control. We are not human, Lara, and we may appear tame and civilized, but we are not."

He didn't look tame or civilized to her. He looked powerful and dangerous and far too sexy for a woman as inexperienced as she was. She wanted him with every fiber of her being.

"You have to eat so we can get out of here," he reminded.

If that was what it took, she was willing. She scooped a little of the broth into the spoon and stared down at the bowl of soup. Her stomach lurched unexpectedly. "I don't think I'm as hungry as I thought I was."

Nicolas frowned. He had given one blood exchange as well as giving her blood twice. She was already Carpathian enough that regular food wouldn't sit well with her, but she needed nourishment. She pushed the contents of the bowl aimlessly around. He very gently took it from her hand and held the broth to her mouth.

Lara shook her head. "I've always had a little trouble eating food. Usually soup is one thing I can get down as long as it is only vegetable, but the smell of it is making my stomach rebel. I honestly don't think I can."

Nicolas reached with his free hand to curl his palm beneath the fall of silky hair to caress the nape of her neck. "You have to eat, Lara. You've had one complete blood exchange and taken my blood twice. You cannot go without sustenance. I'll help you hold it down."

It was the last thing she wanted to do, but he was looking at her with his incredible eyes and she found herself nodding. In her heightened state of awareness, the slide of his mind against hers was almost sexual, a caress, much like the brushing of his fingers against her skin. Her breathing turned ragged. There were so many erotic fantasies playing through his mind, and each one was more shocking than the last.

He certainly wanted to sweep the items off the table and lay her across it, peeling back her dress one inch at a time until he could see and touch her hot satin skin. Lara touched the tip of her tongue to her lips, fighting for breath when her lungs refused to work. His gaze held hers captive, never blinking, never looking away, until she felt consumed by him.

I think that will do. I cannot wait another moment. Can you walk out of here?

She blinked and looked down at the empty soup bowl. While she'd been examining the images in his mind, he'd been feeding her, but as she had looked and fantasized herself, her rising desire had obviously affected him. She smiled at him and this time a good deal of the shyness was gone.

I can make it to the door if you can.

He held out his hand. Lara placed hers in it. The black eyes held hers a heartbeat longer. *The moment I get you out of here, I'm stripping every last bit of clothing off of you. I want to feel you and see you, not just in my imagination, but the real thing.*

There was a warning and a promise in his tone. He was back to being the dangerous predator and this time, she was his prey. The knowledge should have frightened her, but instead, her entire body reacted with heated anticipation. Along with that shiver of anticipation that crept down her spine, she felt the flush of arousal sweep through her body at the drawling caress in his voice.

He yanked open the door and they stepped out into the night, his hand on the small of her back, just at the base of her spine. His long fingers caressed the curve of her bottom under the thin material of the dress he'd fashioned for her. The fabric was heavy and burning against her sensitive skin. They hurried down the stairs into the street, where snowflakes drifted down to melt against their hot bodies.

Nicolas didn't wait, impatient to touch her. He swept her up into his arms, cradled her against his chest, barely remembering to mask their presence when he took two running steps and leapt into the sky.

Lara looked up at his face, almost savagely beautiful, the lines so sensual, the dark eyes hooded and possessive. His arms were enormously strong, his body hot and hard. He buried his face against her neck as if he couldn't wait, not even until they were safely in their underground lair. His teeth scraped over her skin, his lips feathered back and forth, his tongue took small tastes that drove her crazy with every touch.

His breathing roughened, his black eyes filled with torment and shadow as he found her mouth with his. He kissed her like a man starved for more—as if she had become a craving he couldn't resist and he was desperate to have her. Their tongues danced, long, open-mouthed kisses she drowned in. The hot, sweet taste of him was addicting and Lara wrapped her arms around his neck, tunneling her fingers in his thick mane of hair.

The night sparkled. Above, the moon gleamed silver through the fluff of the gray clouds. Snowflakes drifted down, tiny white diamonds that floated lazily to the ground below. Beneath them was a white carpet of dazzling crystals spread across the meadows and draped over the tall trees. Even the shadows had a silvery shine to them.

Lara turned her face up to the night. She'd always felt so out of place unless she was caving, hiding by day so the sunlight couldn't touch her skin, and trying to keep others from noticing. Now, here in the mountains, with night closing her in, she felt truly alive for the first time. She turned her face up again for another kiss, melting against Nicolas, into him, burrowing as close as she could get.

Hayfields and crystallized bogs passed below as he swept her away, floating through the clouds, the flakes brushing her hair and skin, and she turned her face up to try to catch the snow on her tongue. She laughed softly, happy and excited. Her body pulsed with heat from the slow, sultry teasing of his teeth and tongue driving her mad with desire.

I love this feeling. And she did. She wasn't in the least bit afraid when he set her down on the firm rock at the entrance to his lair.

Nicolas could barely breathe with wanting her. He stripped away her long, flowing dress before they were inside the cave, unable to wait one moment longer to be skin to skin. She stood at the entrance with the snow falling softly all around her, the moon sliding in and out of the gray clouds to illuminate the wealth of satin skin.

His lungs burned for air. A fire raged in his belly and spread to his groin. "Lift your arms over your head and turn around," he instructed, his voice roughening.

Lara felt the power of being not only a lifemate, but a woman, in that moment. She stretched her arms above her head, a slow, graceful movement that lifted her breasts. She heard him growl, a deep rumbling that only added to the slick heat gathering between her legs. Her hair spilled around her face and flowed down her back, a silky, sensual slide that added to the gathering heat.

His gaze burned over her, making the ache in her body grow with each passing second. She began a slow turn, just a little self-conscious, watching the tension in his face, watching as each muscle tensed, grew taut. He stepped toward her and her mouth went dry.

"You are so beautiful, Lara."

He made her feel beautiful whether she was or not. He made her feel sexy, the only woman alive that could make him burn. He crowded her close to the cave entrance, his body aggressive. Her hands came up to press against his chest. He caught both wrists and slid her palms down the heavy muscles of his chest. As he did so, his clothing was gone, leaving behind hard, hot skin. Beneath her palms, his stomach muscles tightened and knotted in anticipation.

Her breath caught in her throat. She gasped at the heat pouring from him. Her gaze slid down his taut body.

"Look at me."

At the rough command, her gaze jumped back to his eyes. The dark arousal caught and held her there as he continued to press her palms down his body to his heavy, aching erection. Her lungs burned as he closed her fingers around the thick, hard shaft, pulsing with life, with hunger, with such need. The naked lust blazing in the dark depths of his eyes nearly had her body rippling with shock. She felt her deep response, slick hot heat, her inner muscles contracting and spasming, desperate for him.

"Do you know what I want from you?"

She shook her head, unable to look away from the demand in his eyes.

"Complete surrender, *fél ku kuuluaak sívam belső*. Beloved, nothing less. I want everything you are. That is who I am."

She had known all along he would want that. Her fingers stroked caresses along the thick shaft. He felt like velvet-encased steel, so hard, jerking and pulsing compulsively beneath her exploration. She traced each beloved line with the tips of her fingers, wanting so many things.

"Taking my blood is a part of Carpathian lovemaking."

He refused to release her from his black, demanding gaze. "There can be no compromise here, Lara. Not for either one of us. You have to trust me with your body or we can wait until you do."

She was suddenly afraid. She shivered with need, her body desperate for release, her mind craving him, wanting the experiences his hot gaze promised. He would accept nothing less than total surrender, putting herself into his hands and trusting that he wouldn't do anything she couldn't cope with. His mind was left open to hers, allowing her to see every erotic image, everything he wanted from her. Color swept up her neck, into her face, but she didn't look away. She wanted whatever he would give her, but along with the hot kisses and his body possessing hers, she saw clearly how he planned to seduce her into accepting his taking of her blood.

"If I can't?"

He bent his head to hers, holding her gaze captive. "Then we will certainly enjoy ourselves along the way."

She didn't pull back, instead, she turned her face up to his. His mouth was hard and hot and demanding, sweeping her into a storm of desire so that she shuddered beneath his kisses. His lips moved over her face, tracing each detail, her high cheekbones, her smooth jaw, the small dimple in her chin and then took possession of her mouth again.

He lifted her into his arms again, never breaking the kiss. She wrapped her arms around his neck, pressing as close as she could get, rubbing her body along his, desperate to relieve the building pressure deep inside of her. She was so wet, so hot, so frantic to have him.

Nicolas took her through the tunnels fast, straight to the chamber where the large bed stood. As he lowered her to the mattress, he waved his hand toward two soft candles, wanting to see her face, to see the need there for him. She reached for him and he caught her hands and pinned them to the mattress.

"Do not move." It was a hiss of a command.

He bent over her, drinking in her body, sprawled across his bed, open for his exploration. He actually trembled, hot lust clawing at his stomach and pouring into his groin. He knelt on the bed, still locking her wrists to either side of her head. Very slowly he lowered his head, forcing himself to be patient, to slowly savor the texture of her skin.

He nibbled his way down her throat to the curve of her breast. She writhed beneath him, her hips bucking, a flush spreading across her body.

"I'm so sensitive."

He smiled as he flicked his tongue over her nipple. "You are supposed to be."

Lara gasped, unable to comprehend anything but the feel and need driving her. The sensation of his tongue and teeth rasping against her nipple sent electricity arcing to her belly and thighs, and sizzling deep within her feminine core.

He took her breast deep into his mouth, suckled strongly, teeth scraping with deliberate intent along her nipple. She cried out, arching her back, unable to remain still as he ordered. The combination of pain and pleasure sent shock waves rippling through her system. His mouth was relentless, driving her wild. He took his time, dividing his attention between her breasts, flicking his tongue fast and hard, then suddenly using slow, long licks as if savoring each stroke.

His fingers slid down her arms to caress the sides of her breasts before cupping the soft weight in his palms. His fingers tugged until she came off the bed with frantic little whimpers of mindless pleading.

She wasn't holding back at all. She left herself, mind, heart and body, open to him and it was humbling. She trusted him with her body, and her trust was a priceless, overwhelming gift. After everything he had done, she gave herself wholly into his keeping, trusting him to know what he could and couldn't do, trusting him to stretch her limits without going too far. More than anything, he wanted to be worthy of her faith in him.

His mouth moved over her skin, down her flat stomach to dip and play in her belly button. He felt a rush of desire for her so strong it shook him. He had always known that when he found his lifemate, he would want—no, need—to rule her until the dawn broke, yet never once had it occurred to him that he would feel the intensity of love. It shook him as nothing else could, the need to worship her body, show her with his body, without words, how he felt.

His need was no longer about the lust driving him so hard. It was no longer about sating his own appetite for her. He needed to love her with every touch of his hand. Every stroke of his tongue. Every thrust of his body. He wasn't a gentle man. He didn't have pretty words to tell her how wrong he'd been. He only had his body and the terrible love that shook him beyond anything he'd ever known.

Her skin was warm silk, so soft he wanted to burrow deep. She tasted like the night, clean and perfect and so damned beautiful it made his heart ache. He caught her thighs in his hands, pulling them apart, stopping for a moment just to drink her in.

Lara's face was flushed, head tossing side to side on the pillows, her breasts heaving, her hips bucking. She didn't try to hide her reaction to his touch and her stark need of him made him want her even more.

Lara looked at him, his expression almost savage as he lay between her legs. His black eyes glittered, even glowed a little. More than once she'd felt the scrape of his teeth over her skin—over every pulse point. Her heart had thundered in alarm, but he never broke the skin or took advantage of the frantic desperation building inside of her. Now he looked a conquistador, his midnight-black hair spilling around his face, lines etched deep, his sensual mouth set in firm, ruthless lines. He slowly bent his head and she stopped breathing.

His mouth clamped over her, tongue stabbing deep and she heard her own keening wail. He licked her like a tiger, almost an attack, not the gentle lapping of a kitten, but long, rasping strokes that stole her mind. He held her down when she tried to crawl off the mattress, black edges around the exploding stars in her mind. She felt the edge of his teeth nipping and scraping at the pounding beat of her pulse, so deep inside of her—and somehow fear added another dimension to her pleasure.

Lara shuddered, the firestorm in the center of her body building until it was out of control. She couldn't think. Couldn't breathe. Couldn't stop the pressure. She thrashed beneath his marauding mouth, the wicked tongue and teeth that drove her higher and higher. And then his finger slipped into her channel and her hips bucked wildly as every muscle tightened to the point of pain. His tongue fluttered against her most sensitive spot.

She cried out his name, her hands fisting in his hair, holding him to her as her body flew apart, the flames scorching her from the inside out, burning white-hot and spreading like a storm from her center to her breasts and down her thighs.

Before she could catch her breath, Nicolas knelt between her thighs, lifting her legs over his arms, the thick head of his erection pressed tightly against her entrance. He felt hard and hot, yet velvet encased, adding to the building inferno. Her breath caught in her lungs and she stared up at his face, carved deep with sensual lines as he began to invade her. He slid deeper, slow inch by slow inch, stretching her tight muscles, forcing his way through the stranglehold of hot slick walls, sending lightning whipping through her body.

Lara gasped when he halted, coming to the barrier of innocence.

"Breathe for me, *hän ku kuulua sívamet*. Take a breath and relax."

Keeper of my heart. The words in his native language were beautiful when he uttered them, soft and tender, turning her heart over. She forced her body to relax. Nicolas surged forward, the bite of pain increasing her sensitivity so that her nails bit deep into his shoulders as she tried to anchor herself.

He began to move, long hard strokes that sent flashes of heat spiraling over her body, searing her thighs and scorching her belly. Her muscles tightened more, clamping around him as he plunged even deeper, angling her body so the friction on her most sensitive spot was hot, demanding and never let up. She felt the pressure gathering and building until she was afraid she might lose her mind.

He picked up the pace, pistoning into her, the sound of flesh meeting flesh loud in the silence of the cave. Her breath came in gasps as the fire continued to build, stretching her beyond her ability to cope. She could only plead for release in between breathing raggedly. She was going to burn from the inside out, just go up in flames or die from sheer pleasure if he didn't stop.

She heard his heart thundering in her ears. Her mouth filled with the taste of him and her teeth lengthened, pressing against her lips. Before she could think, before she could fear her own reaction, he reared back, then began a harder rhythm, pounding into her, that drove everything but pleasure from her mind. She was burning alive, screaming, as her body nearly convulsed, clamping down on him to squeeze and milk.

He yelled hoarsely, emptying himself into her, leaning over her, his eyes glowing hot with flames, his teeth in evidence. He made no attempt to hide from her dazed, shocked stare. Aftershocks rocked her as he bent slowly to her neck. She couldn't move, couldn't breathe, even with her body still shuddering with pleasure. A part of her screamed inside, another part wanted to feel his teeth sink into her neck.

His lips feathered over her pulse. She felt the teasing scrape of his teeth, but he never penetrated her skin. He kissed his way up her neck to the corner of her mouth and when he smiled at her, his teeth had receded. Still buried deep, he moved and sent electricity arcing through her all over again.

"I can't move."

"You do not have to move. It is going to be a long, pleasurable night, *pã́lã́fertiilm*," he promised softly.

13

Lara stood at the wide entrance to the cave, listening to the soft melody coming from within. Women's voices. The faint sounds produced instant memories of her aunts singing to her when she was alone and distressed, deep in the maze of caves beneath the ice mountain. For a moment, she stopped to listen.

"I know this song. It's a lullaby," she said. "It sounds beautiful in the Carpathian language. I used to sing it for the children in the camps where I lived. When I realized no one understood the language, I switched to the English version. I was never certain exactly what the last line meant, but the melody and lyrics always comforted me, and also the children I sang to."

"The song is sung by mothers before the child is out of the womb," he explained. "While the mother is waiting until the night she can hold her child in her arms."

Nicolas sang to her in a melodious voice, one that sent touches of heat streaking along with the comfort. *Tumtesz o wäke ku pitasz belső. Hiszasz sívadet. Én olenam gæidnod. Sas csecsemõm, kuńasz. Rauho jone ted. Tumtesz o sívdobbanás ku olen lamt3ad belső. Gond-kumpadek ku kim te. Pesänak te, asti o jüti, kidüsz.*

She interpreted the lullaby. "Feel the strength you hold inside. Trust your heart, I'll be your guide. Hush my baby, close your eyes. Peace will come to you. Feel the rhythm deep inside. Waves of love that cover you, protect, until the night you rise." She looked at him. "What does that last line mean?"

"So many women were losing their babies," Nicolas said. "Women tell them that love will protect them until they are ready to be born, to come into our night."

"It's so beautiful."

Everything about the night seemed beautiful now. Nicolas had spent hour after hour making love to her, seemingly insatiable. They had taken a short break to enter the warmth of the mineral pool, only to have him take her there as well. He knew every inch of her body and the hot look he gave her made her blush, as if, with just a small encouragement, he might take her right there at the entrance to the women's cave.

"I don't really feel like I belong here, Nicolas." She twisted her fingers together. "I don't know anyone. Natalya isn't going to be here."

It wasn't that she was terribly shy, but gathering with the Carpathian women at such an emotional time, when she already felt raw and emotional, was a little daunting.

"Raven asked for all women to attend and she asks very little of our people."

"I don't think she meant me. She doesn't even know me."

"Everyone knows about you, Lara. This is a very small community and we share a common communication path. When she put out the call for all the women to join her, she definitely meant you as well. I would attend with you, but it is a woman's ceremony."

"Natalya's a woman," she said stubbornly, under her breath. "And she isn't coming."

Nicolas framed her face with both hands. "I know I am asking a lot of you, Lara, but this is an ancient ceremony and one small detail may help you remember more of what you saw in the ice cave. Our children rarely survive the womb, let alone outside. They cannot go to ground as they should where the parents can protect them. Our women cannot even provide food for them. We need to know why these things are happening and you might have valuable clues that will aid us. This could be the single most important time for our people."

She moistened her lips with the tip of her tongue. "I can't make the memories come back. When I look too hard, everything is just a blank slate."

"Protection for you," Nicolas said. "But your aunts were not hiding these things from our people. If that were so, they would have erased your memories, not preserved them."

"Nicolas?" A woman materialized quite close to them. "Is this Lara?" She smiled in welcome, her face unlined and serene, in spite of the strain she had to be under. Her hair was bright red and hung in one thick, elaborate braid down her back. "I'm Shea Dubrinsky, Lara, Jacques is my lifemate. We can't thank you enough for coming. Nicolas tells us that you may be able to give us a few more pieces to the puzzle to help us find our answers."

Lara took a deep breath, glanced at Nicolas and then back to Shea. "I can't just conjure up the memories, but I catch a glimpse now and then. If it helps, I'm more than happy to tell you about them."

"We do plan to enter the ice cave as early as tomorrow evening," Nicolas added. "If you can give us that extra time, by aiding Raven and Savannah to hold on a little longer, there is the possibility of finding out more clues."

Shea frowned. "I've been researching this problem for some time. We know at this point we're working against a combination of things, including toxicities in the soil. In order for the soil to rejuvenate and heal us, we absorb necessary minerals through our skin. Every area has different minerals and various levels of richness, but we're finding more and more toxins as well. Our species is tied to the earth and we can't survive without the soil. If Xavier introduced something, a compound, a parasite that over the centuries has slowly killed our species, if we find out what it is, I believe we have a chance to combat it."

Shea was trained as a doctor and a researcher before Jacques claimed her.

"I have a memory of Xavier when I was about seven or eight, just a glimpse of a woman who must have just lost her baby. There was soil in the room with her. Xavier was very pleased that she lost the child."

Small lines appeared along Shea's forehead as her brows drew together. "He has had several centuries to perfect his attacks."

"Or introduce something that took place over time," Nicolas suggested. "I have to take my leave." He bowed low in a gesture of respect toward Shea. "We have a warriors' council this night."

She made a face at him. "The all-important 'keep the women at home barefoot-and-pregnant,' council? Yes, I'd say you have decisions to make. Maybe I should stay home and forget all about my research, just leave it to Gregori and Gary. I do have a son to take care of."

Lara frowned. "I don't understand."

"Nicolas didn't tell you? The men are having a meeting tonight and discussing whether or not women should be allowed—*allowed*—to fight vampires, or whether we would do much better staying home having babies."

"I believe it would be a good idea to leave now," Nicolas said, and cupped Lara's face in his hands, bending to kiss her right in front of Shea.

Lara blushed, but she kissed him back, her eyes shining. Before she could protest or ask questions, he began to shift. He wasn't going to debate with Shea Dubrinsky over whether or not women should be out fighting vampires. It was going to be a heated enough discussion between the men. It was not a decision any of them would take lightly, but something had to be done to save their species. He sent Lara a wave of warmth and disappeared into the night.

Lara stared after him, not quite believing that he'd abandoned her to a group of strangers. Besides, she frowned after him, he'd taken the coward's way out and left before she could voice an opinion on the issue of men allowing or not allowing anything a woman did.

Of course I will listen to your opinion.

The intimacy of his voice made her blush all over again. *Don't leave me too long.*

I will return as quickly as possible.

She could hear the reassurance in his voice and it made her smile as she looked down the tunnel leading to the deeper chamber inside the cavern. "Are there many women here?"

"At the moment, we have about a dozen, so we're more than glad that you have joined us. There aren't that many of us here in the mountains. We've had to send delegates to the warriors' council to speak for us as well as report back to us. Unfortunately, the men may have a legitimate argument and if so, we'd all like to hear it so we can have a chance to agree or disagree for ourselves."

It was obvious to Lara, Shea was trying to keep an open mind, but the subject irritated her. According to Nicolas, she was a modern woman who had gone through medical school, had a reputation as a valued researcher and felt the men were moving the women backward instead of forward, but she was trying to be fair and wait to hear all the facts. Lara liked her.

Shea waved her hand toward the interior. "Let me introduce you to the others."

Lara followed her down the narrow, winding tunnel that

led deeper beneath the mountain. Like the caverns Nicolas occupied, this one was warm rather than part of the network of ice caves beneath the glacier, and as they descended into the depths, the warmth increased. Sconces lit the way, small flickering subdued lights that glowed rather than danced. The muted lights played across the crystal growths in tunnel walls. Varied with color and shape, the lights created a dizzying display, making the wall almost surreal. In the dreamlike state, she felt almost as if she was walking backward through time to the warmth and safety of the womb.

As she entered the main chamber where the women were gathering, the illusion became even stronger. Two women, Raven and Savannah, lay in the center where black soil, rich in minerals, covered their bodies. Around them, in a loose semicircle, women had gathered to sing the Carpathian lullaby softly, swaying back and forth as if rocking a baby.

Two other women, one tall and elegant and one thin, young and very fragile-looking, stood on the outer edges of the soil, hands lifted, both singing a soft, melodious rhythm as they moved their feet in an intricate pattern.

"Syndil and Skyler," Shea whispered. "They rejuvenate the earth itself. They're calling on the minerals and healing properties to come forth to aid us in saving our children. Both have been invaluable in restoring toxin-free soil to us. Skyler is working as Syndil's apprentice and already she's very good."

It was a beautiful sight, the two women performing an ancient ritual of cleansing the earth, and calling on Mother Nature to help save their children. Lara listened to the introductions, but all the while she was watching the ceremony, her heart swelled, and her mind followed every graceful sway of hands and feet. She knew the ceremony, in some part of her mind. The phrases were familiar to her, the rhythm and patterns, as if long before she was born she had been given the tools to cleanse the earth.

Her feet ached to join the two women, her hands fluttered, rising to trace a flowing arc in the air. She felt the pulse of the earth beneath her. Her heart began to change rhythm to match the song and the beat. Oh yes, the words were there, ancient and beautiful and filled with the power of women.

Oh, Mother Nature, we are your beloved daughters. Lara dipped low, bowing out of respect, her feet turning of their own accord to pick up the graceful spin Syndil and Skyler completed on two of the four corners surrounding Raven and Savannah. Instinctively, Lara took the third corner. *We dance to heal the earth. We sing to heal the earth. We join with you now. Our hearts and minds and spirits become one.*

The music was already there in her soul. But they needed a fourth. The other women danced and sang, their voices growing in strength, but they needed one more voice. They weren't strong enough. Lara looked to Syndil, a faint frown on her face. They needed to adjust their footing. "Do you feel it?"

A hush fell over the women. The warm cave pulsed with the suspension of power. Lara should have felt embarrassed to have all eyes on her. She had never done this before. She wasn't certain she was right, but something felt—off. She looked to Syndil. Power emanated from the woman, vibrated in the air around her. Her aura even pulsated.

Syndil frowned. "The dance is off balance, but there is little we can do about that." She glanced at Skyler. "What do you think?"

"It's working, but it's not exact." The teenager shrugged. "We can only do the best we can do. We need four and we have only the three of us."

Syndil nodded. "I adjust the dance and notes of the song

by the amount of toxins I feel through the soles of my feet. With this soil we have to be especially careful because we're preparing it for the babies."

Lara nodded, still frowning. She raised her hand to feel the power pulsating through the room. "Some of the weaves are off a bit. We need a fourth weaver."

"There is no one. The others can contribute to the power, but they can't produce the healing song of the earth."

"There is no other from your lineage?" she asked Syndil.

Syndil shook her head. "Not that I know of. We suspect Skyler is of the Dragonseeker line, but we don't know. She heard the earth screaming, so if she isn't, she, like me, is empathic toward the earth."

"She has Dragonseeker eyes," Lara agreed.

Skyler's eyes were too old in her young face. And Lara could see traces of Razvan there. This, then, was probably one of the children Xavier had forced Razvan's body to produce in order to feed off of her blood. Somehow, the girl had ended up with the Carpathian race. The thought was unsettling and for a moment she wanted the comfort of Nicolas's arms. Without thinking, she reached for him. At once he was there.

You have need of me?

She felt foolish. She wasn't about to lose a child, yet she was shivering because a teenage girl had the eyes of her father. *No. No. Everything is fine.*

You have only to touch my mind with yours, Lara. I am with you.

His reassurance made her feel safe and comforted and for the first time in her life she felt as if she belonged.

I'm fine. This time she said it with conviction. She spoke directly to Raven, meeting her troubled gaze squarely. "We need Natalya."

The women all looked at one another. "Natalya is a warrior. She says she cannot feel the earth," Shea said. "She doesn't have the sensitivity for it."

Lara's eyebrow shot up. "Really? Is that what she said?"

Shea and Raven exchanged a long look and then Raven frowned. "Mikhail told me she could not heal the earth in the way her family could. Is that not true?"

Lara pursed her lips. "Natalya pulses with power. I would be shocked if she could not."

"Call her in," Raven said.

"She's at the warriors' council, speaking for us," Shea reminded.

"Call her back," Raven said again, and this time it was a command. "If there is hope to save these children, then this is far more important than the discussion going on with the men. In the end, Mikhail will come to a decision on whether women will fight with their men or not and we will all abide by it."

No one was going to point out that the reason they needed Natalya at the meeting was to make certain their voices were heard. Raven rarely—if ever—pulled rank as Mikhail's wife, but there was no doubt she wanted Natalya *summoned*.

Raven's face was streaked with tears, and her anguish weighed heavily on the women. Raven had survived one loss, and now another child was slipping away. Beside her, Savannah was pale and drawn, closing her eyes, concentrating on holding her babies to her.

Both women could communicate with their unborn children, which made the loss all the more difficult to face. The babies were real, with personalities already developing.

"Call her now, Shea," Raven insisted.

Shea reached out to Razvan's twin.

"Why is Shea reluctant to call her back?" Lara whispered to Syndil.

"Natalya is different," Syndil answered. "She's the oldest surviving female Dragonseeker and as such, her blood is extremely powerful. Beyond that, she is a force to contend with in every other way and she walks her own path. I think having to hide from Xavier, she became a loner over the years. She's always pleasant and respectful, but she has a tendency to keep to herself. One rarely sees her without Vikirnoff."

Lara wasn't surprised that Natalya was a loner. Natalya exuded the air of a very confident woman, but she was Razvan's sister and the granddaughter of one of the most evil men ever born. She'd most likely spent her earlier years looking over her shoulder and afraid to trust anyone at all. Lara wasn't certain she could overcome her own traumatic childhood in order to commit fully to Nicolas. She could certainly understand her aunt's reticence.

Natalya strode in with her easy, casual grace, her blue-green eyes wide with questions. "Raven? You have need of me?"

Raven nodded. "Lara and Syndil feel you are the only one to aid us in this and I am—we are—*desperate* to save our children."

Natalya glanced around the cave and then to Lara. "I don't have any experience in healing rituals, but if you tell me what to do, I'll do my best."

Raven let out her breath. "Thank you, Natalya."

Savannah's long lashes lifted. Her eyes were swimming with tears. "My daughters thank you as well. They're trying to hold on, but my body is rejecting them." She wrapped both arms around her middle and rocked gently. "I tell them I want them to stay with me, but they feel my body attacking them."

Raven nodded. "I can't bear to lose another child."

The naked sorrow in her voice tore at Lara's heart. A tall, elegant woman with waist-length thick black hair immediately knelt between the two pregnant women, laying a hand on each of them.

"Francesca," Natalya supplied. "Lifemate to Gabriel, healer, and adopted mother to Skyler. She's an amazing woman. Now tell me what you want me to do."

Lara was happy to have her there. She didn't know any of the women, and looking at Skyler was like looking at herself as a young girl. A little lost. Very much alone. Traumatized. The teenager made her feel exposed. Natalya was clearly a puzzle to the women, although it was obvious they admired her.

"This is about healing the earth first," Syndil explained. "We've found the richest soil we could and have coaxed more minerals in it, but we have to heal it from all toxins."

"And parasites," Lara muttered under her breath.

Shea spun around. "What did you say?"

Lara wished she hadn't spoken, but they were all looking at her expectantly. She pressed her fingers against her suddenly throbbing temple. "I'm sorry. I was thinking out loud."

"No, I need to know what you said," Shea insisted.

Lara shrugged. She didn't want to talk about her childhood, or even think about it. "Xavier always experimented with parasites. He was never satisfied with them and always looked for ways to use them. He once said they had been more useful than any of his most gifted mages. I can't imagine that he would do anything without that being his first thought. He could create toxins for the soil, but what if he created a parasite that entered the host body and prevented pregnancy?"

Francesca stood up slowly, her eyes meeting Shea's over the tops of both Raven's and Savannah's heads.

"We checked for foreign microbes. We scan the bodies of the women all the time," Shea said. "Gregori would never miss something like that."

"Maybe," Lara said, "but Xavier is a master at working with microscopic amoebas. And when you're dancing to heal the earth, you're looking for modern-day toxins."

Shea frowned. "Do you have any idea how many toxins are found in a newborn's umbilical cord or in breast milk? The soil is what we live in, what rejuvenates us, yet our children can't go to ground with us or use the most perfect nutritious milk nature can provide. I could name every chemical we've found in the soil, most of which cause cancer and…"

Raven laid a restraining hand on her sister-kin's arm. "Lara, our water supply and our soil are fed from the purest of sources, the glacier. Even with that, Syndil has to heal the earth."

"I'm just saying maybe your glacier isn't the purest of sources. Xavier owns the ice caves. The caves run for miles beneath the mountains, an entire city really. His mountain is above your homes and his glacier feeds your water supply and seeps into your soil. You've discounted him because you think he's dead. Well, he's not. No one is going to kill him. And he hates the Carpathian people. If he could have, he would have found a way to introduce something into your systems to make your bodies reject a pregnancy."

Lara ran a hand through her hair. "I'm not saying it isn't modern toxins, I'm only saying you might want to look to your past for answers as well."

She couldn't believe she was voicing her opinion to the circle of women. Growing up outside the ice caves, she had stayed under the radar by remaining as quiet and meek as possible. She had learned that if she wanted to remain with a family or in a camp, she had to keep from being noticed—not too easy when her hair banded with color and her eyes changed as well. The gypsies she had been with had been kind to her, but they were superstitious and her strange appearance along with her psychic abilities often made her unwelcome.

"Don't be uncomfortable," Francesca encouraged. "We need as many new ideas as possible."

"Well, Xavier isn't just a possibility as far as I'm

concerned, he's done something to cause this. He might be spreading toxins to the land, and the water, but I would bet my life that he introduced something to Carpathian women that causes them to reject their children."

"We checked the women thoroughly," Francesca said. "And not everyone has the problem."

"Let's get this started again," Syndil said. "Raven and Savannah need rich soil to aid them in strengthening their bodies."

"Oh, my God!" Shea spun around, wide-eyed, her gaze meeting Francesca's. "We've checked the women, but men determine the sex of the child, both in human and in Carpathian. We didn't check the men. Our problems started with a disproportionate number of male children."

Francesca obviously tried to suppress her own excitement, opting for caution after so many disappointments. "Maybe. It's logical, but we have to continue to explore every avenue open to us."

Shea nodded her head several times, but squeezed Raven's hand. "We're going to help Syndil and the others make this the best soil possible for you and Savannah," she said. "And then I'm going to my laboratory and figure this out. All you have to do is hold on a little longer."

Raven nodded, but there were white lines around her mouth and desperation in her eyes. Lara had to look away from the open grief on her face.

Some of the other women must have seen Raven's face. They once again formed their loose semicircle. A fire in the corner held a large pot and Francesca put several large stones of various composition into the water along with bunches of the small blue flowers and the bitterroot mandragora. While she added other herbs and ingredients, several other women lit aromatic candles. At once the scents of lavender and jasmine filled the air. The women began to sing the Carpathian lullaby.

Lara found herself joining them, lifting her voice,

feeling the overwhelming sense of love for the unborn children, calling to them to stay in the womb, safe and protected, waiting until the moment they were born and could be held in loving arms.

Power surged in the room and it held a subtle difference. Feminine energy was every bit as potent as male, but it held roots of nurturing and compassion. Part mage as she was, Lara was very sensitive to the differences, sorting through individual threads and finding that the layers being woven around Raven and Savannah held genuine love and absolute harmony. The women had come together with one purpose—to save the babies—and no matter how each was different, from different backgrounds, their minds and hearts held the exact same objective and intent.

The strength of the combined women was amazing. She felt bolstered by it and encouraged not just to be part of the amazing sisterhood, but to feel balanced and confident in herself and the others as a whole.

Lara looked around the cavern at all the women, drinking in the sight, soaking in the feeling of unity. Power lived in each of them, as it did in all living things, and they gathered that positive energy and used it for the best of all purposes—saving lives.

She added her voice, a soft melodious plea, a soothing comfort to the unborn children. The women connected, so that they could feel each other, close in their minds, and they also felt Raven and Savannah, and through them, the children.

Savannah's two daughters were nestled close, listening intently and trying to ignore the spasms that occasionally clamped down on them. Raven's child was a boy. Her body was desperately trying to abort, laboring hard to rid itself of the intruder. The boy was in great distress, torn between fighting to stay with his mother, and gaining peace by leaving. Raven crooned softly to him, rocking gently, her empty arms folded over him as if she was cradling him.

Syndil signaled to Skyler to take her position at the corner of the immense bed of soil prepared for the two pregnant women. Natalya and Lara took the lower corners. A hush fell over the cave until the only sound heard was Raven's labored breathing.

Syndil's arms rose into the air and the other three women followed suit. Her feet began a pattern of dancing, her body swaying gracefully as her hands flowed in elegant lines. Skyler waited several heartbeats, humming the melody in perfect tune with Syndil until her feet took up the rhythm and she started the first line of the chant two lines behind Syndil. Lara took her cue from Skyler, waiting instinctively until her feet and hands, of their own volition, began to move. She felt the song of healing rising from inside to burst out. The air shimmered with power. And then Natalya joined them.

Their voices rose in song and they danced an intricate pattern to the sound of their bare feet patting the dirt as if drawing music from the very center of the earth. Lara felt the song, felt the dance, through the soles of her feet. She knew each step before she took it, each graceful movement of her hand and sway of her body before she made it. The song was loud in her mind, in perfect harmony with the other three dancers, perfectly tuned to the notes of the earth itself.

Oh, Mother Nature, we are your beloved daughters. We dance to heal the earth. We sing to heal the earth. We join with you now. Our hearts and minds and spirits become one.

As she sang the song, this time it was right, the women merging into one unit with the earth, in accord with the sky above them and the hot core beneath them.

Oh, Mother Nature, we are your beloved daughters. We pay homage to our mother and call upon the North… Syndil bowed low and swept into a circle. *South.* Skyler repeated the move in perfect synchronization with Syndil.

East. Lara dipped low, a sign of respect, spinning with the other two women as Natalya went next. *West.* All four women completed the fourth bow and turned at the exact same moment. *Above and below and within as well.*

Power burst through the chamber, alive now, visible threads linking all of the women in the room, drawing on their energy.

Our love of the land heals that which is in need. We join with you now, earth to earth. The cycle of life is complete.

The soil warmed beneath their feet. Raven and Savannah gasped as the wave of heat washed over them. The color of the soil darkened even more into a rich, fertile black, sparkling with minerals.

Lara felt the joy of the earth through the soles of her bare feet, moving up through her legs to infuse her body with strength and happiness. As part of a cosmic whole she was one with the women, one with the universe and had a complete feeling of confidence and accord. For that one moment in time, she had no fears, no vulnerabilities, was part of a greater whole. She was flooded with almost a euphoric feeling of well-being, transcended by the energy and peace surrounding her.

The dancers stopped swaying and the women buried their hands in the richness of the fertile soil, far more valuable to them than the richest gold mine. They all should have been drained and weary, but the soil infused them with energy.

Syndil's face reflected the joy Lara was feeling, her eyes shining with wonder.

"This is what our soil should be for our women," Syndil said. "And with four of us, we can do so much now."

"I feel a difference already," Savannah said, relieved. "My cramps are far less."

Raven bit her lip and shook her head. "It isn't helping me. The contractions are getting stronger." Despair was in her voice.

Lara, one with the other women, reached to connect with the child. Fear swamped her mind, pain followed. She had the sensation of being torn from her safe haven. She choked back a ragged cry. The little boy was conscious of what was happening to him and he kept reaching out to his mother.

Raven tried to shield him from the pain and the continual battering on his tiny body. More than the physical assault against him, Lara felt the subtle flow of something else. She frowned, glanced at Natalya and then the others to see if they caught it as well. They were all caught in the same fear and grief of losing the child.

Lara touched her tongue to her suddenly dry lips, reaching instinctively for Nicolas. At once he was there, his warmth surrounding her, his strength giving her confidence. Steadied, she took a breath and let it out, trying to follow the thread of dark influence working against both child and mother. Before she could find the source, the child slipped farther away.

Raven began to cry, deep wrenching sobs that tore at Lara's heart. "I can't lose another child. He's too tiny to send into the next life without a mother. I have to go with him."

A collective gasp went up and the women visibly paled.

"You cannot," Shea stated. "Absolutely not."

"Mother," Savannah protested.

"Raven," Francesca's voice was the sound of calm. "If you choose to follow your son, Mikhail will follow you into the next world. Our people need both of you. You are distraught and not thinking straight."

Raven continued to weep brokenly. Shea sank down into the soil beside her, wrapping her arms around her while Savannah clasped her hand.

"I don't understand what that means, that Mikhail will follow her," Lara whispered to Natalya.

"Lifemates cannot exist without one another. If Raven

chooses the next life with her child, Mikhail will have no choice but to follow, or he will turn vampire. This cannot be a choice for Raven, especially with Mikhail. He is our leader. Unless Savannah could take his place, our enemies have won and our species will be extinct."

Lara went very still, fingers of fear trickling down her spine. Nicolas could have turned vampire. She had left the world by her own choice, never fully understanding the dire consequences to him or to the people around him. He had never said a word to her, not one word of recrimination. Nicolas was an experienced hunter. Had he turned, he would have killed many before he was destroyed.

She scooped more of the rich soil into her fists as she looked at Raven's tear-streaked face. "You cannot take the chance with your lifemate's life." As she had done. Selfishly, without thought of the consequences to anyone else.

Looking around the chamber at the women gathered together to heal the earth and to save the lives of three children, she realized that each person was valuable in their own way, that each contributed to the greater good. She was part of the circle of life just as Nicolas was, just as Raven and the unborn children were. Each of them was special and important and had a contribution to make. Maybe none of them knew what it was, but they had to revere life—fight for it—count each individual as important.

"Raven, you're needed here by so many," she murmured aloud, understanding for the first time that individuals made up the whole. "We would all be diminished by your passing."

"I need you," Savannah said, gripping her mother's arm. "I need you with me. I'm your daughter. If you only have me, aren't I worth staying here for?" She looked panic-stricken, very white in contrast to the black soil. "Mom, you can't leave me."

"I know. I know." Raven put her arms around her daughter. "I just can't bear losing another child. He's so tiny and he wants to live. He's so far away."

Francesca caught her arms, gave her a little shake. "Raven, look at me." She waited until Raven focused on her. "You're panicking. You have to be calm so he can stay calm. You have to believe we can save him so he'll believe it."

"It hurts him and he's in shock," Raven protested.

"I know, honey. And you're feeling his pain and his fear and it's amplifying your own, but that won't help him. We can. All of us. Look around you. We're all here with you. We'll help."

Savannah nodded her head. "I'll help, too, and so will the twins."

Lara reached again for the thread. "There is a dark art at work here. I feel it when I connect with you and the child. You're being influenced to give up and so is your son. You have to fight back, Raven. Don't let Xavier have this child. Don't let him take you and the boy. Buy me some time."

Francesca and Shea whipped their heads around to stare at her in shock. "Are you certain?" Francesca demanded. "Really certain?"

"It's subtle but it's there. Believe me, I can recognize Xavier's influence anywhere, no matter how light his touch is."

"I need to feel what you're feeling," Francesca said. "Natalya? Do you feel it?"

Natalya went very still. She nodded slowly. "Yes, she's right. And the same influence is working in Savannah as well. Not as strong yet, because the twins are merging to bolster their strength, but the weave of dark art is attacking them as well. They won't be able to hold out against it if it continues, at least not until they're ready to be born."

Savannah placed both arms protectively around her stomach. "What can we do?"

"We have to destroy whatever is attacking them," Francesca said.

"Should I call Gregori back?"

"And Mikhail?" Raven's voice wavered.

Lara frowned. "We can't take the chance of it retreating once it feels the threat of a male. Carpathian men are the protectors and guardians. It doesn't perceive us as a threat."

"Can you follow it?" Natalya asked. "Because if you can give me a target, I can destroy it." She spoke with absolute confidence.

"I can follow it," Lara said.

"Raven?" Francesca said. "This is your call. Yours and Savannah's. If you believe Mikhail and Gregori should be called back to try to deal with this attempt to murder your children, then we'll summon them immediately."

Raven and Savannah exchanged a long look. Silence settled into the cavern. The water in the huge pot continued to boil and the soothing scents of lavender and jasmine filled the air. Raven looked around at the women who waited, the women who had all come for one purpose—to save their children.

Raven lifted her chin, leaned over and kissed her daughter and met Lara's blue-green gaze. "Find this thing and let's destroy it."

14

The hum of the crystals greeted Nicolas as he entered the deep caverns. The formations of the giant crystals never failed to astonish and impress him. Only nature could have provided such a wealth of beauty formed with rich minerals. Gypsum, not uncommon in many areas, was not as well known in the Carpathian Mountains. A thousand feet below the earth, with the hot magma burning even farther below it, the soft limestone bed had been cut through by the wash of hydrothermal liquid bubbling up, breaking through from the magma chambers below and filling the chambers before draining away, leaving behind a thick forest of selenite, some over seventy feet in height and a good seven feet in diameter.

Nicolas had seen the giant redwood forests in the States and he had found the trees impressive and grandiose, but not even they could compare to the magnificent forest of crystals. He knew the gypsum columns were very rare throughout the world as they were so deep beneath the earth, steeped in heat and bathed in one hundred percent humidity, which made the underground grottoes difficult for even the most expert of cavers to discover, but the Carpathians thrived in the underground environment.

He looked around the labyrinth of chambers, one leading to the next, at the shape and colors of the enormous crystals, and felt awed. He stopped a moment to admire the beauty and soak it in, wishing Lara was with him to share the moment. He felt at peace, as if he might be in the greatest cathedral, as if this place was a gift from the heavens for his species alone. No other species could withstand the high temperatures and humidity for any length of time without being cooked, yet his people thrived here. Standing at the foot of a giant crystal column, he felt very close to any deity that might be looking out for him.

As he descended deeper into the inner chambers, the vibrations increased, tuning to his body so that he felt power ripple through him. As he moved through the separate chambers to get to the warriors' council room, the walls, heavy with crystals, appeared to undulate, a slow rhythmic wave like the gentle ebb and flow of the tide. The continual movement enhanced the feeling of being one with the earth, another tie to the planet itself and the mountains so rich in everything the Carpathian people needed.

At least for the first few centuries, the mountains had provided for them, but now he suspected Xavier had somehow managed to change that. He hoped to address that suspicion and give credence to his need to re-enter the high mage's black arts labyrinth of caves. The network ran miles beneath the mountains, spread out like a village. There was no way of knowing if any of it was still occupied. Xavier had left powerful safeguards that were death traps.

He and Vikirnoff intended to find another way into the chambers of the dark mage after the council meeting. The entrance they had been using was closed to them, and the parasite venom in the guardian's teeth was a powerful dissuading argument for trying to go through a door primed to kill.

Many of the Carpathian males had already gathered and he hailed them, using the more formal forearm-to-forearm greeting out of respect. With his emotions so new, the camaraderie he felt was somewhat overwhelming. He had always been aloof. For the most part, other than his brothers, very solitary. Within the confines of the large warriors' chamber, he felt the strength of the Carpathian people, the wisdom of the ancients and especially the connection they all had through their prince.

He realized, once inside the deep chamber, that an air of sobriety ran through the men—and the three women waiting there. He raised an eyebrow as he greeted Vikirnoff.

"Raven is having more trouble. Gregori has called most of the women and want them to do their woman magic, as we all referred to it in ancient times. He has no idea what is wrong, but hopes Syndil and the others can stop her from miscarrying."

"And Savannah?"

"Gregori has not allowed her to get up other than to attend to Raven. He is very grim, so I fear the odds of her keeping the babies are not good either."

Nicolas glanced at the three women present in the warriors' chamber: Natalya, Jaxon and Destiny. "Shouldn't they be with Raven?"

"The women are aware we are raising the issue of female fighters and have formally asked the three of them to speak on behalf of the others."

Nicolas shook his head. "We could have a fight on our hands."

Vikirnoff shrugged. "In the end, the prince will have to make a decision on the issue. Natalya has hunted the vampire and has been independent for a long time. Destiny has hunted her entire life. I am not even certain she could put it down. She was enslaved by a vampire and suffered greatly at his hands."

"I am well aware of the arguments," Nicolas said.

"And I have discovered it is not so easy to say no when your lifemate is insistent on doing something dangerous. I have strong reservations against taking Lara back to Xavier's cave, but she is probably the one who will be able to unravel the safeguards. She will recognize clues we might miss, and the journey may open her memories even more—memories we may need to aid us in solving the problems our women face."

"I had not considered those things," Vikirnoff said. "In truth, I had decided we should just go in tonight if we find a suitable entrance, and leave the women behind."

"Your woman would not follow you?"

"Of course she would think to follow me if she knew." Vikirnoff sent Natalya a look of utter devotion. "She does not know the meaning of 'quit.' On the other hand, I have more experience and, if necessary, could throw her off for a few hours in order to do the necessary exploring. She would be angry with me later, but I would much rather have her safe."

"And if you tell her to stop hunting?"

"If Natalya decides it is the right thing to do to stop hunting the vampire, she will stop, but that is the only way. I could dictate to her until the end of days, but she goes her own way and I am proud of her for doing so."

"You are not going to be much of a help," Nicolas pointed out.

Vikirnoff frowned. "I've always had a quick learning curve and in dealing with women, I've found it is much easier avoiding a confrontation."

"We need to have Mikhail make a ruling on this issue."

"I will add my voice to yours and Gregori's. I believe if we do not act soon, it will be too late. We must have more hope for our males. And we have to find a way to produce more children as well as search the world over for lifemates. The only real hope we have left to us is for our women to produce more children."

Dayan of the Dark Troubadours strode up, obviously overhearing what Vikirnoff said. "Perhaps we should take a page from our enemy's book and open a psychic center where we can interview women without them being aware we are doing so."

Gregori moved through the giant crystal forest, Mikhail at his side. Both men looked strained and tired. A hush fell across the council hall.

"Any news?" Lucian asked his younger brother.

Gregori shoved a hand through his thick hair, the gesture weary. "There is little we can do now. I am holding the twins to their mother. They want to live. That is something."

"And Raven?" Lucian prompted.

Mikhail shook his head. "She is trying to hold on. Jacques and I are both holding the baby to her, but they are getting weaker. Soon I will have no choice but to allow the child to slip away. I dare not risk Raven. She says no, but I cannot take chances with her life."

"If we can aid you in any way," Lucian offered, "we are more than willing."

Mikhail nodded. "The women gather now. There is much magic in the old ways. Syndil is providing the richest soil and Shea has come up with a strengthening drink to aid their bodies in gaining nutrients they seem to be lacking."

"There is some reason to believe that Xavier has a hand in this," Nicolas said, raising his voice so all could hear. He related the small cracking open of the door to Lara's memory. "We hope she will remember more when we go to the ice cave. Perhaps there is a piece of the puzzle that we can find in time to help."

"Xavier's lair is dangerous," Lucian said. "If he is alive, he would not have abandoned it completely. He had too many of his secrets stored there." He looked at his brother. "As a healer, Gregori, what kinds of things could he have done, centuries ago, that would cause our women to have these problems?"

"The fact that the problems changed over the years leads me to believe that whatever Lara saw could be real. First we noticed the lack of female babies," Gregori noted. "The precedence occurred over a long period of time. Because our women as a rule only give birth every fifty or so years, no one noticed that the male count was rising as the female count dropped."

"His first attempt?" Lucian asked.

"Perhaps," Mikhail mused. "We would have to talk to Shea about the way he could have influenced the sex of the children, but many of our people were attending his school. In those days, Xavier was a trusted friend. He set up the safeguards for us, weaving strands of magic with natural energy to protect the places we rested. No one ever guessed his jealousy of our longevity would lead him to commit the atrocities that he has over the centuries."

Gregori shrugged broad shoulders. "His jealousy has led him down the path of madness."

"He is entirely evil now," Nicolas declared, "if he wasn't already before."

Natalya stood suddenly, touching her lifemate's arm with gentle fingers. "I'm sorry, but Raven has summoned me. I must go to her."

Mikhail's face was drawn and tired as he looked at her. "I appreciate whatever you can do to help us, Natalya." He pressed his fingers to his temples. "She has asked that I do not interfere with what they are doing."

Gregori's face was pale as well. "They want Natalya right away."

Natalya nodded. "Yes, they are calling for me and of course I'll go. Whatever it takes, all of us are behind you."

Vikirnoff brushed a kiss across the top of her head and squeezed her hand as she took her leave. "Natalya isn't always comfortable within a group."

"No one is comfortable right now," Mikhail said. "This is a heartbreaking situation for everyone. If Raven and

Savannah cannot keep these children, do you think any of the women who are now pregnant will feel as if they have the chance to carry? And the ones who are not, do you think they will chance the heartache?"

"They will not have a choice, Mikhail, if our species is to survive," Lucian pointed out. "All of us feel the pain of the loss of our children, but we cannot give up or give in to that heartache."

Mikhail's eyebrow shot up. "I did not realize you and your lifemate had suffered the loss of a child, Lucian."

"All losses diminish us as a whole."

"Words give little comfort when one suffers the loss of a child who is not only the best part of you but part of your beloved lifemate as well," Mikhail agreed, "but we talk with our child. We encourage him, love him, suffer the pain when he is hurt because Raven's body is rejecting him. He is as real to us as if we were able to hold him in our arms. Raven has lost a son once already. Now there is another and she is losing him to an enemy we cannot see or fight. Each rising he slips further from us, inch by slow inch, and we are helpless to save him. Do you think I want this for my lifemate? Or for yours?"

There was a small silence. Gregori stirred. "We are asking that everyone weigh in with these matters because if we do not have answers soon, our species will not recover."

"You are a healer, Gregori," Destiny said. "Do you think our women should continue to try to have children when we have been unable to resolve these problems? Wouldn't it be better to wait until we know what's wrong before we subject our hearts, minds and bodies to such trauma?"

"Our problem is very simple, Destiny," Gregori answered. "If we do not have children, we die out. Every hour we wait to have female children, we lose more of our males. Yes, it is a tragedy and is a terrible thing that our women must risk losing a child, but our men are without hope. No one can continue without hope."

"It seems a useless sacrifice to get pregnant knowing the child will die, just to give false hope to a male. In the end, he has nothing anyway," Jaxon pointed out. "If we cannot safely have children, maybe the solution is to look in another direction. Why not put together a database of female psychics as Dayan mentioned? We could find a way to check them out, record their voices, have our males listen and see if there is a possibility that they can find their lifemates that way."

Destiny nodded. "We're not utilizing modern technologies for our searches."

"If you create a database, our enemies will have their targets laid out before them like a feast," Lucian objected. "Do you think the moment word got out, as it would, that we have stored names and locations of potential lifemates our enemies would not move on that as fast as they could?"

Nicolas frowned. "There has to be a way to protect the database. It does not sound like a bad idea."

"Our enemy thought of it before us," Destiny said. "They have a psychic research center called the 'Morrison Center' in the United States. I'm betting they've established them everywhere. The women go to the center, are tested and then they are targets for murder. The database already exists."

Several of the men without lifemates exchanged long looks of complete understanding. One stepped forward. Nicolas had seen the man once, years earlier, but only when he had passed through the Amazon forest chasing a vampire. Like most males without emotion or color, he had been solitary and rather curt when they had met. His name was André. Nicolas had tracked him and found evidence that the man had been wounded in the ensuing battle, but he was long gone from De La Cruz territory.

André gave a stiff bow toward the two women before

addressing the others. He stood tall and straight, his face a chiseled mask, his eyes hollow. "If there is a database already of potential lifemates, I say we take it over. We have all accumulated wealth through the years, we can buy them out legally, or hack into their system, or just walk in and take over those running the place by using mind control. Once we have control, we turn the site into a fortress."

"It is a calculated risk," Lucian said. "The more we expose ourselves, the chances of discovery are greater. The world of computers and modern technology—with cameras on every cell phone and nearly every public place one goes outside of these mountains—raises the danger to all of us."

"I am more than willing to take that chance if it increases the odds that even one of us will find a lifemate. We cannot afford to wait to give our protection to these women," André declared.

There was a note in his voice that told Nicolas he was asking permission and most likely would go after the database whether it was okayed or not. Judging from the looks on the other males without lifemates, André would have a lot of help.

Gregori started to speak but Mikhail forestalled him by moving into the center of the circle. He looked around the chamber filled with many single males, men who had given their lives to sustaining a dying species.

"This opportunity is far too important to pass up, whatever the risk. In any case, if these women are in danger whether they are true lifemates or not, they need our protection. I will meet with you next rising to discuss this issue and come up with a plan of action."

André again gave a small bow toward the women and slipped toward the back of the chamber where he obviously was more comfortable and less exposed.

Mikhail, many of our males are desperate. They could

abuse this situation, turning into stalkers of these women if we are not careful. This could become a huge problem, Gregori cautioned.

I am well aware of that. But it is a sound idea and one, once voiced, that cannot be taken back. These men are indeed desperate and they will go to whatever lengths it takes to acquire this list of potential lifemates. If we control the list, we can protect the women.

So be it.

"Once this information is acquired, however we do it, we have to make certain the guardian will stand against any and all who would force them to give it up." Mikhail took a careful look around the chamber to ensure everyone understood him. "These women are targeted for murder. We do not want to expose them to any more risk than they already are under."

"It's all part of the master plan to destroy our species," Nicolas said. "If our enemies can successfully eliminate our women and children, and all potential lifemates, all hope is lost and a good portion of our males will join their ranks."

"Do we pull back and protect ourselves by calling everyone back to the Carpathian Mountains?" Gregori asked. "We have a better chance of protecting our own by gathering together. Our enemies' numbers have increased and they are now running in packs." He indicated Nicolas. "We've had disturbing news all of you should hear, including reports of the vampires trying to open the shadow world so their dead can join their ranks against us."

Nicolas revealed the plot his brother Manolito had uncovered when he had awakened still partially in the shadow world after the attack on Shea. "The Malinov brothers have made an alliance with Xavier. We do not know if Razvan is part of their conspiracy or if he is a prisoner at this point. With the parasites Xavier developed, the vampires appear to recognize one another and yet can hide their presence from us. We can no longer trust that we can so easily detect an enemy."

Gregori nodded. "The enemy has corrupted many of the jaguar-males. We'll be asking Zacarias and his brothers to act as emissaries and try to get those not already lost to join with us."

The silence in the room was broken only by the humming crystals. The news wasn't good. Mikhail eventually stood. "Many of you may have heard that Manolito has found his lifemate. She is lycanthrope. That species has always gone their own way, but they wield a lot of power and would make a tremendous ally. We need to locate them and send someone to convince them to join with us."

There was a brief murmur of conversation as the men discussed the possibility of finding the long-absent lycanthrope species.

"And humans?" Jaxon asked.

There was a long silence. Mikhail sighed. "This has been a long-running debate. Most think it is still not the time for acceptance."

"Perhaps expand our trusted circle. Cullen, Gary and Jubal certainly have proven to be more than reliable," Jacques said, naming three of their human friends. "Without Gary we wouldn't be nearly as far along in our research as we are. He works hard and keeps our hours. He also watches over the children who cannot go to ground. Mikhail has several friends in the village who have proven trustworthy time and again."

"And have we considered aligning ourselves with the community of mages? Not all of them followed Xavier, and most were abused and tortured under his rule," Nicolas added.

Immediately, at the suggestion, heated discussions broke out. Mikhail said nothing, simply let the men discuss the possibility of asking aid of other communities—ones

they had protected but had been careful not to reveal themselves to.

Mikhail sat quietly, his senses flaring out to bridge
with the power emanating from the forest of crystals. Each
geode hummed a slightly different note and as he listened,
turning his mind to the notes, he heard the quiet voices
of the ancient warriors who had gone before. Each told of
the old days when all the species existed in harmony. The
reclusive lycanthrope, as powerful as the Carpathians in
their own way, but running on a short fuse, the males every
bit as protective of their females as the Carpathians, which
made for a volatile situation when so many Carpathian
males were unable to find lifemates among their own kind.
Would an emissary be welcome if they were found? Or
would he be killed to protect the lycanthrope society as a
whole? Whoever he sent would be at risk.

Leadership wasn't about knowing the right thing to do,
it was about making decisions and being willing to accept
the responsibility that came with inevitable mistakes. If
he allowed his men to reach out to the various species,
he could put his people at terrible risk. Over the years the
vampire myths had grown and become legends. Few would
distinguish between a Carpathian and vampire. Jaguars
had turned on their women.

Mikhail rubbed his eyes wearily. Their world seemed
too long at war. He had so many problems trying to keep
his dying species alive, yet at that moment, surrounded
by his fellow warriors, his mind continually tried to reach
for his lifemate and check on his child.

When the discussion looked as if it might go from
heated to outright mayhem, he broke in. "Mage and Jaguar
have mixed with humans and I would guess lycanthrope
have done so as well over the last few centuries. Many of
the shifters have diluted their blood. They carry the gene,
but they no longer can shift. Shea had a human mother
and a Carpathian father. We do not know whether Razvan

deliberately impregnated human women or whether he was forced to do so, but we know the children carry Carpathian blood. Our species is not so far removed from any other. We have to have allies and we need to actively find them."

Mikhail's voice was quiet, but carried the weight of his absolute authority. "We cannot abandon other species to fight the vampire alone. We need to change with the times and become more open to friendship and alliances."

"The more we let into our circle, the more difficult it will be to protect our women and children," Gregori pointed out. "We are surrounded by enemies and we do not know friend from foe at this point."

"Then all of us need to be trained in destroying vampires," Jaxon proposed. "It should be mandatory, so no matter where we are, we have a chance to get out alive."

"We train the male children from the time they are born now," Mikhail said quietly. "I am already passing my knowledge to my son who is in Raven's womb."

"What about your granddaughters, Mikhail?" Jaxon asked. "Is anyone teaching them?"

Gregori scowled, his silver eyes glittering with something close to a warning. "My daughters and my lifemate will never be allowed into a dangerous situation."

Destiny's eyebrow shot up. "You can't possibly know that. You can't. No one, not even you have that kind of control throughout a lifetime, especially a lifetime as long as we have. Absolutely all women and even our children should be trained in how to destroy a vampire," Destiny said. "It only makes sense."

Jaxon nodded her head. "Why should you only train the male children? Even if a woman never has to use her knowledge, she should have it. You never know when she may be attacked and males are not always by our sides."

"Why not?" Nicolas demanded. "Your lifemate and every other male, whether he is attached or unattached, should be with one of our women when they go anywhere.

Each and every one of you, and especially our children, should have bodyguards. Ivory died because she left the safety of her family. We lost Rhiannon for the same reason. The moment Xavier closed his school to males and took only our females, we should have refused to allow them to attend."

There was a murmur of agreement in the chamber and several nodded their heads. Destiny glanced at her lifemate, clearly asking him questions. She scowled at his answers.

"You're talking about something that happened centuries ago, Nicolas. Times are different and the world is different. You can't live in the past."

"No, but we can learn from it," Nicolas said. "We lost everything by not protecting our women. *Everything.* We are down to thirty or so women who can maybe provide one or two lifemates for our males, if we manage to figure out what is killing our children. We cannot afford to think in terms of humans or any other species that have numerous numbers to fall back on. If they choose to forget their women and children, that's their problem, but we cannot. We have to do everything in our power to protect the few that we have."

"You can't lock up the women, Nicolas," Lucian said, "as much as we may want to."

"We could try," Dimitri, one of the single men, muttered under his breath.

Jaxon shot him a hostile look. "You can try, but I wouldn't count on it ever happening."

Gregori stirred, drawing all eyes instantly. "Destiny is correct in that our women and children should be taught how to defend themselves. But I agree with Nicolas on this point. No child and no woman should go unescorted. We have too many enemies and if we can no longer detect them, they could walk through our village and we would never be aware of the danger."

Jaxon frowned. "Do you really think any grown woman

is going to sit in her home waiting for an escort when she has things to do?"

"We all make sacrifices in times of need," Gregori said.

Jaxon rolled her eyes. "Then you wait in your house for one of us to come escort you. Try it for a few risings and see how you like it." She turned her head and met her life-mate's icy gaze. "If I feel like visiting a friend or relative, I'm certainly going to do it."

"Now you sound like a sulky child deliberately misunderstanding what I am saying to you," Gregori said. "No one wants to dictate to you. The reality is quite simple. We need children, not fighters, and women have babies, not men. We have a surplus of fighters and very few women, so the task of giving birth falls to the women."

"Really?" Destiny's eyebrow shot up. "So what I'm hearing is that Nicolae should be allowed to fight the vampire, but not me because if I get killed we lose me as a brood mare."

"That is not what I said," Gregori denied.

"That's what it sounded like to me," Jaxon said. "And if she stayed home like a good little pregnant woman, and Nicolae was killed, what do you think would happen anyway? This entire argument is ridiculous. Maybe you're looking for some sign that we should know our places in the home and stay there, but we were not born or raised Carpathian. We have our own baggage that comes with each individual and some of us need to act. Others need to stay in the home and still others want to heal or research or carry on with whatever work interests them. And that, my friend, is our right."

"I disagree," Gregori said, his voice quiet, but carrying easily through the cave. "You are Carpathian and as such, there are certain differences in our species we cannot get around. Your first loyalty is not to yourselves, but to our people as a whole. We do what is best for all of us, not just individuals. For instance, our first duty is to the prince of our people. Without him, we cannot exist, so his protection must come first at all times. Every man, woman and child should be taught that, respect that and whole-heartedly serve."

"I think all women have proven we're willing to serve the Carpathian people," Jaxon said. "We just don't want to go back to the dark ages when men dictated to women."

Swift impatience crossed Gregori's face. "Do you honestly believe this is about male versus female? This is about saving a species, not women's rights."

"So how is it saving the species to have my lifemate go out and fight the vampire, leaving me at home to worry whether or not he's coming home? If he dies, we both do. The risk is great either way. In a perfect world, neither of us would be fighting vampires, but the world isn't so perfect, is it, Gregori? If I feel the need to stand by my lifemate and help to bring him home safe, you bet it is about my rights."

Gregori leaned close, his silver eyes slashing at Jaxon. "Why would you think, for one moment, that your presence does anything but jeopardize your lifemate's ability to fight? He is our greatest warrior. No one compares to him in battle. He has fought a thousand years, has more experience than any other, yet you, a female, once human, with so few years you are considered a child in our species, you think that he is not divided when he now battles? That his risk is lessened by your presence? It is more than doubled. He has to have one eye on you at all times. He has to keep his mind merged with yours in order to ensure your safety. Even directing you, he is divided, not wholly focused on the kill."

"Gregori," Lucian warned, his gaze going flat and cold.

Jaxon held up her hand. "No, this is why we're here, isn't it? To hear both sides of this argument. I want to hear why Gregori and so many others are opposed to the women fighting the vampire. If I don't understand why he is opposed, I will never have a chance to agree with him."

Then be very careful, little brother, how you address my lifemate.

I speak the truth to her and you know it. You have a thousand times the risk when she is along. She has to understand that.

Lucian's cool gaze swept over his brother. *Perhaps, but it is my risk to take.*

I disagree. We cannot lose you, nor can we afford the loss of your lifemate. You have lived too long in a solitary world, going your own way and making your decisions based not on saving a dying species, but on Vlad's directive to seek and destroy the vampire. We have a new prince and a new threat that must be addressed.

You are very close to getting your ass kicked, little brother.

You are more than welcome to try.

Jaxon glanced from her lifemate's cold gaze to Gregori's slashing one. "I know the two of you are arguing over this, but I really want to hear what Gregori has to say. Lucian, please."

She slipped a restraining hand up his arm in a loving gesture that made Nicolas turn his head away and long for Lara's touch. Again he tried to reach out to her but only heard the sounds of the long-forgotten Carpathian lullaby. He turned his attention back to the discussion raging around him, but this time, he couldn't quite shake the feeling that something wasn't right.

Lucian slipped his arm around Jaxon's waist, but nodded his head toward Gregori.

Gregori folded his arms across his chest. "Look at your lifemate in this moment. There is no threat to you, yet he is protective, ready to come at me if I say a word out of place to you. It is our nature, ingrained in us from before our birth, to protect our lifemate. Words and circumstance cannot change that, nor would we want it to change. Do you think this is less so in battle? Before you, he had only strategy and his own life to think about, now he must divide his attention and watch out for you. Even with the knowledge he shares with you of battles, even with his vast experience for you to draw on, you cannot be nearly fast enough."

"Every warrior has to start somewhere," Destiny countered. "You have young men practicing. We can do the same."

"Why would you want to?" Nicolas demanded. "Why would you want to face such a monster and risk your life when it is so precious to so many?"

"I cannot stop," Destiny answered truthfully. "Perhaps if Nicolae no longer hunted, I would be able to lay it down, but in truth, I am not certain I can."

Jaxon shrugged. "I've spent my entire life hunting monsters. I don't know what else I'd do."

"If you had a child?" Mikhail's voice, as always, was low, but swept through the room.

The crystals hummed low, the sound more melodic and soothing as if trying to bring the two women peace.

André and another tall Carpathian once again made their way through the ranks of warriors. Nicolas recognized the lone warrior, Tariq Asenguard, beside André. Vlad had sent him out centuries before. Even then he had stayed to himself, losing his ability to see color and feel emotion quite quickly after losing his family. His mother had suffered the loss of several children and in the end his parents had chosen to follow their young ones into the next realm. Nicolas had never seen him smile after that. Vlad had sent him to the North American continent and it was rumored he lived wild for a long time, although now he looked very civilized and would have blended with any business community.

Both Carpathian males bowed toward the women. Again it was André who spoke. "If one of our women wishes to go into battle and her lifemate allows such a thing..."

There was a hint of scorn in his voice. "...obviously that is their decision, but knowing this is going on, when we have spent lifetimes battling the vampire and have more experience and are willing to sacrifice our lives so that even one woman will live and give us a female child, then we have no choice but to ban together and protect those female warriors. When you go into battle, look behind you, there will be a legion of warriors defending you."

Jaxon frowned. "Thank you very much, but no. I don't want anyone defending me. I have a partner. We work together. I don't want anyone putting his life on the line for me."

"If you choose battle and you believe that is your right," Tariq said, "then our surviving males who look to you and all of our women for hope have the right to see to your protection when your lifemate chooses not to do so."

Immediately pandemonium broke out. Power surged in the room and the crystals vibrated with anger as the males with lifemates turned on the warriors without.

"Enough!" Mikhail's voice was a whiplash through the room. Instantly there was silence. "What did you think our males would be feeling over this issue?" he demanded of his males with lifemates. "Even among you, the opinions are divided. Most feel very strongly one way or the other about our women putting their lives in jeopardy. Our single males have a huge stake in this discussion and their voices carry as much weight as any other man here. They have sacrificed for centuries and it is their lives—their very souls at stake."

Lucian nodded his head. "That is so." It was the closest they were going to get to an apology. "But no one will threaten or dictate to my lifemate. What we do is our decision."

"Then you are willing to divide our people?" Gregori asked. "You are willing to go against a decision our prince makes?" He threw the challenge in his brother's face, uncaring that Lucian was a legend in their community.

Before Lucian could reply, Jaxon lifted her hands to his face. "Tell me the absolute truth, Lucian. When I go with you on a hunt, is your attention divided as Gregori says? Are you more at risk?" She refused to let him look away from her, her gaze on his.

"It is my risk to take."

Jaxon took a deep breath and let it out. "You should have told me."

"To what purpose? You cannot sit at home. If you could, I would have commanded you long ago, but your nature demands you be actively seeking justice." He pulled her close to him, his large body protective. "I have every confidence in my ability to protect both of our lives, or I would never risk you." He sent his brother a cool, razor-sharp glare. "There was no need to hurt you with what others consider their truth."

"Truth is truth, Lucian," Jaxon said.

Mikhail studied the couple. "You have need of action and to aid the men in ridding the world of the monsters we face. I have need of women willing to be taught, to learn to fight and then to teach our women and daughters. We need women willing to guard other women and be the first line of defense should the battle be brought to our doors. Perhaps this is something you would be willing to consider. If not..." He directed his gaze at André and Tariq. "Then I believe you will not be facing the vampire alone in battle—ever."

rose quartz was the mother stone and often used to effect change and open the heart.

She took the smoothest stones of rose quartz and ametrine from the pouch and gave them to Raven and Savannah to hold in their hands and rub while the ceremony took place. Next she took braided cowrie shells and placed them around both pregnant women's necks, another call to energy. She scattered rosebuds over the rich soil and added pomegranate to aid in the ceremony of renewed life.

Once Francesca had prepared Savannah and Raven, she took up a small drum, hand painted with a map of the shadow world and various animals of power and wisdom. She took a soft mallet and began to thump in a monotonous beat, using the rhythm of the women's collective hearts.

Lara seated herself close to Raven and Savannah, forming a triangle, while around them, the other Carpathian women formed a tight circle. Now, braids of sweet grass and copal tree resin were added to the smoking sage on the hot rocks along with herbs so that the room surrounded them with the scents of nature. Lara inhaled the scent, allowing the fragrance to carry her jitters away.

This was the most important task she might ever accomplish and she had nearly ended her own life. Had she succeeded, how many children would be lost? She felt she had been put on earth to fulfill this moment, to make this journey and save the three children. Xavier had destroyed so many lives and she was determined that he would not take these women and children as he had so many others.

Rubbing her fingers over a clear quartz crystal for clarity and focus, she pushed all thoughts away and allowed the waves in her mind to come and go and then recede altogether until her mind was a calm body of water, lapping at the edges relentlessly, ready to expand.

In her calm state, she sifted through her memories, long forgotten, and found the faint tracks of mage. She followed the path until she could open the door she needed.

Dragonseeker blood might flow through her veins, but she was mage—her mother from a pure line. The mystic ran strong in her, and everything she had been taught by the aunts was ready to feed her instincts should she need aid. This underground chamber the ancient women had instinctively chosen to use for their rituals was a place of power where the physical world merged with the spiritual realm. She felt the energy flowing into her, heard the rhythmic sound of a drum and the distant feminine voices chanting. The melodic notes carried her deeper into another sphere.

Smoke filled her vision. Clouds of mist and fog drifted in the smoke. She inhaled sharply, drawing the smoke and air into her lungs, as she set her soul free to travel. She found herself at the border of the two worlds, the chamber where she sat composed and tranquil, at the first stage of travel.

As her vision cleared, she could see a large tree with a labyrinth of roots and a jungle of wide-reaching branches standing before her. Mist of varying colors swirled through and around the branches. Leaves rustled as if alive, silvery green in color, fluttering in the soft breeze. The wind was just strong enough to stir the mist, not dislodge it, so that she caught glimpses of the thick twisting trunk, leading upward toward the sky and down beneath the soil.

Lara concentrated on the tree. The trunk appeared quite old, grayish in color. There were a few dark knots in the trunk and branches and one or two places where it may have lost a limb over time, but the tree appeared healthy. She continued moving over the ever-expanding meadow toward the tree, her bare feet skimming the fresh grass. As she moved across the field, flowers sprang up under the soles of her feet as if she scattered seeds along the fertile ground. The closer she got to the tree, the more missing branches she spotted, and beneath the tree, held within the cage of roots, old dead limbs lay like broken bodies in a mass grave.

As she approached the tree of life, she heard voices
crying out, the sound of weeping, and she felt wet drops
on her upturned face. Tears rained down on her, the tears
of ancient women who had gone before, losing child after
child to the unknown killer. The tears splashed on the
ground to form a stream, each tear merging with another
until the stream became a river.

Lara waded through the rising water to get to the wide,
thick trunk so she could examine it up close. Faint, shallow
marks were burned into the trunk leading up toward the
branches where new life waited. Raven's son. Savannah's
two daughters. Their souls clung to the gently rocking
limbs far above her. She could see the two branches were
blackened and hollow, twisted from some disease. Above
them were several other brand-new souls as well, clinging
to relatively healthy branches, but she could already see
signs of the unknown disease eating at the limbs. These,
then, were the most recent Carpathian pregnancies. The
killer had targeted Raven's child first and then Savannah's,
but these children were in jeopardy as well.

There was a taint to evil. Xavier had used the dark arts
against the Carpathians, corrupting his gift, twisting it for
his own purpose, and now she could see not only the faint
track marks, but smell the odor of the malevolence along
the trail of dark alchemy. The path led up toward the high
branches, but also followed the trunk down to the maze of
roots below the earth. She went down the trunk and followed the root system, seeking the source.

Lara drifted down the long trunk, pursuing the tracks,
using scent and sight. Once on the tangle of roots, the trail
was much more difficult, as the tracks appeared everywhere. Shadows leapt out at her, great greedy claws,
extended toward her. Moans and wails rose around her.
The river of tears continued to rise.

She pressed the pads of her fingers deep into the smooth
surface of her crystal and waited patiently. The croak of a

frog drew her attention. The small creature floated to her on a lily pad. It leapt from the streaming water to the trunk of a tree, looking at her with large, earnest eyes.

She smiled and greeted the creature formally and with respect, her spirit guide in the underworld realm. Frogs were amazing, magical creatures, potent in both land and water energy. To Lara, the frog symbolized everything the Carpathian women sought. Transformation, rebirth, the bond of mother and child and Mother Earth to her daughters. Unblocking the energy and creating a path for a smoother flowing so healing could prevail, ridding the earth and water of all toxins was exactly what Lara wanted to do. And the symbolism continued further; when frog populations were strong, the ecosystem was in balance and harmony was restored. She was on the right path.

She followed with even more confidence. The frog hopped easily along the root system, moving from stalk to stalk until he found one extremely large and twisted root that seemed to lead away from the rest. It bored deep into the earth and the farther down it went, the more twisted and black it became. Holes pierced the root and the stalk wept black tears.

Lara traced the faint footprint of evil farther, spiraling down the long taproot. The impression of hatred and despair grew stronger until she was caught in its flow and felt the influence pressing on the mother's body to reject the small intruder nestled in her womb. The illusion was strong, mother hating child, wanting it to leave, to get out, that the *thing* inside was a monster not a beloved child.

She resisted sending the little boy reassurance. That wasn't her job. Far away she could hear melodic voices singing a lullaby softly. She concentrated on the heartbeat, on the crystal in her hand that kept her focused on her journey.

The shadows grew stronger and darker. Waves of despondency washed over her. Threads of hatred and rage mixed with the flow of desolation. A weave of incredible power, but restrained, so subtlety was at work here. She knew that touch. She'd felt that touch all too often as a child. Xavier had humiliated her. He'd made her feel weak and defenseless, unwanted and unloved. He had made her feel as if the people who had brought her into the world rejected and despised her. This was his work. His signature was everywhere. Whatever microbe he had devised to carry out his cunning conspiracy was very close. She was nearing the home of the killer.

She tapped Natalya's mind. She couldn't afford detection until Natalya was ready to strike and she dared not continue until Natalya followed her clear path and joined her spirit to spirit. This part was the most dangerous. Lara was light and airy, floating along the realm with little to alert others to her presence. Natalya was a warrior, skilled in the art of killing, and now, in spite of the fact that she had been mage, she was fully Carpathian. She had lost none of her mage skills, but it was possible the entity could feel her presence as a threat. Lara stayed very quiet until she felt Natalya's spirit join hers.

Lara continued forward, taking Natalya's spirit with her. The entity had burrowed beneath the earth, the negative energy raising the toxicity of the ground so that Lara's sensitive soul wanted to weep. She pressed her fingers against her clear crystal and pushed on, focusing on her mission. Used to the ice caves and the extremophiles she found there, she spotted the killer as it clung to a bit of fungus. It didn't surprise her at all that Xavier had chosen to use such an organism to deliver death.

Extremophiles were given the name because they could survive and thrive in all kinds of extreme conditions, hot or cold, darkness or light, even a salty environment. The microbe was perfect as an assassin. Of course, Xavier had mutated this one to serve his purpose. It was tiny, a chameleon microbe able to merge with cells and appear part of whatever it chose to mimic. She felt the moment the microbe became aware of her presence and the danger to it.

Alarm spread, resounding waves swamping her, and she leapt aside as the microbe spit chemicals at her. Droplets of acid hissed through the stem of the root. The tree shook under the assault. She had known that extremophiles spit chemicals at other microbes to protect themselves and their territories, so she'd been somewhat prepared, but the sudden aggression surprised her. The microbe went on the attack immediately, raining acid over the taproot in an effort to eradicate the threat to it.

Lara had to lure the thing to the surface so Natalya could kill it and she had to do so immediately. The attack could kill off the last of the baby's strength. *Baby.* The extremophile was programmed to kill an infant. No baby would be a threat to it. Knowing Xavier, he would have given his assassin the scent of both Dubrinsky and Dragonseeker blood.

For the first time she hesitated. She would have to go back to her childhood and face her demons again. There would be no Nicolas to stand between her and her traumatic memories, but she could not fail this child.

I am here, Natalya reassured.

The echo of female voices surrounded her, uplifted her, gave her renewed confidence with their offer of sisterhood.

Lara looked to her spirit guide. Without hesitation, the little frog, who had started in water and transformed to land, began the journey along another root. She felt the warp of time and knew the frog was taking her back so that she would appear as an infant to the assassin.

At once the acid stopped raining down, but now the attack was different, sharp and focused and very complex. It began as a feeling, dread stealing into her mind. A voice whispered to her in the Carpathian language, a repetitious message of hatred. The insidious tone was poisonous, seeping into her mind even though she knew she wasn't an infant. The disgust was all too reminiscent of her childhood.

She forced herself to continue up the taproot, knowing the microbe followed, feeling its presence as it whispered hideous things. No one wanted her. She was worthless. The body carrying her rejected her, fighting to rid itself of such a parasitic creature. Go! Go! Abandon the host. She detested carrying such a weak, pathetic foreign object. Not a person, an object.

Without warning, something stabbed at her, a vicious hot poker that tore through her outer shell to her soul. The microbe had gotten close enough to attack with a retracting stinger. She saw the probe disappear back into the chameleon of an extremophile. The pain was excruciating. Lara stumbled. At once sharpened points raked at her ankle. She nearly panicked, terrified of being injected with a mass of parasites. It was only the crystal in her hand and the sound of feminine voices rising in melodious harmony that kept her from abandoning her infant state.

She moved faster, her baby cries clearly spurring the microbe on to more vicious action. The murmur of the voice continued, relentlessly pushing at her to give up, to go away, that the body she resided in wanted her gone. Despair was an ever-present companion and now her environment became hostile as well. Attacks came in the form of an army of antibodies. Small chains lashed at her, beating at her in an attempt to drive her out. She realized the stinger had tagged her for attack and now the chains of proteins whipped around and through her.

This was happening to Raven's son and Savannah's daughters.

Outraged, Lara pushed upward toward the traveler's entrance where one realm met the other. No matter the cost to her, she would be bait and bring this hideous killer to the surface where Natalya waited.

As she moved upward, she felt a burning sensation, not on her outer shell, but deep inside, as if her blood was boiling. The stinger had injected her, not with a parasite, but with an incompatibility to her host's blood. Already cells were breaking down, causing hemorrhages. And all the while that voice continued to tell her how worthless she was and how much her host didn't want her there. Waves of despair swamped her continually.

Sound began to drown out the voice as pressure built all around her, squeezing down on her while the sound thundered in her ears and her heartbeat picked up pace. The comforting sound of the ebb and flow of life-giving fluid changed to a fast, hard race that roared in her ears, sounding like a frightening freight train coming at her from all sides.

Lara struggled up the tree, clinging to the sound of the lullaby, forcing the pads of her fingers into the crystal to maintain some semblance of reality. She wept, spurring the microbe on, letting her baby cries whip it into a frenzy so that the organism didn't realize she was doing anything but trying to flee its presence. In response, sensing victory, the killer increased its attacks, pressing despondency deep into her mind while it increased its assault.

Terrified, she fixed her sight on the smoke and mist swirling all around just out of reach. Time slowed, and she felt as if she was wading through quicksand. Her environment became less and less stable, small earthquakes rocking her, pressure squeezing down on her, shrinking her world from every side, fluid building all around her so that she felt as if she was drowning. A swarm of tremors shook the tree from branches to root deep within the ground.

Just when she thought she might not make it out, the little frog was there, swimming beside her, guiding her through the crumbling walls as violent shock waves attacked her. Fissures opened up around her as stability decreased. She made one last desperate push to regain the surface, to find her spot of entry.

Gasping, she inhaled sage and sweet grass. "Now, Natalya, now!" She slumped to the floor of the chamber, in the dark, fertile soil, exhaustion gripping her body and the echo of her childhood nightmares resounding in her mind.

Natalya crouched over Raven, her body as still as a tigress, unmoving, every sense alert, trained on her prey, waiting—waiting. She struck quickly when she detected a faint trace of mage and the taint of dark art. Her weapon was an egg. She rolled it carefully over Raven's wound, drawing the microbe into the center of the egg.

Lara couldn't talk, but she sent Natalya a warning using the common Carpathian path her aunts had taught her. *Watch out, it's nasty. Don't let it sting you.*

Already the egg was rocking, darkening in color, the microbe sending waves of hatred and despair out into the chamber. A mixture of the foul stench of decomposing flesh and rotten eggs assailed Lara, deepening the feeling of being back in the ice cave. In spite of the heat rising from the chambers beneath them, she shivered with cold, and icy fingers of fear traveled down her spine.

The smoke and incense quickly absorbed the negative energies. Natalya, mindful of the lashing stinger, rushed the new host from the cavern. She called for an electrical storm so that for a moment the night sky lit up as she called down the lightning to incinerate the microbe held within the egg.

Lara rolled over and stared up at the ceiling. Gentle hands touched her face and body as the women searched for injuries. She didn't have the energy left to tell them it wasn't her body that needed to be healed, but her mind. She pried open her eyes and watched as Francesca examined Raven.

Did we get it? Is the baby all right? She didn't have the energy to speak aloud.

Natalya strode back in, going straight to Lara, taking her hand.

Raven closed her eyes and touched her son's mind. Her hands fluttered over her stomach, rubbing gently. "He's at peace. Finally, he's at peace and I feel different. I don't think my body's trying to reject him."

Francesca immediately sent herself outside her own body, to go seeking in Raven's. A smile of joy lit her face. "This is a miracle. Shea, her blood pressure is fine, there are no more contractions, she isn't bleeding, and her body isn't treating the baby as a foreign invader and trying to dispose of it."

Lara closed her eyes, pressing both hands to her pounding head. She wanted to weep and laugh at the same time. She was happy she'd been able to find the microbe, but now childhood memories beat at her, images of blood and torture and screaming men and women. More than that was the feeling of utter hopelessness, a seed planted from long ago that she could barely rise above. Her self esteem plummeted, the insidious thread of dark magic preying on her mind.

She didn't want Raven to know what the journey had cost her, but she felt sick to her stomach. Too many doors had opened along the way, and remembering wasn't a good thing. There had been a reason her aunts built a barrier to protect her, and the shield seemed to be in shreds. She needed to be alone, far from everyone else where she could pull her fractured mind back together. The problem was— she was too weak to rise.

Around her, voices rose in excitement. Shea and Francesca whispered in consult, their body language animated. Raven's child was safe and the culprit had been found. The other women rejoiced and Raven wept with happiness.

"What about my daughters?" Savannah's quivering voice quieted the room. "Do I have one of those things in me attacking the girls? Is that why I'm having contractions and bleeding?"

Gregori! I need you. Her cry was heartfelt, a mother's instinctive need to protect her children.

Lara stilled, her heart beginning to hammer inside her chest. She knew what was coming, but she *couldn't*. There was no possible way, with her mind so fragmented, that she could go back and face her childhood a second time. Without conscious thought, instinctively her traumatized mind reached out to Nicolas.

Nicolas. Hurry. I fear I'm lost.

"Lara?" Raven asked. "Does Savannah have a parasite in her body attacking the girls?"

For a moment she was paralyzed, her mind frozen, refusing to process information. She was still that child in the cave with Xavier standing over her telling her she was worthless and had killed her own mother.

"Get it out of me! Get it away from the babies," Savannah cried. "Get it out of me now."

She could hear herself screaming silently, deep down where no one could hear.

I hear. I am with you. Nicolas's voice was quiet and gentle, but carried absolute confidence. *Hang on, hän ku kuulua sívamet, I am almost there.*

He was coming and he had called her "keeper of my heart." Lara tried to cling to that, shivering with cold, aware of little around her but the whispers of her past.

Natalya dropped on her knees beside Lara. "You need blood." She used her teeth to open her wrist, extending her hand toward Lara.

Lara's horrified gaze fastened on the elongated teeth, then touched on the red droplets welling up. The thin crimson trickle turned her stomach. Crablike, Lara scrambled backward away from Natalya, feeling trapped.

All eyes seemed on her and for a moment the expressions seemed greedy and disdainful. Her wrist burned and ached. She rubbed her fingers over the scars, looking toward the chamber entrance, judging the distance to make her escape.

Worthless, pathetic creature. You killed your mother. It is no wonder your father wants you dead. I should let him drink you dry.

Wide shoulders filled the doorway and silver eyes glittered and raked over her face. The scream echoed through her mind, built and built until it was a giant tsunami, bursting out of her, growing and expanding as energy exploded outward.

Nicolas threw Gregori aside and took the brunt of the assault, the powerful energy waves slamming him backward and down. Both he and Gregori shifted into mist as they moved. The force of the blow shook the chamber. Several sconces exploded, showering the cavern with wax and flame. Gregori materialized, his body blocking Savannah and Raven from falling debris.

Lara pulled herself into a standing position and staggered toward Nicolas, remorse adding to her feelings of humiliation and self-loathing. He was there instantly, sweeping her up into his arms and glaring at the women. She buried her face against his chest, clinging, wanting to disappear. She felt fractured, fragile, raw and exposed.

"I trusted you with her." Fury burned through Nicolas, his strong body vibrating with power as rage took hold. He knew Lara's emotions were cutting into his self-control, but it mattered little. She had come here already in a fragile state and instead of being bolstered by the women, they had torn her to shreds. He wanted to annihilate them. To maintain control, he stepped back toward the entrance.

Gregori spread his arms wide in a gesture of challenge and there was real anger breaking through the usual cold-stone demeanor. "Take your woman and go. Mage-born, daughter of Razvan, great-granddaughter of Xavier, what do we really know of her? It is bad enough that she endangered our prince with her lack of control, but she has placed every woman in this room in danger."

Nicolas dragged in his breath, the rage in the pit of his stomach coming to a boil. "You dare to imply that she is a spy in our camp?"

Power shimmered throughout the cavern and the walls undulated. The ground beneath them rolled.

"Stop!" Raven cried out.

"Gregori, you don't understand," Francesca intervened.

"What is going on?" Mikhail appeared, standing squarely between the two Carpathian males. "You are in a sacred place."

"She's done a great service, Gregori," Francesca said. "She found and brought to the surface the parasite threatening Raven with miscarriage. We thought the baby lost to us. She's exhausted and needs blood."

It was more than that. Merged as he was with Lara, Nicolas felt the press of Xavier's torment. He whirled around with Lara in his arms and took two steps, but Savannah cried out, pushing past everyone to block the entrance to the chamber.

"She can't leave. She can't." Tears swam in her eyes. "I'm sorry for what Gregori said, but she *has* to get this thing out of me. It's trying to kill my children."

Gregori put a gentle hand on her shoulder, ignoring Nicolas, who was still shaking with fury. "I can get rid of it, Savannah, now that I know what to look for."

Savannah shook her head. "It hides from men. Xavier was very clever. He knew every male scans his lifemate's body to ensure her health. Lara detected it because she lived for years with Xavier's taint all around her. She was able to go on a soul journey to find it dwelling within Raven. She used herself as bait to bring the entity to the surface, and allow Natalya to destroy it."

Lara slipped her arms tighter around Nicolas's neck and buried her face against his throat. Nicolas nuzzled the top of her head with his chin and then looked at Gregori, dark anger rolling like thunder in his eyes. "Too bad you have condemned my lifemate to banishment as a spy from the camp of the enemy."

He stepped around Savannah only to find his way blocked by Gregori's solid body. "You will not condemn my children to death because you are angry with me." His body crackled with electricity, tiny sparks snapping around him.

"Get the hell out of my way," Nicolas snapped, not in the least intimidated.

When Gregori didn't move, Nicolas placed Lara carefully on the ground well clear of a possible fight zone and stepped up, chest to chest, staring straight into Gregori's eyes, two dangerous predators not yielding an inch. "Do you really want to do this with me?" The anger faded from his eyes so they went flat and cold and a killer stood where a man had been.

"If I have to," Gregori replied.

A collective gasp went through the cavern. Mikhail sighed and waved his hand toward the two men. The energy field around Gregori snapped off with a small, brightly lit surge before going dark, and both men found themselves on the floor, sitting side by side on the edge of the rich soil.

"Enough. You can both leave if you refuse to do other than posture." Ignoring both men, Mikhail crouched down beside Lara, looking into her eyes. "This is more than needing blood. Francesca? Come take a look at her."

"Get away from her," Nicolas growled, his first thought to get to his lifemate, but the women surrounded them, pushing in close to the two men, trapping them inside a circle of protection.

Savannah caught at Lara's hand, tears streaming down her face. "I'm sorry. Please, I'll do anything. Anything at all. Don't let my babies die."

Lara's body jerked. She'd heard those words before. A man's voice calling out in a desperate plea. *Xavier turning to look back at Razvan, his silvery eyes glittering with such contempt and triumph.* She gasped, her shocked gaze hunting for Nicolas, her only anchor when the truth clawed at her, tore her open.

Nicolas. He did it for me. He allowed Xavier to take him over so I would be allowed life.

Razvan had inadvertently opened his soul to Xavier when he had sought to save the life of his child. He'd exposed his soul and Xavier had snatched it, able to control his grandson's movements, taking over without having to drain his energy by possessing the body. For her. To save her. Razvan had paid the ultimate price—not death, but soul destruction.

"Nicolas!" She called for him, covering her face with her hands. She was slipping backward into her mind.

"I am here, *fél ku kuuluaak sívam belső*, and I am not going anywhere."

"She came back too fast," Francesca said. She pushed past Mikhail to kneel beside Lara, slipping her arms around her. "She's freezing. Gregori, I need help."

"She's back in the ice cave," Nicolas said. He was already there, gathering Lara into his arms and holding her close, his mind merging with hers to hold her steady. He crooned softly to her, rocking her back and forth. "She should never have gone there without me."

"What has she done?" Gregori demanded, crouching beside Francesca to examine Lara. His hands skimmed over her.

"She used herself as bait. The entity destroyed babies so she regressed and became a child so it would follow her," Natalya explained.

Nicolas swore under his breath. "She shouldn't have gone back without me," he repeated.

"She fears me," Gregori said abruptly. "You have to get her to come back with me to retrieve what has been lost."

Nicolas searched Gregori's face for a long moment, then he nodded.

Gregori crouched quite close to Lara and looked into her eyes. He nodded at whatever he found there and murmured instructions to Francesca, who once again took up her position at her drum.

"She needs to feel safe and loved, Nicolas," Gregori said. "Bring her into the center of the circle and hold her so she feels your presence. Stay connected to her mind. A part of her is so stressed from the painful revelations of her past that she's unable to deal with more of her memories. We have to invite that part of her to return and it must feel safe to do so."

"Invite it?" Nicolas echoed.

Gregori shrugged. "Do not worry, I will get back what is lost for her. We dare not leave even a small fragment of her soul in the lower realm too long. If Xavier is alive, he will sense her there and like Lara tracking his evil, he will be able to acquire a piece of her."

More sage and sweet grass was laid on the hot rocks. The women began the healing chant, the longer version often used to retrieve the soul of someone who had died. Nicolas found every muscle tight, his stomach muscles bunched and knotted in apprehension. He would much rather face a dozen skilled vampires than have to rely on someone else to aid Lara.

I am a healer and I cannot help my children or my lifemate.

Nicolas accepted the brief statement as the closest thing to an apology he would get from Gregori. And he understood what would drive a man to rage now. Impotence. Helplessness. The inability to defend what was his.

Nicolas bent his head and brushed kisses along Lara's cold forehead. She shivered continually, but she was aware of him. Her gaze clung to his and there was trust there. He was grateful for that much from her.

Gregori wasted little time, shedding his physical body and traveling, first into Lara, and then guiding them straight to the tree of life. His experience showed, Nicolas thought. He moved with complete confidence, meeting animals along the way, showing respect as he made inquiries, tracking what Lara had left behind in her haste to bring a killer from Raven's body.

Gregori's manners on the journey were impeccable, even when he found what was lost, politely inviting it home, persuading the stressed fragment it would be returning to a safe environment. The soft healing chant added to the healer's persuasive voice, and in the end, the fragment returned to Lara without much trouble.

Gregori swayed a little from the drain of energy. "She needs blood and rest." He had seen the wealth of childhood memories pouring into Lara's mind.

"I am taking her home," Nicolas declared.

"No!" Savannah pressed both hands over the rounded curve of her belly. "I feel that thing tearing at my children, hurting them. Making them feel unwanted. I can't wait another rising." She reached out her hand toward Lara in a pleading gesture. "I swear to you, I would if I could. I know what this costs you, but they're hurting." Tears streamed down her face and she turned to Gregori.

He was there instantly, cupping the back of her head, pressing her damp face against his chest, but he said nothing—simply waited.

Lara turned back on shaky legs, her stomach knotting at the prospect, but Savannah was right. They couldn't allow the babies to suffer any longer than necessary.

"Absolutely not," Nicolas said. "I forbid it, Lara." He ignored the stubborn look on her face. "You barely made it out last time in one piece. If it has to be done, I will do it."

"How? If a man could do it, the healer would have already. It has to be a woman and that woman has to recognize Xavier's touch. It's very faint and difficult to follow."

"Natalya can go," Nicolas said. He was beginning to

feel desperate, his skin too tight, his skull pressing down on his mind.

"She cannot and I think you know that. There is no one else." There was quiet despair in her voice and it shattered him.

The chamber was quiet, but he could feel all eyes on him. His gaze was locked with Lara's. She didn't want to go, and a part of her even wanted him to stop her, but both of them knew she had no real choice. How could she live with herself if she allowed two unborn babies to suffer as she had suffered, when she knew the lasting effects? When she knew the killer would double his efforts to rid the world of the grandchildren of the prince?

Nicolas.

She whispered his name and for the first time he heard love. His heart jerked hard in his chest. This, then, was love. This terrible wrenching inside, an ache that was unrelenting. The terrible need to make her world right.

Sívamet—my heart. And he meant it.

I will need blood to make this journey.

He swallowed his protest. She had to go and he had to let her.

Gregori stepped forward, drawing their attention, extending his wrist. "I offer freely, my life for your life."

There was a small silence. Lara forced a self-conscious smile. "I'm sorry. I have an aversion to taking blood. I'm just learning to be able to take what my lifemate offers."

Gregori inclined his head. "I understand. And I offer my sincere apologies for my conduct."

"There really is no need."

Lara turned in Nicolas's arms, the pads of her fingers skimming beneath his shirt, seeking hot skin. She needed and he provided. It was that complex—and that simple. Nicolas moved back into the shadows and blurred their image to hide his reaction. No matter that she needed blood for survival, for him it was an erotic intimacy that would forever stir a physical hunger. His body hardened as he felt the skim of her teeth, of her lips and the bite of pain that gave way instantly to a flood of pleasure. He stroked back her hair, fingers caressing as he gave her his strength. Even when she sealed the twin pinpricks with a lick of her tongue, he continued to hold her tightly, not wanting to let her go.

Are you certain?

She opened her eyes and looked up at him, her blue-green gaze colliding with his. For a moment no one was there but the two of them and, beneath the fringe of long lashes, love—for him—shone bright and enduring. He felt the impact, like a hard punch to the pit of his stomach.

I'm certain. Just don't go anywhere.

He had no intention of going anywhere without her.

The microbe bent on destroying Savannah and Gregori's daughters proved to be faster and more vicious than the one in Raven. It was only the combined strength of the parents and the fact that the entity had to work on both babies simultaneously that gave them the resistance needed to hold out.

She lured the extremophile to the surface and it was destroyed, but not without a cost to Lara. Without Nicolas she knew she never would have managed to survive. He gave her blood, shielding her fragmented mind to prevent the childhood trauma from destroying her. She wasn't aware when he finally took her back to their cavern.

16

Lara woke to a flood of erotic sensations. Nicolas lay on his side, his hot, hard body pressed against her, his hand cupping the underside of her breast while his mouth suckled, pulling strongly, teeth scraping while his tongue flicked against her nipple. He massaged her other breast, pulling and teasing her nipple into a hard peak. His mouth was rough and possessive, claiming her body, branding her forever his.

Another strong pull of his mouth sent arousal spreading in a heated rush from breasts to toes. She felt his arms, strong and protective around her, a safe haven when his mouth was so demanding. His thigh wedged in between hers, giving him access to the welcoming haven between her legs. His hand slipped down her stomach to caress the damp folds.

I want to wake up to you forever—just like this.

His voice slid against her mind, over and into, a gentle thrust much like his hips made, pushing his heavy erection against her thigh. She felt the push of his fingers, the stretch and glide, creating a slick heat that sent waves of pleasure rocketing through her. All the while his mouth stayed busy, lapping at the tight bud of her nipple.

Desire for his touch, his mouth and hands, his hard body, ran deep, rushing through her like a drug. Gentleness gave way to aggression as he feasted on her, his teeth and mouth and tongue claiming her breasts for his own. All the while his fingers moved over her and into her, one moment deep, the next shallow, until she was pushing into his hand, and her body was flushed with heat.

He slid down her body. *His.* His own personal playground. Her skin was hot satin, her sheath, living silk, and he wanted to know every inch of her. He kissed and licked and bit his way to her thighs, then pulled her restless legs apart to reveal the ultimate treasure. She was already wet and swollen with need, too beautiful to resist. He lay between her thighs and, cupping her bottom, pulled her to his mouth.

Nicolas ran his tongue over her folds, lapping at the moisture there, then straightened his tongue, stabbed deep and used his teeth to rake at the little sensitive bud peaking at him. She screamed and writhed, trying to use her heels to dig in to the mattress and push her body out from under him, but he pinned her there and feasted. She tasted like a spring meadow under a full moon and he wanted all of her.

His large hands kneaded her bottom, the pads of his fingers catching the warm cream and massaging it into her body and exploring every shadow and hollow while he lapped at her like a great cat. His tongue took long, deep strokes, then stiffened and plunged over and over until she was panting, twisting, begging him for release. He watched her with hooded eyes, darkened with lust, soft with love, paying attention to every detail of her reaction. When her breath hitched, when she arched up, and her hips bucked. He felt her muscles contract and bunch in her stomach, felt the ripple of arousal through her thighs.

His body matched hers heat for heat, flame for flame. He loved the dazed look on her face, the whirling green-blue of her eyes sliding to opaque. The rose flush to her body and the tight buds of her nipples. Every gasp. Every moan. It all heightened his raw hunger.

He stabbed at her sensitive bud with his stiff tongue, flicking and teasing before using the edge of his teeth. She gave a broken cry, thrashed and caught a fistful of his hair. He responded by sucking and then using a circular motion with the flat of his tongue. When he thrust two fingers into her she gasped, her orgasm washing over her, giving him another rush of warm honey.

Lara went limp, panting, watching him with that dazed expression. Nicolas smiled and crawled up her body, rubbing his tight balls and the thick length of his shaft over her belly and breasts, leaving a pearly trail behind.

He knelt over her, his knees on either side of her shoulders, leaning forward to brace himself on one hand. He guided his shaft to her mouth, his gaze on her lips as her tongue slid out and touched the velvet tip, licking at the pearl drops like a kitten licking cream. He rubbed the broad head over her lips. Her lashes fluttered, her breasts rose and fell.

"Open your mouth."

Lara was certain he was too big to accommodate, but he didn't give her a chance to protest. The moment her lips parted, he slipped inside and threw back his head, eyes closing as if in ecstasy. It was that expression of rapture that made her want to learn, to follow the images and instructions in his mind. She wanted this for him, wanted the heat and fire and the loss of control, and she wanted to be the one to give it to him.

She experimented with technique, getting used to the feel and size of him, the texture and musky scent. She ran her tongue up and down his thick shaft, teased and nibbled at the underside of the flared head. When his breath rushed out of his lungs, she knew she was making head-way. She flicked her tongue in much the same way he had until he jerked in her mouth. She tried a small suction and was rewarded with his gasp of pleasure.

You like that?

He swore softly in his native language. *I need that. Harder. Deeper.* Nicolas couldn't believe that was his voice, the commands really nothing but throaty growls.

Lara complied, wrapping her lips around him, taking him deeper until he was engulfed in hot, moist velvet. His hips bucked. His hand went to her hair, tangling in the red-blond silk while she cupped and stroked his balls with one hand and wrapped the other around the thick base of his shaft. Her lashes fanned her cheeks, her lips a sexy pout as she took him deep and flattened her tongue to draw him out.

Her breath hitched and he felt the warmth fan over him as he thrust deeper, her mouth, hot and wet sliding over his shaft, consuming him. He didn't let her get away with pull-ing back, forcing her out of her comfort zone again, push-ing deeper, breathing for both of them.

I want to feel your throat squeezing all around me. Take me deeper.

I can't. But she wanted to. She was desperate to take him deeper. She felt every wave of pleasure rolling over him and reveled in her ability to bring him the kind of pleasure he gave her. She was just a little intimidated by his size.

You will, because if you don't I won't live another two minutes. He thrust down into her mouth, felt her throat squeeze around him, tight and wet and so wonderful he nearly lost his mind. Her mouth slid up and down him, and then she licked and sucked on his sac before swallowing him again.

As her throat closed around him, he took control, ris-ing a little, shifting his angle so he could thrust, taking her breath, watching her eyes go wide. Even her trepidation as he slid deeper sent flames rolling in his belly.

I can't.

You will. Relax. Breathe. Feel me, Lara. Feel what you're doing to me.

He opened his mind to her, sharing the hot slide, the clamp of her throat, the stroke of her tongue on his sensitized flesh. He reared back, using the silk of her hair and his knees to keep her in place while he began to move.

She followed the instructions he bit out through bared teeth. The harder she sucked and used the flat of her tongue, and the edge of her teeth, the wilder and more aggressive he became, but she couldn't stop—didn't want to stop even though a part of her was nervous. She felt him grow thicker and she tried to pull away. He held her, the seductive whisper moving in her mind, telling her exactly what he needed from her.

Nicolas suddenly withdrew, moving off of her. She cried out, reaching for him. He flipped her over and with one strong arm around her waist, lifted her, dragging her to her knees, pressing his shaft tightly against the curve of her buttocks. He licked his way down her spine, teasing the firm globes and tasting heat and spice down her very center. She gasped, unsure what he intended, but he held her submissively in front of him, forcing her to wait while he took his time, exploring her body, the body that was his to love, to worship, to play with.

Keeping one hand on the nape of her neck, he held her down, thrusting the broad head of his erection against her soft, wet entrance. She gasped and rocked back. He held her firmly, stopping when she tried to impale herself. He waited until she remained still and pushed deeper through the tight folds, inch by inch, filling and stretching her while her heart beat with his and the air moved through her lungs in rhythm with his.

Her muscles were tight and hot, a fiery inferno encasing him in silk. He caught her hips in his hands and thrust hard, burying himself so deep his balls met her bottom with a slap of sensitive flesh and he nearly howled with pleasure. He began to ride her, a hard, rough ride, slamming home, deliberately going as deep and as hard as possible with each stroke, taking her breath, not giving her time to do anything but rock back with sobbing breaths.

Her breasts swayed with every hard, pounding thrust and he leaned forward, angling his body to get a different position, to go even deeper. Her muscles clamped tighter and tighter, and suddenly fire raced over him as her orgasm took her, but he didn't slow down, didn't let her catch her breath, driving her right back up the pinnacle as hard and fast as he could.

Again. It was a demand, a growl rumbling in his throat. He gripped her hair and pulled her head back, leaning toward her shoulder, his teeth lengthening. All the while his hips pounded with real urgency, pushing her up and up, building the tension until she screamed, the lightning streaking from groin to belly to breasts, ripping through her like a tidal wave.

He moved again, turning her, lifting her, wrapping her legs around his waist so he could feel the slide of her breasts on his chest, so he could take her mouth with his, so that he could drop her down over the hard, rigid length of him and hear her scream with pleasure.

Tet vigyázam. I love you. He couldn't say the words out loud. They didn't seem to be enough to express what he felt inside.

He slowed the pace, savoring the tightness of her channel, the slick heat surrounding him and the way she gave herself so completely to him. He tipped her backward until she was lying half across the bed and he was kneeling, hips surging, never wanting the moment to end. Her eyes were glazing over when he caught her hips and drove desperately into the very core of her again and again.

His jaw ached as his teeth lengthened, his shaft was so hard he was afraid it would burst, but he couldn't stop. He was nearly at the point of no return. His teeth ached. His body ached. Every cell demanded he take her blood. He couldn't quiet the roar in his mind, or the thunder in his ears. He bent over her slowly, letting her get used to being pinned down by his larger, heavier body. He couldn't stop the deep thrusting of his hips, savoring the milking of her tight muscles over his pulsing flesh.

He looked into her eyes, let her see his intent. He kissed her breast, nuzzled her nipple and felt her body's instinctive rush of heat. His heartbeat was tuned to the rhythm of hers and he could feel her pulse beckoning—seducing beneath his tongue. He tasted her soft skin. Warm satin, the feel of her as addicting as her scent. He bit very gently right along the swell of her breast, the smallest of nips and felt her heart flutter. Felt her sheath pulse around his shaft, felt the hot flood of glorious cream bathing him with her need.

He nipped a second time, a little harder, breaking the skin this time. The taste of her burst into his mouth and flooded his system so that he thickened, his erection growing heavier. Her muscles reacted, clamping down around him like a vise, holding him to her.

Say yes, Lara. Tell me yes.

His tongue lapped at the little sting. His hips took a long, slow, leisurely stroke, going deep and hard, pressing down on her sensitive bud so that as he raked over her, she shuddered with pleasure and arched into him.

He never asked if he could have her body, he took her over and over in any way he chose, driving her to bliss with his insatiable appetite, but he asked permission to do the one thing so natural to him she could feel the need beating and clawing at him.

His lips feathered over her pulse, teeth sinking a little deeper. She cried out, arching her back, her hips bucking hard, sheath clamping down again. Heat rushed through her, flames licked at her skin.

Please, she whispered.

He surged forward, another long stroke that nearly drove her over the edge, but he stopped with the walls of tight muscles pulsing all around him and her keening cry.

Please what?

Do it now while I am so desperate for you. Because it was all part of the erotic pleasure and she was desperate. Every part of her ached for this, this connection, the completeness between them.

Nicolas sank his teeth deep, thrust into her mind and body, all simultaneously, sharing his joy, heightening her pleasure, giving her everything he was and ever would be. Her taste burst through him like fireworks, hot and addicting and so perfect he knew he'd never get enough of her blood or her body. He was careful to keep her body at a fever pitch, to not allow her mind to hold any thought but pleasure and he didn't linger, although he wanted to.

He took enough for a true blood exchange, sliding his tongue over the curve of her breast to close the pinpricks even as he shifted again to lock his arm around her hips and begin another wild ride. He thrust faster and harder, watching her face, watching her eyes go, seeing that dazed look of delight, the sexy pout to her mouth as she gave a husky scream when her orgasm tore through her. Her tight sheath clamped down hard, squeezing and milking and tearing his own orgasm from him. He poured his seed into her, his hoarse cry mingling with hers.

With her body rippling around his, he caught her and rolled to his side, bringing her head into the cradle of his arm. *Now, Lara, finish it.* He didn't ask. It was a demand, dark and filled with lust, with desperate hunger.

Lara couldn't have resisted if she wanted to. The waves of pleasure rocked her, took her from breasts to belly to feminine channel and back again. The call of his blood was loud, the taste of his essence already burning the back of her throat. She licked over his pulse and bit down, sinking her teeth into his chest.

His hips slammed into her hard, lifting her body, the bite of pain stimulating him even more. She closed her eyes and drank him in, taking him into her veins, her heart, every cell in her body, while he pumped in and out of her tight sheath. His taste was as primal as he was. A blend of dominance and heat, male and the night. She would forever crave him. It took a great deal of self-control to seal the pinpricks, but she was rewarded instantly.

Her orgasm hit her hard, driving the breath from her body and constricting her muscles tightly around Nicolas. He roared, clamping his hands on her hips while her body locked down unexpectedly on his shaft, tearing hot jets of semen from him. The climax continued, a brutal hot release that tore through his body, so that he plunged into her tight depths repeatedly, flooding her with his seed.

When he could move, he rolled them over so she could pillow her head on his chest. His arm circled her possessively, one hand cupping the underside of her breast. It took a few minutes for his burning lungs to manage to get air. "I want to stay here forever with you, Lara."

She managed a smile. "We might have to."

His thumb brushed the soft underside of her breast, back and forth. "I love your skin."

She ran her hand down his chest to his belly. "I love yours." She stretched her neck to nibble on his chin.

"Thank you."

Her gaze shifted away from his. "You know what I have to do, don't you?"

She was going to avoid talking about making a blood exchange. Nicolas hesitated, unsure whether to force the issue, but then followed her lead. She needed to come to terms in her own way. Because she had managed to let him take her blood this one time didn't mean it would be easy the next time—or even that she could. He accepted that in her, just as he accepted his own peculiar quirks, formed from a lifetime of experiences.

"We have to do it together," Nicolas corrected. "You lured the entity, for lack of a better word, to the surface and Natalya was able to get it out of Savannah, but it was much easier with me there, wasn't it? Admit it."

Lara nuzzled his chest with her chin. "Yes. I don't mind admitting it. It seems a bit of a daunting task to check every single woman, and Francesca said it would have to be done. She plans to try to journey with me so she can learn Xavier's touch in order to help."

He rubbed his palm up and down her narrow rib cage, savoring the feel of her soft skin, the movement more absent-minded than voluntary. "I do not understand how these things got into the women. Are there more than one?"

She frowned. "It doesn't appear so, at least not in Raven or Savannah. Extremophiles can be very aggressive about defending their territory and basically that's what these mutated microbes are."

"So once they're gone, everything is back to normal? It seems too fast."

"I think it is too fast. How did the organism get there in the first place? Whatever the source is, we haven't found it. I overheard Shea talking to Francesca right before we left. She thought there was a good possibility it was transferred from male to female and that they live in the soil first."

"She is wrong about the males," Nicolas said, his hand stilling on her breast. "And they better not think you are taking journeys through every male."

Her body felt so warm beside his, fit so perfectly and when she laughed, that soft melodic sound, teasing at his senses, he felt absolutely content—right—complete. He had always known he was highly intelligent, that he'd been gifted to be fast with natural hunting instincts, but finding her had made him a better person.

"What about you? If you are infected, then I would become infected as well."

He swore beneath his breath, a time-honored *o köd belső*—darkness take it! The husky male timbre combined with the words made her smile, and she leaned upward to kiss his jaw.

He cupped her breast, his thumb sliding over her nipple. "I did not even consider that."

"I think all Carpathians have to consider it."

There was a small silence. "Would you check?"

She frowned and rolled over, pressing her soft breasts into his chest so that his body reacted with a shudder of awareness. "If a single microbe first enters the male body and then is passed to the female, it would leave the male's body open as a host for a second microbe. As long as one resides in the woman, the second would stay in the male. But if Raven or Savannah, who are now without a microbe, have sex with their partners, and Mikhail and Gregori are infected, then they would be reinfected. This could be a very vicious circle, Nicolas." Especially if she was the only person able to detect the extremophile.

Nicolas sat up, pulling her with him. Her face was pale, dark circles under her eyes. She wasn't eating anymore, not even broth. And he read her mind. What if she couldn't detect the microbes once she was fully Carpathian? Natalya couldn't seem to do it on her own and she had been part mage. That would leave the entire weight of a dying species falling directly on Lara's shoulders.

"I don't understand how this happened, Nicolas. I just got up one evening and decided the Carpathian Mountains was the next area I was going to search for the ice cave, mostly because of the gaps in the memories of those I spoke with about the ice caves. Now I've got you and all this responsibility I never dreamed of. But I'm afraid for us. I'm afraid to look inside of me and see a microbe. I'm afraid to look inside of you." She framed his face with her hands, coming up on her knees beside him. "I want children and I don't want them to suffer like that, or to ever believe they weren't wanted."

He leaned forward and took her mouth, his kiss gentle, pouring as much reassurance into it as he could. "They will know they are wanted, *fél ku kuuluaak sívam belső*.

She loved the way he whispered "beloved." The Carpathian phrase had music to it, a tenderness that shook her each time he said it to her. It was always more than just the word, but the true meaning behind that word as well. His overwhelming emotion for her. And she believed him.

Because he made her believe a man like him could love her and accept her, even damaged from the trauma of her childhood, she found the strength to hunt for the microbe, to see for herself if either was infected—and only she was. The one inside of her was newly there, and hadn't had time to establish itself. Her body was still treating it as an intruder. So that meant either the men weren't infected, and Shea's theory was incorrect, or that because she had only recently gotten together with Nicolas, he had passed her the microbe and had not yet been exposed to reinfection.

"You didn't sleep in the soil, Nicolas. You stayed on the bed with me."

"We need to go talk to Francesca and Gregori about this," Nicolas said.

She would never feel comfortable around Gregori with his strange-colored eyes, but she nodded. She had to journey into the other pregnant women this evening and hopefully Francesca would be able to follow the faint trail of the killer to aid in removing the microbes from all the other women. And she wanted the one in her out—this rising.

Lara felt drained when she came out of the healing cave with Nicolas at her side. She had aided two other pregnant women and also led the microbe within her to the surface for Natalya to destroy. They had experimented, taking both Natalya and Francesca along, but Francesca, try as she might, could not detect that faint, tainted path, and something in Natalya served as a warning to the extremophile and it successfully hid its presence from them, ruling out the possibility of Natalya tracking them.

A microbe was found in Mikhail and one in Gregori. Shea was excited that she might actually be on the right track at last to solving the problem of miscarriage. She, Gregori and a man Lara had never met named Gary, retreated together to try to explore ideas on how to combat the microbe.

Nicolas walked through the village with her. She wanted to visit Gerald and check on Terry while he and Vikirnoff finally searched for another entrance to the ice cave.

"I will not be gone long," he assured.

"And you won't go in without me," she added, giving him a quick, warning look.

At the bottom of the steps leading to the inn, he wrapped his arm around her and pulled her close. "No, I told you I wouldn't. You look pale, though. If you can manage to get some broth down, do so. If not, Lara, we cannot wait much longer to convert you."

She moistened her lips. "I have avoidance issues, I think. When I don't want to think about something, I just put it out of my mind and pretend it will go away. I like being mage. I rely on being mage."

"Mage blood aids in casting and learning, but Carpathian blood does as well. Our two species were intertwined for centuries, Lara. Xavier came up with the safeguards, but in the end Carpathians improved on them. Mages had longevity, so did lycanthrope, but even mortal wounds could sometimes be healed by Carpathians, leading others to believe our species is immortal. But we can be killed."

She tilted her head, facing her worst fear. "And that's what all the experiments on Razvan are about, aren't they? It's the reason Xavier has kept him alive. He's trying to find a way to kill Carpathians."

Nicolas held her close to him. "I am afraid of that, yes."

"Then if there is a chance he's alive, Nicolas, we have to find the evidence in the ice caves. I owe him that."

He tipped her face up and kissed her gently. "I will only be gone a couple of hours. Stay in the inn with the innkeeper and wait for me."

Lara nodded and with reluctance, left his side, stepping onto the first stair. Standing there in the dark, she watched him go—a tall, handsome man striding down the walkway, long coat swirling around his legs, his silky hair flying behind him—and her heart hammered out a rhythm of love.

He shimmered, his formidable physique nearly transparent and then he was gone, swallowed up by the darkness. She stood there listening to the night, hearing so many things she hadn't heard before. She saw differently, and the night took on a special beauty. She enjoyed just standing there, drinking it in, the solitude, the peace, with the murmur of life going on behind the scenes.

A few minutes later, Lara pushed open the door to the inn and slipped inside. It was warm and cozy, the open beams giving the inn a sense of space, the fireplace giving the room a homey feel. Slavica, the innkeeper, greeted her with a smile.

"I was hoping to see you. How are you?"

Lara was aware that few villagers were aware of the Carpathian people. Of course there were rumors, old legends whispered around a fire at night, but few modern people believed the old tales. She had heard that Mikhail Dubrinsky and the innkeeper's family went back years, but she didn't want to make the mistake of drawing too much attention to herself. She smiled and nodded. "I wanted to check on my friends. Have they been down at all?"

Slavica shook her head. "I called them to see if they wanted me to bring them food, but they refused, so I've left them alone."

"*Neither* of them has been down to eat? Not even Gerald?" Lara frowned. Both men normally had hearty appetites. "Did Gregori check on them?"

"Early last night, your friend Nicolas came and then much later Gregori stopped by. He knocked, but they were already asleep. He told me he'd be back sometime this evening."

"Did you ask them if they wanted food tonight?"

"Each meal we've asked and they've declined."

Lara was very uneasy with Slavica's answer. Terry might not feel like having food, but Gerald should be starving. "I'm going to check on them." She crossed to the stairs and began to climb, Slavica keeping pace.

"Would you like me to go with you?"

Lara bit down on her bottom lip. Her apprehension grew. *Nicolas? I'm here at the inn, but when I asked Slavica about Terry and Gerald she said...* What could she say? They'd refused a couple of meals. It was very possible Gerald would turn down one meal, but three? More than three?

Wait for me. I am not far from you and I will come back.

She felt silly standing at the top of the stairs facing the hall with the innkeeper looking at her as if she wasn't quite bright.

"What's wrong?" Slavica asked.

"Nothing. I think I forgot my key." Color rose as she told the ridiculous lie. She rubbed her palm over her left side, down low. The spot burned a little.

"Won't they let you in if you knock?" Slavica asked, moving briskly down the hall toward the door.

Lara dragged her feet. "Maybe I'll wait for Nicolas. He was going to stop by and Terry and Gerald will want to see him."

Slavica started to turn back toward her, but stopped abruptly, wrinkling her nose. "What is that terrible smell?"

A cold finger of fear raced down Lara's spine. "Slavica, come away from there," she said softly. Her side burned hotter, that small telltale dragon that warned her when the taint of evil was close. She held out her hand, lowering her voice even more. "Hurry. Right now."

Slavica reacted to the urgency in her voice, not stopping to ask questions, but hurrying back toward Lara. Lara caught her arm and yanked, an instinctive, primal gesture, nearly throwing the innkeeper onto the top of the stairs. It saved Slavica's life.

The door splintered outward, shooting spears of sharpened wood into the hall where Slavica had been standing. Gerald emerged, his face twisted into a grotesque mask. Blood tracked like tears from his eyes and trickled from his nose and mouth. He tore at his chest with his fingernails, gouging trails of flesh in madness.

Horrified, Lara stepped in front of Slavica. "Get downstairs. Don't let your other guests up here. He's infected."

He was deranged. The madness in his eyes told her that. He looked around him with a blank stare until he spotted them—spotted her. At first she thought he recognized her, but then he sniffed the air like a dog.

She reached to her belt to find the comforting hilt of her knife with trembling fingers. "Go, Slavica. I don't know if I can stop him."

Gerald growled and hissed, his eyes glowing red-hot. He turned toward her, stumbled and raked his fingers along the wall, gouging huge chunks of wood from the polished surface. Her heart jumped.

Nicolas. Now would be a great time for you to show up.

You know all that crap about women fighting vampires? I'm on your side.

This was her friend. She didn't want him dead. She wanted him fixed. When Terry had ripped out the snake's head, blood had splashed all over the car. Gerald must have had an open wound somewhere and parasites had entered. She hadn't thought to have the healer check him, she'd been so disoriented from that long-forgotten foul stench. The odor permeated Gerald. The infection had spread rapidly or...

Her stomach lurched. She moistened her lips. "Gerald? Where's Terry?"

Gerald lumbered toward her, his steps jerky and plodding. His head tilted to one side, a cunning, animalistic expression crossed his face. "Worthless traitor," he hissed.

Spittle sprayed into the hall and she couldn't help but follow the droplets with her gaze, fearing the tiny parasites would be strewn all over the floors and the entire inn would be infected. She had visions of zombies breaking through walls and eating people.

Slavica caught her arm and tugged, slowly backing down the stairs. Lara didn't want to be on the staircase, but she didn't have a lot of fighting room.

Gerald wrinkled his nose and sniffed the air more. Growls emerged from his throat, a rumbling challenge. The dragon mark burned hotter. She gripped the knife.

"Gerald!" She said his name sharply, trying to find the man inside the beast.

He blinked rapidly, tilting his head to one side, his body tensing. She gripped the knife harder and set herself on the balls of her feet. She couldn't let him get downstairs where many of Slavica's guests had gathered for dinner or drinks.

Gerald suddenly moved, lightning fast, a blur of preternatural speed that scared the hell out of her. She leapt to the side, over the banister and onto the landing, barely escaping his slashing claws. Slavica nearly fell backward down the stairs, stumbling and then recovering, backpedaling as fast as she could to get out of reach.

Screams broke out below them as guests looked up to see a wild-haired man covered in blood lunging at the two women. Two of the men rushed up the stairs to try to help.

"Stay back!" Lara called out, terrified someone else would be infected. "Gerald, who am I? Try to remember who I am and who you are."

They'd been colleagues and friends for several years, had gone caving together in some of the most dangerous caves in the world, relying on one another and forming a family of sorts.

"Gerald." Maybe if she said his name enough times, it would jog his memory.

He has no memory. Get out of there. The parasites have consumed his brain. I mean it, Lara, get away from him.

Nicolas strode up the stairs, waving a hand to calm the group below, blurring the scene so no one could quite see what happened. He had scanned Gerald and Terry the moment he set foot in the inn. Terry was dead and Gerald was the walking dead.

"Don't kill him," Lara pleaded. "There has to be a way to save him."

Nicolas caught her around the waist and shoved her behind him. "He's already dead, Lara, and he's programmed to find and kill you."

Gerald sniffed the air again, looking confused with Nicolas blocking access to Lara.

"He's my friend. You can't know that."

"He's not your friend. Go now. Wait for me outside."

"But..." She couldn't just walk away and give up. "This is my fault. I should have checked on them."

Hands dropped to her shoulders. Startled, she swung around, the knife in her fist. Gregori shook his head and took the weapon. "Let us handle this, little sister. The fault does not lie with you. I should have checked him."

Lara backed down the stairs. The Carpathian males had a difficult time detecting the parasites, but she should have scented the taint of Xavier. She *should* have sensed it, but she'd been too busy feeling sorry for herself. She wiped at the tears streaming down her face. She hadn't achieved any of her goals since her arrival. She'd only managed to get her friends killed. She hadn't recovered the aunts. Their bodies were still locked away in the labyrinth of horror where Xavier had ruled.

She couldn't leave, couldn't look away. She owed it to Gerald to be with him, to stay while they destroyed the mass of parasites eating him from the inside out. Nicolas turned his head slightly to glance over his shoulder at her. She saw his long hair swing out and then—nothing at all. They were gone.

She stood staring up the staircase, one hand pressed to her mouth, trying to push back the sobs welling up. She'd lost her friend. Both of them. Lara backed away from the stairs into the lobby. Gregori and Nicolas could deal with the memories of Slavica's guests. She needed air fast. And she was going to the caves with or without Nicolas. She was going to find the bodies of her aunts and bring them home.

The cold air hit her face and it was only then she realized she was outside with Slavica standing beside her, a look of concern in her dark eyes.

"I'm sorry about your friend."

Lara ducked her head. "None of us had any family, so we kind of hung together. And we shared a love of caving. I can't believe this happened." *Nicolas, is Terry dead?*

I am sorry, fél ku kuuluaak sívam belső. Gerald killed him. We have to ensure that all the parasites are destroyed.

Lightning arced across the sky, zigzagged and lit up the clouds in a fiery display before slamming down to earth. For a half-second the inn lit up and then everything went dark again. Lara stood beside Slavica with an occasional snowflake drifting past her.

"You aren't terrified by all this," she said to the innkeeper.

Slavica shrugged. "Life can be frightening if you dwell on things you can't control. I choose not to be afraid if I can help it. Mikhail will see that my guests are safe, or at least as safe as we can keep them when the undead walk the night. Most outsiders think it is superstition when we caution them, but locals know such things walk among us."

"I wish I'd been more careful. I should have been more careful."

She didn't realize she was weeping until Nicolas turned her into his arms and pressed her face against his chest. She caught a glimpse of Gregori before she closed her eyes and let herself cry for the loss of her two friends.

"The inn is no longer contaminated and there is no evidence of any problem, Slavica," Gregori said. "Your guests will not remember anything took place."

Slavica nodded and went back inside, leaving Lara clinging to Nicolas.

Nicolas stroked his hand down her hair. "I'm sorry, Lara. I should have checked your other friend."

Gregori added his own apology.

Lara lifted her head and looked up at Nicolas. "I can find a new entrance to the caves. I want to go now—tonight. I need to go, Nicolas."

He nodded. "Then we will go tonight."

"You cannot," Gregori protested. "You have a higher purpose."

She lifted her chin at him. "I came here for one purpose and that was to find my aunts, and I'm going to do it, with or without help. I've tried to help Francesca learn how to recognize Xavier's touch..."

"But she's unable to do so," Gregori pointed out.

Nicolas dropped his arm around Lara's shoulders. "She

needs to do this and she has more than done her duty to our people, Gregori. In any case, what we find there may be invaluable. If Lara can recognize the source, we can stop our women from miscarrying for good."

Gregori sighed. "There is truth in that."

"She goes," Nicolas stated.

17

Nicolas studied the snow-covered mountains rising sharply above them. Ringed in swirling mist, the mountains appeared a peaceful place of cold beauty, but he heard the soft voices murmuring continually, and felt the steady flow of energy, a force field subtly sending out signals tuned to brain waves. *Stay away. Fear this place. Forget this place.*

Even the locals avoided the mountain. The upper peaks were inhospitable. Nothing grew but a few straggly plants in the midst of boulders and once you climbed past the boulders, there was the glacier itself. Unwary travelers who braved the uneasy, disturbed feeling often found themselves victims of falling boulders or a heavy avalanche. The mountain shook and rumbled the moment anyone dared set foot on it.

He walked along the base, studying it from every angle, looking for anything that might conceal an entryway. Natalya, Vikirnoff and Lara spread out several yards apart and did the same, all of them careful not to get too close and trip any hidden traps or alarms that would trigger the mountain to protect itself.

"What do you think, Lara?" he called.

The wind whipped his words away from the mountain, slamming his voice back down his throat. It was an aggressive move and he'd been unprepared for the attack. They weren't actually on the mountain. He exchanged a long look with Lara.

She nodded her head and moved toward him. Nicolas signaled to Natalya and Vikirnoff to watch above their heads and below their feet, in the ground itself. Lara placed her feet carefully, all the while scanning along the snow-covered ground for the slightest movement.

If we triggered an alarm, then we have to be close to an entrance. It will be something ordinary, easily overlooked, but simple.

Nicolas spotted a crack that ran the length of the overhang at the base of the mountain. The line was narrow, tiny really, no more than an inch thick running just under the overhang, nearly hidden in the shadow of the limestone cliffs. He scanned along the crack, inch by inch, but couldn't see where there could be an opening.

From the air, Nicolas had noted the pattern of rocks, which looked, with its ice cap, like an undulating sea of blue beneath the glacier—a sure sign that far below meltwater had carved canyons and formed large ice caves beneath the surface. He might know a labyrinth of chambers was beneath the mountain, but finding a way in was difficult.

It's here, Lara said with confidence. *Very close.*

Now that she knew she was in the right area, she knew what to look for. No, not look. "Feel" for. Scent. Xavier had sealed the entrances, but they were there and she shouldn't be looking for an opening, she should be following the taint of evil, just as she had when she searched the women's bodies for mutated extremophiles.

A short distance from them, deer moved out onto the meadow, but none approached the thicker grass a few yards

from where she was standing. She touched their minds.
Gentle creatures as a rule, interested in feeding. A few
pawed the snow to reveal short stalks of grass beneath the
white layer. Not one looked or scented the thick offering
pushing through the snow.

She closed her eyes and inhaled the night, taking in
the information her surroundings offered. The night was
crisp and cold. The snow had ceased to fall but the smell
was there, a clean feel to the air until you went deeper. She
caught the whiff of tainted magic and wrinkled her nose,
turning in the direction where it was strongest before opening her eyes. She was looking at that patch of tall grass that
poked through the snow, yet didn't tempt hungry deer.

She took a couple of steps closer to the green stalks
now rippling as if wind drove them—but there was no real
breeze on her face. The ripples increased, until the grass
undulated as if water ebbed and flowed around it. Something moved in the forest of green, a stealthy crawl that
drew her eye. A bat emerged, using its wings as legs, coming out of the deep grass to creep silently toward the grazing deer. A second and third bat appeared, and then the
ground seemed covered by them, a stealthy, dark-furred
army, circling an unwary doe, cutting it off from the rest
of the herd.

Lara gripped Nicolas's arm as the bats swayed back and
forth, walking on the tips of their wings, to close the net on
the deer. *Vampire bats just take a small amount of blood.
They don't behave like that.* As if they were stalking the
deer for darker, more sinister purposes.

Before Nicolas could reply, the bats rushed the doe,
wings flapping, so that the circle appeared solid. She
caught a glimpse of huge teeth, not like a vampire bat, but
more like a shark, razor-edged and rows of them filling the
muzzles. The sheer weight of numbers drove the doe to her
knees and then down to the grass. Blood ran onto the snow.

The herd whirled and raced away from the meadow, back into the forest.

The bats swarmed over the doe, her sides heaving, her pitiful bleats tearing at Lara's heart. When she would have moved, Nicolas stopped her.

There is nothing to do for her. Look at what they are doing.

The bats tore great chunks of flesh from the deer to get at her insides, but even while some fed, others began to use their teeth to pull the weight of the carcass across the meadow toward the taller grass. Behind them, they left a trail of blood. Several bats licked at the blood before hurrying to help drag the doe.

Have you ever seen something like that before? Lara asked. She glanced at Vikirnoff and Natalya and they looked every bit as stunned as she was.

Nicolas shook his head. *They aren't vampire bats.*

A mutation then. Lara watched the deer carcass disappear into the longer grass. Dirt and snow boiled up, spewing like a small geyser. The grass shook. Under the swarm of bats, the deer rolled over, legs up in the air, and then sank beneath the earth. The ground was quiet again. *I think we've just met the guardians of the gate,* Lara said. *And they aren't going to be alone.*

"Did you see the teeth on those things?" Vikirnoff asked.

"Maybe we should try another way in," Natalya ventured.

Nicolas watched Lara closely. She moved in a semicircle a few yards from the patch of green grass, pacing back and forth, counting under her breath, one hand out, palm facing down toward the earth.

"What's she doing?" Vikirnoff asked.

"Testing the strength of his safeguards," Natalya said. "Mage magic is all about elements and energy. She's obviously extremely sensitive to Xavier's signature. Every mage has one and when you work with them you get to know their particular fingerprints."

"That's why she can detect the microbe in the women?" Vikirnoff asked. "You're mage. And you're actually Xavier's granddaughter. She's his great-granddaughter. You knew him, too."

Natalya shook her head. "Not like Lara. I stayed away from him. I was good at mage spells, Razvan wasn't. I was more mage, and I thought Razvan wasn't mage or Dragonseeker, but I was wrong. I was wrong about so many things."

Vikirnoff stroked a caress down the length of her hair. "He wanted you to be. He misled everyone on purpose to protect you."

"It seems he did that all the time," Nicolas said.

He stayed close enough to Lara to protect her, but far enough away to allow her to get a good feel for the traps Xavier left behind to safeguard his lair. He noted her hair banded, the red stripes moving through the blond. Tiny electric sparks gathered around her and he felt the buildup of energy as she gathered power to her. She lifted her arms into the air.

Air, earth, fire and water, hear my call. See your daughter...

The air grew heavy with the combination of elements gathering and spinning into a combined force.

Air unseen, seek that which is closed. Earth that does hold open, unfold. Fire that burns, eat that which would harm, water that flows, break open this door.

As she spoke, the ground beneath their feet shook. The mountain rumbled in protest. Rocks and snow rained down, as though hurled from above, showering the entire area where Lara stood, but she didn't move, trusting Nicolas to keep her from harm.

He waved his hands to form a protective shield over her,

careful to give her room to work. Her hands moved in a graceful pattern, parts of which he recognized. She was reversing the tight weave of a safeguard, reversing the spell so she could open the entrance.

The wind rose to a piercing whine. The earth quivered and then shook in earnest. Fire spiders webbed along the base of the mountain right above the patch of green. Racing along tiny, unseen cracks, fire rained down on the patch of green. Right behind the silken strands of orange-red flame came a flood of water to pour over the blaze and into the cave entrance to finish eroding the safeguards.

Lara's hands continued to flow gracefully. *That which was set in place to harm, now give forth a warning alarm.* A fine-spun pattern began to appear. *Spiders, spiders of finespun ice, hear my call, spin and splice. Create a web of finest thread, to give a warning against harm and dread.* The pattern burned brightly in the air for a brief moment and then slowly faded away.

Stone creaked and groaned as if rubbing against itself. Snow slid from the mountain in a long rush of white. The patch of green sunk in so that dirt, snow and vegetation fell in on itself, revealing the deep hole penetrating the earth.

Nicolas caught Lara and shoved her behind him as he and Vikirnoff examined the entrance. Even as they watched, a thin layer of ice stretched and then covered the hole so he appeared to be looking through a window into the black interior. The ice walls were textured in spots with mud, grass and a dark stain that could only be blood. In direct contrast, the rest of the wall looked pristine and beautiful, like a great ice sculpture, thick and carved into a round tube of shimmering glass.

Lara caught Nicolas around the waist from behind and peered down into the hole, noting the darker spots lining the tube, most of which dotted the first two hundred feet of the shaft. The stains of grass and blood formed a distinctive trail to the scattered spots. They looked solid, but on closer inspection, that same sheet of thin ice that formed the window covered holes.

She indicated them with her chin. "That's where the guardians live."

"Bats with big teeth that will crawl out of their little holes and drop on us to gnaw our heads off as we descend," Natalya said. "Great. Someone ought to make a movie."

Vikirnoff grinned at her. "You and your movies. She has the worst taste in movies."

Natalya blew him a kiss. "Just for that, you can go first."

Lara shook her head. "Let me remove the ice cap and then I'll weave a holding spell. We should be able to get past them without too much trouble." She sent Nicolas a faint smile. "And I'd rather have someone protecting me from above."

She made a move toward the hole and Nicolas caught her arm. "You do your mage spell, but you do not set one foot in there by yourself. Vikirnoff can go first to make certain we land without too much harm and I will bring up the rear to protect you from above."

Lara put a hand over her heart and sent a quick grin in her aunt's direction. "I love it when he does that."

Natalya rolled her eyes. "He-Man and She-Ra."

Nicolas frowned. "Who?"

Vikirnoff groaned. "Do not *ever* make the mistake of asking." He looked up at the night, took a deep breath. "The safeguards are down?"

Lara nodded. "In theory, you should be able to go right through the thin layer of ice and straight down the tube without disturbing the guardians. Once into the lava tube, avoid touching anything that might trigger a response."

"Great, thanks," Vikirnoff said. He shimmered into mist and slipped through the layer of ice covering the entrance.

Natalya followed him immediately.

"I will hold the image for you," Nicolas assured.

Now that she'd had some experience with shifting, she knew what to expect so the sensation of her body disintegrating into vapor didn't alarm her and she just let it happen. Oftentimes, when caving in an ice cave, the ropes used could collect a thin layer of ice. There were hazards from falling icicles and great chunks of ice bursting out of the walls due to the tremendous pressures from the sheer weight. Becoming mist seemed so much easier.

The world beneath the earth, inside the ice cave itself, was, to Lara, a world of uncommon and magnificent beauty. As she descended into the dark moulin, essentially a deep pit, she whispered a brief spell, calling for soft light to spill along the walls and floors wherever they walked. Using her childhood spiders, the only friends she had to light the way, she chanted softly.

Spiders, spiders of crystal ice, spin your webs of softest light. The little spiders appeared instantly out of the walls of ice, spinning and dancing to freely form a continuous fine web of translucent icy silk, covering the walls and rushing ahead of them down toward the floor. *Spin and dance, surround and form, so our eyes may see to prevent all harm.*

At once the tube turned blue, a beautiful, surreal world of ice. The water spraying continually from above had caused an avalanche of various-sized ice balls to cascade down the walls so it appeared as though a waterfall of blue ice rushed downward, when in reality, the ice balls were stationary, attached to the thick walls surrounding them. She was used to the sound of creaking ice punctuated by the thunderous roar as the tremendous pressure sent giant chunks hurling out of the wall to slam against the opposite side and fall to the floor below.

As she passed the darker holes, she realized the entryways were a maze of dwellings woven into the ice to allow the bats communal living. Through the thick window of ice, she could see bones and hair and blood from discarded carcasses. The cave dwellers feasted on their kill, lived for a while on the remains and then every so often swarmed to the surface to drag a hapless victim to their lair. Anything or anyone venturing too near at the wrong time was fair game.

They floated past a ledge that ran the circle of the tube, not very wide. Hanging below it was a variety of long icicles, each one coming to a lethal point.

We need to break those off, she told Nicolas. *He'll use those against us and we don't want to be caught on the floor when they come flying at us.*

At once sound echoed through the tube, a high note that set the icicles rocking. Some shattered. Others broke loose and fell to the cavern floor several hundred feet below. The sound was loud—too loud—too abrupt. The bats flew at their entrances, the movement frightening to watch through the ice, but Lara's safeguard held against the battering bodies. Tiny fire spiders rushed down the sides of the walls, using their silken threads of flames. As the bats emerged from the holes, using their wings like arms to creep out onto the sheer wall, the nets made of flames and silk dropped over them, consuming them entirely.

A noxious odor permeated the moulin. Despite being insubstantial mist, Lara felt sick.

Nicolas flashed into human form, waved his arms to create a breeze, and then before any of the falling debris could strike him, was back to vapor form.

Thank you.

He seemed to think of everything for her comfort and she was grateful, because this place brought back too many horrific memories. She had to steel herself to the idea that she would find her aunts dead and bring them home. She didn't want their bodies to remain imprisoned, as they'd spent their lives that way.

The cave floor was just beneath her and she hovered

there, studying the layout, the way the chamber widened and ran into a maze of galleries. She took her time, not wanting to miss the slightest taint of dark magic that would herald an attack. This was Xavier's private realm. She recognized the high ceilings and network of lava tubes leading to various chambers where he conducted his gruesome experiments.

We got lucky. This is Xavier's exclusive domain. The entire mountain is a maze of tunnels and chambers and we were lucky enough or crazy enough to find his private quarters.

Her voice shook and she pulled back to get a better grip on her emotions. She hadn't considered what it would do to her to be surrounded by Xavier. He was everywhere, his mark on everything. His smell filled her with dread. He had been there recently. No matter what anyone said, his pipe tobacco mingled with the pungent scent of blood smelled all too fresh. No matter how long ago it had been, she couldn't forget the difference between old blood and new and the way his tobacco intermingled, making her gag.

If at any time, Lara, you have to leave this place, Nicolas reassured, *tell me and I will get you out. And I will come back and search for your aunts.* He wanted to hold her, to wrap her up in comfort and make her feel beautiful and safe. No one was ever going to understand what it cost her to come to this place, to be haunted by the torment of that young child.

Thank you. She sent him waves of warmth. *He's been here, Nicolas. Very recently. And if he's still using these chambers, he would never leave them without serious traps. The floor is washed in magic. I think the entire room is a trap.*

Nicolas shifted to the common Carpathian path. *Do not touch anything. We should move on to the next chamber.*

Lara tried to remember where she had seen the young woman miscarrying. *Take the left tube and move slowly. Even the disturbance of air could trigger an attack.*

The four of them went as carefully as they could down the twisting ice tunnel until they came to a series of smaller chambers. Lara sucked in her breath, the smells hitting her like a punch in the stomach. Water trickled from the walls, dripped from the ceiling and poured out in other places so that she heard a continuous echo, loud and growing even louder until it rang in her ears and filled her mind with confusion.

She remembered that sound from her childhood. The sound seemed to be an alarm, roaring through the chambers, or whispering quietly, but warning her of the monsters lurking everywhere. Her heart beat too fast and she could barely draw air into her lungs, but she kept moving, directing Nicolas toward the terrible chambers where the screams of victims drowned out the relentless sound of water.

Lara stopped just inside the room where Razvan had been kept chained. Memories rose along with bile and she couldn't hold the form even with Nicolas helping her. She needed to kneel on the ice floor and put her head down to keep from passing out.

Nicolas dropped a hand on her shoulder. "You do not have to do this."

She drew a breath and nodded. "I do. I do have to do this."

But she couldn't look at that alcove where her father had been chained so much of the time. Where she had been kicked and beaten, where the flesh had been torn from her wrist so sharp greedy teeth could bite deep and drain her to the point she was dizzy and wheezing for air. She remembered crawling across the floor, the cold biting into her knees and arms, on her belly, like a dog, he'd said, too weak to get up.

"There's fresh blood here," Natalya said. "It's all over the place." She touched a manacle, smeared the blood on her fingers and held it to her nose. Her face paled. "Razvan. This is my brother's blood. He had to have been here within a rising or two." The blood was sticky and congealed, but not dry.

Vikirnoff examined the manacles. "Vampire blood to burn him while he's chained."

Lara shuddered. "There's so much blood, and stab wounds in the ice. Look at that," she pointed to the wall. "It looks as though he was stabbed and the instrument went through him and out the other side."

Natalya skimmed her palm down the wall without touching the blood spatter. Lara could hear her heart pounding and the rhythm matched the drumming of the water coming out of the walls. Natalya's body trembled as she kept her hand over the blood of her twin.

"There's something here."

Lara put out her palm to feel the energy band. It was low, humming, very much alive. "The energy doesn't feel dark."

Natalya shook her head. "It's Razvan. He left something here. When we were children we used to leave messages for one another right under Xavier's nose." She frowned and paced the length of Razvan's prison, both hands palm out away from her body as if feeling the air.

Lara tried not to be that little girl, worthless and lonely in the cave with only ice spiders for friends. She detested how pathetically jealous she was that Natalya had good memories of her father. She rubbed at the ridges on her wrist.

Nicolas reached over and took her hand, bringing it to his chest. *I love you, sívamet.*

Her heart fluttered. She wasn't that lonely child anymore, living in terror, feeling worthless and unloved. She looked up at him, at his beautiful face, so masculine and strong. There was love in his eyes, tenderness in the way the pad of his thumb swept back and forth over the palm of her hand. This tall, dangerous man loved her. *Loved* her. With all her failings, even her aversion to letting anyone take her blood, he loved her, and that was everything.

Nicolas turned up her wrist and brushed his lips over the fading scars. *I am very grateful that I found you.*

She sent him a quick, teasing smile. *Actually, I found you.*

Natalya's gasp drew her attention.

"I found it. He left a message behind." Natalya leaned over the ledge of ice, waved her hands gracefully, murmuring low.

That which is hidden from all sight, created between two who shared the fight. Blood of blood, twin and twine, show me now the twining rhyme.

The ice lit up from within and an image wavered, a hologram of a man ravaged by time and torture. He was manacled to the wall, no shirt and his trousers in shreds. Lines cut deep into his face. His hair was in dreadlocks, streaked with gray, but it was his eyes that Lara couldn't look away from—so filled with sorrow and pain.

The hologram began to glow and the man spoke, but his words were garbled, unintelligible, a twin talk devised and scrambled between the brother and sister. Natalya's hands moved, gently weaving another unlocking spell, rearranging the notes of his voice, working to make sense of the message left long ago—and meant only for her eyes and ears. Slowly she began to see the pattern of the language, unraveling it until he made sense.

"Natalya. Beloved sister. I pray you find this message I've hidden at great cost. I dare not let Xavier ever touch you or my Lara. He's evil beyond all imagining. I no longer have the strength to fight him, although I believe I've put up a worthy battle. He uses my body to produce children he can feed on and, although I have tried, I cannot stop him." He shuddered, pain crossing his face. "The knowledge that it is me he uses to cause such harm to others, to those I love, is far worse than any physical torment he has ever devised."

Natalya let out a soft cry of distress. Vikirnoff circled her waist with his arm.

"When I could, I helped their mothers escape him and take the children far from him, but I do not even have that ability left to me. I opened my soul in a moment of weakness and he owns it now, commanding me for his foul purpose and, though I am aware on some level, I cannot resist his commands. I think that amuses him so much he wants to keep me alive. Few things amuse him these days."

"Razvan." Natalya whispered her brother's name and turned her tear-streaked face up to Vikirnoff. "Look what Xavier did to him."

There were scars. Horrible scars on his neck and throat, on his arms and chest, his wrists, even his legs. The links of the chains smeared in vampire blood had burned the images into his skin—Carpathian skin that didn't scar.

Natalya drew in a sobbing breath. "He is Dragonseeker. He would never turn. I should have known and believed in him. Instead I tried to kill him."

The hologram continued. "I beg you to find my daughter. She is so like you. Tatijana and Branislava have agreed to help her escape. I've convinced them not to tell me their plans. Xavier still likes to occupy my body and I'm afraid if he does, he'll discover the plan and we won't be able to get her out of here. I dared not let Lara know too much because if Xavier suspected anything, he would torture her until she told him everything."

He hung there, his chains cutting into his flesh, his tangled hair hanging down his back and around his shoulders. He was painfully thin. Even talking tired him out, that and the use of magic as he recorded his message to his sister. He moistened his cracked lips.

"He keeps us all drained of blood and weak. He's using me to find a way to kill the Carpathians. Everything from poisons to parasites. He has to be stopped. Find the prince and tell him, Xavier has to be stopped. But first, find my child. Her mother was not my lifemate, but the mage in me loved her dearly. She was sunshine in a world of madness. Find Lara for us and love her, Natalya. It is the last thing I ask of you."

He looked to his left. His body shuddered and his skin took on a grayish tinge. "He's coming for me and I'll hold on as long as I can until Lara is out of his hands, and then I will find a way to force him to kill me. Natalya, do not ever come back here. And don't look for me. Find Lara and let that be enough." He turned his head and looked straight at them.

Lara could feel his piercing gaze right through to her soul. The mental anguish he suffered was far worse than any physical torture Xavier could conceive. She didn't even realize she was sobbing until Nicolas turned her into his arms and held her close.

"I've hated him for years. I thought of him as a monster," she whispered. "He wanted me to think of him that way so he could protect me."

"He's alive," Natalya said. "He's out there, Xavier's prisoner, and he's alive."

"We don't know that," Vikirnoff objected. "There's so much blood here, *sívamet,* and it is all his. If he survived this, it would be a miracle." He caught her to him. "I know what you're thinking, but he does not want you to try to find him. Either of you." He glanced at Lara before turning his attention back to his lifemate. "Don't you see? You and Lara are the two people he loves most and he's managed to protect you. We have to give him that. It's all he has to hang on to to keep him sane. This man has given up his life, his soul, everything he is or ever was in order to ensure you and Lara have a life. You cannot take that away from him."

"I can find him."

"What do you think it would do to him if you fell into Xavier's hands after all of his sacrifices?"

Natalya shook her head, refusing to answer.

Lara knew she would never give her word not to go looking for her brother. Lara wouldn't either, if Nicolas asked it of her. She took a deep breath, let it out and looked cautiously around her. The others, always so confident in their power and skills, weren't as nervous being in Xavier's lair as she was. And they were growing in confidence the longer they went without anything attacking them, but the lack of resistance only made her leerier.

She stayed very still, watching the cave as the others fanned out in an attempt to find more clues. Natalya used her connection with her brother, hoping to find more messages, while Nicolas and Vikirnoff examined the devices shelved in the ice where Razvan was chained to the wall. Obviously the various instruments had been stored where he could see them to build anticipation of torture.

"Xavier is one sadistic *hän ku tuulmahl elidet*," Nicolas commented.

Life-stealer, Lara translated, and thought the phrase more than appropriate. Xavier was definitely a stealer of life. He took from everyone—family, species, everyone he met—and the Carpathian meaning was so much more, not just the words, but the inflection, the darkness behind the words.

Vikirnoff bent down to examine marks gouged into the ice. "What is this, Nicolas?"

Lara followed his gaze as both men crouched beside what appeared to be claw marks running along the ice floor. Her heart jumped. The aunts in the form of dragons? Could it be? The marks were recent. Had they been there? Hope sprang even though she knew it was impossible. Both had been so ill all those years ago.

Nicolas and Vikirnoff stroked fingers along the grooves

in an effort to figure out what had made those marks. Heart hammering, she crouched down beside Nicolas.

Nicolas turned his head to look at Lara as her shoulder brushed his. The scent of her enveloped him. Although she'd braided her hair, stray strands curled around her face, making him want to brush them aside just for the pleasure of feeling her satin skin and the silky texture of her hair. He had lived long, battled hard, seen beautiful places and none of it, not one thing, compared to the treasure he had been given. The gift. *Lara*. He whispered her name in his mind, wanting to take the anxiety from her.

Their eyes met and his heart slammed inside his chest in reaction. His belly knotted at the intensity of his love for her. The emotion seemed to grow each rising, filling him so completely, he barely recognized himself anymore. There was a gentleness in Lara he was drawn to. Maybe because he felt there was little in him. Maybe she brought out the best in him—made him a better man. Whatever it was, he ached inside for her. He thought of her, watched for every expression to chase across her face. He didn't even know exactly when it had happened to him—the growing love and need of her—but he accepted that it was only going to get stronger.

"What?" she asked, a small smile chasing away some of the shadows in her eyes.

He smiled back. "Just looking at you."

She blushed and looked down at the claw marks, running her palm over the area to get a feel for what had made the gouges. At once she felt the taint of darkness. Gasping, she scrambled back. "It's a trap. Don't touch it. Get away from there."

Nicolas caught her hand and pulled her to her feet. Vikirnoff and Natalya turned back to back so they faced outward, looking for an enemy.

Large icicles rained down on them from the ceiling. Others hurled themselves like spears from the walls. The men threw up shields to prevent injury or even death from the heavy, sharp, daggerlike ice formations.

The ice cave rumbled and shook. Water gushed from a crack on the wall above them, pouring down with a roar. The ice splintered and a spiderweb of tiny lines spread from ceiling to floor. Water seeped, began to trickle and then pour from the cracks, widening them into deeper crevasses. The ice quivered and then sloughed off in great chunks, crashing to the floor. The grinding and cracking noises increased, as if the walls were moving closer together.

"This chamber is mutating. We have to get out now," Lara warned.

"They do that?" Nicolas asked, already running toward his right where a long, narrow tunnel looked more hospitable.

"This one does," Lara said and rushed after him with Vikirnoff and Natalya close behind.

As the water filled the chamber and began to leak into the tunnel, Lara turned back and murmured her own safeguard. Let Xavier deal with a solid wall of ice several feet thick in his torture chamber.

Water that runs, shift and grow, rise high now to fill these walls. The water began to form layer after layer, growing quickly into a block of ice as big as a tower.

Satisfied that the water had halted at the entrance to the tunnel and begun refreezing, she turned and ran after the others. As she ran, she heard the steady drip of water again, the same monotonous pattern she'd noted earlier. She could actually hear each individual drop plop into a puddle. A shiver went down her spine.

Something isn't right, Nicolas. Xavier's chambers know we're intruders and we're in for a fight. Watch everything, no matter how trivial. That's his specialty—the subtle, creeping up on you before you notice anything.

Out of the narrow tunnel they found themselves in a

much larger room, this one intensely beautiful with ice sculptures and prisms and many orbs. Lara halted, her heart pounding. She had been in this room many times. She glanced over at the tall pillars, terrified she would see Xavier standing there with his grotesque mask of a face, his fierce eyes and the twisted smug smirk he always seemed to wear.

Shadows moved and stretched. She gasped and stepped back.

"What is it, Lara?" Natalya asked. "What do you feel?"

Lara shook her head, twisting and turning, spinning in a circle to see everything—everywhere. "Apparitions. Shadows. We shouldn't be here. Through there," she gestured toward another narrow tube, "is his laboratory."

"We need to take a look at it," Vikirnoff said, moving toward it.

"Stop!" Desperation was in her voice. "Don't take another step. Don't breathe hard."

The others looked warily around the room. Water dripped, a steady plop into the puddle forming at the base of the wall beside a wide column. Lara turned toward the sound. Another loud drop hit a second puddle, this one closer to her, right near the tallest pillar. She stared into the water as rings expanded outward toward the edges of the small pool of water.

"Elements. Water. He's all around us. He's everywhere."

Nicolas glanced at her, alarmed by her rambling. "Lara!" He said her name sharply to snap her out of it. "He isn't here."

"You don't understand," Lara said. "He's here. He locks himself into things, into elements. He can travel that way. You don't know him."

Nicolas moved cautiously to wrap his arm around her. He was worried about her and it showed on his face. "Lara, monsters always appear larger and much more indestructible when you are a child. He may have been here recently..."

"I smell his tobacco."

Natalya inhaled, shook her head and shrugged. "If he is, Lara, he's hiding from us."

The men were cautious as they made their way across the open floor. Natalya and Lara followed, both watching above and around them. The water dripped monotonously. As they approached the archway leading to the next series of open caverns, they could see just inside the entrance. Water sprayed from the ceiling, the droplets falling into a series of pools. Each pool was a bit lower than the first and each was a different color.

Tiny frogs croaked, the notes mournful. A dark red stain dripped down from the ice and dropped into one of the pools, staining it a deep crimson. Several of the frogs stuck to the side of the wall, long tongues dipping in the blood, licking at it as it ran down. Although there was no breeze, each pool of water rippled slightly, as if something lived in them. The scent of blood and bodily fluids was heavy in the air.

"This is it," Lara said. "This is what you've been looking for, Nicolas. He mutates them here. He's experimenting with extremophiles and this is where he tests and corrupts them for his own purpose. We've found his laboratory."

18

Standing at the entrance of the laboratory, watching the light spray of icy water come down from the ceiling to feed the pools, Nicolas felt his gut tighten. If Lara was right, and Xavier was experimenting with microbes, then it was the mage who had virtually brought the Carpathian people to near extinction and none of them had ever suspected the extent of his true treachery all those centuries ago. As if sensing his need, Lara slipped her hand into his. He closed his fingers tightly around hers and drew in a deep, shuddering breath.

"Without you, Lara, he might have succeeded."

Vikirnoff looked over their shoulders. "Is that spray natural?"

Steam curled over several of the pools, as if they were somehow warm and the icy spray created a foggy condensation. Droplets froze on the walls and congealed in the trail of blood.

"It appears so," Lara said, "but you can't trust anything in these chambers to be what it appears."

She held out her hands, palms up. The spray from the

ceiling was so fine, it appeared more mist than anything else. "It's ice," she said, "tiny particles of ice."

"There has to be a purpose for it," Natalya added. She also put her palms out to test the "feel" of the spray. "Are you getting anything?"

Lara frowned. "Yes, I feel Xavier's hand in this. There appears to be subtle influence in the mist, but I can't tell what it is yet. Why can't you feel it?"

"I can in the outer chambers, but it was difficult," Natalya said. "But in this room, I wouldn't have even been able to tell you Xavier had been here." She looked around. "And I have to say, this is creepy, like in those spooky old movies where the mad scientist conjures up mutated zombies. These are all vats with extremely disgusting gunk bubbling in them."

Nicolas stepped into the room, waited until the mist touched his face and arms before signaling the others inside. "It's cold, but I expected that."

"The room isn't cold," Lara pointed out. "In fact, that pool over there is steaming. I'll bet it's fed by an underground volcano. Xavier's tapped into something hot."

"Wouldn't that kill anything he's trying to grow in here?" Natalya asked.

"Extremophiles are called just that because they live in extreme conditions." Lara looked around the room. "And it looks to me as if he's testing every condition. Hot. Cold. Acid. Blood. Salt. Minerals. You name it, he has it in here. This is his breeding program."

"Why all the frogs?" Vikirnoff asked.

Lara approached the little creatures, ignoring Nicolas's restraining hand. Again she placed her hand just inches from them. "They're male. All of them."

Nicolas's jaw tightened. "This is where it started then. He found a way for the microbe to force male offspring and suppress female."

Lara indicated the first pool. "See those stalks with that

gelatinous mass, the tiny black specks wiggling inside? I'm betting those are all male. He's still working at perfecting his methods, I see."

Things can always be improved. The hated voice whispered in her ear and Lara spun around, eyes wide with terror, expecting to see the mage standing behind her with his smug expression and his hate-filled silvery eyes.

She drew in a deep breath and pressed a hand to her thudding heart. He had always said that when he injected something into Razvan's body. The memory poured into her mind, the image vivid and sharp. Razvan fighting, sweating blood, her mother crying while Razvan writhed and convulsed on the ice floor. Bile rose. She was going to be sick.

Nicolas pressed his hand against her stomach, his mind merging with hers. *I am here. He cannot harm you, Lara. You are not the little helpless child anymore.* He poured strength and love into her mind.

"I'm sorry. I can do this. We have to do this. I want to find my aunts." Lara lifted her chin and managed a faint smile. "Be careful in here. I don't trust anything." Her chest felt heavy and she pressed her hand against it hard as she took another nervous look around. He was there. Maybe not physically, but Xavier permeated the room. His evil nature seemed permanently pressed into the layers of ice.

She took another deep breath to steady herself and forced her body closer to the tanks. One was filled with fluid and when she sniffed it, she drew back horrified. "I think this is amniotic fluid. Where would he get that?" The one beside it was blood. The blood coming from above ran steadily into the pool. Dense clusters of organisms floated in both pools.

"Where's that blood coming from?"

Nicolas stepped closer and sniffed it. "That is from the deer the bats took down earlier, but look at the other trails, Lara. This one has two separate blood trails. They are older, but the blood is Carpathian."

Natalya waved them to the corner wall. "This is Razvan's blood. It's not as old as those trails and it also goes into that pool."

"How old do you think Razvan's blood trail is, Natalya?" Vikirnoff asked.

She shook her head. "Not very old. A day or two. Just like in that chamber, his blood is congealed, frozen even, but it isn't old."

"Then he's been here recently, which means Xavier has been here. Right under our noses," Nicolas said. "He's been conducting experiments and sending his little microbe army after us this entire time. How could he hide from us?"

"He's had centuries to perfect his methods, and he appears to be sharing them with vampires," Vikirnoff pointed out.

There was a small silence while all around the ice seemed alive, creaking and groaning. Lara looked around her. "The deeper the ice cave, the more unstable the ice, unless guarded by magic. Ice caves never stay the same, not like this one. Water can pour in from a melt above, creating a very strong waterfall, and then a few days later, when it's cold again, that can be completely frozen. And it moves. The walls move on you. You measure them to make certain they aren't closing on you. This ice is very stable in spite of the fact that we are hundreds of feet down. The walls move when he wants them to move. He's been here."

Her lungs burned. She realized she was breathing shallowly. She detested this place and she wanted out.

"Lara," Nicolas said, "can these two other blood trails be your aunts? I do not recognize the scent, other than knowing it is Dragonseeker."

Natalya hurried over, pressing both hands to her chest tightly. "I did not know them. I thought them long dead."

Lara felt sluggish, reluctant to move. "If that's their blood, we should be able to track it back to them. He kept them weak and sick because he was afraid of them, but he wanted their blood and he drained it from them often."

Nicolas whipped his head around to look at her. "Lara! What is wrong with you?" He looked from her to the other two. "Something is wrong. None of us are breathing right."

Lara tried to clear her foggy brain. "A natural hazard. He would use the elements and it would be simple." She lifted her face to look at the ceiling and spray hit her. "Nicolas, we have to get out of here. Warm up your lungs. He's freezing our lungs using the ice crystals. The particles are so tiny and we inhale them."

Nicolas yanked her out of the laboratory and into the next chamber. It was free of the icy spray. Vikirnoff and Natalya followed them out. Nicolas turned to her, his hands pressing on either side of her body, spreading warmth through her lungs and chest. Pins and needles ran along her skin, but the terrible pressure was gone.

"We were lucky," she said. "Ice particles in the lungs can kill you very fast. And suffocation is a lousy way to go." She rubbed Nicolas's arm. "Can you track the blood trail of my aunts?"

"They are above us and toward our left. We go in that direction."

Nicolas took the lead, choosing a wider tunnel leading upward. The ice was banded tightly with white and blue thin stripes. Crackles and grumblings and the ever-present trickling of water were constant companions. The weight of ice and rock pressed down heavily on them. As they hurried, the floor became more and more uneven, as if the earth had pushed chunks of ice upward. They took to the air, skimming over the surface, following the twisting tunnel upward.

Several other galleries opened, but other than glancing inside, the four continued upward. They'd been inside Xavier's lair for some time: They needed to find Tatijana and Branislava and get out. The shower of ice was constant, small pieces breaking off and raining down on them, so it was necessary to keep a shield above them. As the floor sloped up, icicles began to vibrate. Water dripped faster. One wall began to web into tiny cracks. Water trickled out.

"I detest this place," Vikirnoff said. "We should just get out of here."

Natalya scowled at him. "I'm not going to leave without finding my aunts' bodies. You saw the blood. What if they're still alive?"

Nicolas muttered something foul under his breath. "They are not alive. After all this time, it would be impossible. This is a fool's errand and you are going to get us killed."

Vikirnoff whirled around, baring his teeth. "This was not Natalya's idea. *Your* lifemate dragged us here."

Nicolas responded with aggression, his black eyes smoldering with red flames, with the need for action. "Do not use that tone when speaking of my lifemate."

Lara frowned as she stepped between the two men. With the ice spiders weaving luminescent threads to light the way, the silky strings cast shadows not only along the blue and white ice, but over both men's faces, and they seemed dark and sinister in the shimmering glow. Along the wall, the shadows seemed to move of their own accord, growing and extending, reshaping with each movement within the tunnel.

Lara lifted her hands palms up and sang to her spiders. *Tiny spiders of crystalline ice, spinning threads to make us light, throw and cast your finespun threads, digging deeper into what we dread. Enter the ice, search it well, reveal to me what's hidden by spell.*

Dark streaks appeared along the ice wall and crisscrossed the tunnel itself. She drew in her breath. "He's controlling emotions. It's Xavier. Don't speak. Don't think. Keep your mind blank while I find a way to counter this."

Again she lifted her hands and wove a counterspell. *That which has been cast to control and be hidden, can be undone by the song of a maiden.*

Within the icy walls, a face and form of a young girl began to take shape, and then a perfectly formed ice sculpture of a young girl emerged. She appeared to be reaching down into the ice. As she bent over, she began to sing and the notes appeared like a cold wind, blowing across the walls and up across the tube itself, coating the dark streaks with ropes of ice so that each streak froze solid. Her notes pitched higher and higher until the frequency shattered the ice ropes and they fell, harmless, to the floor. The maiden climbed back into the ice and disappeared.

Nicolas grinned at Vikirnoff. "That's my woman."

Natalya smiled at her, pride on her face. "You really know your stuff."

"The aunts taught me everything. It's all them." Technically, they were her great-aunts and Natalya's aunts, but Lara would never think of them any other way. "I have to find them."

"We will, *sívamet,* we all want to find them and bring them home," Nicolas assured.

Still the shadows on the walls continued to grow and lengthen. The male Carpathians put the women between them, deadly snarls on their faces. The danger in the tunnel was palpable. The shadows swirled on the blue-white walls, pushing through the layers of ice so that smoke drifted out.

Natalya gasped. She gripped Lara's wrist. "I know what this is."

Both looked at one another, horror on their faces. "Shadow warriors," they whispered together.

Nicolas drew in his breath and looked up and down the long tunnel. They were in the middle of the tube and all along the walls, in front and behind them, smoke began to push through the cracks in the ice. "Not even the most seasoned hunter can hope to escape the shadow guardians," he said. "We have to get to the next chamber before they emerge from the wall. If we are caught in between them, we die here."

"Movement attracts them," Natalya pointed out.

"I would have to say they already know we are here," Nicolas replied.

"If we can get to a safer place and give Natalya some time," Vikirnoff said, "then she can perhaps deal with them, but it takes time."

"I could because I had mage blood running in me, I think," Natalya said. "I'm not as certain I could control them now."

"I have mage blood," Lara said.

"Talk later! Run now!" Nicolas caught Lara's wrist and, without waiting for an argument, put on a burst of preternatural speed.

Vikirnoff and Natalya stayed right on their heels, all four blurred they moved so fast, but the action caused a reaction from the whirling shadows. The dark smoke poured even faster from the ice wall and began to form into life-sized apparitions of swirling smoke, shadow and substance.

They barely made it to the entrance to the next chamber before the shadow warriors were after them, gliding silently through the twisting ice tube, swords raised high. The smoke swirled and shifted, often revealing an armor-clad warrior, face obscured completely, but sword gleaming and polished.

Nicolas kept moving to the opposite side of the chamber, heading for the left entrance, but several warriors spread out quickly through the room, cutting off that escape route. The only choice they had was a narrow right passage, still leading up, but away from the direction they wanted to go.

Shadow warriors were made of whatever elements were available, molecules and water. Once the most skilled and honored fighters of their time, their spirits were ripped from them and forced into service by the dark mage. They were already dead, insubstantial and nearly impossible to defeat in battle.

The warriors fanned out and the Carpathians retreated farther into the narrow corridor of ice. The men kept the women firmly behind them, walking backward, facing the enemy.

"They'll have to face us one at a time," Nicolas said with some satisfaction.

Natalya tried to stem the flow of shadows into the room. She halted and raised her arms.

Hear me now, dark ones, torn from your resting place. I call on earth, wind, fire, water and spirit.

The warriors should have put down their swords and waited for commands, but instead, they rushed toward the two women, the smoke going from gray to black.

"That's not working so well without the mage blood," Natalya said. "Run!"

The Carpathians whirled and ran again, using their blurring speed. Lara had a difficult time keeping up, although Nicolas was pulling her along and her feet didn't really touch the ground. She kept forgetting to regulate her body temperature and it was so cold, she ached and shivered continually. Her legs and arms felt stiff and her chest hurt from the cold. As they continued up the narrow corridor, the air changed, warming a bit, which gave her some relief, but she worried with the temperature a few degrees warmer, the ice might melt.

Lara glanced over her shoulder and saw that the warriors had finally come to a halt. Perhaps the holding spell Natalya had cast had finally taken, or they were guardians of a specific area and could not go any farther.

"They aren't following us," she announced.

The others stopped to look back. The warriors had halted at the entrance to the tube and stood, smoke whirling around them, swords raised.

"Keep moving," Nicolas said, his hand on the small of Lara's back. "Who is to say they will not attack again? Let's keep going, but look for a corridor leading to our left and we can take that and get back on track to find your aunts."

Lara checked the ice surrounding them. Even a few degrees difference in temperature could trigger large chunks of ice to come flying out of or off of the wall. This tube was narrower than most and lined heavily with rows of dagger-sharp icicles. On either side of them, above and below, were two solid rows of icy stilettos in strange colors of faded brown, very unusual for an ice cave. The floor was covered in round ice pods, also very unusual. The slightly raised bumps were everywhere, as if some strange form of bacteria grew along the floor of the tunnel.

As they continued, it grew darker and she realized the ice spiders were not emerging from the walls to light the way with their luminescent silk. The floor curved upward and with each step there were more of the pods and the temperature increased.

"Stop." Lara took a careful look around.

She had good night vision, but the Carpathians could see in the dark without any light and it looked as if a few more steps would take them over the slight rise and into pitch blackness. Before she went blind and had to rely on the others, she wanted to check out the stability of the ice. She noted two particularly sharpened, curved icicles—one on either side of them near the opening—were dripping. Each drop was yellowish in color and formed a small pool before running along the base of the icicles on the floor. The liquid fed the small ice pods, slowly staining them a pale amber. As the pods went amber, she detected movement, tiny microbes wriggling inside the pods.

She swore under her breath. "This isn't good."

Nicolas had continued forward a few steps in order to

put the light far enough behind him for his night vision to kick in. At the top of the slope he peered down into the darkened tunnel.

"The sounds are different," Natalya said. "I don't like this."

Vikirnoff moved up beside Nicolas, surveying the only way open to them. "What do you think?" Both scanned all around them continuously.

"Something is down there waiting for us," Nicolas said. "It is unfamiliar to me, but I feel movement. I think the shadow warriors herded us into this tube for a reason and the reason is crouched in the dark, ready to attack."

Vikirnoff glanced over his shoulder. The shadow warriors had not melted away. They were holding their position and waiting for something.

Lara crouched down beside the pods, studying them carefully and then, careful not to step on them, examined the double rows of brownish icicles. She passed her palm over the formations without touching them. "These icicles are swarming with bacteria, but that's not why they're such an odd color." She leaned closer and sniffed delicately. "This is diluted blood. At least I think it is."

"Whatever is moving down there is coming this way," Nicolas warned.

For the first time since entering the cave, he felt truly trapped. Whatever was creeping toward them out of the dark sounded, to his ears, as if it was not alone. His vision cleared as the thing got closer and at first he thought it was several large snakes, thick like anacondas. The heads were large and each opened its mouth wide, forked tongue testing the air, sniffing for prey. The snake heads looked suspiciously like the ones taken from Terry's leg.

"How many?" Vikirnoff asked. "I'm counting six visually, but hearing more behind them.

"It's only one," Nicolas corrected. "One with tentacles. I think it's planning on dragging us into its mouth."

"We are already in its mouth," Lara said.

There was a small silence while they all looked around the tube. The double rows of bloodstained icicles were teeth. The two curved teeth held venom. The mouth was a breeding ground for bacteria, all kinds of strains, many fatal. The bumps along the tongue were the nesting pods. And the tentacles reaching for them would pull them back where they could be digested.

"Vikirnoff and I will hold the tentacles back, but we have to get out of here. Find a way through the shadow warriors, Lara. You're mage."

She rolled her eyes. "Whatever happened to your women-not-fighting campaign?"

"No, we just have to fight a legion of shadow warriors," Natalya said sarcastically. "No biggie."

"You've done it before," Vikirnoff pointed out. "I think you can handle it."

"Are you certain you don't want to impregnate me and send me home while you play Superman? Because I'm all for it," Natalya said.

"The snake heads have stopped sniffing and they're coming for us," Nicolas said. "You might want to get on those shadow warriors right now."

"As my absolute hero in *The Abyss* would say, 'Keep your pantyhose on.'" Natalya sniffed indignantly.

"Come on, Lara, let's show them how to fight a shadow warrior."

Lara reluctantly followed her aunt back toward the double rows of teeth. "Be careful, don't step on the pods. I think this is parasite breeding ground, not the microbes. I'm fairly certain that laboratory was for the extremophiles. He collects them from the ice and tests them in the first few pools, mutates them and sends them into the blood and amniotic fluids so they learn to survive in those conditions. And then he lets the glacier take them down to the soil where the Carpathians rest. This thing, whatever it is, breeds his parasites. Look at them wiggling inside the pods." She was very suspicious that the yellow-colored venom feeding the pods was the same liquid injected into Razvan.

"Oh dear," Natalya quipped. "I do believe we're inside mommy dearest."

The tiny maggots became excited, even agitated when they stepped close to the pods.

Behind them, the first attack came. Nicolas and Vikirnoff fashioned swords of ice, spreading out to give themselves room to maneuver, hovering inches from the floor in order to keep from stepping on the pods littered all over what had to be the creature's tongue. The huge heads bobbed and ducked, slashing from side to side. The attack was well coordinated, the heads moving in a mesmerizing pattern, like a cobra hypnotizing its prey.

Both women steadied themselves and picked their way through the maze of bumps to stand just in back of the bacteria-encrusted teeth. There were flashes of light, swearing, a spatter of blood along the walls that sent the parasitic worms into a frenzy. The floor swayed and bucked beneath their feet. More venom dripped from the fangs and ran down along the floor.

"Remind me to call down the lightning to make certain we're clean before we go back to the village," Natalya said.

Lara was grateful Natalya thought they'd actually get out of the ice cave alive.

"Look out, Vikirnoff," Nicolas shouted. He'd severed a head and blood filled with parasites spewed across the walls and floors. "Do not let them touch you. Lara, Natalya, keep out of their way."

Lara sent a scowl over her shoulder. "We're concentrating here. Do you think this is easy?"

"We can't kill them, they're already dead," Natalya said, thinking aloud. "We can't freeze them, they came out of the ice."

"We should be able to get their attention and wrestle the command away from Xavier. His way is always simplicity. He rips their soul from them and takes command, much like he did to my father," Lara mused. "So there's no loyalty there. They're enslaved against their will."

"Lara!" Nicolas called. "It's grown another head. What are you doing up there?"

"Playing dolls," Lara called back, a bite of irritation in her voice. "This isn't easy, Nicolas. I need to concentrate."

"You can do it," Natalya encouraged. "You have a feel for him and I've noticed the ice responds to you."

Lara hadn't considered that. She was at home in ice caves. They felt natural to her and the mage spells flooded her mind, faster and faster the more she used them. The aunts had prepared her for any trouble, it seemed, and more than ever she was determined to bring their bodies home. In life, maybe they'd been prisoners, but not in death.

"Keep the venom and parasites off of me, Natalya," she said.

"You got it."

Lara took a breath and let it out, lifting her hands and weaving a pattern in the air directed at the shadow warriors.

Ancient warriors of the past, who stood with honor and favored tasks. Now controlled by the dark and unseen, I call to you—listen to me. Bound by darkness that has no honor, I call to your spirit—fight once again as warriors. I send to you strands of strength, allowing you the ability to think. I ask a boon and release your souls, stand as one that has been froze.

The shadow warriors froze, dropping their swords, points toward the icy floor. Through the swirling smoke, Lara caught glimpses of the red pits for eyes set into black masks where their faces should have been. Facing the mirror of ice, the warriors remained frozen, staring sightlessly into that which reflected their empty souls. It saddened her that these men, who had lived their entire lives with honor, could be commanded by one so evil as Xavier.

Lara lifted her hands once more and began to weave a pattern, this one even more intricate and detailed than the one before. This time when she chanted, her voice rang with respect.

Those who have suffered evil wrongs, who have fought in battles standing strong, look into the ice and see, that which may be reclaimed by thee.

Holding her breath, she waited as each warrior began to move, awakening as if from a long sleep. They stretched their arms toward the mirror of ice.

Lara continued to chant softly. *Warriors of strength, time and valor, take back that which is yours and ascend with honor.*

The ice began to form and give birth to floating lights, each a different color and shape. As the lights descended, the warriors stepped into them, glowing for a moment. Then each, bowing low toward Lara, simply vanished.

The moment the last of the shadow warriors disappeared, Lara called to Nicolas. "The way is clear. We have to get out of here. Don't step on the pods."

Vikirnoff and Nicolas joined their lifemates, hurdling over the snapping teeth to get out of the mother parasite.

"That was well done, Lara," Nicolas said, sending a small salute after the warriors. "You honored them and rightly so."

"What are we going to do with that?" Vikirnoff asked, as the hideous creature snapped her jaws at them. She couldn't move, frozen as she was, her body part of the ice cave.

"Destroy it, Lara," Nicolas said. "I cannot call down the lightning here, but you can destroy that breeding machine. It sits there waiting for victims to feed to its young. You command all the elements."

"So do you." She tipped her head back and studied his

face. He wanted this for her—to feel powerful and in control. He wanted her to know she could kill the monster that preyed on his people. She nodded. "I wish we'd had time to think of a way to destroy his laboratory."

Nicolas's smile held no humor, he simply bared his teeth in a wolfish way. "I'm giving it some thought. It is necessary to see where he is slipping the infected microbes into the soil."

"He has to be using the glacier to deliver them to either the soil or the water," Lara said. "My guess would be the soil because the villagers don't seem to be infected."

"We will find it now that we know what we are looking for," Nicolas said with confidence. "But in the meantime, destroy that creature."

Lara looked back at the ice monster with its blood-stained teeth and dripping venom. Xavier had created the perfect mother for his parasites. Lara needed fire, and air to feed the fire. She lifted her arms and faced the monster, while the others stood back, knowing Nicolas had given her a perfect opportunity to thwart Xavier. Destroying his parasite factory would set him back a great deal.

"This is for Razvan and Gerald and Terry," she whispered softly and held up her arms, hands sketching a pattern in the air.

I call on the power of the west, air hear my call. I draw on the power of the east, fire come to me.

A rushing of wind could be heard as small, flickering particles began to gather, swirling round and round, creating a wind tunnel. The faster it turned, the higher the flames leaped, gathering more and more particles until it became one large tube of fire. Lara gave a flick of her hand and shot the fire funnel straight and hard at the monster breeding the horrific parasitic worms, enveloping it entirely.

That which is mother and bound by deed, let fire consume the parasites that feed.

The great jaws gaped open in a silent scream and the

fire hissed and fought against the ice, blazing white-hot, incinerating and melting the creature fast.

Nicolas blew Lara a kiss. "That is *my* woman," he said. "Let's get out of here."

Xavier's ice caves were well aware of their presence and were beginning to fight back in earnest. The sun would be rising soon and they had to leave. They needed to find the bodies of the aunts and get out before they were trapped by their own weaknesses.

They used blurring speed, not touching the ground, moving fast through the twisting, sometimes very narrow tunnels, always going to the left and up.

Lara's heart began to pound. *This is it. This is the chamber where I last saw them and they helped me to escape.*

Immediately, Nicolas halted. Natalya and Vikirnoff stopped as well, looking around.

Lara recognized the cathedral ceilings and the two rows of tall, intricate crystal-and-ice-carved pillars running the length of the room. Globes of various colors sat in niches built into the columns. Life-sized ice sculptures of various mythical creatures were scattered around the room, looking like fierce guards. The sculptures had frightened her as a child, especially when she'd seen them come alive at Xavier's whim and stalk her across the floor. Set inside chiseled archways were bloodred pyramids that gave off an unholy glow.

"Don't look into the globes, especially the cloudy ones. They come alive and can trap you." Lara reached for Nicolas's hand, needing the contact.

"Natalya and I have been here before. I pushed the ice through the opening to close it in order to prevent the prince from coming down here to aid us," Vikirnoff said. "Xavier had set a trap for Mikhail using vampires to help him. We were forced to close the opening to protect him, and Natalya and I barely made it out alive."

"We went through the floor," Natalya said. "He has trap-doors built in to escape."

Beneath the ice floor was a starburst, squares and pyra-mid pattern that ran through the floor. In the center of each shape were hieroglyphics, each symbol carved deep into the various shapes.

"And I saw the dragons encased in ice," Natalya said. "The ice around them was several feet thick. They looked like water paintings. At first we didn't realize there were two of them."

Lara nodded to her right. "There's an alcove just through there." Now she could barely breathe. Would the bodies still be there? And if so, where had the blood come from? They couldn't still be alive, could they?

"Do you want me to look for you?" Nicolas asked.

She shook her head. This was her quest—her promise. She would do this herself. She squeezed his hand and let go, straightening her spine and forcing her body to put one foot in front of the other. Vikirnoff, Natalya and Nicolas fanned out to protect her, watching the room closely for an attack—certain one was imminent.

Lara crossed over the ice squares, ignoring the horrific memories pouring into her mind. Deliberately she reached for the good—and there had been good—all because of two women. She'd never seen them in their human form, only the dragons, but their voices had kept her sane, made her feel loved, taught her everything she knew and then some. These women had been her only real family and she desperately wanted to bring them home. Xavier couldn't have them any longer.

Please. Please. Her throat felt swollen. Her heart ham-mered loudly. Her chest was tight and her eyes burned. *Please.* It was a litany. She wasn't certain she could face not ever knowing. They had done so much for her, kept her sane, given her values, taught her right from wrong, given her a chance at life, sending her out into the world with as much knowledge as they could give her. They had loved her, and because of them, she knew what love was.

I am with you, Nicolas assured.

She realized he was merged with her, his strength and love flowing into her, bolstering her. Lara clung to him for a moment and then rounded the corner to enter the alcove. Her breath exploded out of her lungs and silent tears tracked down her face. She could see Aunt Bronnie, one beautiful emerald eye staring at her through the thick wall of ice. Scales covered the serpentine neck and ran up the wedge-shaped head. One claw was outstretched, had obviously been digging at the ice before she froze. Behind her, shielded as usual by Branislava, was Tatijana, her body almost impossible to see.

They're still here, Nicolas. If I can get their bodies out of the ice, can you float them? They're enormously large and impossible to carry.

Whatever you need.

He wouldn't tell her the cost to his strength while he was keeping her warm and scanning constantly for the enemy. He never would and she knew that. She also knew it was getting closer to dawn. They had to get out.

Lara stood back away from the wall and lifted her hands. This would be the most important spell she would ever cast. She had to command her spiders to bore through the ice, to cut huge chunks away to release the dragons, but she also needed to stabilize the ice so it wouldn't collapse in on them.

The ice constantly groaned, reminding her just how unstable it really was. First, she needed to know if the walls were moving, because she was fairly certain they were. She took a breath. She needed a web stretched taut from wall to wall to warn her if the passage was narrowing.

Tiny spiders of crystalline ice, weave your web, make it tight, cast your silk from wall to wall, making sure no ice shall fall. Spin your patterns, weave them tight, watch your lines command the ice.

The spiders raced out of the ice, spread across the thick walls and began to weave and spin their luminescent threads until the shiny, glowing web was stretched in an intricate pattern from wall to wall. Satisfied, Lara wove a pattern with her hands, graceful and loving movements, tracing each weave carefully, her voice thick with emotion as she commanded the spiders to begin boring holes into the ice all around the dragons, like a giant cutout.

Spiders, spiders, form a line, use your skills, cut— bore—and bind.

The spiders swarmed over the wall encasing the dragons. It took some time to bore several feet inward and around such a large area.

"Hurry, Lara. The globes in here are changing colors, swirling with what looks like blood through each orb," Natalya called. "We have to get out of here."

Lara refused to hurry her next spell. This mattered too much. She wouldn't chance losing the aunts when she was so close. She added a holding spell for the ice, knowing it wouldn't last too long against the tremendous pressure of the glacier and Xavier's wrath that she could already feel in the ice itself.

I call thee water in frozen form, hold your place though cracked and worn. Tiny particles of water, ice meld and mold, fit and splice.

The ominous creaking and rumbling faded to whispers, but the sound of water continued to surround them. This was it then. She took another breath and with all the hope and love and knowledge she had, she wove her next spell to open the ice block the spiders had cut for her.

Thrice around this ice do bound, evil sink into the ground. Little spiders of crystalline ice, hold your webs, keep them tight. Cast them round, protect and be, so I may reach those who sleep.

The spiders wove their silken fire strands through each bore hole and pulled the threads tight, sawing back and forth until chunks of ice broke free. They continued to work until they exposed the dragons, and then they carved holes around the bodies until the dragons slipped free.

The dragon carcasses slid out of their ice prison, still frozen, hitting the floor with a cracking sound.

19

Lara crouched down beside the dragons, weeping. She put one hand on each of the ice-cold necks, bowed her head and whispered to them softly. "I'm setting you free. Just the way you did me, he doesn't have you any longer." Maybe it wouldn't matter to them in death, but it did to her. She would never want Xavier to have any part of her—in any form.

"Lara! Look at the web," Natalya said sharply. She peeked around the corner of the alcove and gasped aloud, staring in awe and dismay at the two dragon carcasses.

The ice spiders were making a mass exodus, rushing across the thick ice wall. The web they'd spun tight sagged in the middle by a few inches, but that was steadily increasing. The creaks and rumbling in the ice increased to an almost angry roar.

Nicolas rounded the corner of the alcove at a run and slid to a halt so fast that Vikirnoff, on his heels, bumped into him.

"You got them out," Vikirnoff said. "You found them and got them out."

Nicolas frowned and walked around the two bodies. He glanced at Vikirnoff. "They really are in dragon form."

"You knew they were," Lara said, "I told you. And you were with me..." She trailed off, glancing at Vikirnoff and Natalya, who were walking around the two dragons. Lara stroked loving caresses over the scales, usually shimmering with iridescent color, but now drab and dull.

"But they are part mage. How can they shift?" Nicolas murmured aloud.

"You said I could shift," Lara pointed out.

"You can, as long as I'm holding the image for you. Your Dragonseeker blood is strong but..." He trailed off and looked at Vikirnoff.

Vikirnoff crouched down beside the two women. "Natalya, reach for them."

"I don't understand."

"Lara should. She's spoken numerous times with them telepathically," Nicolas said. "Lara, reach deep along the path you used to speak to them. Call them to you."

"You can't possibly think they're alive. Look at them. They're frozen solid. They're thin and drab."

"They are not mage," Nicolas said. "They are Carpathian. Fully Carpathian. How that came to be, I do not know, but they could not have survived all these years frozen, encased in ice—and you said they were kept in ice even when you were a child—unless they are Carpathian. Mage would die. I do not know how I missed that. How any of us did. How could they be caught in the bodies of dragons?"

"You're saying they're still alive?"

"It is a possibility, yes," Nicolas said.

The ice continued to protest, crackling as icicles rained down on them, as large chunks sloughed off to crash to the floor. The trickle of water became louder.

Lara cleared her mind and reached. She knew the path

intimately, had clung to it as a child, her only stability in a world of absolute madness. She reached with a mixture of love and hope. *Aunt Bronnie. Auntie Tatijana. Can you hear me?*

There was a weak stirring in her mind. Lara lost all color and gave a little cry. "I felt them. They're there. I felt them."

Nicolas looked grimly at Vikirnoff and then to the spiderweb, which was now sagging by at least a foot more. "I'm calling in aid. Let us go now."

Warrior to warrior! We have great need. We have found two of our women in the ice caves and we are under attack.

Nicolas sent the call and immediately levitated the dragons' bodies. "Let's get out of here. Vikirnoff, you take the lead, I'll hold the rear."

Vikirnoff glanced back at him in total understanding, and then turned and ran. The look that passed between them said a multitude of things. Nicolas was entrusting the other half of his soul to Vikirnoff. He was telling him not to guard his back, but to take the women to safety no matter what happened behind him. Vikirnoff accepted the responsibility of the women and also the consequences should Nicolas die in the ice cave protecting their flank.

Natalya grabbed Lara's wrist and yanked her into a blurring run, racing after Vikirnoff. Behind her, the bodies of the two dragons burst through the tunnels, sheering bits of ice off the walls.

Nicolas ran behind them, his senses fully alert for any movement, any danger. He had given Vikirnoff the responsibility of getting the women out of the caves. An army of Carpathian males were on the way and they would first go to defend the women, so Vikirnoff's job was to get them as close to a meeting point as fast as possible. Relieved of watching out for the women, Nicolas was left with only one task. He would fight whatever came at them and see to it that Vikirnoff had the time needed to meet up with their relief forces.

The creaking and groaning grew to rumbles of protests. The rumbling became a roar of fury. The ice cave came alive, furious that they were escaping with Xavier's greatest treasures. Thunder crashed, echoing through the chambers, shaking the walls all around them. The pressure of the glacier, the weight of the ice itself, along with Xavier's wrath, forced out huge chunks of ice, squares and rectangles, several feet thick and wide, from the ice wall. The chunks shot out across the chamber, destroying everything in their path.

Vikirnoff shepherded the women back down along the tube winding through the chambers, leading back toward the entrance where they had originally entered the cave. Large chunks of ice slammed down, the caves crumbling as they ran. Nicolas waved his hand and stayed the huge weight, holding the ice chunks just a few seconds so the women could run through, towing the dragon bodies and then hastily staying the next series. It took tremendous concentration and timing to stay just ahead of the small group while he ran, too.

Water went from a trickle to a continuous pour, so that from every wall and the ceiling water flowed into their escape tunnel.

It will only take minutes for this to become a waterfall, Lara warned. *The force of the water alone can kill. It's designed to sweep anything surviving back into his lair.*

Just run!

Nicolas had already figured out what the next attack would be. He was beginning to know his enemy. Xavier was mage, and mage, like Carpathian, used the elements and whatever was simplest and available. Xavier was a master at simplicity. Water was turning torrential, hammering down in a long fall from several steep places to roar to the floor.

The water kicked up an icy spray, the particles tiny such as Xavier had in his laboratory, so the danger was inhaling and freezing the lungs. It was Vikirnoff he warned, because he had to shut himself off from the danger to Lara in order to be one hundred percent focused on keeping them all alive.

Mask everyone.

Vikirnoff did so ruthlessly, not asking, simply constructing and fitting masks to everyone as they ran. Twice Natalya glanced over her shoulder as if she might fall back to help protect the flank, but Vikirnoff said something sharply and she renewed her efforts to drag Lara through the tunnel and with Lara, the two dragons.

The water burst through every wall, broke through the ceiling. Nicolas used the huge chunks of ice against it, hastily building ice dams several feet thick, staying the water from filling the tunnel. The waterfalls were cold, so it was the battering rather than the temperature that took the toll on the ice dam.

Vikirnoff veered off through a series of chambers. The moment they exited the tube, Nicolas sealed it—a temporary hold, but he only needed to buy them minutes. As he raced after the women and Vikirnoff, Nicolas noted the change in the feel of his surroundings. His scanning of the chambers ahead picked up movement, although nothing registered as a life form.

It is possible you are going to be running into shadow warriors again. Before entering the chamber leading to the entrance, back off and let me take the lead. I will draw their attention and let you slip past with the women.

Nicolas noted that the dragons were thawing along with the ice cave. The bodies were harder to control. He was going to have to give them completely into Vikirnoff's care.

They are awakening and will need to be reassured. You, Natalya and Lara will need to cope, Vikirnoff.

He glanced at the dragons as he put on a burst of speed and slipped past. The moment Vikirnoff halted their forward progress, the two bodies lay on the floor. As the blood began to unfreeze, the muscles locked and contorted. He couldn't imagine the pain they had to be in.

Lara knelt beside her aunts, murmuring reassurances, trying to touch their minds and let them know what was happening. Bronnie looked up at her, blinking her enormous emerald eyes, tears swimming there.

Auntie Bronnie. It's Lara. I came back for you.

The dragon turned her head and stretched to cover her sister with her chin, her touch gentle when her body went rigid, contorted and then relaxed again. *Starved.* The single word was a croak.

Can you shift to human form? Natalya can clothe you and we can give you blood. The idea made her stomach lurch, but to save her aunts, she was willing to do anything.

The great emerald eyes blinked and then turned to look at Natalya. She stared at her niece for one long, emotion-laden moment. *No strength.*

Put the images you need in Natalya's head and she can hold them for you. Vikirnoff will help send you strength. We have little time. Xavier is sending his guardians after us.

Natalya and Vikirnoff held the images Branislava provided and the dragons disappeared, leaving two women lying on the floor of the ice cave. Natalya had provided clothes for them, warm leggings and sweaters to help heat their bodies. Their hair was long and thick, far past their waists, and Natalya hastily braided both with a wave of her hand and then covered them with warm caps to keep the strands from freezing.

Lara held their heads in her lap while Natalya immediately offered Tatijana her wrist. There was no hesitation. Natalya smiled at her aunt and murmured the ritual offering.

"I offer my life freely for yours."

Lara took a breath and held out her hand to Branislava. "I offer my life freely for yours." Her heart thundered in her ears. Her mouth went dry. Terror filled her mind, but she ruthlessly pushed it aside. This was her beloved aunt, who had sacrificed everything for her. She would save her and she would do so gladly. She meant her offering. She owed her life to Branislava and Tatijana—more, she owed her soul to them. Razvan's soul had been stolen by a madman and he could just as easily have used her, but at great cost to themselves, they had saved her.

Teeth bit down into her wrist. Her stomach lurched, but she held on, breathing through the need to be sick, grateful her aunt was too ill to notice. It took a moment to realize her aunt wasn't hurting her. The teeth didn't tear at her flesh, but rather pierced with two small holes. There wasn't the erotic feel that there was when Nicolas took her blood, but more of a giving, a sharing, an act of camaraderie, giving her a deeper connection.

Her aunt's body warmed faster with the influx of blood, but it wasn't enough for the shriveled cells and organs. As soon as Branislava swept her tongue over the pinpricks to close the wounds, Vikirnoff knelt beside her.

Branislava shook her head. *You need your strength to get us out of here.* Even that small effort exhausted her.

The continual sound of water became overly loud, drawing Lara's attention. She caught Natalya's wrist and gestured with her chin, not wanting to alarm her aunts. The water dripped onto the floor and ran along a crevice, forming a long, narrow tube. Within moments of hitting the icy floor, the water refroze, forming the long body of a snake. The moment one formed and slithered off, another took its place until a good portion of the floor was taken up by hissing snakes.

Tatijana swung her head toward them, although she was too weak to lift her neck to see. *Don't let him take us. Kill us if you have to.*

Lara tightened her arms around both of them. "He will never get near you again," she assured fiercely.

"I'll deal with the snakes," Natalya said. She raised her arms and gathered power to her. She was tired of Xavier's relentless pursuit and happy to find a target. "Those people on *Snakes on a Plane* should have tried this."

That which does slither, bites and strikes, feel the wrath of fire-cold ice. I call thee fire, cold of flame, fit to my hand, strike this bane. As Natalya gathered the energy force, converting it into cold fusion fire, she directed it straight at the icy serpents.

The snakes shattered into a million pieces, the ice crystals melting. They were absorbed by the floor. Natalya looked grimly satisfied. "We've got to get out of here fast. I hear the water beating at the dam Nicolas built, and if we're caught..."

"Nicolas will find us the way out." Lara said it with absolute conviction because she believed in him. She lifted her head to try to see what was happening in the chamber leading to the escape corridor.

～

Nicolas stepped into the cavern, alert for whatever trouble Xavier had left as his last line of defense against losing his daughters. He had held Branislava and Tatijana prisoner for centuries, and he wouldn't let them go so easily. He could see shadowy figures moving in the darkness of the chamber, and there were more than he wanted to think about. Not shadow warriors. As much as they seemed insubstantial, they didn't appear to move with the same swirl of smoke and grace. No, these were different.

He felt the rush battle brought, the one feeling he was familiar with and embraced. He knew what heightened senses brought, and the power flowing through his body. *Come to me*, he sent into the darkened chamber. *Come to me and die.*

As he moved into the center of the chamber, the first attack came as a shadowy figure charged him. Nicolas leapt smoothly into the air, slashing as he did so, razor-sharp talons slicing across the throat of the aggressor. His claw went through the air, touching nothing solid at all. He landed in a crouch, recognizing his opponents. Not shadow warriors, men of honor whose souls were ripped from their resting place, but death slaves, mercenaries who willingly pledged their service after death in order to rape and pillage with the aid of the dark arts to protect them in life. They were already dead and they were nearly as bad as vampires.

Three rushed him and he whirled around and through them, drawing energy from all around him until he could fashion a sword of blazing light—light he knew they avoided. If the light remained too long, they would grow accustomed to it, even with their sensitive eyes, so he flashed it on and off. Colors pulsed through the light, giving off a strobe effect, but each time the light came near, the death slaves retreated.

Take them through now, Vikirnoff. Death slaves guard the way. Hurry.

Vikirnoff didn't wait. He sent Natalya ahead of him with Lara, and caught up with the other two women, trusting Natalya to get Lara through. *Faster,* he ordered.

Natalya muttered something that sounded like "chauvinist pig" in his mind, but it sounded more of a caress than an insult.

The death slaves let out an eerie cry and, sensing the women, charged in spite of the light. Nicolas closed in on them, clearing a path, sweeping his light sword through the ranks, driving them back. Two managed to slash at him, in spite of his speed, their numbers overwhelming. One opened a cut on his arm, another on his side. He sealed off both wounds, weaving in and out of their ranks, his light sword hacking through them.

Like shadow warriors, the death slaves were already dead and therefore insubstantial, but light was a bitter enemy and enough of it could destroy them if he managed to strike them in the heart. In the dark, surrounded by enemies, it was nearly impossible to choose his target accurately at the blurring speed he needed to survive.

Natalya and Lara stopped to look back in spite of Vikirnoff's gruff command to keep moving. They could see Nicolas moving in and out of the death slaves with fluid grace and astonishing speed. He seemed a machine, flowing rather than stepping, never flinching even when the tip of a dagger or sword tore open his flesh.

Lara hesitated, but Natalya grabbed her arm.

"Look at him," Lara whispered. "He was born for this."

Carpathian males burst through the tube, catching at the women and passing them to the front out of harm's way, paying no attention to their resistance. Vikirnoff relaxed visibly, but he didn't relinquish his charges.

What do you need, Nicolas? Lucian asked.

Gregori, leading a large group, charged into the foray to take the pressure off of Nicolas.

The sun, Nicolas answered, taking his time, now that he had reinforcements, to plunge the sword of light into the nearest heart. The death slave exploded, burst into molecules and rained down onto the ice floor.

Again that eerie cry went up as one of their own was sent for good to the land of shadows.

I'll see what I can do, Lucian said.

Natalya peeked through the solid wall of tall, grim-faced Carpathians. Lara did the same. For the first time,

Natalya saw the difference in the coordinated movements of the warriors. Without women to protect, they moved with double the speed, graceful and precise, utterly without fear, their attacks well orchestrated.

The first wave of Carpathian males charged the center of the mass of death slaves, Nicolas leaping over the first line of the enemy, forcing them to either come after him and turn their backs on the other Carpathians or fight the men coming at them. The death slaves had no choice but to defend themselves against the newcomers, giving Nicolas more time to fight the three facing him.

It was obvious the battle was well coordinated on the part of the Carpathians. They each knew how the other worked, never once having to look to see if their backs were guarded. They flowed together, almost like a ballet, cutting through the ranks of Xavier's guardians.

The ice cave expanded and contracted as more death slaves poured into the battle from all directions. They must have been guarding other entrances and, with the disturbance, came running. They swarmed into the chamber, slicing at Carpathians with lethal swords, attacking with a fury born of desperation. Xavier punished any who failed him and even the dead were careful not to cross him.

Lucian waited until the fighting was at its most ferocious, when the chamber was arcing with energy. He began to gather the energy into a ball, pulling power from every conceivable resource. The ball spun brighter and hotter, so much so that he was forced to cloak it, to keep from blinding himself. Still, he drew power to him, collecting every bit he could summon to him without draining his companions. When the ball pulsed with power, threatening to detonate, he called out to Nicolas.

Your sun is ready.

Mist. Nicolas gave the command on the common path and shifted.

The other Carpathians shifted at exactly the same moment.

Lucian released the whirling mass of energy, a bright white light spinning out of control through the chamber. The ice cave lit up like daylight, only brighter, as if a bomb had gone off, the flash as bright as the sun.

The death slaves screamed a collective cry of denial, the note shattering the ice chamber, causing cracks all along the walls and ceiling. Their bodies glowed bright, burst outward into molecules and scattered across the floor.

Out! Nicolas was already streaking for the tube.

Vikirnoff and the others burst into the open. Branislava and Tatijana cried out, covering their eyes. Neither had ever been out of the ice caves before and the wide-open space was terrifying. The male Carpathians gathered around them, shielding them from the early-morning dawn and providing a tighter group so they felt safe.

Lara didn't look back as they set out for the home of the prince. She never wanted to see the ice caves again. She held tight to Nicolas's and Tatijana's hands as he whisked them through the skies to the deep forest.

Francesca had already been alerted and she was waiting along with Mikhail to greet Rhiannon's daughters. The two women were thin and weak, their bodies' wracked with pain, muscles cramping continuously. Lara sat between them, holding their hands while the two healers worked on them. Mikhail gave them his blood and Gregori followed suit, while outside, the unmated Carpathian males formed a ring of protection.

"How is it you are fully Carpathian?" Lara asked, feeling guilty that she was asking questions when both were so weak and needed to go to ground to rejuvenate.

"Our mother," Tatijana explained. "It was the only way

she could think to help us fight him. And we did the same for Razvan, your father, after Xavier killed our brother."

Nicolas knelt beside them. "I am Nicolas, lifemate to Lara. Lara and I would be honored to take you home and watch over you until you are at full strength, but we will take you wherever you are most comfortable."

"Of course with Lara," Branislava said. Weakly, she touched Lara's arm, love filling her gaze. "We never thought you would return for us."

"Thank you, Lara," Tatijana added. "We had lost all hope."

"Do you have news of my brother?" Natalya said. "We thought he had turned."

"Xavier torments him with the idea that you believe he betrayed you, that all Carpathians abhor him and that his own daughter believes him a monster."

"I did," Lara admitted. She rubbed her wrist where it burned and ached.

At once Nicolas took her hand and turned her wrist up to feather kisses over it. *You had reason. Do not feel guilty when you have just saved your aunts. No one else would have freed them. Without you, they would have remained prisoners for all time and everyone would still believe Razvan followed in Xavier's footsteps.*

"We were not allowed out of our prison for several years now," Tatijana explained. "We were frozen, asleep most of the time since you were gone, only awakened when he wanted to drain our blood. I am sorry, but we only know of the past."

Branislava blinked rapidly. "I want to visit with you, both of you, all of you, and thank you for our rescue, but I am much too weak and disoriented. Nicolas, would you take us home?"

"It is best," Gregori said. "They need the soil. They have been denied it their entire lives. On the rising we can give them more blood and slowly, over time, they will be strong again."

"The soil could be contaminated," Lara objected.

"Most likely," Gregori agreed, "but it is all we have for now. We can only do one thing at a time. If your aunts are comfortable with you, that is where they must go to heal. We will deal with all else another time."

Lara nodded, although she abhorred the idea of her aunts becoming infected.

"Most likely it is the man infected first," Gregori added, to try to reassure her.

Excitement was tangible throughout the Carpathian community as word spread that two Dragonseeker women had been recovered. Nicolas, Vikirnoff beside him, went out to address the unmated males guarding the home of the prince. As Dominic was suspect with the parasites in his blood, Nicolas and Vikirnoff—as the two related males— were now the official guardians of the two Dragonseeker women.

Light was pouring into the sky and Nicolas winced automatically. He loved the night. Even in the early-morning light, he felt his skin burn, although he had to acknowledge it was more psychological than anything else. He knew some Carpathians enjoyed walking around the village in the early-morning hours—he wasn't one of them.

He thanked the men who had come to his aid, told them all what they'd found and confirmed that yes, Branislava and Tatijana were Rhiannon's daughters. He confirmed they were ill and would be resting for some time before being introduced into Carpathian society, trying to be tactful when he was telling them they couldn't be introduced immediately. What he really wanted to say was to leave the women the hell alone, that they'd been through enough already and didn't need the men circling around like a pack of wolves. As he spoke, he could feel Lara's amusement.

He couldn't see her, she was inside Mikhail's house with her aunts, but she was laughing at him.

What is so funny?

You prefer to tell everyone what to do.

His stomach tightened in reaction to her teasing tone. He had forgotten fun in the midst of duty. *I want to go home.* He wanted to hold her close to him. *And I only want to tell you what to do.*

She laughed at that. *You would dictate to the world if you could get away with it.*

Maybe that's the truth, but only because I am always right.

He left it to Mikhail to tell the others they needed to let Branislava and Tatijana alone until they were fully healed, but he made it clear the two women were under his protection.

Lara gave him the mental equivalent of rolling her eyes and he gave a shrug back. *It is always better to be safe, especially when one guards our treasures.*

They took Branislava and Tatijana to their home. Lara fussed over them, insisting on checking the soil for the richest and most fertile they could find within the cave. Used to the cold of the ice, the warmth of the cave was nearly as disconcerting as the open spaces.

"We will get used to it," Branislava assured. "We have dreamt of freedom all our lives. Razvan tried to keep us up with what was happening in the outside world. He shared his knowledge with us as much as possible."

Tatijana stretched her arms wide. "I have wanted to do that for so many years." She leaned over and kissed Lara's forehead. "I could not do something so simple as to stretch."

Nicolas opened the earth for them. "We will be resting just above you. Your protection is paramount not just to Lara and me, but to all the Carpathian people. If you fear anything at all, you have only to send a call."

"But we'll be close," Lara assured. She could barely let the two women go.

Nicolas slipped his arm around her, holding her while the earth welcomed her aunts.

Lara looked up at him. "You are covered in wounds."

"I am?" He looked down at his body, a little shocked to see the scattered cuts. "There isn't anything really serious, certainly nothing to put that little frown on your face." His thumb caressed her lips and then slid along the small dimple in her chin.

She caught the edge of his shirt and tugged, pulling it off of him. "You can get in the pool and then I'm going to make certain none of those cuts are serious."

He decided he liked her bossy tone. Nicolas took his time stripping, mostly because she looked like he was unwrapping a gift. The look of tenderness and concern had him feeling soft inside, weakened in some way, but gave him strength in so many others.

"Now you."

Her smile was slow and sensual. "Now me what?"

"Now you take off your clothes." He was already growing hard, his body reacting with insatiable hunger to the way she was looking at him.

Her gaze dropped to his thickening erection. He circled the base with his hand, sliding a stroke along the hard length, watching her eyes darken and the tip of her tongue dart out to moisten her lips.

"I'm supposed to be taking care of you."

His smile widened. "That is taking care of me." He continued the casual stroking while she slowly pulled off her top and flung it aside. "You can take care of this particular part of me." He drew her attention to the thick length of him, so hard now he ached. She looked mesmerized by the movement of his hand and the tiny pearl drop of liquid smearing across the broad, flat head. When she licked her lips, his shaft jerked in anticipation.

Her nipples beneath the lace bra were already stiff, pushing at the lace. He couldn't resist leaning over to catch her breast in his mouth, flicking at the tight bead through the material. He sucked and teased, using the lace to scrape over her nipple so that she arched into his mouth and gave him that little gasping sound that he found particularly sexy.

He lifted his head and stepped back to watch her shimmy her knit pants off her hips. She wore little boy shorts, skimming over her hips and cut up across the curves of her bottom. The lace stretched over her creamy skin, enhancing his desire to see her without a stitch. His breath caught in his throat as she unhooked her bra and her breasts tumbled out, the soft rounded curves inviting, her skin gleaming in the soft glow of candlelight. Her boy shorts were next, sliding off her skin, making him ache inside, just to touch her.

He gestured for her to wade out ahead of him into the pool, just for the pleasure of watching her body move. She was conscious of him watching her, giving him that little extra enticement, drawing him to her with her sexy come-on. Standing waist-deep in the bubbling water, he drew her back against him, cupping her breasts and bending his head to her neck, his body flattening along the back of hers, pressing deep, using his height and weight to bend her over just a bit, so he could press even tighter against her.

His arm circled her waist to hold her in place while his other hand slid up her satin thigh to find the nest of red-gold curls, strumming along the secrets folds, tunneling into the warmth of her moist, tight channel. She moaned, her bottom pressing back into him, rubbing along his already aching shaft, sending arrows of pleasure darting through him. He sank his finger deep, feeling her muscles clamp down and suck on him, dragging hard. His shaft pulsed and wept, wanted to feel that hot, hungry clasp around it.

His fingers stroked down her neck and over the creamy swell of her breasts, his teeth scraping suggestively over her neck. Her breathy little moan sent heat sweeping through his belly. His fingers curved and plunged deep inside her. Her hips bucked, pressing against his hand while her firm buttocks slid tantalizingly over his heavy erection.

He turned her into his arms and found her mouth. His kiss was hard, a little rough and very possessive. His tongue teased and enticed her, cajoling her into giving him anything he wanted. He whispered hot, sexy, very graphic suggestions that left her heated and a little shocked.

She kissed him back, blushing, her skin flushed and damp. "I have to take care of this first," she whispered. "Stop making my knees weak."

She pressed her mouth to the laceration on his arm, her tongue dipping and sliding in small caresses, healing the wound as she kissed him better. Next was the one on his side, a little deeper, the silk of her hair sliding sensuously over his skin as her tongue lapped at him and the bubbles in the pool fizzed over his hardened shaft.

He caressed her breasts with his long fingers, stroking and kneading, occasionally leaning forward to suckle while the water lapped at her as well. She bent her head again and swept her tongue across a graze on his lower abdomen. Every muscle in his belly bunched and knotted. Suddenly nothing was as important as feeling her mouth around him, tight and wet and hot. He pulled her to the shallow edge where the pool was lined with boulders, seating himself on a higher one so she could remain in the bubbling water.

His hands fisted in her wealth of hair and dragged her head down to his lap. He murmured in his ancient language, the harsh tone and explicit instructions making her hot all over. She loved the urgency in his voice, the control in his hands, the way his hips thrust against her mouth. It took a moment to pick up the rhythm; he didn't give her much of a chance to get used to the thickness and length of him.

Harder. His head was thrown back, his eyes closed, his throat exposed as he urged her on. She couldn't tell if he was talking to himself or to her, but the clipped, graphic need sent desire shooting through her. *Take me deeper. That's it. That's what I need. Squeeze harder, suck on me.*

His voice continued each whispered command rougher and wilder. *All of me. Take more. You can do it.* He was no longer looking to her comfort, or helping her breathe, and the demands only made her want to give up everything to him. He was fast losing control and she had never thought he ever would.

She increased her attentions, sliding her mouth over him, flattening her tongue, hollowing her cheeks until he was gasping for mercy, until he spilled over, his hot essence jetting strong before he could regain control.

More than satisfied with her success, she took over, climbing onto his lap, wrapping her arms around his neck and settling her body over his still-hard erection with exquisite slowness. He pushed through her tight sheath, filling her, stretching and burning until she was completely seated and she felt full and deliciously stuffed.

She began to ride him, lifting herself up and dropping back over him, squeezing her muscles, getting a feel for what robbed him of his breath and sent streaks of fire racing through his body. She loved taking his body and making it her own. There was a heady excitement in watching the breath slam out of his lungs. Of moving up and down his body, using it for her own pleasure. She rode him slowly, leisurely, refusing to give in to the urgency of his hands biting into her hips or the enticement of his tightening thighs. She took her time, letting the waves build in her, pushing her higher, sending fire streaking through her womb so that she all but vibrated with the building tension. All the while she watched him as his breath hitched, as his expression grew darker, more filled with lust.

Nicolas fought himself to allow her to keep control, watching her face through half-closed eyes, enjoying the way she moved her body, the feel of her sheathing him like a tight glove. She was driving him insane with her slow, leisurely ride. She would rise up, twisting a little, contracting her muscles so her hot, silken sheath would tighten like a greedy fist around him. His body just kept building and building pressure until he was afraid he would spontaneously combust.

"Lock your ankles around my waist," he ordered, through bared teeth.

She looked amused. "What do you want me to do?"

"I am not joking around with you." Because she was torturing him slowly with her sensuous ride.

"Really?" Her eyebrow shot up and she lifted again, moving her hips in a small spiral as she locked her muscles around him.

Her creamy buttocks were far too tempting and he didn't try to resist, turning her skin a rosy red while reminding her who was the boss. She just laughed as she locked her ankles, gasping a little as he swung her around, setting her on the boulder and leveraging over her, locking her beneath him so he could have his way with her.

He slammed deep, driving into her the way he needed, burying himself into her so deep she went wild, exploding around him, gripping him hard as her orgasm tore through her. He continued to pound into her while her body squeezed and milked his until, with a hoarse cry, he jerked hard, thrusting mindlessly, his hot release flooding her.

Still buried deep, his body rocking, he bent his head to her breast, teeth aching, mouth filling with the taste of her. He flicked his tongue, nipped at her.

Nicolas's teeth scraped along her breast and her toes

curled. Butterfly wings brushed the inside of her stomach. His lips feathered over her pulse, his tongue rasping a light caress. She felt his bite of pleasure/pain.

Her wrist burned. A flashing image of teeth tearing at her flesh intruded. Her stomach lurched and she ground her teeth together to keep from crying out. Everything in her tensed. Waited. Screamed at him to stop.

Nicolas lifted his head, his black, hooded gaze, so sexy, so dark with desire, drifted alertly over her face. "What is it, *hän ku kuulua sívamet*?"

His voice was a velvet stroke, a dark caress as he called her "keeper of my heart." How could she be the keeper of his heart when she couldn't give him everything?

"I don't think I can," she whispered, tears burning behind her eyes. She'd managed to give blood to her aunt and that was all her mind would allow.

She detested disappointing him, especially now when she was feeling totally satisfied and loved. She wanted that for him as well. She wanted him to know she would give him everything if he asked—but she couldn't quite overcome the aversion she had. She knew giving blood was natural, even erotic between lifemates, she'd enjoyed it once, but now her stomach churned and panic set in. Everything had been so perfect and she had ruined it.

"I'm sorry," she whispered, shamed. "I'm so sorry."

He cupped her chin, lifted her face to kiss his way along her cheeks, collecting her tears with his tongue along the way. "Do you honestly think taking your blood every time I make love to you matters to me, Lara?"

Nicolas kissed her pulse and swept his tongue over the pinpricks there. "*Tet vigyázam*. I love you, it is that simple. Nothing else matters. You. Just you. I love to touch your body and make love to you, but it is you, who you are inside, that counts to me. If I cannot take your blood, will I miss that? I am certain I would occasionally. But truthfully, I

20

Lara and Nicolas rose early the next evening, bathed in the pool and made leisurely love. The naming ceremony was in a couple of hours and Lara was looking forward to it. She could feel the excitement building in the air all around her, even from within their cave. As she dressed she studied Nicolas. The wounds were gone, but she could see the raw edges not yet healed.

"When are you going to ground? You haven't been since we've been together."

"I will go when you are ready," he said.

She frowned. "That's not good enough, Nicolas. I can only check a few people a day for the microbe. I'm not through with all the women, let alone starting on the men. And if the microbe is in the ground, it will be an endless, vicious circle."

"You have to be converted, Lara."

"I will be, just not right now."

"Within the week. Check the women and you are done."

She didn't reply, knowing when he got that edge to his voice that he was worried about her. She knew what that felt like when she looked at him and saw his wounds that should have been healed. And she was very aware how often Nicolas suppressed his need to protect and keep her healthy. He knew the drain the journey was on her when she was hunting the microbe and she was having trouble keeping even broth down.

Nicolas suddenly looked alert, his fingers settling around her arm, pulling her behind him. "We have company. Let us meet them at the entrance to the cave, away from where your aunts rest."

To Lara's surprise, Shea and Jacques Dubrinsky stood waiting for an invitation to enter, Jacques holding their infant son in his arms. It was the first time Lara had ever gotten a good glimpse of the man who was lifemate to the Carpathian's researcher. He reminded her in some ways of her father, that ravaged look, with lines etched deep, eyes that had seen too much pain and suffering. She had heard the rumors of this man, of his splintered mind and how truly dangerous he was, but watching him hold his son so tenderly, it was difficult to believe.

"We've come asking more from your lifemate, Nicolas," Jacques said without preamble. "I understand these journeys she makes are difficult, and I would not ask, but Shea thinks it is necessary." His gaze slid to his lifemate and the tenderness in his expression was touching.

"It isn't so bad now that I know what I'm doing," Lara said. "And I have Nicolas as well to anchor me." She cleared her throat, thinking to confess her problem with giving or taking blood, which made the journeying difficult. She could only take blood from Nicolas and she didn't want to take a journey without him close. Reliving her childhood repeatedly was taxing.

It is no one's business. Nicolas reached out and took her hand, bringing her palm to his chest.

Shea touched her son's foot and looked up at both of them, blinking back sudden emotion. "He isn't doing well.

Our son. He's struggling and I've tried everything I know how to do, and he's still losing ground. Gregori and Francesca have both examined him repeatedly, but he has the same wasting disease the other children we've lost has had. I cannot feed him properly and the mixtures I've tried for him are not nourishing him."

"Shea, I'm so sorry," Lara said. "We had no idea. No one's said a word."

"We thought it best to keep it private," Jacques replied. "A few of our women are pregnant now and we do not want to chance causing them more stress."

"What can I do?" Lara asked.

"Journey and see if he is infected with the microbe."

Lara and Nicolas exchanged a long look of sudden comprehension. "You think I'll find one, don't you?"

Shea bit her lip, nodding as she did so. "I think a microbe finds the male first and when he has sex with his lifemate, the microbe travels to her, leaving him open territory. While he lies sleeping in the soil, another enters, through his skin most likely. The first microbe has found the female host and lies in weight for conception. If she becomes pregnant, the organism forces her to miscarry by continually attacking the baby, but if it isn't successful, I believe the microbe then travels into the baby, again leaving her without one. So the cycle starts all over again with the man once again infecting the woman. Once inside the baby, the microbe slowly kills it."

Lara closed her eyes briefly. Shea's theory sounded very sensible, especially since they had found Xavier's laboratory and his series of pools. Each was a different environment for the extremophile.

"Unfortunately, your theory matches evidence we found in the ice caves. These microorganisms are very difficult to kill as a rule, Shea. We're burning them one by one, but if everyone is continually infected each time we go to ground, it will be impossible to keep up."

Nicolas's hand curved around the nape of Lara's neck. "Especially when, so far, Lara's the only one who can find them. And when I convert her, she may not be able to do so anymore. Natalya cannot."

Shea gasped. "You can't convert her, Nicolas." She shook her head. "I know how much you both must want to, but you can't. We can't take any chances. This is too important to all of us. Until I can find an antibody that will fight this thing in the ground, Lara is our only hope."

"Xavier corrupts the extremophiles. If someone collects them for you, perhaps you can use the original superpowered bugs to fight his corrupt ones," Lara offered. "I've collected them for research before and scientists all over the world believe the extremophile can be used to cure many diseases. They actually will defend against other microbes, so maybe the answer is the simplest of all. Use the original."

Shea's expression brightened. "You saw evidence of mutation?"

Lara nodded. "I've seen normal extremophiles hundreds of times. Xavier definitely mutated these."

"If that's true," Shea said with confidence, "I believe we'll be able to find an antidote, or vaccine, or something to combat this. Finally. Hope. Real hope."

"But you are talking experiments to get it right," Nicolas said. "That takes time." He tugged Lara to him protectively. "She is caught between both worlds, Shea. She can barely manage to keep any food down. She cannot go to ground, but she cannot be in the light either. Is it right to ask my lifemate to live in a half-world?"

"No," Jacques answered for both of them—for the entire Carpathian people. "No, of course it isn't, but we have no choice. We have to ask you to save our children."

Lara looked at the baby in his arms, so innocent, already slipping away from them. He was pale and thin, listless, his eyes dull. Her gaze met Nicolas's. She tried not to let him see or feel her despair. She couldn't sacrifice this child or any other—and neither could he. Until they could find a way to counteract the microbes already living in the soil she couldn't be converted.

You can, Nicolas said firmly. *We have no idea what could happen to you living a half-life. No one can ask this of you.*

I love you, too. She smiled at him. *And you know there is no choice. This child belongs to all of us.*

Nicolas swore and looked away from her, once again feeling helpless. His centuries of existence had failed to prepare him for failure. He had driven her to the very end of her endurance. He had been unable to protect her when she'd relived her childhood. He'd failed to save her friends, and now he could not take her from the half-life. What kind of a lifemate was he? Protection had always—*always*—come first in his mind, but now he was an utter failure at the one thing that was the most important.

Lara wrapped her arms around him, right there, in front of Jacques and Shea, leaning into him and tilting her head. "You are the best lifemate. That's what you are, and right now, I need you to help me find whatever is trying to harm this child. We'll need Natalya to draw the microbe out once I lure it to the surface and you'll have to be ready to give me blood. And then—" She smiled at Shea. "—then we have a celebration to go to. Everyone is so excited about the naming ceremony."

Shea managed a weak smile. "Please find it, Lara. If you don't, I have no idea how to save our son."

"I'll find it," Lara said with more confidence than she felt.

A hush fell over the gathered crowd. Anticipation and excitement heightened awareness of details. The incense burning, the fragrance of sage and lavender blended with the aroma of candles. The chamber was warm, the direct opposite of the ice caves and Lara couldn't help but compare this child's welcome to the one given her. She wished her aunts could have been there to participate, but after the healers had examined them, and given them more blood, both decreed it was too soon and the women needed far more time to regain their health in the ground. She looked up at Nicolas and smiled.

Nicolas tightened his fingers around Lara's. Pride welled up in him in spite of the fact that a part of him wanted to throw his lifemate over his shoulder and take her back to South America where he could see to her health. If it wasn't for Lara, this child would never have had a chance at life. She had taken the journey into the small body and discovered Shea's theory was right. The microbe had passed from mother to child and was slowly killing the baby.

The journey had been more difficult than he had expected. The baby was small and already weak and sick. Lara had to be careful and go in as an infant almost before she really got started. The microbe would have run from an adult. The continual reliving of her childhood was taking a toll on Lara, but when he tried to put his foot down and tell her enough was enough, she only smiled at him and pointed to the baby. With the microbe out of his body, he was already hungry and active, bouncing back fast.

He watched Jacques carry his son into the center of the chamber while the Carpathian greeting chant swelled in volume. Everyone present would pledge their love and support to the child, become family to him, vow to raise him should anything happen to his parents.

Jacques handed his son to his brother and the prince raised the child high into the air. A roar of approval went up. Shea slipped her hand into her lifemate's and looked over at them.

Thank you both. You enabled this to happen.

Nicolas felt his throat tighten. He brought Lara's hand to his mouth and pressed a kiss to the center of her palm.

"Who names this child?" Mikhail asked.

"His father," Jacques replied.

"His mother," Shea said.

"His people," the crowd of males and females, lifemated and single, added.

"You are called Stefan Kane," Mikhail announced, "born in battle, crowned with love. Who will accept the offer of the Carpathian people to love and raise our son?"

"His parents, with gratitude." Jacques and Shea looked at one another with joy.

Nicolas felt the emotion spread through him. Joy. He knew the meaning of the word and it was Lara.

And now, a special preview of

Street Game

by Christine Feehan.

Coming January 2010 from Jove.

And be sure to continue reading for special
deleted scenes from *Dark Curse*!

Black night. No moon, no stars. Just the way he liked it. Mack McKinley crouched in the alley, close to the tall dirty building, allowing his senses to become tuned to the familiar sounds. A cat raked through a garbage can, a drunk moaned and shivered in the cold. Waves rose, folded over with a slap and sloshed against the pier just behind the building. Three stories up, lights went out, leaving the long row of windows like giant gaping black mouths. McKinley smiled at the image, smiled up at the windows. His smile was not pleasant.

This was the all-important tip. Tracking the explosives through Lebanon, Beirut, the South American freighter, San Francisco. Always one step behind. He had moved fast to check out the information, praying it was correct. They had less than twenty-four hours to find the guns and the five-man unit of Doomsday he knew was planning to buy the weapons. He sneered at the name of the terrorist unit, but he had to give them kudos for scaring the crap out of every country they had visited. They left behind wreckage and carnage and death. More—they left behind fear.

Urban warfare was an art, any way one looked at it, and his team had knowledge of the streets, were the best there was. But it was dangerous work and one had to have a cool head. Too many civilians, too many potential hostages, too damn many things to go wrong. And yet his men were good at it, more than good—he counted them the best. Sergeant Major Theodore Griffen wanted Doomsday taken out, and when the sergeant major gave an order, it was carried out immediately and to the letter.

The warehouse was wired. He knew it, could "feel" it. But something . . . His men were in position, waiting for him. As always, Kane Cannon was at his back. They'd started on the streets together, two kids trying to stay alive, eventually pulling in six other boys and two girls, all with "different" abilities to make up their ragtag family.

From the streets, Kane and Mack and one of the girls—Mack didn't want to think about her—had gone on to the University. The others had gone into the Marine Corps. All had a gift for languages, as well as too many other things, such as what he was doing now. They were recruited right out of school and trained as operatives until the psychic testing. That had been a huge mistake, and all of his family had followed him—as they had all along.

Special Forces. Psychic testing where they'd all come back together just like on the street. More specialized training. SEAL training. Urban war games. Even more specialized training until they were pretty much killing machines. They had stuck together and knew one another's every move. They trusted one another and no one else, not in the business they were in. Well . . . with the exception of the new kid, but that was a whole other story. It was no good thinking about that right now, not when he was surrounded with the ones he loved, leading them into a situation that was explosive at the very least.

Mack signaled for the others to pull down their night goggles, making it easy to see in the blackness of the night.

He and Kane didn't need them. They could both see in the dark as easily as during the day. Something to do with the experiments they'd lent themselves to. Stupid, but they'd done it for the good of the country and their need for a home. Yeah, he knew the psychological bullshit everyone spouted. It was probably all true too, but he didn't much care. It was also one hell of an adrenaline rush.

Still, he waited, hesitating before signaling his team forward. His men were coiled and ready. He had a bad feeling, deep in his gut, and he never discounted his instincts. Something wasn't quite right, but he couldn't put his finger on it.

What is it? Kane questioned, using telepathy, communication they had perfected as children and which the military had enhanced when they volunteered for their psychic GhostWalker program.

Something's wrong? Not wrong, maybe, just not right. How the hell could he explain that strange kick in his belly?

I feel it, too, but I'm not sure what's out of sync here. There was another long moment of silence. *Abort?* Kane asked.

Mack took a breath. Let it out. *No, but let's all be very cautious.*

Of the eight of them, only the new kid the sergeant major had insisted they train couldn't communicate telepathically. That had been the common denominator that had drawn them together on the streets. They were all different and they'd all recognized the psychic gift in one another. Mack had been the acknowledged leader and Kane had always, *always*, had his back.

He glanced at the man and saw he was doing what Kane did best, searching the huge warehouse with his strange eyes. He could see right through the wood and metal to the heat inside, a gift from Whitney and his experiments. There were several new things in them. Animal DNA.

A new genetic code. They hadn't signed on for that kind of experiment, but when they woke up, they had been changed for all time.

He signaled his men forward. It took minutes to bypass the alarm on the side entrance door, far longer than it should have. The alarm was too complicated for a wharf warehouse. Who put together a triple, sophisticated alarm system so complex it took Javier, his best tech, precious time to unravel it?

We've got ourselves a pro system, here, Mack, Javier said. *One I've never seen before. Whoever put this mother together, knew what they were doing.* There was frank admiration in the voice.

No activity in the lower warehouse that I can spot, Mack, Kane said. *I can't detect heat on the second floor either, but someone's on the third floor.*

Just one person? That made no sense.

Just one.

Mac moved first, his brain more reluctant than his body. He rolled inside the door of the first floor, under a trip wire, crawled military fashion beneath the maze of track beams. The entire room was empty, deserted, with the exception of scattered building materials here and there. The sophisticated alarm system seemed ridiculous. Something was nagging at the back of his mind, refusing to leave him alone.

Where are the sentries, Kane?

I don't know, bro, but this is all wrong.

The roof was clean, protected only by an alarm. His man, Gideon, was up there now, with a rifle and a radio. Gideon could see in the dark, hear like an owl and shoot the wings off a fly in the middle of the night if necessary. Mack should have been feeling good, but that punch in his gut was getting stronger. And where the hell was the sentry on the ground level? Was this an elaborate trap? Had Doomsday been tipped off that they were coming?

The little band of terrorists had no cause, no politics, no religious war to fight. They were mercenaries, a brand-new type spawned by the times. They showed off their talents, sparing no country, no man, woman or child, with one idea—working for the highest bidder. They sold their services to the highest bidder, which made them a little difficult to track, as no one could ever figure out who they worked for and where they would be next. This was the GhostWalkers' one opportunity to get them, following the weapons, yet he just couldn't shake the feeling that something was wrong.

Even as his mind struggled desperately with the problem, he was aware of every detail around him, aware of the kid, young Paul, exposed an inch too high, close beneath one of the beams. Mack hissed and all movement ceased. The warehouse was utterly still. His cold gaze pinned Paul. Mack signaled with a flat hand. The rookie's body hugged the cold cement. Despite the cover of darkness, Mack knew Paul flushed crimson.

The kid blushed a lot. What the hell he was doing with their team, Mack couldn't figure out. Basically, they were babysitting, and that could get them all killed. No one on the team wanted the kid with them, but Sergeant Major Griffen had been more than insistent. It wasn't that the kid wasn't highly intelligent—he was. He also was psychic, although none of them had gone through Dr. Whitney's program with him. All the GhostWalkers tended to know or at least recognize one another. Paul was an exception. Mack didn't like question marks, and the kid posed too many.

Mack rolled free of the interlocking track beams. The loudness of the freight lift was out of the question. It had to be the stairs, each one more perilous than the next. There would be two flights to get to that third floor.

Where the hell are the sentries? The question nagged at him, would not let him go.

Everyone was on high alert now, the question as disturbing to them as it was to him. He waited a heartbeat, but couldn't find a reason not to continue.

He moved cautiously. Four stairs—seven. He felt it on eight. The wire puzzled him. It was an alarm, not a mine. His mind seized on that, worried at it.

Mack had done this so many times that he knew exactly how each one of his men was feeling. Adrenaline pumping, heart racing, fear choking, guns rock steady. Something was off-kilter. Wrong. The word fluttered in his head, beat at him like tiny wings.

Definitely off.

Kane's anxiety heightened his own.

Mack gained the second floor. Where the first floor had been mostly empty space and building materials, this one was packed with electronic equipment. A bank of computers was built into the far wall, the only thing completed. Everything else was in boxes, all electronics equipment, high-end.

"Bingo," Paul's whisper came over the radio, trembling with excitement. "Moving day."

Check it, Kane. Maybe we're looking at how they transported the guns.

Inside electronic equipment? This is satellite tracking, cameras, stuff like that. Not guns. We've stumbled onto something, but I'm not certain it's what we're after.

Mack wasn't certain either. He shook his head, his mind screaming at him now. This was all wrong. No sentries. This type of equipment was far too advanced for the kind of terrorists the Doomsday organization were.

He moved up the staircase. Third stair this time. No explosives. Seventh stair. He rolled beneath the beam on the landing, came up on one knee, breathing deeply. *Here! Here!* His men were spreading out, back-to-back, in a standard search pattern.

What is it? What's wrong? Find the answer! Find the answer! Mac moved carefully through the furniture.

The furniture, Mack. All wrong, Kane hissed in his mind.

A long plush couch, a hand-carved wooden coffee table, a priceless Persian rug. Beautiful, expensive. A small object on an end table. A dragon. Like in a living room. A home. Knowledge came a heartbeat too late.

Something stirred just a few feet from him, a weapon glinted.

"Break off! Break off!" He yelled it even as he launched himself toward the small figure crouched behind the recliner. His body, solid, heavily muscled, hit the smaller, softer one squarely, knocking the woman flat, pinning her to the floor.

She shocked him by fighting hard, going for pressure points, obviously having a working knowledge of hand-to-hand combat tactics. It took some strength and finesse to subdue her without hurting her. He successfully blanketed her body with his, tensed for the bullets he was certain would tear into him. His team was well trained, superb even. Not a shot was fired. Even so, as a precaution, Kane caught Paul's weapon, pushing it away from McKinley's body.

There was a long, deadly silence. Mack could hear her breathing, her heart racing. There was no struggle once he'd pinned her; she lay perfectly still beneath him. For a moment, he was afraid he had knocked her unconscious, but her breathing was too ragged.

"Is anyone else up here?" he whispered the words in her ear.

She shook her head.

Kane and the others began a standard search pattern. McKinley hoped she was telling the truth. She smelled fresh and faintly exotic, her skin satin smooth, petal soft. The scent, the feel of her, was oddly familiar. Too familiar. His body recognized her before his brain did, reacting with enough testosterone for his entire unit, mixed with more adrenaline than any of them could possibly handle.

McKinley, slowly, carefully, eased his weight until he
was certain he wasn't hurting her, yet still kept her pinned.
As each member of the team barked "Clear," he shifted
enough to get a good look at her face. One leg remained
firmly over her thighs, a warning not to move.

Behind them, a lamp was switched on. "All clear, sir."
That was young Paul. His men were all staring, yet trying not to stare. The woman was in a long nightgown.
See-through. One of those diaphanous, filmy things that
clung to every curve and sent a jackhammer through the
middle of a man's skull. Her gown had pulled up her thigh,
revealing a more than generous expanse of gleaming skin.

She had tousled hair, a riot of curls, and large, haunting
eyes. He would know her anywhere, anyplace.

Jaimie. He said her name, at least he thought he said it,
but no sound emerged. Maybe he just breathed her name.
He touched her thick mane of silky, midnight black hair,
his fingers sliding into one of the curls and tugging, letting
the strands slide through the pads of his fingers, trying to
regain the breath she'd stolen.

"Get off me, McKinley." The fear was in her voice, but
she was striving for control. "What are you doing here? Hi,
boys. I missed—most of you," she greeted from the floor.

"Hey, Jaimie," Kane said.

"Man, Jaimie," Javier added. "Sweet damn security system. I should have recognized your work."

"Great to see you, Jaimie," Brian Hutton added with a
little grin. "Although we're seeing more of you than brothers are comfortable with."

"What the fuck are you wearing?" Mack demanded.
Lust punched hard and mean, his entire body tightening,
his cock hard as a rock. He was furious with her, scared for
her. Shocked at seeing her. What was going on? She had
fucking left him. *Left* him. Disappeared without a trace.

His hand gripped her throat and he trapped her there on
the floor, letting her feel the strength of his anger—of his

need. He leaned close. "Did you find yourself, Jaimie? Did you find everything you were looking for?" *Did you miss me the way I missed you? Did you bring my heart back, because I have a damn big hole where it should be.*

He stared down into her eyes—eyes he always fell into—eyes he'd always drown in. *Damn you, Jaimie. Damn you to hell for this.* The attraction was worse than it had ever been, flooding him until his body was no longer his and discipline and control had gone out the window. "Don't you dare look at me that way."

She swallowed hard. He felt the movement against the palm of his hand. "What way?"

"Like you're afraid of me. Like I'm going to hurt you." There was panic in her eyes, fear almost amounting to terror, and it sickened him.

"Mack." Kane's voice was very soft. "You've got your hand around her throat and you're sitting on her. That could be interpreted by some as aggressive action."

Mack hissed, his head snapping around. "Anyone else have anything brilliant they want to contribute?"

No one else was that stupid—or brave.

He loosened his hold on her throat, but retained possession, feeling the satisfying frantic beat of her pulse. "What the hell are you wearing?" He demanded again. "You might as well be wearing nothing at all."

"It's called a nightgown," Jaimie replied, her voice sarcastic. "Mack, let me up. In case no one's ever told you, you're heavy."

He was solid muscle. And right now every single inch of him was as hard as a rock. Moving was going to be painful, one way or the other.

Sighing, because everyone was going to know exactly what she did to him, he shifted very carefully. "Get some clothes on." Abruptly, Mack was on his feet, pulling her up with him. A quick flick of his eyes and his men suddenly found the ceiling interesting.

They were grinning like idiots. All of them. Even Kane. He resisted swearing at them.

"Have the decency to turn around," he ordered the others.

Morons. Every single one. He didn't turn around. He glared at her. Daggers. "That's a hell of a thing to wear unless you're entertaining, Jaimie. Are you entertaining?" His hand slid down to the satisfying hilt of his knife. He'd do some entertaining of his own if some son of a bitch was moving in on Jaimie. Not waiting for an answer, he tore off his jacket and threw it at her. "Cover up."

"Go to hell, Mack. This is my home. My bedroom, in case you haven't noticed."

Still, she slipped her arms into the jacket and inhaled, rubbing her cheek along the material without thinking, and then stalked across the room to yank open a drawer.

"You're a long way from home." Jaimie made the observation as she donned a pair of charcoal sweatpants. "Not to mention you're a little overdressed for these parts."

He noticed her hands were trembling as she pulled the edges of his jacket together. Her voice was exactly as he remembered. Soft, husky, beautiful. Like clear running water. It hurt him to look at her. Her chin was in the air—same defiant Jaimie he'd known forever. But she wasn't looking at him—not directly—and that wasn't like Jaimie.

"The next time you want to drop in, local custom demands that you do me the courtesy of knocking." She paced away from him, back again, unable to rid her body of the adrenaline. "What are you doing here, Mack?"

"We followed a shipment of weapons."

Her eyebrows shot up. "To San Francisco? To my home?"

"Right to your front door, baby."

She winced. "I'm not your baby, Mack. That was a long time ago. What are you really doing here?"

"Our information . . ."

"Mack, come on." She crossed to the window and looked out over the pounding waves. "You and I both know this is too big of a coincidence. If you weren't the one to arrange it, then your informer wanted you here. Wanted us together."

He wanted them together, so whoever had done this deliberately or not, he owed them. Jaimie had disappeared out of all of their lives some time ago. She'd been a big part of their street family and now, here she was—practically in his lap.

He crossed to stand behind her, gently taking hold of her shoulders and moving her back away from the window.

Kane cleared his throat. "The information was, the shipment we're after was offloaded and stored in this block of warehouses. Corner. High security. That's this warehouse, Jaimie."

Her sapphire gaze touched his face, jumped away. "Actually, it's not. You want the one at the end of this block. Mysterious trucks in the middle of the night. Hard cases, trying to look friendly. You want that warehouse, not mine. They have a lot of shady deals going." Her gaze swung back to Mack. There was something faintly accusing in the depths of her eyes, but then she glanced away from him, as if she couldn't bear to look at him.

Deep inside, there was a stirring, an answer. Mack could feel his body's reaction, taut, dangerous, a man's reaction. Jaimie Fielding. His fists curled. His Jaimie. Stubborn Jaimie, with her outrageous sense of humor, her computer brain and her pure ethics. Her small teeth bit nervously at her lip, drawing Mack's immediate attention to the fullness of her soft mouth. He had always wanted to crush her lips beneath his. She had *left* him.

"I think my rights as a United States citizen have been severely violated," Jaimie pointed out. "You just invaded my home."

Mack swept a hand through charcoal hair. "Can it, Jaimie," he snapped. "This isn't funny." Seeing her threw him. Drawing her scent into his lungs sent his body into some kind of permanent overdrive. He was supposed to be disciplined, but somehow, with Jaimie around, his body went haywire, thinking with other portions of his anatomy rather than his brain.

"Do I look like I'm laughing?" Her eyebrows arched in inquiry. "I can assure you, I wasn't trying to be funny." At his look, her full, lush lips curled, pursed. "Well, so, all right," she conceded. "Maybe I was a bit. Your hotshot intelligence group made a big mistake. Left you with egg all over your faces. Not to mention I was waiting for you."

Mack snatched up the frying pan lying beside the sofa. "I suppose you thought you were going to bean the entire team with this."

A low rumble of laughter swept through the room. Jaimie smirked at them. "Laugh all you want, hotshots. If I'd been your enemy, you would be dead or wounded right now."

"She has a point." Mack's glittering eyes swept the room. "We're lucky this isn't the place."

Cannon watched McKinley watching Jaimie. It looked like trouble to him, but then, it always had been trouble when the two of them had been in close proximity. Combustible. Like a match to dynamite. He found himself grinning. "Did you provide the anonymous information?"

"Not a chance," Jaimie denied staunchly. "I'm sort of doing my own thing here and wouldn't call attention to myself. Nor do I want an angry neighbor torching the place with me in it, if I set the hounds on them."

"Why all the security?" Paul demanded, unconvinced. "And what's with all the electronic equipment?"

"I'm a spy for Russia," Jaimie snapped. "Where's your search warrant? This is still the United States, whether you have an invisible badge or not."

"He's new, Jaimie," Cannon said softly. "Cut him some slack."

"He's a hothead." Her hands were still trembling. Jaimie

felt her stomach lurch uncomfortably. "And he'll get one of you killed." She pressed one hand to her midsection, hard.

"Take them out of here," McKinley ordered Kane, frowning at her action.

"You can go down to the first floor. There's heat, but little else," Jaimie said.

"I wouldn't mind looking at your equipment on the second floor," Javier said. "Looks like a sweet setup."

"I'll just bet you'd like a look. It's my new business, Javier." She flashed him a smile. "And I'm not letting you anywhere near those computers. I don't need the competition."

"Maybe you don't want us to look at them for a reason," Paul said.

Jaimie shrugged, her gaze cool as she looked the man up and down. "Maybe."

"I'll take them to the first floor," Cannon said. "And contact the sergeant major to see where our information went haywire."

Jaimie switched off her elaborate security alarm to speed things up. Mack waited until they were alone. He followed her into the kitchen area and watched as she reached for the teakettle. Tea. Of course. She always made tea when she was upset.

"Are you all right?" he asked gently.

"You took ten years off my life," she admitted.

He leaned one hip against the cupboards, drinking in the sight of her. "What are you doing here? What is all the equipment?"

"Just something I'm working on."

She refused to look at him. Her shoulders were stiff. Her body posture screamed at him to go. "I've missed you, Jaimie." Stubborn, he wasn't about to back off from a confrontation. She'd taken his heart and soul when she'd left. He'd been a zombie, a machine without a direction. He couldn't take his eyes from her. He knew there was accusation in his voice, in his expression, but damn it all, she deserved it. "You disappeared without a trace."

"You had a choice, Mack," she reminded. "You made it very clear to me where your priorities were. They weren't with me. With us. It's called self-preservation."

"That's bullshit. You knew I had no idea you'd just disappear."

"As I recall, you said in no uncertain terms you weren't ready for any kind of commitment. I took you at your word. What did you think I'd do?"

Weep for him. Wait for him. Crawl back and beg his forgiveness. Not fucking disappear. Never that. She'd taken his life. She'd taken everything he was from him. "I expected you to realize I was busy."

She kept her back to him, her hands shook as she lifted the whistling teakettle. "Busy? You mean your drive to make the world right? Your need to save everyone? You walked out on us, Mack. If you want to pretend you didn't, if that makes it all good for you, it's all right with me. I survived. You survived. You have the life you want. I'm good too. I moved on, so I'm guessing we're both good."

"Is that what you're guessing?" He waited until the kettle was safely back on the stove before gripping her arm and spinning her around to face him. "Guess again, Jaimie."

She didn't struggle as he'd expected her to. She simply went very still and looked down at the fingers circling her wrists like a steel vise. Her gaze flicked up to his face, lingered on his mouth for a heart-stopping moment before her eyes met his. He had the curious sensation of tumbling forward.

"Mack, let go of me."

He nearly didn't. He nearly jerked her against him and took possession of her mouth. That perfect mouth that could drive a man out of his mind, take him to paradise. He knew she'd melt into him. He knew she belonged to him—every last inch of her—but he wanted more than her body. He'd had something precious and didn't know it until he'd lost it. He dropped his hand and was annoyed when she rubbed the mark of his fingers from her skin before turning back to her task.

He stared at her back for a long moment, trying to find a way to reach her. Anything. The rage and pain of his loss was too close to the surface, rendering his quick brain useless. This was his Jaimie, yet not.

"Jaimie," he said softly. "Talk to me."

She kept her back to him. McKinley. She'd never called him McKinley, even when they'd been best friends. Cannon, McKinley and Fielding. Where one had been, there was the other, but he had been Mack, always Mack.

"Was this really an accident? A coincidence?"

His fist tightened until his knuckles turned white. "Of course it was an accident. What else?"

She turned around then, her large eyes luminous, beautiful. Eyes a man could get lost in. "It's a bit far-fetched, don't you think? You just happen to get the wrong warehouse and find me in it."

"It's a small world."

"Don't give me clichés, Mack," she cautioned. "You scared me to death. I thought you were a burglar."

"And you were going to attack him with a frying pan? What the hell's the matter with you?" He had to keep his hands in check when he wanted to step forward and hold her trembling body against the shelter of his. When he needed to touch the silk of her hair and smooth the frown lines from her face.

"I'm keeping a low profile. Shooting a burglar or beating the crap out of him is a good way to advertise my presence, now, isn't it?"

He drew in his breath. "You're working undercover."

She leaned against the sink and looked at him with her killer eyes. He felt the impact like a wicked punch to his gut and then lower, the pain reminding him he was more than alive.

"I'm starting a new business that requires a good reputation, privacy and respectability."

"That's a load of bullshit. I'm family. If I'm nothing else to you, at least I'm that."

Her eyes flashed fire at him. Threw sparks. "You broke my heart, Mack. You threw me away for your adrenaline rush. Well, you've got the life you wanted. I learned my lesson, and believe me, it was a hard one. You wanted sex and I was handy. I'm attracted to you and was willing to give you just about everything. I didn't see for a long, long time that *that*," she jerked her chin toward the thick, rock-hard bulge in the front of his jeans, "was all that mattered between us, all that you were ever going to give me. It isn't ever going to be enough for me. I've got a life, now, Mack. I'm never going to feel like that again, the way you made me feel. I hated myself. I don't want to see you again. I'm asking you to just stay away from me."

"Like hell. Like hell I'll stay away from you." He stepped closer, his breath coming in ragged gasps. He burned for her. Every moment of every day. He couldn't think straight without her. She stilled his mind. Made him human. "I can't breathe without you, and damn you, you know it. You don't get over what we had together. You can't. I can't. We belong no matter what bullshit you're telling yourself."

She shocked him by standing her ground. Staring at him. Her body was still, coiled and ready. She was trembling and there was a slight quiver to her perfect mouth, but she didn't crumble under his demand as she always had.

"It was your choice to throw us away, Mack, not mine. I'm not going to argue with you about my feelings. You just aren't entitled to know what I'm feeling anymore. You aren't entitled to anything of mine. Not my body and not my heart."

"Think again. If I kissed you, touched you, you'd still belong to me."

She gave him that casual shrug that ripped his heart

out and made him madder than hell. "Probably, Mack. We always had that firestorm to fall back on, but I realized something when you walked away from me. That's all we had. You told me what to do and I did it, like a puppet. Your puppet. I was good in bed, but you didn't need me for anything else. There are millions of women who are great in bed—find one of them, one that just wants sex. I want more and I deserve more. I *need* more. You can't give me what I need, Mack. I've accepted that."

He could hear the quiet acceptance in her voice and panic welled up. She wasn't stringing him along. She was serious. He risked a breath when his lungs burned for air. He took his gaze from her and looked around the huge warehouse. It was a home. Unique. Like Jaimie. She was far from Chicago, where they'd grown up. As far as she could get. She really hadn't provided the information. This wasn't her plan. Someone else had gotten them together. She had made a new life for herself.

There were flowers in a vase on a table. Roses. Red and white. Jaimie's favorite.

Jealousy burst like a dam, flooding him with poisonous rage, a dark red strain that spread fast, gripping like a demon. She'd killed him when she disappeared, left him half a man and, damn her, she'd just moved on as if he wasn't part of her heart and soul the way she was his.

"Is there a fucking man living here with you?" He bit out each word. Wrenched the sounds between gritted teeth.

"I'm not doing this with you. I told you I wanted a family, Mack."

"We were a family. We *are* a family. It's always been us." And what the hell did that mean, exactly? He continued to look around the spacious floor for signs of another man.

"Do you remember what you said to me when I asked about getting pregnant?"

"I told you it was fine."

She shook her head. "That is not what you said, Mack. First you looked angry and you demanded to know if I was pregnant. When I didn't answer you, you said if I was pregnant, we'd handle it."

"Well, we would have."

"*Handle* it? That's not wanting a family, Mack, that's making the best of a bad situation. Or worse, maybe your 'handling it' was to suggest an abortion."

"Damn it, Jaimie, I would never suggest you get rid of our baby. Is that what you thought? You know me better than that."

"I thought I knew you. I thought we both wanted the same thing out of our relationship. It was a shock when I discovered I was wrong." She shrugged. "I handled it. But it's best if we don't see each other."

"Because we belong together." There was smug satisfaction in his voice.

"Because we aren't good for one another." There was finality in her tone.

"Jaimie, are you happy?" Everything in him stilled. Waited. Her answer would determine his fate. He wouldn't ruin what Jaimie had if it was really what she wanted. Jaimie would never lie. She might avoid the question, but it wasn't in her to lie. He knew her too well.

The tip of her tongue touched her lip. She blew on her tea, avoiding his eyes. "You didn't need a family, Mack. I was always surprised that so many didn't. I wanted desperately to belong. That was why I joined you in the first place and later did undercover work. I needed to belong somewhere, to feel I was part of something. I haven't found that yet, but I will. At least I know what's important to me and I'm going after it." She flashed him a small smile that didn't quite reach her eyes. "I'll be all right."

Everything in him settled again. If she wasn't happy, that meant he had a chance. It might be a slim one, but he was a GhostWalker and he thrived on slim chances.

"I'm coming back. I have to go to work, Jaimie, but I'm coming back. If you have another man in your life, get rid of him. He isn't making you happy."

Her eyes flashed again, tiny sparks. He felt the answer in his gut. He had never been able to stop his response to her, and since his psychic enhancement, the pull between them was electric. He remembered her as a teenager, a young girl, all eyes and hair and that awesome mouth. When she smiled she could make the sun rise. He'd never met anyone else as intelligent. She could keep up with him on any subject, her mind quick, like the computers she loved so much. He'd spent hours just talking to her back then, watching the animation on her face, knowing she was his—that she'd always been his.

Very carefully she set the teacup onto the sink, more to keep from throwing it at him than to prevent him from seeing her hands shake. "I'm not starting up with you again, Mack. It took too much out of me. I loved seeing all of you. I've felt terribly alone these past couple of years, but I can't go there again. I'm asking you to please leave me alone."

He stepped close, crowding her body with his so she could feel the heat radiating from his body and the brush of hard muscles against her soft curves. "Honey." His voice was gentle, tender even, as it only managed with Jaimie. "You might as well ask me to stop breathing." He caught her chin in his hand and lifted her face to force her to meet his gaze. "You're home to me, Jaimie. I'm tired of being without you. I've never wanted anyone else. I'm not walking away from you. Not after finding you again. I don't care if someone threw us together on purpose. I don't care how it happened. And don't try disappearing. Don't do it, Jaimie. This time I'll come looking, and God help both of us if I have to kill a man over you."

She jerked her chin out his hand. "I hate the way you have to be so alpha, beat your chest all the time. I'm not a bone to fight over."

"No, you're a woman worth everything on this earth to me."

"Well that's a big change, isn't it?"

"I'm not fighting with you. God knows we did enough of that. I'm done fighting with you. I want to come home."

She pushed at the wall of his chest. The shove didn't even rock him. A flicker of anger crossed her face. "You haven't changed at all."

"You always loved me just the way I am, Jaimie, alpha or not."

"I was a kid and anything you did was incredible and cool. I'm all grown up now and I know the difference between physical attraction and love. I want love. I want a family. I won't settle for anything less, and you don't have that kind of commitment in you. You aren't tearing out my heart, Mack. Go do your thing, get your adrenaline rush. But when you come back all hot and bothered, find another woman to expend all that energy on, because I'm not available."

A muscle ticked in his jaw, always a bad sign. It took discipline to keep his hands off of her. "We'll see, Jaimie. I'm coming back and I'd better find you here, alone."

He turned on his heel and stalked out.

In this special section,
you'll get an exclusive look at
three deleted scenes from
Dark Curse

The shadow warrior spun around, sword flashing, cutting straight at Vikirnoff's throat. He ducked and parried, sparks raining down as the metal edges collided with enormous force.

"Having a good time there, honey?" Natalya called out. "You're looking a little slow. You've got a trio coming up on your right." She folded her arms and tapped her foot as three more warriors rushed into the fray.

Vikirnoff went vertical, leaping into the air, kicking at one.

"Way cool, babycakes. I'm so impressed with that move. Very Jackie Chan!" She fanned herself. "My little heart is all aflutter."

"Okay, I've got the point. Get in here and help me." Virkinoff threw a dark scowl over his shoulder and ducked another sword coming at him, spinning to take him through the ranks of smoky warriors, his movements drawing them away from his lifemate.

Natalya clutched her side and batted her eyelashes. "I think I'm ovulating and this is the optimal time. Can we call a time-out so you can do the dastardly deed and get me with child?"

One of the shadow warriors drove hard at Vikirnoff. The Carpathian raced up the side of the ice wall, then flipped over, driving the blade of his sword across the warrior's neck. It should have beheaded his opponent, but as the shadow warrior was already dead, Vikirnoff's blade cut through air.

Natalya clapped her hands. "Hey! If you were shorter and green, we could call you Yoda. Didn't he teach that move to Luke Skywalker?"

"Natalya," Vikirnoff bit out through clenched teeth. "You aren't funny. I've got five of these warriors coming at me, and you're just standing around."

"But I'm looking pretty. You have to admit I look good standing here. And I'm cheering for you, babe." Pom-poms appeared in her hands and she was suddenly wearing a short skirt. She did a little demonstration for him. "Go Vik, go. Destroy those bad boys."

She stopped moving when one of the shadow warriors turned his head toward her. Movement always attracted them.

Vikirnoff fought through the ranks until he had placed his body between his lifemate and the warriors. His sword flashed in and out as he spun gracefully, dropped low, went high and kept a whirling movement impossible to anticipate. "Stop kidding around!"

"Are you going to go before the warrior's counsel and tell them you think women should be allowed to fight? 'Cuz it looks like you could use a little help. But I could just stand here braiding my hair if you'd rather I sit this one out."

"*O jelä peje teräd—Sun scorch you*, Natalya!"

She raised an eyebrow. "Did you just curse at me? I'm only following my man's wishes." She glared at him. "Like Donna Reed."

"Sun scorch the warrior's counsel. And sun scorch Donna Reed as well."

"That's so not nice when Donna Reed is your dream girl."

"Warrior princess is my dream girl and she'd better get her spectacular ass in gear." Vikirnoff parried two swords coming at him, then spun and took the flat of a blade across his shoulder.

It rocked him, but he kept moving fast, getting out of the way by ducking low and sliding through the warrior's ranks.

Natalya flinched, taking two steps toward Vikirnoff and then forcing herself to stop. "That looked like it hurt big time. I'd help out, but you know I might mess up the polish on my fingernails. It's so pretty and pink."

"I'm going to beat you when I get out of this."

"I'm not sure you're going to get out of this without some help, but unfortunately for you, I think I'm ovulating right now. We women have to stay home and be impregnated."

"What's it going to take?"

"Changing your position on women fighting, oh mighty dictator." But she was already lifting her arms into the air, ready to take command of the shadow warriors. Because she wasn't about to let them kill her man, even if he was an idiot.

Hear me now, dark ones, great warriors torn from your resting places, while I call on earth, wind, fire, water and spirit.

She expected the semitransparent warriors to halt and lower their swords, but they continued to battle Vikirnoff.

"Holy smoke, Batman, they aren't listening to me." Natalya drew her sword and leapt into the fray, back-to-back with Vikirnoff. "I no longer have mage blood. We're in a little trouble here."

Vikirnoff glared at her over his shoulder. "You think?"

～

Lara stood at the top of the cliffs, her heart pounding hard. She looked across the expanse of rock at Nicolas, her heart in her throat.

"Are you certain you want to do this, Lara? I can do it for you," Nicolas offered.

She shook her head. "Terry and Gerald were my friends, the closest thing I had to family, really. I was passed around so much as a child, I had problems with the concept of trust and camaraderie. A team of expert cavers was formed in order to conduct a study in Greenland. I was looking for extremophiles for the university to study, and both Terry and Gerald were part of a team studying global warming."

Nicolas studied her drawn face. She really needed this, whether he liked it or not.

"The conditions were extreme cold and very dangerous; the winds were terrible. Unlike Carpathians, who can shift and float down a moulin, we have to go down on a thin rope, terrified the rope is going to ice up. When you do that with someone, when you rely on them for your life, they come to matter to you. Gerald and Terry were like me. Neither had anybody and we'd sit together, huddled in a tent, listening to that awful wind. Terry would tell the funniest stories."

Feeling the heavy stone weighing her down, the sorrow and guilt pushing at her, Nicolas framed her face with his hands. "You didn't do this, Lara."

"I honestly didn't think my childhood was real. It seemed such a hazy dream, but I kept searching and I kept taking them with me."

"You can't go into an ice cave alone," he pointed out. "You need climbing partners."

Lara looked down at the two urns, both containing the ashes of her two friends. Nicolas's explanation wouldn't remove the guilt she felt, not for a long time—if ever. Both had suffered terribly before they'd died. When Terry had yanked the snake head from his ankle, he'd dumped an entire mass of parasites into his system. Gregori had fought long and hard to remove them and everyone had thought he was okay, that he just needed rest. Gerald had gone back to his room to shower and no one had checked him. But she should have. She'd been preoccupied with her past rearing up and with Nicolas claiming her, changing her life for all time.

"There isn't an excuse—not for any of us," Lara said. "They were good men. Brave men. Both descended five hundred feet into rapidly changing caves in order to get what was needed for research. And both of them were so funny. I didn't really know how to have fun until I met them."

Nicolas caressed the top of her head. "I'm glad the three of you found each other. You probably enhanced their lives as much as they did yours." He wished he hadn't been so jealous, his primitive side refusing to share her, not thinking to check on her friends. Mikhail was right in thinking they needed to enlist the aid of humans, widen their circle of trusted friends. His family had a symbiotic relationship with a human family, and had for many centuries, yet they still didn't trust others. If they were going to survive the coming war with Xavier, the Carpathian people were going to need allies.

"The blue and white stripes in the caves indicate age, the summers and winters, just like bands on a tree. As the years pass, the bands compress into these very thin lines. Gerald was obsessed with counting them." She laughed softly, remembering. "One time we were in this rapidly changing pit. We'd measured the walls and knew that the conditions were deteriorating much faster than we'd anticipated. Terry and I were practically running for our lives. The walls were creaking and groaning and we were showered with ice shards. Terry was getting claustrophobic. And there was Gerald, calmly counting the bands, like we had all time in the world. Terry finally clipped a carabineer to his rig and jerked on it like a leash attached to a dog to get Gerald moving. I was laughing so hard I could barely make the climb."

She rubbed her wrist, a habit she couldn't seem to break.

"The ice world is beautiful, with unbelievable color, but it's so cold. Even waiting for the right conditions, huddling in a tent with the wind whipping around you and your hands so numb you can't grip anything, just going to the bathroom is a hazard. Ice explodes around you and it rains shards and slivers. You only have each other."

Nicolas pulled her into his arms. "We will keep some of their ashes in our cave. They would like that. We can find a niche for them and you can have a memorial there, but let me do this with you. Instead of you shifting and trying to harness the urns on you, let me carry you through the skies. I'll fly over the mountains they loved so much, and if you want do scatter some of the ashes, you can. If not, we'll give them a send-off to the heavens."

"Both always wanted to fly. They climbed so much, but both of them would spread their arms out sitting on a rope and pretend they were flying. I want to give them that."

Nicolas nodded. "I'll shift and you climb onto my back."

He was already changing, feathers spreading across his body, his form morphing, wings dipping to allow her to climb on. Lara wiped at the tears on her face and picked up the urns. She couldn't bring them back, but she could give them their dream.

~

Lara shuddered as she crawled on her hands and knees through the twisting, narrowing ice tube that led from the interior of the cave to the outside world. At least she hoped it led outside, because there was nothing but death for her inside the cave. The ice creaked and groaned continuously, always alive, always on the move, never still, never silent. The cold seeped into her bones, even though she was regulating her body temperature.

The layers of ice, white and blue, were difficult to see without the light from the sconces illuminating her grandfather's grandiose chambers. She had her father's excellent night vision, but she was crying so hard, the tears blurred everything and fear compounded the shadowy figures that weren't really there. With the biting cold, she could tell the tears were turning to ice on her face, freezing her skin.

The cries of the dragons became muted, and she unconsciously strained to hear them. She didn't want her aunts to die. She hesitated, thinking to go back to help them, but what could she do? Shaking, she huddled in the ice tube, frightened to go forward, terrified to go back.

The mountain trembled, shaking around her. For a moment her lungs seized, burning for air. She heard the cry of the dragon, a pain-filled shriek that rose through the caverns, and then the answer as the second dragon bellowed in anguish.

She covered her face with her hands. There was no going back now. The aunts hadn't gotten away, and Xavier was punishing them. His punishments were terrible. She had no idea what lay ahead in the outside world, no idea what to expect, but it had to be better than living the way she'd been living.

Her wrist throbbed and she rubbed it, forcing herself to look ahead, not behind her. She was terrified the sun would burn her as Xavier had always told her. The sun was a huge burning mass of magma, churning and terrible, waiting to set her on fire. She shuddered and began to crawl again.

Almost immediately she heard the whispers start. Voices. Muffled. Persistent. Ugly. *Monsters will eat you. The sun will fry you. Your skin will melt off your bones.*

She pushed herself to continue, to inch forward. She became aware of the cold seeping into her body, destroying her ability to think clearly and forced herself to try to regulate her body temperature. The further she got from the ice cave and Xavier, the more she realized her father must have been helping her maintain her body heat.

The climb to the surface was endless, her knees scraped and bloody by the time she reached the next level. The tube

branched off in two directions. She had no idea which way
to go. Above her head the mountain groaned and creaked
with the pressure of the weight of the ice. All around her the
ice broke off and showered shards down on her. She sat in at
the junction in the tunnel and tried to figure out which way
to go. She couldn't just sit there. Xavier would send something terrible after her. She was certain he already had.

Spider, spider my friend who is bright
Spider, spider, help me this night
I need direction, I'm in doubt
Spider, spider, show me the way out

Tiny ice spiders, lethal, with poisonous fangs, rushed
from the cracks of ice, dropping down to console her. They
fanned out, their silken, crystalline webs sparkling in the
dark, catching light from a source she couldn't see and
dazzling her with displays of color as they rushed along
the walls of the tunnel, spinning webs to show her the way
along the left-hand tube.

She heard scratching behind her and knew she was minutes from capture. Her heart beat too fast, slamming hard
in her chest, her blood roaring like the sound of ice breaking in her ears.

Spider, spider, help me now
Remove the threat to me somehow.

An army of spiders broke off from the main body to
rush behind her, spinning webs fast, building a barrier
across the tunnel, thick and strong and glistening with poisonous threads.

Lara scrambled after the other spiders, following the
dazzling silken threads along the walls. Without having to
worry about what was ahead, or where she was going, she
traveled faster, crawling at a rapid pace in time to the slamming beat of her heart. The tunnel angled down as it wound
back and forth in various directions, taking her back the
way she'd come and then abruptly swinging to the opposite
direction. Openings broke off in every direction so that it

was a labyrinth she knew she never would have been able to maneuver on her own. The spiders made it easy, lighting the way with their glittering threads.

Wind touched her face. Icy flakes bit into her exposed skin. Shivering nonstop, her teeth chattering, she crawled until there was little flesh left on her knees or the palms of her hands. In front of her she saw light. At first she thought her eyes were playing tricks on her, but as she continued forward, more light spilled into the tunnel. The walls widened and the ceiling was much higher.

She stood up, her body aching, tears frozen on her skin. She ran, chanting:

Spider, spider, thanks to you all,
A debt to you, I will recall
Ask me when you have great need
Spider, spider, and I will heed

Lara picked up momentum, running faster and faster, frightened that since she was so close, Xavier would find a way to stop her. The opening loomed before her and she ran toward it, never seeing the drop-off. Her bare, bloody feet hit empty space and she fell with a thin, scared scream, dropping like a stone to the snow below.

She landed hard, the air driven from her lungs, her eyes widening in terror as a large animal reared up, legs slashing the air above her head. A man rushed around the animal, calming it with a gentle hand, then looked down at her terrified, bloody face. His expression changed to one of kindness and concern. As if she were a frightened animal, he bent slowly toward her and lifted her body into the warmth of his arms, crooning to her in a language she didn't understand.

A woman appeared, dressed in a long skirt, and she drew off her wrap and pressed it around Lara's shivering body, speaking to her husband in the same language. He carried her back to the colorful wagon they were traveling in.

A MUCH-ABRIDGED CARPATHIAN
DICTIONARY

This very much abridged Carpathian dictionary contains most of the Carpathian words used in these Dark books. Of course, a full Carpathian dictionary would be as large as the usual dictionary for an entire language (typically more than a hundred thousand words).

Note: The Carpathian nouns and verbs below are word stems. They generally do not appear in their isolated, "stem" form, as below. Instead, they usually appear with suffixes (e.g., *"andam"*—"I give," rather than just the root, *"and"*).

agba—to be seemly or proper.
ai—oh.
aina—body.
ainaak—forever.
ak—suffix added after a noun ending in a consonant to make it plural.
aka—to give heed; to hearken; to listen.
akarat—mind; will.

ál—to bless; to attach to.

alatt—through.

aldyn—under; underneath.

alə—to lift; to raise.

alte—to bless; to curse.

and—to give.

arvo—value (*noun*).

arwa—praise (*noun*).

arwa-arvo—honor (*noun*).

arwa-arvo olen gæidnod, ekäm—honor guide you, my brother (*greeting*).

arwa-arvo olen isäntä, ekäm—honor keep you, my brother (*greeting*).

arwa-arvo pile sívadet—may honor light your heart (*greeting*).

arwa-arvod mäne me ködak—may your honor hold back the dark (*greeting*).

asti—until.

avaa—to open.

avio—wedded.

avio päläfertiil—lifemate.

belső—within; inside.

bur—good; well.

bur tule ekämet kuntamak—well met brother-kin (*greeting*).

ćaδa—to flee; to run; to escape.

ćoro—to flow; to run like rain.

csecsemõ—baby (*noun*).

csitri—little one (*female*).

eći—to fall.

ek—suffix added after a noun ending in a consonant to make it plural.

ekä—brother.

elä—to live.

eläsz arwa-arvoval—may you live with honor (*greeting*).

eläsz jeläbam ainaak—long may you live in the light (*greeting*).

elävä—alive.

elävä ainak majaknak—land of the living.

elid—life.

emä—mother (*noun*).

Emä Maγe—Mother Nature.

én—I.

en—great, many, big.

én jutta félet és ekämet—I greet a friend and brother (*greeting*).

En Puwe—The Great Tree. Related to the legends of Ygddrasil, the *axis mundi*, Mount Meru, heaven and hell, etc.

engem—me.

és—and.

että—that.

fáz—to feel cold or chilly.

fél—fellow, friend.

fél ku kuuluaak sívam belső—beloved.

fél ku vigyázak—dear one.

fertiil—fertile one.

fesztelen—airy.

fü—herbs; grass.

gæidno—road, way.

gond—care; worry; love (*noun*).

hän—he; she; it.

hän agba—it is so.

hän ku—prefix: one who; that which.

hän ku agba—truth.

hän ku kaśwa o numamet—sky-owner.

hän ku kuulua sívamet—keeper of my heart.

hän ku meke pirämet—defender.

hän ku pesä—protector.

hän ku saa kuć3aket—star-reacher.

hän ku tappa—deadly.

hän ku tuulmahl elidet—vampire (*literally: life-stealer*).

hän ku vie elidet—vampire (*literally: thief of life*).

hany—clod; lump of earth.

hisz—to believe; to trust.

ida—east.

irgalom—compassion; pity; mercy.

isä—father (*noun*).

isäntä—master of the house.

it—now.

jälleen—again.

jama—to be sick, wounded or dying; to be near death.

jelä—sunlight; day, sun; light.

jelä keje terád—light sear you (*Carpathian swear words*).

o jelä peje terád—sun scorch you (*Carpathian swear words*).

o jelä sielamak—light of my soul.

joma—to be under way; to go.

joŋe—to come; to return.

joŋesz arwa-arvoval—return with honor (*greeting*).

jörem—to forget; to lose one's way; to make a mistake.

juo—to drink.

juosz és eläsz—drink and live (*greeting*).

juosz és olen ainaak sielamet jutta—drink and become one with me (*greeting*).

juta—to go; to wander.

jüti—night; evening.

jutta—connected; fixed (*adj.*). To connect; to fix; to bind (*verb*).

k—suffix added after a noun ending in a vowel to make it plural.

kaca—male lover.

kaik—all.

kaŋa—to call; to invite; to request; to beg.

kaŋk—windpipe; Adam's apple; throat.

kaδa—to abandon; to leave; to remain.

kaδa wäkeva óv o köd—stand fast against the dark (*greeting*).

Karpatii—Carpathian.

käsi—hand (*noun*).

kaśwa—to own.

keje—to cook; to burn; to sear.

kepä—lesser, small, easy, few.

kidü—to wake up; to arise (*intransitive verb*).

kim—to cover an entire object with some sort of covering.

kinn—out; outdoors; outside; without.

kinta—fog; mist; smoke.

köd—fog; mist; darkness.

köd alte hän—darkness curse it (*Carpathian swear words*).

o köd belső—darkness take it (*Carpathian swear words*).

köd jutasz belső—shadow take you (*Carpathian swear words*).

koje—man; husband; drone.

kola—to die.

kolasz arwa-arvoval—may you die with honor (*greeting*).

koma—empty hand; bare hand; palm of the hand; hollow of the hand.

kond—all of a family's or clan's children.

kont—warrior.

kont o sívanak—strong heart (*literally: heart of the warrior*).

ku—who; which; that.

kule—to hear.

kulke—to go or to travel (on land or water).

kulkesz arwa-arvoval, ekäm—walk with honor, my brother (*greeting*).

kulkesz arwaval, joŋesz arwa arvoval—go with glory, return with honor (*greeting*).

kuly—intestinal worm; tapeworm; demon who possesses and devours souls.

kumpa—wave (*noun*).

kuńa—to lie as if asleep; to close or cover the eyes in a game of hide-and-seek; to die.

kunta—band, clan, tribe, family.

kutni̱—to be able to bear, carry, endure, stand or take.

kutnisz ainaak—long may you endure (*greeting*).

kuulua—to belong; to hold.

lääs—west.

lamti (or **lamt3**)—lowland; meadow; deep; depth.

lamti ból jüti, kinta, ja szelem—the netherworld (*literally: the meadow of night, mists and ghosts*).

lańa—daughter.

lejkka—crack, fissure, split (*noun*). To cut; to hit; to strike forcefully (*verb*).

lewl—spirit (*noun*).

lewl ma—the other world (*literally: spirit land*). *Lewl ma* includes *lamti ból jüti, kinta, ja szelem:* the netherworld, but also includes the worlds higher up *En Puwe*, the Great Tree.

lõuna—south.

löyly—breath; steam (*related to* lewl: *spirit*).

ma—land; forest.

mana—to abuse; to curse; to ruin.

mäne—to rescue; to save.

maɣe—land; earth; territory; place; nature.

me—we.

meke—deed; work (*noun*). To do; to make; to work (*verb*).

minan—mine.

minden—every, all (*adj.*).

möért?—what for? (*exclamation*).

molanâ—to crumble; to fall apart.

molo—to crush; to break into bits.

mozdul—to begin to move, to enter into movement.

myös—also.

nä—for.

ŋamaŋ—this; this one here.

nélkül—without.

nenä—anger.

nó—like; in the same way as; as.

numa—god; sky; top; upper part; highest (*related to the English word: numinous*).

nyál—saliva; spit (*related to* nyelv: *tongue*).

nyelv—tongue.

o—the (*used before a noun beginning with a consonant*).

odam—to dream; to sleep.

odam-sarna kondak—lullaby (*literally: sleep-song of children*).

olen—to be.

oma—old; ancient.

omboće—other; second (*adj.*).

ot—the (*used before a noun beginning with a vowel*).

otti—to look; to see; to find.

óv—to protect against.

owe—door.

pajna—to press.

pälä—half; side.

päläfertiil—mate or wife.

peje—to burn.

peje terád—get burned (*Carpathian swear words*).

pél—to be afraid; to be scared of.

pesä—nest (*literal*); protection (*figurative*).

pesäsz jeläbam ainaak—long may you stay in the light (*greeting*).

pide—above.

pile—to ignite; to light up.

pirä—circle; ring (*noun*). To surround; to enclose (*verb*).

piros—red.

pitä—to keep; to hold.

piwtä—to follow; to follow the track of game.

põhi—north.

pukta—to drive away; to persecute; to put to flight.

pus—healthy; healing.

pusm—to be restored to health.

puwe—tree; wood.

rauho—peace.

reka—ecstasy; trance.

rituaali—ritual.

salama—lightning; lightning bolt.

sarna—words; speech; magic incantation (*noun*). To chant; to sing; to celebrate (*verb*).

sarna kontakawk—warriors' chant.

śaro—frozen snow.

sas—shoosh (*to a child or baby*).

saγe—to arrive; to come; to reach.

siel—soul.

sisar—sister.

sív—heart.

sívad olen wäkeva, hän ku piwtä—may your heart stay strong, hunter (*greeting*).

sívamet—my love of my heart to my heart

sívdobbanás—heartbeat (*literal*); rhythm (*figurative*).

sokta—to mix; to stir around.

soŋe—to enter; to penetrate; to compensate; to replace.

susu—home; birthplace (*noun*). At home (*adv.*).

szabadon—freely.

szelem—ghost.

tappa—to dance; to stamp with the feet; to kill.

te—you.

ted—yours.

terád keje—get scorched (*Carpathian swear words*).

toja—to bend; to bow; to break.

toro—to fight; to quarrel.

torosz wäkeval—fight fiercely (*greeting*).

tule—to meet; to come.

tumte—to feel; to touch; to touch upon.

türe—full; satiated; accomplished.

tyvi—stem; base; trunk.

uskol—faithful.

uskolfertiil—allegiance; loyalty.

veri—blood.

veri-elidet—blood-life.

veri ekäakank—blood of our brothers.

veri isäakank—blood of our fathers.

veri olen piros, ekäm—blood be red, my brother (*literal*); find your lifemate (*figurative: greeting*).

veriak ot en Karpatiiak—by the blood of the prince (*literally:* by the blood of the great Carpathian; *Carpathian swear words*).

veridet peje—may your blood burn (*Carpathian swear words*).

vigyáz—to love; to care for; to take care of.

vii—last; at last; finally.

wäke—power; strength.

wäke kaδa—steadfastness.

wäke kutni—endurance.

wäke-sarna—vow; curse; blessing (*literally:* power words).

wäkeva—powerful.

wara—bird; crow.

weńća—complete; whole.

wete—water (*noun*).

NOW AVAILABLE
An all-new Carpathian novel from
#1 *New York Times* bestselling author

Christine Feehan

DARK SLAYER

The Dragonseeker Razvan is considered an enemy of both Carpathian hunters and vampires. But when Ivory, a rare female Carpathian, encounters Razvan after he has escaped from captivity, she senses that Razvan is more than what he appears to be, and she is willing to go against the entire Carpathian race to help him. But will her belief cost them their lives?

penguin.com